VALLEY OF
TERROR

VALLEY OF
TERROR

ZHOU HAOHUI
TRANSLATED BY BONNIE HUIE

Text copyright © 2009 by Zhou Haohui.
Translation copyright © 2017 by Bonnie Huie.
All rights reserved.

Previously published as 《摄魂谷之雅库玛的诅咒》 in 2009 by China Pictorial Publishing House and《摄魂谷》 in 2015 by Hainan Publishing House in Shanghai, China.

Translated from Simplified Chinese by Bonnie Huie. First published in English by AmazonCrossing in 2017.

Published by AmazonCrossing, Seattle.

www.apub.com

Amazon, the Amazon logo, and AmazonCrossing are trademarks of Amazon.com, Inc., or its affiliates.

ISBN-13: 9781542046558
ISBN-10: 1542046556

Cover design by M. S. Corley.

Printed in the United States of America.

VALLEY OF
TERROR

Prologue

It was nightfall, but the streetlights had not yet been turned on. The sky outside the window was obscured by the figures of trees, making the long, narrow corridor seem even dimmer than usual. The ceiling and walls had been scrubbed to a ghastly shade of white. Combined with a murky gray concrete floor, it gave the entire space an oppressive atmosphere.

The clicking of footsteps suddenly cut through the silence. A young woman hesitated at the door from the stairwell, her wide eyes surveying the dark and eerie passageway.

An elderly gentleman outfitted in a white doctor's coat pushed past the young woman.

"Come with me."

His quick footsteps made not even the slightest sound.

The young woman stood still, anxiously watching him disappear into the darkness. Then she hurried to catch up, her heels striking the hard floor.

She followed close behind until they reached a dead end. A closed wooden door appeared in front of them. The gentleman took out a key and turned to face the young woman. She bit her lip nervously, then nodded. The elderly gentleman inserted the key into the lock, the slight sound reverberating loudly.

The gentleman cleared his throat. "Uh—"

A bloodcurdling scream tore through the room. Though the young woman seemed to have anticipated it, she couldn't help shuddering. The elderly gentleman was long past being startled. As if nothing had happened, he turned the key.

Behind the wooden door stood a wall of wrought-iron bars. A human figure could vaguely be seen huddled in one corner of the cell. Visibly terrified, he was shaking from head to toe. The shriek of despair had come from precisely this source.

The elderly gentleman flicked a switch by the door, and the fluorescent lights in the room instantly turned on. The light seemed to make the man curled in the corner calm down somewhat, and he stopped screaming. His eyes widened as he peered out the door and at the visitors, though he still looked horror-struck. A moment later, he abruptly opened his mouth, and a stream of odd-sounding words burst forth.

The elderly gentleman turned quizzically toward the young woman.

The young woman nodded. "That's right. This is the native dialect of the Hamo people."

The elderly gentleman's eyes lit up. "So what is he saying?"

The man was jabbering excitedly, his pitch rising as if trying to stress an important point.

The young woman furrowed her brow, straining to make out the words. "The Valley of Terror . . . Demons are coming?"

"Demons?" the elderly gentleman asked. "What demons?"

The young woman shook her head and looked at the man, asking him in the Hamo dialect, "Demons? What demons are you talking about?"

The man suddenly stood up and began to walk toward the metal bars. He stared into the woman's face, his gaze like a dagger.

The elderly gentleman rubbed his palms together, unable to contain his excitement. "This is wonderful. You can communicate with him!"

At that moment, the man reached the side of the cell. He thrust his arms through the bars and grabbed for the young woman, but the elderly gentleman reacted quickly, pulling her just out of reach. The man's hands brushed against her face, leaving behind the sensation of cold.

The man violently shook the bars. Then, staring foggily into the distance, he let out a bone-chilling cry: "Ya—ku—ma!"

It was as if all the world's terror, despair, and pain were concentrated in that single inhuman cry. The elderly man and the young woman trembled. They couldn't help looking all around themselves, searching for the abominable horror about to descend.

Demons!

Chapter 1

YOU CAN RUN, BUT YOU CAN'T HIDE

The city of Longzhou in Hebei Province

When the case first began to unfold, Chief Inspector Luo Fei thought it was a prank.

The incident report was filed by three students from the Natural Resources and Environmental Engineering Program at Longzhou Polytechnic Institute.

The first student, Zou Wenbin, was the resident adviser for the other two, a male and a female. It was late, 11:47 p.m., when they filed the report. According to their account, the following events took place:

That evening, around 8:10 p.m., a boy named Yu Ziqiang suddenly screamed and rushed out of the classroom where several engineering students were studying. Before the others knew what was going on, he had disappeared into the night, and he failed to return to the dorm by lights-out. Attempts were made to reach him on his cell phone, but no one answered. His RA, Zou Wenbin, contacted Yu Ziqiang's roommate, Zhang Hong, and Xu Ting, who had witnessed it. Together, they went to file a report.

"Unfortunately, there's not much we can do right now," Luo told them. "The party has to be gone for at least forty-eight hours before they're considered a missing person. What you can do in the meantime is alert everyone you know. And don't worry too much. He may turn up on his own tomorrow."

It was evident the three students were frustrated with the detective's response. Xu Ting in particular seemed to want to say more, but in the end, she left with the others.

Luo did not feel that he had handled the case inappropriately. Not only had he followed procedure, but the case just didn't give cause for serious alarm. Yu Ziqiang had run away of his own accord, even if the reason was unknown. *These students are just overreacting,* Luo thought. *If you took it seriously every time something like this happened, you'd drop dead from overwork!*

But the situation quickly grew complex. Early the next morning, some senior citizens were exercising in an out-of-the-way spot on the south bank of the Yudai River, which encircled the city of Longzhou. The roads running along both banks were little used and poorly maintained—they didn't even have lights. As the sun rose, the seniors spotted a body. Cards in his wallet confirmed it was Yu Ziqiang.

Accompanied by forensic specialist Zhang Yu, Luo hurried to the scene, where they found the victim lying facedown on the riverbank. He was fully clothed, and his posture appeared natural. There were no indications of a struggle, no traces of blood, and no suspicious items anywhere nearby.

However, when they rolled the body over, what they saw on the victim's face set off alarm bells.

Yu Ziqiang's face was frozen in a grimace of pain. His facial muscles were so contorted, his nose appeared askew. But even more unsettling were his eyes.

Brimming with fear, his eyes were open so wide they were practically bursting out of their sockets, and the veins were clearly visible. It was enough to make even the seasoned investigators shiver.

"What do you think?" Luo asked.

Zhang Yu carefully examined key areas along the body. "The corpse is fully intact and undamaged on the surface. There are no signs of a violent blow. The mucus and saliva around the nose and mouth suggest that he may have been in the early stages of expelling some form of toxin. It doesn't appear to be a homicide, but as far as cause of death goes, we'll need to wait for a full examination. It's possible he had some kind of congenital condition, but that's just a guess."

"What about the time of death?"

"Mmm, nine to eleven hours ago, so between eight and ten last night," Zhang Yu said after giving the victim's wrist a quick squeeze.

But Luo had his own routine. After gripping the victim's other wrist, he flashed a grin. "Last night at 8:47 p.m."

"Huh?"

"The time of death. Last night at 8:47 p.m."

"How can you be so precise?" Zhang Yu shook his head in disbelief. "Even with all my years as a medical examiner, I can't pinpoint the time like that."

"My forensics expertise is no match for yours, but I have my own methods." Luo turned over the victim's wrist to reveal a watch. "Take a look. When the victim fell, his watch struck the ground, breaking the glass and stopping the hands!"

Further investigation revealed that the victim was quite physically fit, and medical records showed no significant illnesses in his family. The investigators spoke with students who'd been in the classroom and learned they had been completely absorbed in their work until Yu Ziqiang's bloodcurdling scream and subsequent flight. None of them could offer an explanation for the boy's behavior, and Luo was frustrated by the lack of clues.

But then he got a call from Xu Ting, the female student who'd seemed so upset the night before. She asked to speak with him privately at the institute.

Xu Ting was a demure, gangly girl with thick black glasses. She had been sitting behind Yu Ziqiang during the study session, and one look told Luo that she was distraught.

"The whole time, I felt like I was seeing things. Everyone else was acting normal, so I thought it must've just been me. But then Ziqiang—why would he drop dead for no apparent reason? I'm—I'm really scared."

"Scared? What are you scared of?" Luo prodded.

"Last night, all these things appeared. I don't know what they were, and no one else seemed to see them—" The girl stared at Luo as if seeking courage from him.

Luo knitted his brow. "I'm sorry, I don't follow. Things appeared?"

Xu Ting kept rubbing her hands together anxiously. "It's hard to explain. My classmates would laugh at me, but I have to tell you. I could feel that there was something terrible there, floating in the air in the classroom. Or maybe it was outside the window, in the dark. But it was there; it was real. I could hardly keep from screaming myself."

"So what you're saying is that you think you and Yu Ziqiang felt the same thing?"

Xu Ting nodded vigorously. "Yes. He must have sensed it before I did. I noticed that he seemed panicky, and he was looking around like he was searching for something—probably for like five minutes. Then I got scared, too. Suddenly, I realized there was this terrible thing, and it was right there beside me!"

Luo felt as though he were listening to a campy ghost story. Yet he could not refrain from asking, "And then what happened?"

"Then Ziqiang turned around and stared at me. His eyes seemed kind of unfocused, like maybe he wasn't even looking at me, exactly. But he definitely saw something, because the look on his face suddenly got even worse. I was terrified, and I started shaking all over, but I couldn't say a word. It wasn't until Ziqiang screamed that I snapped back to my senses." The girl gasped for air. "You know what happened next. Ziqiang rushed out of the classroom like he'd gone mad, and he never came back."

Luo could only presume that Xu Ting was telling the truth. He shook his head sadly, then asked, "What about you? How did you feel afterward?"

"After Ziqiang took off, I felt much better. The terror went away as quickly as it came. Maybe the thing followed him."

"The thing?" Luo couldn't stifle a chuckle. "What thing? If all those kids could see Yu Ziqiang, what kind of 'thing' could possibly have followed him?"

"No one else saw it, but it was really there. I really felt it!" the girl exploded. "And it must have followed Ziqiang! Otherwise, why would he have taken off running, and why did he die?!"

There was nothing more Luo could say. He squeezed the girl's hand and tried to calm her down, thinking, *I'd better check out that classroom myself.*

No matter how Luo looked at it, the classroom was completely normal. There was nothing out of the ordinary about the desks, the podium, the walls, or the blackboard. The only notable features were the north-facing windows and the Chinese parasol tree outside. At night, the silhouette of its swaying branches might cause a person to imagine all kinds of ghosts and monsters. Even so, there was no way it could provoke the level of terror Xu Ting had described.

Luo questioned the other students again to find out if any of them experienced what Xu Ting did, but his efforts were futile.

"Did I feel terrified? I mean, yeah, maybe a little after I heard that Yu Ziqiang died, but I was just kinda shocked when he screamed and all."

"Scared? No, man. Actually, I was in a great mood last night! Why would I have been scared?"

"Something in the room? I dunno. I sure didn't feel anything. Maybe I was studying too hard—I have an exam coming up. Speaking of which, I have to get back to work, okay?"

When Luo left the engineering school, he couldn't help wondering if Xu Ting was pulling his leg. He stopped to eat at a tiny restaurant, and by the time he returned to the station, it was already past 2:00 p.m. Zhang Yu had been waiting for a long time with the autopsy results.

"Well," Zhang Yu declared, "you can put the interrogations of local cab drivers on hold."

"Why is that?"

"The victim did not take any form of motorized transportation."

"Wait, how do you know? And how could he have traveled such a long distance in such a short time?"

Zhang Yu handed over the autopsy report. "See for yourself."

Luo's eyes honed in on the most important line on the page, the cause of death.

"Physical overexertion?" Luo mumbled. He'd been on the police force for many years, but this was the first time he'd seen those words in an autopsy report.

"Basically, the victim ran himself to death. From the time he left the school, he remained in a constant state of running until his heart gave out and he died."

"You're saying he ran six miles in under forty minutes?" Luo was gaping in disbelief.

Zhang Yu nodded.

"But how could someone in such good shape run himself to death? And why?"

Zhang Yu shrugged. "That's your job to figure out."

Luo remained standing there, dumbstruck. There was just no logical explanation. Had Xu Ting been right after all? Had Yu Ziqiang been chased by a demonic force?

Chapter 2

An Ostrich Is Frightened

At noon on the same day, an unusual wedding was being held at the Jinhua Grand Hotel. The young newlyweds were ethnically Korean, and the celebration featured their heritage. Members of the immediate family were seated at two tables at the front of the hall, all of them flamboyantly outfitted in traditional Korean dress.

After three rounds of drinks, the bride and groom stepped to the center of the floor to dance gracefully, hand in hand, to the song being boisterously sung by their friends and relatives. Soon, some of the other ethnically Korean guests moved up to the front tables, dancing exuberantly alongside them.

Naturally, this delighted the Han Chinese guests, who were accustomed to rowdy wedding games and pranks. Though they could neither sing nor dance along with their Korean counterparts, they drank to their hearts' delight, chattering away and likewise making merry.

Everyone was having the time of their lives—except Chen Bin. Not yet thirty years old, Chen Bin was an old classmate of the groom's who'd just happened to be in Longzhou and was invited at the last minute. There was a strange look on his face as he surveyed the crowd, panting uncontrollably.

He hadn't had all that much to drink, yet he felt a knot in the pit of his stomach. The feeling gradually intensified until he staggered from his chair and raced to the men's room. Back in the rowdy hall, no one noticed that Chen Bin had left, and no one wondered why he never came back.

Two hours later, the last of the giddy guests had dispersed. A member of the hotel staff was cleaning the restroom when he discovered Chen Bin—by that time, already an ice-cold corpse.

When he received the call from the Jinhua Grand Hotel, Luo was staring blankly at the autopsy photos of Yu Ziqiang. Upon hearing there had been another bizarre death, Luo called Zhang Yu and proceeded straight to the scene.

The hotel manager was at the restroom entrance, fearfully awaiting the arrival of Luo and his team. "This happened out of nowhere. It makes no sense! It makes no sense!" he said, shaking his head repeatedly.

Luo gave him a courteous nod before asking, "Who found him?"

"Me." A middle-aged man in a custodial uniform raised his hand.

"Come with us. Everyone else, wait outside." Luo led the way into the restroom.

The custodian pointed at a bathroom stall whose full-length door was shut. "He's in there. You have to see for yourself. It's horrifying."

Luo gingerly pulled open the wooden door, and a bizarre scene unfolded before his eyes.

"What on earth?" murmured Zhang Yu.

A man was half kneeling at the toilet with his head stuck deep inside the bowl. It was obvious that, up until the very moment of his death, he had been trying with all his might to stuff his own head down the toilet.

The custodian cleared his throat. "Around two this afternoon, I came by to clean up. The stall door was locked from the inside, so I thought someone was using it and decided to clean the rest of the

13

bathroom first. But over half an hour passed, and no one came out. I tried knocking on the door, but no one answered. So I peered through the gap under the door and saw someone kneeling there, not moving. I immediately pried open the door, and the guy was hunched over, just like this. I wanted to pull him out, but he was really stuck in there. Then our manager came and told me not to move him since he's already dead, and to call the police right away."

Luo didn't say a word the entire time the custodian was telling this story, but his eyes swept every inch of the scene. The first thing he noticed was the sliding lock on the stall door. It was a basic bolt lock that could only be opened and closed from the inside. The partitions were taller than an average person, and there was nothing in the room that someone could climb on. Combined with the custodian's account, these conditions seemed to eliminate the possibility of another person at the scene.

The forensics assistant had already photographed every last detail of the scene, so Luo and Zhang Yu entered the stall. They grunted and sweated before finally managing to pry the corpse's head from the toilet bowl, exposing a pallid face and bloodshot eyes that bulged in terror just like Yu Ziqiang's. Wastewater trickled down from his hair, streaming over his eyes as though the victim were crying.

Luo stared into the victim's face for a long time. He could practically hear the victim's last sobs—desperate, almost inhuman sounds.

While Luo and the corpse were having this tender exchange, Zhang Yu set about determining the cause of death. When the call came in, Luo and Zhang Yu had both suspected excessive alcohol consumption. A quick test indicated that the blood alcohol level was 0.012 percent, which indicated he'd had roughly one beer or an ounce of hard liquor—not enough to get a person drunk.

However, the cause of death was not difficult to determine. A froth had formed around the victim's mouth and nose, and the membranes in his eyes were inflamed. Zhang Yu drew a preliminary conclusion: "This man drowned."

"He drowned?" Luo was still trying to get his head around it.

"Yes. He bolted the door and held his face in the water, which led to his suffocation." Zhang Yu shook his head in disbelief, then let out a bitter laugh. "Say, you don't think there's gold hidden in that toilet?"

But Luo had his arms crossed and eyes down, stroking his chin in thought.

The team recognized their leader's posture and waited in anxious silence, afraid to interrupt.

After a long while, Luo lifted his head. He looked once more at the victim's face and nodded gravely. Then he muttered: "Ostrich."

"Huh?" Zhang Yu asked.

"Ostrich," Luo repeated emphatically. "The bird."

Everyone in the room looked at each other, baffled.

"When danger is coming and there's nowhere to run, ostriches stick their heads in the sand out of desperation. This man, he's like an ostrich."

Zhang Yu caught on. "What you're saying is that he came across something that terrified him, and there was no escape, so he stuck his head in the toilet?"

"He would've shoved his whole body in if he could've." Luo's low voice sounded eerily detached, chilling everyone in the room.

"But what could he have been so afraid of?" Zhang Yu asked in frustration, peering in all directions.

That was precisely what Luo wanted to know. What had taken place inside that tiny, closed-off space that was so frightening it could cause a young man to drown himself?

Inside the restroom, apart from the corpse, there was nothing unusual. But Luo couldn't deny that a strange, fearful presence seemed to emanate from every corner.

Zhang Yu took the corpse back to the forensic center while Luo and the others tracked down the wedding guests who'd been at the same table as Chen Bin, hoping that a chat with them might yield valuable clues.

They had little luck.

"Chen Bin? I don't know who—oh, was that the kid with the crew cut? I didn't really pay much attention to him. We clinked glasses during the toasts, I think. Why, what happened?"

"Oh yeah, he was sitting next to me. We chatted a bit. He's not from around here. I don't know why he left so early. Everyone was having a great time!"

"Chen? Chen Bin? Oh, from the wedding! Give him a call, and we'll go out for another couple rounds. We'll see who can really hold their liquor around here. You—you'll be wasted in no time!"

Among the guests at the table, not one knew Chen Bin well, and no one could say what time he'd left or why. Everyone had been too busy celebrating. Even hours later when Luo caught up with them, they were still basking in the afterglow.

Luo, on the other hand, was exhausted. He'd spent the evening running around town, all for naught. After dinner, he took a break to regain his energy, then called Zhang Yu and arranged to meet back at the office.

"Any news on your end?" he asked.

"Not really," Zhang Yu said. "We confirmed drowning as the cause of death. And like you said, the victim's actions and expression suggest that he suffered a tremendous scare."

"Uh-huh." Luo nodded. "Any other thoughts?"

"Well, I wonder if these two strange deaths should be investigated together."

"I know what you mean," Luo said, "but from a criminology perspective, I'm not sure that makes sense. First of all, the victims—an engineering student and a visitor from out of town—don't seem to have a single overlap in terms of their professional or social networks.

Plus, the engineering school and the Jinhua Grand Hotel are totally unrelated. You could say that the only common connection between the cases is that both victims apparently suffered a scare just before they died."

"But that's also the most perplexing part." Zhang Yu smiled wryly and shook his head. "I've been working in forensics for years—there isn't a horror I haven't seen. But I have no idea what could scare a person that bad."

"It's hard to imagine." Luo looked up, stroking his beard. Then suddenly he asked, "Have you ever read Sherlock Holmes?"

"Sherlock Holmes? Umm, I guess I've read a few stories?"

Luo leaned forward, his eyes shining. "In *His Last Bow: Some Reminiscences of Sherlock Holmes*, there's a story called 'The Adventure of the Devil's Foot.' Do you know it?"

Zhang Yu laughed awkwardly, then shook his head.

Luo arched an eyebrow disapprovingly. He leaned back in his chair, collecting his thoughts. "In 'The Adventure of the Devil's Foot,' there's an unusual type of plant that grows in Africa. Half of the plant's root resembles a human foot, while the other half resembles a goat's foot, which is where it gets its ominous name. When this plant is burned, it releases poisonous fumes that cause frightening hallucinations. The killer uses it to scare the victims to death."

"Hallucinations?" Zhang Yu gaped. "You think our victims were hallucinating?"

"It's the best explanation I can come up with." There was a hint of dejection in Luo's tone.

"What produced the hallucinations, then? A devil's foot?" Zhang Yu asked, baffled. "And if they were deliberately caused by someone, what was the motive? And with so many people at the scenes, why would only those two be affected?"

Luo laughed heartily. "No idea. That's why I called you! Medically, could what happened in the story ever happen in real life? What kind of drug or psychological mechanism could trigger such strong hallucinations?"

Zhang Yu shrugged defensively. "I'm afraid that's beyond my training." He lowered his head and reflected for an instant. "But I do know who you should go talk to."

"Oh?"

"Zhou Liwei, the associate dean at Longzhou University's School of Medicine. He's one of the foremost psychiatry experts in the nation!"

Luo had heard the name before. Zhou had earned his doctorate in the US and, in addition to his prestigious role at the university, was the head of psychiatry at the municipal hospital. He was also known for his neurological research. The man was a marvel. "Do you know him well? Can you put us in touch?"

An hour later, they pulled up to Longzhou University's School of Medicine. The towering building was pitch black except for a lone window on the third floor. A young man in his twenties stood at the entrance.

Luo and Zhang Yu got out of the police car and hurried up the front steps.

The young man called out, "Are you here to see Professor Zhou?"

Luo nodded. "Are you his student?"

"My name is Liu Yun." Smiling, the young man turned to lead the way. "You're just in time."

Soon after, the three of them were outside the office. With the utmost courtesy, Liu Yun gently knocked on the door.

A man's voice came from inside: "Come in!"

Liu Yun pushed open the door, and they filed in. It was a roughly two-hundred-square-foot room. The walls on either side were lined with bookcases housing all kinds of highly specialized tomes. Near the window was a desk, and opposite it sat a sofa and a coffee table. There was no other decoration.

Professor Zhou was reading at the desk, but once the three had entered, he stood up and took a couple of steps forward.

This world-weary man appeared to be around forty. Though he wasn't particularly tall, he looked athletic. Perhaps it was because he'd been working long hours that his eyes were a little red. But his steps were energetic and steady. Cowed by the man's reputation, Luo couldn't help staring.

Professor Zhou turned to Zhang Yu and, smiling, asked, "And who's this?"

Zhang Yu promptly introduced Luo, and now it was the doctor's turn to stare, as the situation must have been rather serious for the chief inspector to pay a visit so late at night.

"Please, gentlemen, take a seat. Then you can tell me why you're here."

Settling into the sofa and handing him the autopsy reports and photos from the scenes, Zhang Yu gave a comprehensive account of the two cases, including Luo's "Devil's Foot" theory. There was a grave expression on the professor's face as he listened and paged through the reports, interrupting periodically to ask incisive clarifying questions. The entire time, Liu Yun wordlessly recorded details in his notebook. When Zhang Yu finished speaking, a silence fell over the room.

Luo let the scholar reflect for a moment, then said, "Professor Zhou, we're here tonight because we need your expert advice. I know it sounds crazy, but is it possible that the victims experienced hallucinations? If so, what triggered them? Was there foul play involved?"

"At the moment, I can only respond to your first question with a tentative yes." Professor Zhou heaved a sigh. "As for your latter questions, before the two of you arrived, I was already perplexed."

A puzzled look crossed Luo's face. "You knew? How did you hear about this?"

"No, I wasn't aware of your cases. But you weren't aware of ours."

Professor Zhou turned around and picked up a pile of documents. "When Zhang Yu called me, we'd just gotten back from the hospital. The situation may be far worse than you realize."

Luo's heart sank as he reached out to accept the papers. As he scanned through them, he grew increasingly appalled.

The dozen medical records all involved preliminary diagnoses of schizophrenia made over the last two days. What was more, each and every one identified the same cause: emotional trauma caused by an extreme shock.

"Let me get this straight: Yu Ziqiang and Chen Bin aren't the only ones in Longzhou who suffered an excessive shock in the past two days—they're just the only two who died."

It was the first time that Zhang Yu had seen Luo in such an emotional state. He regarded Luo as a wise and prescient man, courageous and confident. He was the one who everyone at the station could turn to in the face of difficulty, and a chat and laugh later, the problem would be resolved. But now, anxiety shone in his eyes.

To make matters worse, the famed Professor Zhou was equally stumped. "I've undertaken a detailed analysis of about a dozen cases, and from a psychological standpoint, I haven't been able to come up with any significant clues. The first such patient the hospital accepted was a thirty-two-year-old woman with the family name Wu. Yesterday, sometime after 2:00 p.m., she entered a fitting room at the mall. There was a commotion, and one of the sales attendants rushed in to find her passed out from an extreme shock. The second was a nineteen-year-old man. Last night, he and his buddies were doing drugs at a small music venue when he started screaming like he'd seen a ghost. It took four or five bouncers to get him under control. We originally suspected those drugs were the culprit, but when we examined him, he was trembling from head to toe, unable to focus his eyes, and obviously petrified of something. This morning, it was an even stranger case, a seventy-year-old who was doing tai chi in a public park with a group of other seniors. I really can't imagine what, in that tranquil environment, could have so severely startled a person. In short, the cases have involved men and women, young and old, from different social backgrounds and occupations. The times and places in which the incidents occurred follow no particular pattern. The only thing they have in common is that the patients suffered a terrible shock that caused them to psychologically unravel—and they did so surrounded by witnesses, none of whom noticed anything out of the ordinary. Toxicology reports show nothing unusual. How could that be? What unseen thing could scare someone so badly?"

A silence enveloped the room. Everyone hung their heads, lost in thought.

Then Liu Yun, who hadn't uttered a word, suddenly declared, "Demons! The demons have chosen their sacrificial offerings."

Luo looked up sharply, disgusted that anyone would make jokes in such grave circumstances. He looked to the young man's teacher, but Professor Zhou was also staring at Liu Yun, astonishment on his face. In a burst of proud excitement, Liu Yun picked up his pen and began scribbling frantically.

Luo closed his eyes and shook his head. "Professor Zhou, may I take these medical records with me? There are some details that I'd like to have our people look at."

"I think that would be an excellent idea," Zhou replied. "It seems we're going to need to cooperate if we're going to solve this."

Luo had come hoping for answers, and instead he'd only gotten more questions. What he didn't know, of course, was that this was only the beginning.

Chapter 3

A Mysterious Prophecy

Fine morning light shone through the window, but Luo's expression was somber. He sat rigidly at his desk, scowling at the computer screen in front of him.

That morning, an online news portal had featured an eye-grabbing headline: INVISIBLE DEMONS DESCEND ON LONGZHOU; NUMBER OF TERROR VICTIMS UNCLEAR. Within just a few hours, the story had already gotten more than ten thousand hits and had been reblogged almost one thousand times.

Using the most sensational language possible, the writer delivered an exhaustive account of the terror cases. What most astounded Luo was the following paragraph:

> On the evening of the thirteenth, Longzhou City Chief Inspector Luo rushed over to Longzhou University's School of Medicine, seeking the aid of renowned psychiatry specialist Professor Zhou Liwei. The two conducted a formal analysis of the situation based on their respective areas of expertise, focusing on what exactly had caused the victims in these cases to suffer

such a terrible fright and why bystanders remained unaffected. At present, no clues to the answers to these questions have been identified. Could it be that invisible demons are appearing in Longzhou and have made their choice of sacrificial offerings?

Luo dialed Professor Zhou's number.

Professor Zhou answered immediately. "Yes, I saw it. Quite a few journalists have already contacted me for interviews. It's a madhouse. How did the writer get access to confidential information?"

"I'm sorry, Professor, but it must have been that student of yours who leaked it."

"Student?" Professor Zhou sounded as if he had no idea what Luo was talking about.

"Yes, Liu Yun. He even used the words 'demons' and 'sacrificial offerings.'"

"You mean that person from last night? He's not my student. I thought he was a member of your team!"

Luo was momentarily dumbstruck. "Ah, now I understand. I just assumed that he was your student, and he let me. Neither of us caught on, and this person slipped under the radar."

"So who is he?"

"A reporter, I'm betting," Luo chuckled. "He caught wind of the schizophrenia cases and came to interview you. He just happened to run into us as we arrived, and he saw an opportunity to get inside."

"What a disaster." Professor Zhou sounded deeply worried. "Now that this information is out there, it could set off a panic."

Luo was momentarily silent. "The best thing for us to do now is to keep quiet. Don't agree to any interviews."

"Right. My thoughts exactly. Maybe it'll blow over."

◆ ◆ ◆

But Longzhou wasn't that big of a place. When people learned that the terrifying incidents in the story really were true, phones at both the hospital and the police station began ringing off the hook.

Luo was under tremendous pressure to solve the case, and the manpower at his disposal was limited. He dispatched a team of nearly twenty investigators to conduct interviews and comb every corner of the city.

Meanwhile, Professor Zhou had his hands full examining new patients admitted for psychotic episodes triggered by fear. Fortunately, the hospital's psychiatry department was top-notch, enabling him to enlist the aid of exceptionally dedicated and talented doctors.

At nightfall, the investigators returned to headquarters for a briefing. They placed their interviews in front of Luo in a massive pile. But when it came time to speak, they hung their heads—none had come up with significant leads.

What was more, the situation appeared to have gotten even worse. By 4:00 p.m., another four schizophrenia cases had been reported, which raised the specter of a real epidemic. Numerous residents had also reported experiencing a strange feeling of terror, though not enough to trigger a total breakdown.

This made Luo recall Xu Ting and what she'd experienced in the classroom. No one was able to articulate what they were scared of, but they all described being utterly choked with fear.

Luo leaned forward over the table, resting his chin in his right hand. He'd sift through the interviews later. As chief, his most important task right now was to point the team in a clear direction. They had to stop this thing before it became one of the biggest catastrophes in Longzhou's history.

Everyone was hushed, looking at Luo expectantly.

Just then, the conference room door was gently pushed open, and Luo's secretary, Zhang Chenglin, entered.

"Chief Inspector Luo, there's a phone call for you."

"What is it about? I'm in the middle of a meeting." Luo furrowed his brow a little.

"It's a long-distance call from Yunnan. Someone saw the story online and has a tip."

"Yunnan?" That was a long way away from Longzhou. Why would anyone there have a tip? Luo jumped up, walked briskly to his office, and grabbed the receiver waiting on top of his desk.

"Hello, Luo speaking."

"Hello, my name is Xu Xiaowen." Contrary to what Luo had expected, the voice on the other end of the line was warm, kind, and apparently that of a young woman.

"You're calling from Yunnan?"

"That's right. I read about what happened in Longzhou. Did that— did that really happen?"

Luo was silent.

"Oh, don't worry, I'm not some weirdo or nosy journalist."

That made Luo chuckle a little, and he told her frankly: "The article contains exaggerations, of course. But those are indeed the basic facts."

"So it really did happen. I can't believe it," she said with such wonderment that Luo could practically see the excitement on her face.

"What? You knew this would happen?"

After a long silence, Xu Xiaowen replied in a voice that suggested she was trying her best to stay calm. "What I'm about to tell you is something that happened to me six months ago. It may sound preposterous, but I swear to God, every single word of it is true. Do you trust me?"

Although they had never met, Luo sensed her sincerity. "Go ahead, I trust you."

"I'm an Ethnic Minority Languages major at Yunnan University, and my main focus is the colloquial language used in dialects indigenous to the Yunnan area. About six months ago, I received a phone call from a mental institution asking for my assistance—"

"A mental institution?" Luo asked.

"That's right. The institution had taken in a very strange patient, and as for his condition . . . I think you might be able to guess."

"Paranoid schizophrenia?"

Xu Xiaowen gave an affirmative grunt. "When the staff was trying to treat him, they ran into a problem: The patient's speech was completely incomprehensible. Because he kept repeating the same phrases over and over, they suspected it wasn't just babbling, but actually speaking some kind of minority dialect."

"So they brought you in to interpret."

"Yes."

"And did you understand what he was saying?" Luo asked with bated breath.

"He said that now, in August, an evil spirit from the Valley of Terror would descend upon Longzhou."

Each of Xu Xiaowen's words sent icy fear through Luo's veins.

Following his conversation with Xu Xiaowen, Luo told his secretary to adjourn the briefing and headed to the morgue, where he knew Professor Zhou had gone to work alongside Zhang Yu.

By the time he arrived, it was dark outside.

"Wow, it's freezing in here. How do you stand it?" Luo exhaled deeply and crossed his bare arms, rubbing them for warmth.

Dressed in a long white lab coat, Zhang Yu came over to greet him. Then he silently gestured in the direction of the autopsy table.

Professor Zhou stood at the head of the table, hunched over the naked corpse of Yu Ziqiang. The professor's eyes were bright, and he didn't so much as look up.

Luo took a delicate step forward and realized that Yu Ziqiang's head had been completely shaved and his skull had been opened up. Professor Zhou held a small flashlight in his left hand, and in his right was a long metal instrument that probed the brain of the deceased.

Luo watched in amazement.

After a few more moments, Professor Zhou set down his flashlight, heaved a deep sigh of relief, and turned to Luo.

"Hello, Chief Inspector Luo."

Luo noticed a ring of sweat along the man's brow.

"I thought doctors were only interested in living patients," Luo teased. "I had no idea that you studied corpses as well."

"Your perspective is biased." Professor Zhou shook his head. "Treating patients is only one part of our job. In my view, preventing the outbreak of illness is actually more important."

"That's right!" Luo felt as if he'd discovered a kindred soul. "That's something that doctors and police have in common. Law enforcement isn't only about chasing criminals. What's more important is preventing crimes in the first place."

Professor Zhou gave him a knowing smile. "That's why I'm here. We can't let this horrific epidemic spread further. In order to prevent an outbreak, we need to conduct pathological research. And from that standpoint, corpses are more valuable than patients, since the bodies of the dead contain all kinds of vital clues. My objective is to analyze the brain of the deceased for any abnormalities that might be linked to the cause of death."

Luo frowned as he processed this, then shook his head. "I'm sorry, Professor, but this brain stuff is new to me. Maybe you could explain how someone could possibly be so scared that they could run themselves to death or drown in a toilet or suffer a psychotic break? I'm dying to learn more about all this."

"Oh really?" Professor Zhou murmured, rubbing his palms. "Very well, then. Let me give you a quick primer.

"Fear begins with an external stimulus and concludes with a strong physiological response," Professor Zhou began. "This response can include shallow breathing, rapid heartbeats, and clenched muscles. External stimuli can likewise take a variety of forms. Everything from a spider gliding down from the ceiling to the feel of a knife against your throat can cause the sensation of threat."

Professor Zhou walked over to the corpse and pointed to the opening in the skull. "Fear is controlled by an almond-shaped part of the cerebrum known as the amygdala. When the situation is sufficiently threatening, the amygdala sends impulses to the hypothalamus, which then triggers distress signals that initiate autonomic responses to fear throughout the body. The severity of those responses depends on how great the amygdala perceives the threat to be."

"So it's the responses that can kill you?"

"Yes, possibly by sending out so much adrenaline that it sets off a process in which the heart muscle contracts and goes into abnormal rhythms, resulting in sudden cardiac arrest. Or, in this case, by causing our victims to engage in behaviors that kill them. The thing is, there doesn't have to be a real threat for the amygdala to send out those signals—just the chemicals telling it there's a threat."

"I get it!" Luo clapped. "So the fear response could have been stimulated by a hallucination—or even a foreign chemical!"

"The devil's foot!" Zhang Yu cried. "Like the Sherlock Holmes story."

"Correct. Hallucinations would be perceived as a real threat, and if there were foreign chemicals in this man's brain, they might well have provoked extreme fear."

"So," Luo said, stroking his chin, "if chemicals stimulate the fear response, do chemicals also stop it?"

Professor Zhou's eyes shone with admiration. "You astonish me, Chief Inspector Luo. Every one of your questions is on point. Yes. The human brain can secrete a hormone called oxytocin that can control the amygdala's activity in response to fear."

"So you could administer oxytocin to mitigate a person's experience of fear, correct?" This time, it was Zhang Yu's turn to demonstrate his wit.

"Theoretically, but synthetic oxytocin isn't on the market yet. As luck would have it, I've spent the past two years working on precisely that. And this is what I've come up with." Professor Zhou reached into the pocket of his lab coat and removed a tiny medicine bottle of powder.

"If you have a treatment, why haven't you helped the patients?" Luo asked. "The terror in their eyes—I've never seen anything like it."

"Because it's only been successful in the laboratory. We know it can be used to control fear, but it's still unclear what the side effects might be. Before a treatment like this can be put into use, it must undergo years of testing. Just another way in which our jobs are similar, Chief Inspector Luo! Sometimes the police know who the culprit is, but they don't have enough evidence, so they can't do anything about it. It's the same kind of frustration."

Luo laughed, delighted by how well they understood one another.

"Modern medicine is really a marvel," Zhang Yu gushed. "These cases seemed impossible, and yet Professor Zhou has a solution—just like that!"

"Actually, I'm afraid the cases might be more complicated than brain chemistry." Luo adopted a more solemn tone. "This afternoon I received a phone call, the contents of which are sure to confound you."

"What kind of phone call?" Zhang Yu asked, wide-eyed.

But Professor Zhou was unsurprised. "You mean the call from Yunnan?"

"Wait, she called you, too?" Luo asked. "So you already know about the prophecy?"

Professor Zhou nodded.

"Well, what do you think?"

Luo was certain the scholarly, traveled doctor would think the woman's claims preposterous, more than likely a complete fabrication. His answer took Luo by surprise.

"I've already booked a plane ticket. I'm flying to Yunnan tomorrow."

Chapter 4

THE FIRST PATIENT

Kunming Changshui International Airport in Yunnan Province

Though it was still summer, the air in Kunming was pleasantly cool and refreshing. Luo took a few deep breaths to shake off grogginess from the long flight. His nerves, which had been tense for the past two days, finally relaxed.

Professor Zhou led the way, his shoulders and chin held high, clearly accustomed to a jet-setting lifestyle.

At the exit, other travelers fixed their stares on them, wondering at the men's distinguished air.

"Are you Professor Zhou?" An elderly man squeezed out of the crowd and extended his hand. Despite the fact that he was many years Zhou's senior, his tone and demeanor conveyed enormous respect. He was obviously aware that he was in the presence of one of the nation's foremost psychiatry experts.

Professor Zhou politely shook hands. "You must be Dr. Liu."

Luo stood behind Professor Zhou, taking no interest in the formalities. A young woman accompanying the elderly gentleman had caught his eye.

In her T-shirt and jeans, she looked like a typical college student. Slight and energetic, she had jet-black hair that fell past her shoulders, and she came across as quiet and good-natured.

Seeing Luo sizing her up, she smiled, flashing straight, perfectly white teeth. "You must be Chief Inspector Luo. I didn't expect you'd be able to get here so soon."

"Hello. You must be Xu Xiaowen."

"You're the one who called?" Professor Zhou turned to face the young woman. He frowned. "The scenario you described is difficult to believe."

"I can attest that it really did happen." The elderly doctor answered in her stead. "Six months ago, when I invited Xu Xiaowen to the Kunming Behavioral Health Center, she interpreted our patient's dialect. Of course, we assumed it was a fantasy born of the patient's mental illness. But then we read the news from Longzhou yesterday. Professor Zhou, Chief Inspector Luo, with your combined expertise in psychiatry and solving mysteries, I hope the two of you can get to the bottom of this."

Luo and Professor Zhou exchanged a look, and they knew they were thinking the same thing. "Take us to the site and let's see what we can do."

The mental institution was about forty minutes away. On the drive over, Dr. Liu told them more about the strange patient.

"We still haven't been able to determine his identity. In January, a local TV crew was shooting in the forest near the border, and every day this man would appear and steal their food. At first, the crew thought they'd encountered a wild savage like in old legends. But, after a few days, they captured him and discovered he knew how to operate modern devices. What no one could understand was why he seemed to be gripped by tremendous fear. So the crew brought him back to Kunming and sent him to us. But without knowing what caused his condition, it was difficult for us to administer an appropriate treatment. He seemed to understand when we spoke, but he'd only reply in his strange dialect. We wondered if what he was saying might contain meaningful information about the period before this condition emerged."

"That's right." Professor Zhou nodded. "And that information would likely point to the cause of the condition."

"Exactly. So we brought Xu Xiaowen in to interpret, and now, the implications of what he said have created an even bigger mystery!" Dr. Liu threw his hands in the air.

"Well, Chief Inspector Luo and Professor Zhou are here now, so I'm sure that the case will be solved soon enough." Though Xu Xiaowen said both of their names, she had eyes only for Luo.

Luo flushed slightly and let out an awkward, self-deprecating laugh. "Your expectations may be a little high. At this point, I haven't the slightest clue."

"I know you can do it." Warmth flashed in Xu Xiaowen's eyes. "I can tell."

Luo blushed. At that moment, the car pulled up to the mental institution, cutting off the conversation.

Because the patient's condition was so unstable, the institution had placed him in a small, remote building designed for severely ill and dangerous patients. It hadn't been renovated in ages, and the atmosphere inside was oppressive.

They filed up the stairs to the second floor and headed toward the small room at the end of the corridor. Recalling the petrifying events of six months earlier, Xu Xiaowen felt a chill down her spine. Scrunching her neck, she edged closer to Luo.

Dr. Liu stopped at the wooden door and inserted the key into the lock, gently turning it . . .

From behind the door came a bloodcurdling scream. Xu Xiaowen's breathing quickened, Luo's brows furrowed, and Professor Zhou's eyes darted sideways. Only Dr. Liu behaved as if nothing out of the ordinary had happened.

Dr. Liu pulled open the wooden door and switched on the light inside. The patient was huddled in a corner, his entire body shaking.

"Now, now. Don't be afraid. We're not here to hurt you," Dr. Liu said gently.

The patient stopped screaming and shakily lifted his head to reveal his face.

He was a wide-eyed young man with bushy brows. Though his face was stubbled, he didn't look very old—perhaps not even thirty. His face was thin and angular. With some grooming, he would probably be rather handsome. But at that moment, he wasn't the least bit charming, because he was a mess, and because there was something terrible in his gaze. It was as if all of mankind's ugliest emotions—fear, despair, anger, hatred, and more—had coalesced into a spine-chilling stare.

Glowering at the four visitors outside the door, the young man slowly stood up and unleashed a string of incomprehensible words.

Luo flinched and looked away. There was one word he understood very clearly.

Longzhou.

"It's the same as before," Xu Xiaowen breathed. "'In August, demons from the Valley of Terror will descend on Longzhou.'"

"Have you asked him what kind of demons?"

"Yes."

"What did he say?"

Xu Xiaowen looked at the young man. Switching languages, she asked, "What kind of demons?"

The patient stepped forward. Then, with his eyes rigidly fixed on Xu Xiaowen's face, he started toward the door.

Xu Xiaowen, who'd expected this, dodged to hide behind Luo.

A blank, desolate look filled the patient's eyes. Then a grumbling sound rose from his throat, and he let out a deep, bestial cry: "Ya Kuma! Ya Kuma!"

"Ya Kuma? What does that mean?" Luo asked.

But Xu Xiaowen shook her head. "That—I don't know."

Dr. Liu and Professor Zhou frowned as they pondered the eerie words. Meanwhile, the patient was creeping closer to the bars.

"Get back!" Xu Xiaowen cried, but it was too late.

The patient had Professor Zhou by the lapels. Unable to overcome the man's massive strength, Professor Zhou found himself pulled up against the bars. Normally so calm and capable, now he could not refrain from breaking into a cold sweat. The patient stared at him fixedly, their faces practically pressed up against one another.

The man let out a howl: "Ya Kuma!"

The despair and fear made Luo's spine tingle. He and Dr. Liu grappled with the patient and, combined with Professor Zhou's own desperate efforts to free himself, were finally able to wrest the men apart. Professor Zhou stumbled back, panting and red-faced.

A moment later, when he'd regained his composure, he let out an embarrassed laugh. "When someone suffers a psychotic episode, he or she often becomes several times stronger than an ordinary person. Today, I can personally attest to the validity of that theory."

The patient returned to clutching the bars of the cell, still howling with rage.

Luo studied the young man—the first in a string of phobia patients. Was this the same terror Yu Ziqiang, Chen Bin, Xu Ting, and all those others had felt? Would there be more? He shuddered and swore to himself that he'd solve this case no matter what it took.

The four visitors stood there without speaking, each lost in their own thoughts. Luo finally spoke up: "Professor Zhou, what are your thoughts on the matter?"

"All I can say is that Xu Xiaowen isn't making things up and that this patient's condition is similar to that of the patients in Longzhou," Professor Zhou replied after a moment's silence.

Glaring at the professor, Xu Xiaowen muttered, "Thanks so much for trusting me."

Luo didn't have time for petty grumbling, yet he was also dissatisfied. "But what about this patient's prophecy? Can you make heads or tails of it? Are you thinking that the illness originates from the forest?"

Narrowing his eyes, Professor Zhou stared intently at the investigator. "I wonder the same thing. But what does the Yunnan forest have to do with our patients in Longzhou? Is it possible they'd all traveled there?"

"No." Luo shook his head firmly. "My investigators interviewed all the families. They wouldn't fail to report such a significant detail."

"So what other possibilities are there? Could someone have brought the illness from the forest to Longzhou? But this patient has been in Kunming the entire time and hasn't been to Longzhou at all," Dr. Liu inserted himself into the conversation.

There was a flicker in Luo's eyes. "He's not just the first victim, he may also be an informant. What if he knows the criminal's identity?"

"Are you suggesting that all of this has been human-induced?" Professor Zhou tightened his lips. "But who would do such a thing? How? For what purpose?"

Luo shook his head in bewilderment.

Xu Xiaowen was looking at Luo with concern. Then she turned to study the patient. "If only he'd recover his senses . . ."

Luo's eyes lit up. He looked at Professor Zhou. "She's right, you know. If this patient were to be cured, he might break this case wide open—"

"You want me to administer my new treatment?" Once again, Professor Zhou intuited what his colleague was getting at. "No, I'm sorry, that's not something I can do."

"Why not?" There was an obvious look of disappointment on Luo's face.

"It would be a breach of medical ethics. Even if I did agree to it, Kunming Behavioral Health Center would never consent. This treatment hasn't undergone clinical trials."

"He's correct," Dr. Liu added. "From an institutional perspective, an untested treatment absolutely cannot be administered."

"What if we were to treat it as a clinical trial?" Luo angled. "Could we use it on the patient then? How could we go about it so that it wouldn't breach your professional ethics?"

"That might actually work." Professor Zhou's eyebrows went up. "But we'd have to find the patient's next of kin."

"His next of kin?"

"Yes," Professor Zhou said sternly. "A patient needs to understand and consent to any negative effects an experimental treatment might cause. Since this patient is obviously not capable, his immediate family would need to sign consent forms."

Luo nodded. But how would they find the next of kin?

As he contemplated the problem, Luo gazed at the patient inside the cell. Though the man's face was contorted with fear, his features were still easily recognizable.

It would be ideal if his family members could see him, thought Luo. He had an idea.

Chapter 5

A Madman's Science

As an online journalist, Liu Yun always had to be on the lookout for leads to stories odd and exciting, hard to believe, or even sensational. It was a restless society, and people needed stimulation.

A strange fear illness had broken out in Longzhou. So Liu Yun did what he had to do and passed himself off as a medical student to get the scoop. When his story went live, the response was tremendous. He was beside himself with excitement. But he was also nervous. After all, deceiving the chief investigator was no joke, and if the police came after him, he didn't know what he'd do.

Then, a couple of mornings later, he got a message saying that Luo was coming by.

Liu Yun sat on the edge of his desk, waiting for his visitor. When he saw the grim look on the investigator's face, he tried to smile. "Heh, Chief Inspector Luo, so we, uh—we meet again."

Luo's sharp look sliced through him.

Liu Yun forced a laugh. "Sir, what happened last time, I think, was a misunderstanding."

"You can relax." Luo's expression softened. "I saw the story. You're a talented journalist."

"Huh?"

"In fact, I'm here because I want you to write a follow-up."

Liu Yun was baffled. "A follow-up? What kind of follow-up?"

"About the origins of the illness. I just got back from Kunming, and there's a patient there with the same condition, except he came down with it six months ago. I'd like you to do a story about it."

Realizing he wasn't being toyed with, Liu Yun's eyes lit up. He leaned forward. "Well, I would need all the relevant information in comprehensive detail—"

Luo chuckled and tossed a folder onto the table. "All ready for you, including a high-res photo of the patient."

Liu Yun licked his lips, yet he did not reach for the folder. He rubbed his hands, trying to contain his excitement. "What's your angle here?"

Luo laughed. This fellow was sharp as a tack. "We're having trouble identifying the patient, so I'm hoping that the media can help."

"Then you came to the right person," Liu Yun boasted. "There's no way traditional media can compete with our website in terms of audience. I'll put this photo up on the splash page, and you'll find out what the Internet is capable of."

"Let's hope so," Luo said coolly. What if the patient came from a remote mountain village without Internet access? But it was worth a shot. He'd do whatever it took to ID the man if it might prevent the spread of the horrifying illness.

He never imagined the response would be so quick.

The morning after the story was published, Luo received a call from an unidentified number.

"Is this Chief Inspector Luo?" came an excited voice. "I saw the news this morning. My oh my, I cannot believe it! The Internet truly is a blessing. It has changed our world!"

"Pardon me? Are you calling about the photo?"

"Yes! He found me on the Internet, and now it's my turn to find him! This is very interesting. Very interesting, indeed!"

"How do you know the patient? Are you a friend of his?"

"Friend? You might call me that, but bosom buddy would be more fitting! I don't know if I can express just how excited I am! But trust me, I am the person you're looking for. In the past, all of you ignored me. Now you have to listen to every word I say, and I'm going to blow your minds! Oh, what a marvelous feeling, indeed!"

Luo listened impatiently to the man's blathering, one eyebrow raised. He asked brusquely, "Where are you?"

"Are you going to come get me?" The man on the other end of the line let out a bizarre laugh. "No, there's no need. I just left Longzhou Airport. When I saw the news, I knew I wouldn't be able to stand the wait! I'll appear before your very eyes in half an hour. That's right, you'd better call that Professor Zhou over. Heh heh, this is the first time in my life I've gotten to face them with my head held high!"

Luo couldn't take it any longer. "I'm sorry, but who are you?"

"Me? In the past, some called me a lunatic and others called me a quack. But I'm a scholar. My name is Yue Dongbei. And from this day on, everyone will know who I am!"

Amid a fit of unbridled laughter, he hung up.

As soon as he got the message from Luo, Professor Zhou rushed over. He paced the room, too agitated to sit. "Yue Dongbei—I went and looked him up online, and you could say I found a few things. He poses as a scholar—originally it was in history, then later Neo-Taoism. Because he propagated all kinds of superstitions, he was blacklisted in the academic world. In the past two years, he's been active online, taking advantage of the open media environment to publish his own so-called research findings. He's developed a following."

"Yeah, sounds like the guy." Luo nodded. "I take it you're not a fan?"

"I'm a scientist. I'm firmly opposed to superstition! But what connection could he have to our case? Seems fishy."

"Don't worry. Have a seat." Luo gestured politely. "When he arrives, we'll have all the answers."

Yue Dongbei didn't keep them waiting long. He was a short, pudgy man around fifty and had neither a strand of hair on his scalp nor a whisker on his chin, which made his head seem round and plump, not unlike a meatball. His frumpy, long-sleeved shirt strained around his waist, looking as if a button might fly off at any moment.

"Chief Inspector Luo? And the illustrious Professor Zhou?" Yue Dongbei looked them up and down. Without waiting for a response, he walked over to the sofa and plopped himself down. There was something unsettling about the way half his body seemed to be instantly absorbed into the sofa.

"And you're Yue Dongbei, the online scholar?" Professor Zhou's voice held obvious derision.

"Oh, an Internet hater, are we? When people like you suppress the truth, the Internet gives us one last battleground!"

"Truth?" Professor Zhou couldn't help laughing. "You call those superstitions 'truth'?"

"Superstitions?" Yue Dongbei wasn't about to back down. "You scientists are so full of yourselves, but you refuse to see how science has already become the greatest superstition of all! You maintain an iron grip over the academic sphere, not allowing anything that might run counter to your own beliefs! Even when there's a phenomenon that science has no way of explaining, you refuse to accept any other theories. The world of science has, in actuality, become a religious tribunal!"

Yue Dongbei shook his plump fist in the air as he aired these long-simmering grievances.

Professor Zhou laughed coldly. He seemed tempted to say something more, but Luo motioned for him to refrain.

"Interesting, but let's not get too far off topic," Luo said calmly. "Why don't you tell us how you know the patient?"

"You must be willing to hear my theory out, as there are some things that you may find rather contentious. Otherwise, we will never be able to communicate." Yue Dongbei folded his arms, a haughty look on his face.

Luo nodded. "We'll listen respectfully to whatever you have to say."

Professor Zhou groaned faintly, but all he could do was listen patiently as Yue Dongbei began.

"I know it's hard for you to see me as a scholar. But I'll have you know that I was once a historian, and my subject mastery is in no way inferior to that of any expert. It's just that I dug too deep into certain areas and uncovered secrets that had been buried for ages. And those secrets are a challenge for modern-day science to explain. I tried to provide an analysis of some of them, drawing on extensive sources and dabbling in esoteric fields. Ever since, mainstream science has rejected me." Yue Dongbei paused. Though wrinkles of worry appeared on his forehead, they were soon replaced by a look of rapture.

"Let me tell you about an episode that took place during the fall of the Ming Dynasty. In 1644, during the period we call the Southern Ming, most of southern China still hadn't been conquered by the Manchus. The last claimant to the throne was the Yongli Emperor, Zhu Youlang. And the most celebrated military general under his rule was named Li Dingguo."

"What you're saying is common knowledge to any educated person," Professor Zhou interrupted coldly. "The Southern Ming troops retreated to the Yunnan border and, in 1659, the Yongli Emperor was forced into exile in Burma, which is now Myanmar. But General Li remained at the Yunnan border, fighting the Manchus right up to his deadly defeat in 1662."

Frustrated by the history lesson, Luo wondered what they were going on about—until the Yunnan border came up. He sat up straighter.

"Of course, it's in history textbooks." Yue Dongbei made a sour face. "But let me ask you something. When General Li fled to the border, he had no more than ten thousand troops. They were surrounded and outnumbered by the Manchus. Don't you think it's strange they were able to hold out for three long years?"

"What's so strange about it?" Professor Zhou countered. "Li Dingguo was a brilliant general. The soldiers under his command were experienced fighters and famous for their courage."

"You have nothing more than a superficial understanding." Yue Dongbei stared the other man down. "At full strength, they suffered successive defeats. General Li's last remaining fighters found themselves under siege in the forest. The emperor was in exile abroad. Morale was low. And yet they remained undefeated for three years. How?"

Professor Zhou went on the defensive. "So let's hear your theory."

Yue Dongbei chuckled proudly, leaning back into the sofa. "Today, General Li's final stronghold has a name: the Valley of Terror!"

"The Valley of Terror?" Luo and Professor Zhou exclaimed.

"You've heard the name before, right? He was the one who told you." Yue Dongbei's face held immense satisfaction. "But what you don't know is the origin of the name. According to Chinese history textbooks, it's because, during bloody clashes of those years, there were unburied corpses everywhere. Ha! Lies!"

All of the sudden, Yue Dongbei leapt to his feet. "According to my research, the valley got its name because General Li was endowed with the power to conjure demonic spirits. That's how he won so many battles!"

Luo shook his head dismissively.

"Nonsense!" Professor Zhou barked.

But Yue Dongbei was undaunted. "Of course it's not nonsense."

He opened the briefcase he'd brought with him and took out a hard plastic case. He stood up and placed the case on the desk, opening it up to reveal its contents.

Luo and Professor Zhou peered inside. All it contained was a strip of cloth a little less than a foot long. The cloth was old and decrepit. However, a faded column of dark red text in traditional Chinese characters could be made out:

One with the demons, joyous and carefree.

May these schemes be hatched, and may you prisoners of terror be!

"A soldier under General Li's command wore this tied around his head. A few years ago, I had the good fortune to find this, which is how it all began. The text's meaning is clear. General Li told his troops, 'I have the power to conjure demons, my followers, and it is a glorious thing. If you should betray me, you will be dragged into the prison that is the Valley of Terror!'" Yue Dongbei crowed.

Professor Zhou shook his head. "Demons were just a trick that officers used to motivate their soldiers in those days. During the Boxer Rebellion, weren't there claims of spirit possession? Would you take that as fact, too?"

"Fact? Anyone who sits at home reading books has no idea what facts are!" Yue Dongbei rolled his eyes. "I am a scholar. I have a rigorous approach to research. After I obtained this cloth, I undertook a substantial investigation and conducted numerous interviews. In addition, I listened to oral history accounts, which have corroborated my own theory."

"How so?" Luo lifted an eyebrow.

"Just when the situation at the Yunnan border seemed dire, General Li manifested an almighty, supernatural strength. His men were filled with boundless courage, such that they died in combat, their faces beaming with joy. And those too cowardly to fight were punished by the demons—their fate was to die from fear! What a miracle of perseverance!"

"But didn't General Li ultimately die in battle? If he really possessed the power to conjure demons, how do you explain that?" Luo had noticed a flaw in Yue Dongbei's theory.

"Good question!" Yue Dongbei said. "That's the missing piece that I'm still working out, and it's the reason I've come here today. Nonetheless, I can provide an explanation of this strange phenomenon you've recently encountered!"

Luo gestured for him to continue.

"So General Li was entrenched in the forest for years. Not only were the Manchus terrified of him, but the locals became involved and there was tremendous suffering. By then, General Li had become tyrannical, the devil incarnate. Then a high priest from the local tribe concocted a scheme to bring about his demise." Yue Dongbei paused, closed his eyes, and shook his head, his face sorrowful.

"A scheme? What are we talking about?" Luo asked.

"I don't know yet." Yue Dongbei shrugged. A helpless expression crossed his face. "I'm a scholar. Anything I say has to be based on facts. All I can tell you is that, in the end, the bravest of the local fighters cut off his head. And without their leader, his army quickly crumbled. But the locals lived in fear of the demons' retaliation until, in a show of magical powers by the high priest, the demons were suppressed."

"And what factual basis do you have for any of this?" Professor Zhou scoffed.

"Of course there's a basis for it: history books!" Yue Dongbei's eyes shone with pride. "But they're not Chinese. History is written by the victors. Naturally, the Manchus didn't make any record of this humiliating incident. So I consulted Burmese history books."

"Burmese history books?" Slightly surprised, Luo looked in admiration at the chubby man before him.

"That's right. The Burmese forces were involved in the war and attested to General Li's death and the high priest's use of magical powers to suppress the demons. But they didn't take part in the operation itself, so their records are incomplete."

"Haven't you sought out the descendants of the locals? There might be some discrepancies with your erudite understanding," Professor Zhou said mockingly.

"If I could, I would have done so ages ago." Yue Dongbei sounded rather glum. "The Hamo people, including those from the Valley of Terror, live deep in the wilderness. In order to reach them, you would need to be in optimal physical condition and have the mountaineering skills to handle rugged conditions. All I did was publish my findings online, hoping to find a sense of community—as well as someone who might be capable of realizing this wish of mine."

"The patient!" Luo blurted out. "He's the person you found!"

"Very good, Inspector," Yue Dongbei said. "But you got one thing wrong. I didn't find him—he found me. He was very interested in my research, and under my guidance, he set off to find the Hamos. I knew he'd be successful, as he was extraordinarily gifted, as well as tenacious and intensely curious."

"Who is he? What's his name?" Luo asked in a rush.

"He's a professional trekker. His name? I don't know." Seeing the perplexed look on Luo's face, Yue Dongbei mused nonchalantly, "Is his name important? I think it's meaningless. The bottom line is, he found the blood vial. It's truly amazing. It's a thrilling achievement!"

"What do you mean, the blood vial?"

"Oh right, I haven't told you yet. The high priest trapped the demons in a blood vial. As long as the vial remained sealed, they would have no way of manifesting their terrifying powers." Yue Dongbei's face was glowing. He scooted up to the sofa's edge and pulled out a folder, which he tossed in front of Luo. "Take a look. Not only are there written records of the blood vial in Burmese literature and history, but there are also illustrations of it. I made a copy just for you!"

Indeed, the papers inside the folder contained illustrations of a tiny vial, a sleek tube whose body narrowed into a spike at the top.

Suddenly, Luo furrowed his brows and peered at Yue Dongbei. "How do you know he found the vial?"

"Ha ha ha!" Yue Dongbei let out a strange, wild laugh. "Do you really need to ask? He not only found the vial, he must have broken it open! The demons—evil spirits that have been trapped inside for three hundred years—have reemerged! It's a pity that talented young man became the first victim. But in order for the truth to come to light, to give a slap in the face to those die-hard adherents of science, that kind of sacrifice is worth it. The only thing I don't understand is why the demons are coming to Longzhou. It's very interesting. I'll have to look into it."

Luo stared at the drawings, dumbstruck. A moment later, he collected himself and sternly told Yue Dongbei, "I'm sorry, but your theory is quite difficult to believe."

"I expected as much from the likes of you. But it doesn't matter. When confronted with reality, you will submit to me—no, you will submit to the truth!"

"What a lunatic," Professor Zhou said with disgust as he watched Yue Dongbei jauntily walk away. "And a charlatan. He's hoping to take advantage of this opportunity to get famous!" Then he noticed Luo still staring blankly at the illustrations. "Chief Inspector Luo, I don't understand why you're still looking at those. Don't tell me you actually believe in that madman's so-called science?"

"It's not a question of whether I believe in it," mumbled Luo. "This very vial actually did show up in Longzhou not too long ago, and what's more, it had been opened!"

Chapter 6

The Secrets of the Blood Vial

If not for the illustrations, Luo probably would have dismissed Yue Dongbei as a demon-obsessed lunatic. However, the drawings of the blood vial gave him no choice but to keep an open mind.

The only thing to do was to take Professor Zhou to the Cultural Relics and Archaeology Institute. On the way there, Luo briefed him on the vial's appearance in Longzhou.

About four months earlier, the police had received a tip regarding the illegal trade of a cultural artifact scheduled to take place at the Xiyuan Hotel. Given the seriousness of stolen artifacts, Luo himself took part in the stakeout.

The operation initially went smoothly. With the cooperation of an undercover agent, the police ambushed the transaction and took control without a single bullet fired. Apart from the informer, four people were involved in the deal. The seller was the notorious Old Hei, a prolific Longzhou-based relics dealer, who was accompanied by two of his underlings. The buyer was a short, dark-skinned, middle-aged man.

He looked as if he might be from Southeast Asia. As it turned out, he was from Myanmar.

When the police burst in, the relic was already inside the Burmese man's leather briefcase. The police ordered the man to open the briefcase, never guessing what would happen next.

The interior of the briefcase had been painstakingly lined to protect the object inside—a distinctively shaped vial. It was a tube with a spiked top, about four inches tall and one and a half wide. The materials appeared to be of exceptional quality—glass and an unidentified metal.

Luo and his team attempted to interrogate the suspects, but they wouldn't talk. Then, suddenly, the Burmese man seized the vial and leaped out the hotel window.

Because they were on the fifteenth floor, the police hadn't anticipated this possibility. When Luo dashed to the window, he discovered a terrace between the thirteenth and fourteenth floors. The man had landed on it and was bolting to safety.

Luo didn't hesitate to leap down after him. But when he landed, he twisted his ankle and collapsed, watching the man sprint toward an open window on the fourteenth floor.

Luo had no choice but to fire a warning shot. He aimed at the man's leg and squeezed the trigger.

The man dropped to the ground. After getting back up on his feet, he just stood there.

Hobbling over, Luo saw that the man's eyes were filled with terror. He was staring at his right hand. It dripped with crimson blood.

This man had been fleeing with all his might, yet now he was frozen. He seemed stupefied for a moment, then his grip slackened. The vial hit the ground with a clank.

The container had been split down the middle, and blood was gushing out.

Two police officers reached the terrace, surrounding the man and taking him by the arms. The man let out a piercing scream, and in a burst of strength that caught the officers off guard, twisted himself free.

But, to their astonishment, he didn't try to run. All he did was violently fling his hand around, then repeatedly wipe it on the ground. At first, Luo thought the bullet might have hit his hand. But it was unscathed; the blood had come from the vial.

Luo could hardly believe the man's hysteria. If a knife had been available, he would undoubtedly have cut off his own hand.

On the way to the station, the officers could not subdue the Burmese man. He kept repeating the same few words over and over. When they were able to get hold of an interpreter, they learned there were two main phrases.

The first was "It's been opened!"

The other was "The demons will come back to life!"

After some perfunctory paperwork, the agitated foreigner was turned over to Burmese authorities, and Luo's team focused on interrogating Old Hei, the local relics trafficker. According to Old Hei, the supplier kept their identity a secret, providing photos of the goods via the Internet. Under their guidance, Old Hei had easily found a willing buyer: the Burmese man, who unexpectedly offered one million US dollars for the tiny vial and, moreover, made a down payment of three hundred thousand. The mystery supplier then sent the vial to Old Hei by courier.

The police had other questions: What was the vial for? Why was it so valuable? What was the story behind the blood inside? Why was the Burmese man so terrified? But Old Hei knew absolutely nothing. The only thing Luo could do was send the vial to the Cultural Relics and Archaeology Institute for examination. Old Hei was charged with smuggling, and Luo, busy at work, forgot all about following up with the institute.

◆ ◆ ◆

But a few months later, here it was in Yue Dongbei's papers, a vial identical to the one that had been broken open.

When the institute's deputy director, Zhu Xiaohua, got the call from Luo, he was thrilled. After all, what could be more magnificent for a scholar than to have important people inquire about your research?

When Luo and Professor Zhou arrived, the three of them got right down to business.

Zhu Xiaohua looked to be around forty years old. He was tall and stout. On his round face was a pair of black glasses that gave him a simple, honest air. And on the desk in front of him was a rectangular glass case containing the object in question.

Zhu Xiaohua lifted the glass case for them to see, beaming. "Chief Inspector Luo, you came for this, yes? I've spent no small amount of time studying it."

"May I have a look?" Professor Zhou stepped forward and stared at the mysterious vial intently.

"Please." Zhu Xiaohua gracefully handed over the case. "There's no harm in looking. It was constructed with a very special material. Even though it was struck by a bullet, there's only a small crack."

Professor Zhou picked up the case and peered inside. Sure enough, there was only an indentation and a crack where the bullet had hit. The vial's sleek profile had been preserved, along with its mysterious black luster. It really was identical to the vial in the papers Yue Dongbei had left.

"If my hunch is correct, your research has been fruitful," Luo said to Zhu Xiaohua, a man whose every joy and sorrow seemed to be written across his face.

"That's right," Zhu Xiaohua happily replied. "This relic is extraordinary. We estimate it to be about three hundred years old."

Luo and Professor Zhou exchanged a glance. The time frame corresponded to Yue Dongbei's account.

Zhu Xiaohua, who didn't notice their reaction, continued: "It has enormous research value to numerous fields, including history, culture, ethnography, even witchcraft and metallurgy—the list goes on. If it weren't for the bullet hole, it would have been the most exciting discovery of the year!"

Luo couldn't help feeling a tad remorseful. "It all went down so quickly. I was scrambling and there wasn't a better solution. It really is a shame that the vial was broken."

Zhu Xiaohua shook his head. "No, no. You prevented the smuggler from getting away, as I understand it, and a damaged artifact is far better than none at all. Well-preserved human blood from several centuries ago is earth-shattering for medicine, archeology, and biology, among other fields!"

"Seriously? It sure looked like blood, but I couldn't quite believe it. How is it possible that it was preserved so long?"

"That's what's so magical about this vial. Its material and construction are a mystery, but what we do know is that, after the vial was made, it was completely airtight, preserving the contents. Of course, after the vial was split open, the blood began to decay and dry up."

"But why was that blood inside the vial? Could it have contained something dangerous?" Luo's head spun, wondering if the blood contained some sort of fear-inducing pathogen. But there were too many pieces that didn't fit, the most salient of which was that he himself had come into contact with the blood during the Burmese man's arrest, and he was still fine.

"Dangerous?" Zhu Xiaohua laughed. "No, this isn't a science fiction novel. It's just ordinary human blood. Other than the fact that it's a few years older, it's very much the same as yours or mine. And why was it sealed inside the vial? Heh. That question eluded me for quite some time. I spent more than two months poring over all kinds of material, unofficial histories, and even folklore, and in the end, I arrived at the answer."

Luo and Professor Zhou stared at him, wide-eyed.

Zhu Xiaohua seemed elated by their reaction and, licking his lips, told them, "It was done as part of an ethnic custom related to witchcraft. To be precise, it's a curse."

"A curse?" Luo raised his eyebrows.

"That's right." Zhu Xiaohua nodded firmly, his tone becoming more formal, as if delivering a lecture. "In the southwestern part of the country live various ethnic minority groups, including those from smaller Southeast Asian countries. In such places, the local people believe that, after a person dies, his body, blood, hair, and so forth must all return to the earth in order for reincarnation to occur."

"Uh-huh." Luo's eyes flashed. "So that means if a certain person died and their blood was sealed inside the vial, then that person couldn't reincarnate?"

"Correct. Their soul would drift eternally between two worlds. Of course, this is merely superstition."

"That certainly is a venomous curse. Why do you think you hadn't encountered it before?"

"There are two reasons," Zhu Xiaohua explained. "The first is that the blood vial was incredibly difficult to make, with the secret technique being handed down among the high priests. The second is that the curse seems to be strictly prohibited due to its sheer ferocity. Only in extreme circumstances, and with the permission of the tribal leader, would it ever have been used."

"So, for instance, if everyone in the entire tribe utterly despised that person?"

"Perhaps. Or if the person terrorized the tribe."

"Terrorized?" Luo furrowed his brow.

"In tribes like these, past favors and grudges are carried over from one generation to the next. If someone from the past was particularly vicious, people would be afraid that they would reincarnate and do more harm."

"Ah." Luo nodded, one more question burning on his tongue. "So whose blood was actually inside this vial?"

Zhu Xiaohua pressed his lips together, unable to suppress a laugh as he replied, "That I have no answer to! You sent me this vial; I have no other leads."

Luo hesitated for a moment. "Do you know the name Li Dingguo?"

"Li Dingguo? Wasn't he that general who fought against the Manchus?"

"Some people think this blood might have something to do with Li Dingguo."

"Who thinks that?" Zhu Xiaohua was supremely interested in the matter.

Luo struggled to find the right words to describe Yue Dongbei. "A person—uh—a person who's an expert in history."

"I covered a great deal of historical material in my research. How is it possible that I've never heard of this?" Zhu Xiaohua asked.

"He claims to have researched Burmese history books."

Professor Zhou, who couldn't hold it in any longer, finally spoke. "In my opinion, the man's a charlatan."

Confronted by Zhu Xiaohua's alarmed face, Luo broke down Yue Dongbei's theory for him, bit by bit.

"That's absurd. It's sheer nonsense!" Zhu Xiaohua shook his head repeatedly. "Chief Inspector Luo, how can you give credence to such an idea? And Professor Zhou, with all your expertise! What in the world made you come here?"

Luo let out a dark laugh. "It sounds like you've been too busy to pay attention to the news recently!" He gave Zhu Xiaohua an account of the strange things that had occurred.

Zhu Xiaohua was incredulous. After a long silence, he declared, "I'm not the detective here, but this fear disease must be the work of a human being—and I find this Yue Dongbei highly suspicious!"

Professor Zhou turned and looked tensely at Luo. It was clear that he agreed.

Chapter 7

DEMONIC POWERS

A silence fell over Zhu Xiaohua's office. The two celebrated scholars frowned at Luo. There was something hard to describe about the chief investigator, especially his eyes, which sparkled. Given the bizarre twists of the case before them, he was perhaps the only one who could lead them through this dense fog and bring the truth to light.

But at this moment, those eyes were filled with confusion. He stared at the blood vial on the table. His mind shuttled back and forth in time and space, between Yunnan during the Southern Ming Dynasty, Longzhou in August, the long-dead military general, the unidentified relics dealer, and the wildly arrogant metaphysicist. These disparate elements somehow converged in this tiny blood vial, and it was up to Luo to figure out how.

Then he lifted his head, a look of realization in his eyes.

"I'm going to give Yue Dongbei a call," Luo said, taking out his cell phone. The conversation was very brief. "He's coming over right away. He was very excited to hear the news."

A short while later, Yue Dongbei appeared. He didn't even bother knocking, just barreled into the room.

The man's bald head was flushed, his eyes were wide, and he was panting. Huge beads of sweat ran down his face.

"The vial! Where is the vial?" Yue Dongbei demanded, a slight tremor in his voice.

After he received no response from the three men, his gaze locked in on his target. His stocky frame darted with astonishing speed to the desk, and he seized the glass case in both hands.

Zhu Xiaohua scowled at the man's rude behavior. But Yue Dongbei paid no heed, staring into the case with an almost crazed look.

"It really is the blood vial! After all my years of research, I have concrete proof!"

He lifted his head to look at Luo and the others. The bliss on his face and tears in his eyes were far more than Luo had expected.

"It really has been broken. And it's in Longzhou! No wonder the demons have been appearing. But what was inside of it?"

Zhu Xiaohua threw an uncertain glance at Luo.

Yue Dongbei happily cried out, "You! You know the answer. Tell me right now!"

Seeing Zhu Xiaohua vacillating, Yue Dongbei straightened his face. "You must tell me! We're both scholars here. We're working together to unravel a mystery. Don't keep anything back!"

Zhu Xiaohua laughed a little at Yue Dongbei identifying himself as a scholar, but Luo nodded, and the researcher recounted his findings.

Yue Dongbei was wide-eyed as he listened. "Yes! That's exactly right. It makes perfect sense!"

He rubbed his hands together a few times, then turned to Luo. "So how did the vial surface in Longzhou? Chief Inspector Luo, this is the question that I'd most like to hear your answer to."

Keeping his cool, Luo informed him about the relics trafficking and the Burmese man. All the while, he looked intently into Yue Dongbei's eyes so that even the slightest internal shift would not escape his keen perception.

Yue Dongbei displayed no reservations whatsoever about being scrutinized by Luo. "Yes, that's right. Do you still not get it? Well, I have the answers to all of your questions!"

Professor Zhou and Zhu Xiaohua both raised their eyebrows, while Luo only gave a gentle laugh. "Tell us, then."

Not that Yue Dongbei could have kept his mouth shut if he'd tried.

"It's all clear. The Hamo, the Manchu troops, and the Burmese conspired to kill General Li. They feared his demonic powers, so the high priest of the Hamo sealed his blood inside the vial so that he would never reincarnate. The young trekker who I sent to find the vial obviously succeeded, and then someone brought it to Longzhou. To think that you wound up being the person who broke open the vial, Chief Inspector Luo! You let the demons escape! You're searching for the culprit, but the culprit is you!" There was a touch of schadenfreude in his laugh.

Luo was reticent. Yue Dongbei's impertinent remarks didn't seem to have upset him. Professor Zhou and Zhu Xiaohua also looked on with cool detachment.

"You do believe me, don't you?" Yue Dongbei was accustomed to getting the cold shoulder, but this time he had enough ammunition to launch a counterattack. He pretended to cough a few times, then raised his voice. "You act on the part of scientists, so of course you won't accept my views. But can you come up with a better explanation? Ha. You have no other leads. Go ahead and verify each and every thing I've said. I've won. It's funny, you all think you're defenders of the truth, when in fact you lack the courage to confront reality."

"Reality?" Professor Zhou couldn't contain himself any longer. "Or an elaborate hoax?"

"Are you saying that I'm a fraud?" The veins in Yue Dongbei's forehead bulged. "I am a scholar! When I make a claim, it is based on historical data. A hoax? How dare you, sir!"

"All right, we're not here to attack each other!" Luo lifted a hand. "This young man who went to find the vial, who was he? What was his motive?"

"I already told you, I don't really know him. We just met online." Yue Dongbei scoffed as if the question weren't important. "He believed my theories. He had excellent outdoor-survival skills. He was extremely curious about the vial. And for me, that was enough. As for who he was, my guess is he was some sort of adventurer. And his motive, in light of the sale you broke up, was probably money."

"How could you not even know his name?"

"I actually asked him. He gave a very strange answer." Yue Dongbei appeared to have remembered something. He scratched his bald head.

"Keep talking."

"He said it comes before Zhou in the ancient book *The Hundred Family Names*." Yue Dongbei looked at Professor Zhou, then added spitefully, "Professor Zhou, it seems that you two are related."

Luo wrinkled his brow. "'Comes before Zhou in *The Hundred Family Names*?'" It was a strangely worded phrase, and for the moment, he couldn't work out what the speaker was implying. "He didn't say anything else?"

"No, nothing." Yue Dongbei shook his round head. "Though actually, now that you remind me, we did meet in person once. We spent the whole time discussing research related to General Li. We had so much to talk about that we didn't bother with any small talk like names!"

"You forgot that you met him?" Luo had one hand over his eyes. "How could you—never mind. So you're saying he was already interested in General Li?"

"That's right. But his knowledge was superficial." Yue Dongbei couldn't hide his arrogance. "Can you imagine? When he saw the depth and insight of my theories online, he must have been astonished! That's why he got in touch with me right away."

"Did he really believe the whole thing about the demons?"

"Of course!" Yue Dongbei proclaimed. "When he left, he took a copy of one of my books."

"Oh? Can I see it?" Luo trilled, playing to the man's vanity.

Yue Dongbei immediately scrambled to remove a crudely bound book from his bag and handed it over to Luo. "Have a look."

The text was printed on a couple hundred pages of standard copy paper. The title page, set in a large font, served as a rudimentary cover. It read *Secrets of Demonic Power: An Analysis of Li Dingguo at the End of the Ming Dynasty.*

On the second page was a foreword:

> Li Dingguo (also known as Zi Ningyu and Zi Hongyuan) was a native of Yulin in Shaanxi Province. During the late Ming and early Qing Dynasties, he was a celebrated military general of Han descent.
>
> In 1630, at the age of ten, he joined Zhang Xianzhong's revolt, and the rebel leader took him under his wing. In 1637, Li Dingguo commanded twenty thousand troops in Sichuan and Hubei Provinces, killing General Zhang Ling of the Ming Dynasty. In 1641, he commanded a cavalry that captured and killed the Xiangyang Prince, Zhu Yiming. From then on, he was known by the nicknames The Wanrendi (the ten-thousand-man uprising) and Little Yuchi (after the character in *Water Margin*).
>
> After the Manchus seized control, Zhang Xianzhong's troops were defeated and General Li led his brigade the other way, supporting the Yongli Emperor during the Southern Ming Dynasty.
>
> During the Battle of Dingguan on July 1, 1652, he fought Kong Youde, the Dingnan Prince of the Qing Dynasty. Both sides braved thunder and lightning

during the bloodbath, and in the end, Li drove the diminished Qing forces to the very edge of Rongjian County.

Kong Youde retreated to Guilin, but Li launched a relentless assault on the city on July 4. Kong Youde, left with no means of escape, took his own life. Li soon captured the cities of Liuzhou and Wuzhou, thereby taking over all of Guangxi. Within six months' time, he had taken control of twelve prefectures in two provinces—an expanse of over nine hundred miles.

In November of the same year, the Qing government under Nikan, Prince Jingjin of the First Rank, dispatched ten thousand troops against Li. The two sides clashed in Hengzhou, and four days later, General Li himself killed Nikan.

While historical texts highlight Li Dingguo's outstanding achievements in battle, they are incomplete if they overlook the fact that, according to numerous sources, Li Dingguo possessed demonic powers. The few Manchu soldiers who survived the Battle of Dingguan claimed that his army employed demons to torment them, and Manchu officials considered the general himself a demon incarnate.

For reasons that have not been brought to light, General Li's adopted brother—Sun Kewang, the warlord and Southern Ming leader—bore a grudge against him. In the name of "exterminating the demon," Sun Kewang mobilized 140,000 troops against Li, but they were soundly defeated. However, in February 1658, Qing troops set forth on a journey to unleash a massive, three-front assault on Li's forces in Guizhou and Yunnan. And in April, Sun Kewang's former subordinate Wang Ziqi added an attack on the county of Yongchang, in what is now Yunnan. Under siege internally as well as externally, Li fled to the forest in Yunnan near the Burmese border.

Even with his vast army reduced to only ten thousand soldiers, General Li maintained his position in the forest for three years. The area, long populated by the ethnic minority Hamo people, came to be known as "the Valley of Terror," and it was said to be the wellspring of his demonic powers.

In 1662, the seemingly unconquerable Li was abruptly overthrown by the joint forces of the Manchus, the Burmese, and the Hamos. And to this day, the legend of the demons near the border persists.

What were those demonic powers? What secrets was Li Dingguo hiding? This book seeks to uncover the answers to these questions.

Luo paused for a moment, lost in thought. Then he asked, "How did Burma get involved in all this? The Yongli Emperor was in exile in Burma, right?"

"Well, the Burmese feared the Manchus, so they placed the Yongli Emperor under house arrest—which enraged General Li. The history books say ten thousand Burmese soldiers lined up along the opposite bank of the river, preparing for battle, but Li unleashed a surprise attack, and it took only a few hundred of his men to slaughter all ten thousand. Burmese officials were forced to release the Yongli Emperor.

"They say that Burmese children still cry when they hear Li Dingguo's name. You said the buyer of the vial was Burmese, didn't you? He must come from the people living along the border, who have always feared that the vial would be opened. General Li's reign of terror continues!"

Zhu Xiaohua, also a historian, was nodding slightly. General Li's rout of the Burmese army was well known.

Luo scanned through the rest of the manuscript and soon discovered that the following two hundred pages or so only recounted what had been said in the foreword. He closed the book, gently patting its cover. "At the end of your foreword, you raised two questions, but you haven't answered them."

"That's because I still don't have the answers." Yue Dongbei looked slightly embarrassed.

"If there's a question, there must be an answer," Professor Zhou scoffed.

"Of course there is," Yue Dongbei countered. "In fact, there's someone who already has it!"

Luo understood immediately. "You mean the trekker?"

Yue Dongbei nodded, then turned glum. "It's too bad that he's under the influence of demonic forces, so he can't tell us everything that he knows."

Luo was rubbing his chin lightly. He hadn't shaved since this string of strange incidents had begun. As the thick hairs on his chin pricked his fingertips, Luo grew alert.

"Who is he, anyway? And what happened to him in the forest?" Luo muttered to himself.

Identifying the mysterious patient had been his original goal. Then Yue Dongbei had come along with his stupefying theory and sent them running around in circles.

Yue Dongbei's eyes twinkled as he said, "The truth, yes, the truth is hidden therein, and we must pursue it to the very end. Chief Inspector Luo, your job is to uncover secrets. And me, I would like to finish this academic monograph. As for you two scientists, you will reap the greatest benefits of all, as this will help you construct a proper conception of truth."

"Pursue it to the very end?" Luo echoed. "Do you have some sort of plan?"

"Yes, I do. A plan, indeed!" Yue Dongbei rubbed his hands together. "We're going to retrace his footsteps, follow the directions I gave him. This trip will be extremely challenging for us, even dangerous. But we must go! This young man's miserable plight has confirmed my theory! All the secrets of the forest await us."

Luo stared at him, trying to imagine how a man so out of shape could undertake a grueling trek into the forest.

"Chief Inspector Luo, scientists, do you understand? I'm inviting you to take part in my fascinating journey." Yue Dongbei's eyes glittered as he looked at the others one by one.

Luo and the others were dumbfounded for a minute. Finally, Luo laughed and asked, "But why?"

"Strength in numbers!" Yue Dongbei teased, but he then grew solemn. "Even though we have tremendous differences of opinion, you each have exceptional observational and analytical skills. I need your help."

"Sure, why not." Luo turned to look at Professor Zhou and Zhu Xiaohua, who gaped at him. "I know it's all crazy, but like Yue Dongbei said, I did break the vial. And the eyes of all the innocent victims who died of fright have been keeping me up at night. I'll never forgive myself if this fear disease becomes an epidemic in my city and I didn't make every effort to stop it."

Zhu Xiaohua began shaking his head dramatically. "Not me. Not a chance. I do my work in the office and the library. On-site expeditions are for archaeologists."

Professor Zhou was reticent. The others stared at him.

"Fine, I'll go. But it doesn't mean that I accept your theory. Just the opposite." After a pause, he added, "You're going on a spiritual journey, and I can respect that. But I'm going in order to represent science, and I'm not backing down."

"Very well." Yue Dongbei flashed an ecstatic smile. "I already have the directions mapped out. Why don't we all go make our individual preparations and set out a week from now?"

Chapter 8

THE RAIN GOD'S TEARS

At the southernmost end of Yunnan Province, at a latitude of roughly 21° north and a longitude of 101° west, a minor landform protruded southward. This peninsula fell within Mengla County in the Xishuangbanna Dai Autonomous Prefecture, which bordered Myanmar to the west and Laos to the south, and the confluence of nations resulted in a corridor of ports and trade.

The area was famous for tea production. Five of the six major tea mountains where Pu'er tea was produced—Mansa, Manzhuan, Youle, Yibang, and Gedeng—were in the region.

It was also a well-known tourist destination, due to the best-preserved primeval rainforest in all of China. Mengla's rainforest teemed with natural wonder, and it guarded mysteries still unknown to man.

Luo, Professor Zhou, and Yue Dongbei arrived in the county seat and, led by a local guide, headed west over rough terrain toward the China-Myanmar border. They rode on horseback for half a day before approaching Mihong, a village that sat between the foot of a colossal mountain and a dry riverbed. Further west they could see a mountain range and dense rainforest.

Most of the residents of Mengla County belonged to the dozen or so local ethnic minorities, primarily the Dai, Hani, Yao, and Yi. But Mihong stood out in being one of the villages that was predominantly Han. The villagers, who could speak Mandarin, were farmers. Their clothing was antiquated but clearly in the Han tradition.

"According to historical records," Yue Dongbei had explained, "after General Li's death, his soldiers had no choice but to surrender. Since they were unwilling to die in the service of the Qing government, the commanding officer asked that they be stationed along the China-Burma border. The residents of this village are the descendants of those troops."

By the time they reached the stockaded village, dusk had fallen and there was little activity. They saw just two men on the narrow road, who gave the group only a quick glance before returning to their business.

"Given how remote this place is, shouldn't they be more surprised to see outsiders?" asked Luo.

"Mihong serves as a base camp for adventurers," the guide explained, "because it's the closest village to the forest. Thrill seekers set up here and hire the locals as guides, so they're used to strange people turning up. Did all of you come here looking for adventure?"

Luo and the others exchanged glances. Though unsure how to reply, each felt exhilarated deep down. They may in fact have come looking for adventure, but the dangers that lay ahead were beyond anything they could have imagined.

Mihong wasn't by any means small, with several hundred homes within its limits. When they reached the center of town, the guide pointed and said, "That brick house belongs to a man by the name of Wang. He rents rooms, and he's honest. Travelers often stay with him."

Mr. Wang was turning sixty this year, and he lived alone. His wife had died the year before, and his two daughters had moved to the county seat. Upon seeing new faces, he barely said a word. He led Luo and the others to their room, spoke briefly to the guide, then left to take care of other matters.

"The accommodations cost ten yuan per person per night. Meals are another ten yuan per day, but there's no breakfast tomorrow morning," the guide relayed.

"Why not?" Yue Dongbei complained. "Does it cost extra?"

"It's not about money," the guide explained, smiling. "Tomorrow the village is holding a ceremony at the Temple of the Dragon King to worship the Rain God."

"The Rain God?" Luo remembered the dry riverbed. "It hasn't rained here in a long time, has it?"

"Nearly a month." The guide shook his head. "This season, it's brutal. If it doesn't rain soon, the food supply for the entire village will be in jeopardy."

Yue Dongbei flapped a hand at the guide. "All right, all right. But our dinner had better be ready soon. Come get us when it's time."

The guide turned and left the room.

Yue Dongbei flopped down on the giant bed. With his belly arcing into the air, he heaved a sigh and announced, "My, how this day has exhausted me!"

"Exhausted already?" Professor Zhou chuckled a little. "What are you going to do once we actually get to the forest?"

"Oh, don't you worry. I'm not done for yet," Yue Dongbei answered.

Luo didn't involve himself in their squabble. He was busy checking over every last inch of the small room. It was about fifty square feet and furnished with nothing but the bed.

About twenty minutes later, the guide came back and announced that dinner was ready. After a long day of travel, their stomachs were rumbling. They followed the guide into the adjacent room and were met with an enticing aroma. Several large bowls had been set out on the dinner table at the center of the room. The main course consisted of diamond-shaped slices of something white that had been sautéed with meat, egg, and vegetables.

"What is this?" Luo had never seen anything like it before.

When Mr. Wang did not respond, the guide took over. "It's a Yunnan specialty, stir-fried rice cakes. They're exquisite. People here call them the Emperor's Lifeline."

"The Emperor's Lifeline?" Professor Zhou couldn't help asking. "Where did that name come from?"

The guide grinned. "From a folktale! It dates back to when the Yongli Emperor fled to Yunnan. The Southern Ming general Li Dingguo had the local villagers cook up a bowl of stir-fried rice cakes for him. The Yongli Emperor was full of praise for the dish, and he said, 'Stir-fried rice cakes have served as a lifeline for the emperor.'"

At the name *Li Dingguo*, the three travelers were aghast. Appetites momentarily forgotten, they stared hollowly at the dishes, the guide, and each other.

Something occurred to Luo. He pulled out a photograph and showed it to Mr. Wang. "Have you ever seen this person before?"

Mr. Wang studied the photo closely. "He stayed here. It was almost a year ago."

The man in the photograph was, of course, now a deranged patient at the Kunming Behavioral Health Center.

Yue Dongbei looked up smugly. "Looks like I was right! This village was the first place he stopped. He followed the directions I gave him."

Luo ignored the interruption. "How long did he stay?"

"Two days. He asked how to get to the Valley of Terror, and then he left."

"Did he hire a guide?"

Mr. Wang shook his head. "He was alone."

"Oh," Luo said. If the young man had hired a guide, they could have questioned him. Still, this confirmed they were on the right track.

The guide noticed Luo's disappointment. "Why? Do you want to go to the Valley of Terror?"

Rather than answering, Luo responded with his own question: "Do you know about the Valley of Terror?"

"I know about it, all right. But I've never been. It's deep in the wilderness, so people don't usually go. But there should be Hamos and a village nearby."

"Now's not a good time to go there," Mr. Wang pronounced.

Luo immediately asked, "Why?"

"The forest people have been fleeing in droves. They say that the demons have returned." The taciturn man stared intently at Luo, evidently moved by concern to speak up.

"Demons? What kind of demons?" Like a bloodhound catching its scent, Yue Dongbei darted over.

Mr. Wang shook his head. "That's a secret only the Hamos know."

"A secret?" Yue Dongbei laughed. "A secret just waiting to be revealed!"

Luo turned and shot Professor Zhou a helpless look. Absurd as it seemed, Mr. Wang's words supported Yue Dongbei's crazy theory. If they wanted to get to the bottom of this and prevent a massive crisis in Longzhou, they would have no choice but to carry out their journey to the very end.

By the time they finished dinner, it was already seven o'clock. The guide, who had to depart for the county seat the next day, retired early. Though Luo and the others were weary from the journey, they weren't accustomed to going to bed so early, so they sat in the courtyard enjoying the breeze. Soon, boredom set in. Then Mr. Wang came out carrying a large bamboo basket.

Luo asked him a few questions and learned that the basket was filled with offerings for the Rain God. Mr. Wang was heading to the Temple of the Dragon King so that his offerings might have a chance of being placed in a good position, close to the Rain God, to earn him extra care in the coming year.

"Is the temple far? Can we come with you?" Luo asked.

"Half a mile. If there's anything here worth seeing, it's the temple. All the travelers used to go. But it won't bring you good luck. It only brings rain," Mr. Wang said solemnly.

The houses grew fewer and the last evening light faded as they followed Mr. Wang, making Luo slightly uneasy. Then, suddenly, there was a sharp bend in the trail and a large clearing appeared. The ground had been leveled to create a public square. At the east end, with its façade facing south and its back facing north, stood a temple. Though the temple wasn't big, it had a distinctive air. The style and materials revealed that it was very old, but it had been well preserved.

"This is the Temple of the Dragon King," Mr. Wang intoned, leading the way inside.

Perhaps affected by Mr. Wang's pious demeanor, Luo felt a sense of solemnity overtake him. The only light came from two tall lanterns on either side of the altar. In the middle of nowhere, in the flickering candlelight, the temple felt a little gloomy, to say the least.

Then Luo's eyes fell on the towering icon behind the altar, and he couldn't help but let out a gasp.

Professor Zhou and Yue Dongbei were also agape.

Inscribed on the tablet next to the icon were five words: LI DING-GUO, THE RAIN GOD.

Mr. Wang didn't seem to notice the strange reaction of his three guests. As he placed his basket of offerings atop the altar, he explained,

"We villagers depend on the heavens to eat. The Rain God has always blessed us with peace and abundance, and watched over us."

Luo's mind was reeling. Since this village comprised the descendants of General Li's soldiers, it wasn't strange for them to worship him. But there was one thing he didn't understand.

"I thought this was the Temple of the Dragon King, your Rain God. Why is Li Dingguo enshrined here?"

"There was once a different Rain God, but he took our offerings and brought nothing in return," Mr. Wang said. His former stiffness vanished as he told them a story passed down from generation to generation.

According to Mr. Wang, the year before General Li retreated to the forest, troops had been stationed in Mengla. It had been an arid year. Faced with the prospect of no harvest, the villagers flocked to the Temple of the Dragon King to pray for rain—but to no avail. When Li arrived in the village to inspect his troops, he was informed of the situation. He then went to the Temple of the Dragon King and let loose his rage. "You're the Rain God," he declared. "It's your responsibility to make it rain. It hasn't rained for ages, and the people are suffering. You've failed to fulfill your responsibilities. I'm the general. My duty is to protect the country so that the people may live in peace. I'm going to take your place as a deity in order to punish you!"

Then, Li Dingguo and his followers pulled down the Dragon King icon and installed his own in its place. He appointed a high-ranking official to oversee the villagers' daily kowtowing to their new Rain God. Before he left, he told the villagers that if they were so devout they could move the Rain God to tears, the heavens would reward them with a downpour.

The villagers secretly had their misgivings, but given General Li's military might, they had no choice but to comply. To their surprise, after three days of continuous kowtowing, the Rain God's statue really did cry. That evening, there was a torrential rain. The village's drought had come to an end, and General Li was consecrated as its patron saint.

Upon hearing the little-known legend, Yue Dongbei was bursting with excitement. "He brought down the Dragon King and anointed himself the Rain God—what unimaginable evil he must have been capable of! This is incredible! You could write an entire book about it! Unbelievable!"

But Professor Zhou had an entirely different response. Chuckling, he asked Mr. Wang, "The statue cried, and they were rewarded with rain? Ridiculous. It's a folktale, that's all. Don't tell me you people still believe in these superstitions?"

"Of course we do." Mr. Wang's tone was resolute and uncompromising. "For generation after generation in this village, every single one of us has seen the Rain God cry with our very own eyes."

"Have you seen it?"

Mr. Wang nodded soberly.

Professor Zhou shook his head in disbelief, then looked to Luo for support.

But Luo just asked, "Are we going to be able to see the Rain God cry tomorrow?"

"We truly hope so. Once Chief Bai makes his offering, the Rain God will make his presence known."

"Well, then," Yue Dongbei laughed. "I guess we'll find out tomorrow whether it's real or not!"

Luo said nothing more. He couldn't accept the notion that a statue was going to cry, but there was no point in arguing. Then he heard footsteps—someone had entered the temple. One by one, Luo and the others turned to see a young man in his twenties. Though not especially tall, he was powerfully built.

The young man looked taken aback to see so many people inside the temple. He asked vehemently, "Who are you, and what are you doing here?"

"These men are my boarders. They arrived today," Mr. Wang hastily replied. "I just came here to leave my offerings, and they asked to come along."

"There's nothing to see here." Eyes brimming with hostility, the young man scanned Luo, Professor Zhou, and Yue Dongbei, then looked back to Mr. Wang. "The ceremonies are tomorrow morning. Didn't Chief Bai say that no one is to disturb the Rain God before dawn?"

"I know, I know," Mr. Wang said meekly. "But it's still the day before, isn't it? Sorry, we'll be on our way."

The young man gave a grunt. He stepped forward and pushed open the door, waiting in stony silence for them to leave.

Mr. Wang flashed a conciliatory smile as they filed out. Yue Dongbei glared at the young man, who ignored him.

"Who was that? He was arrogant and not hospitable in the least!" Yue Dongbei grumbled loudly as soon as they were outside.

Mr. Wang looked embarrassed. He waved his hand dismissively at Yue Dongbei. He walked a few steps farther, then said in a low voice, "His name is Xue Mingfei. He's one of Chief Bai's people. We mustn't offend him."

Luo saw Mr. Wang wincing and was slightly amused, but then thought better of it. In such an isolated area, the head of a village was something akin to a local emperor—his authority knew no bounds.

By now, the sky was pitch black, and a sudden breeze passed through the clearing, shaking the trees and chilling the air. To the east was a patch of rainforest. Who knew what lurked within it?

Luo stopped short.

"What's the matter?" asked Professor Zhou uneasily.

Luo shook his head, unable to explain. A moment later, he turned his head and peered back through the temple door.

Xue Mingfei stood alone before the Rain God. In the faint candlelight, the statue's face seemed to glow with an ominous savagery.

Chapter 9

THE RECURRENCE OF A BLOODBATH

In order to verify the Rain God's miraculous tears, Luo and the others woke up early the next day and accompanied Mr. Wang to the temple.

The square was already packed with droves of villagers, and more kept arriving. Standing at the entrance to the Temple of the Dragon King were two strong and able-looking young men. They scanned the crowd, each with a stern look on his face.

The villagers had found suitable spots and stood in place obediently, silently. Luo was in awe. Who was this Bai character who commanded such startling deference from his people? He whispered to Mr. Wang: "Is one of those two men the chief?"

Mr. Wang shook his head. "Chief Bai isn't here yet."

"So those men—they work for him?"

But Mr. Wang only nodded in response.

There must have been two thousand people in the square by now, their offerings too plentiful to fit inside the temple. There was a minor commotion, and the crowd turned to face the west side of the square, which led to the village. Luo's heart leapt; Chief Bai must be coming. Sure enough, he saw a lone man taking long strides toward the temple.

He looked to be in his thirties. He was slight but quite tall, with a courageous quality about him.

Luo had guessed correctly: This was Mihong's village chief, Bai Jiane. The two young sentries were his associates, Wu Qun and Zhao Liwen.

Wu Qun spoke in an anxious, hushed tone: "Chief, Xue Mingfei still hasn't arrived yet."

Chief Bai raised his eyebrows. Xue Mingfei was his most capable assistant. How could he have failed him on a day like this? With his hands clasped behind his back, Chief Bai thought for a moment. His piercing gaze swept over the crowd.

He immediately spotted three unfamiliar faces and zeroed in on the man standing in the middle. There was a sober expression on the chief's face and a penetrating incisiveness in his eyes.

Without hesitation, Chief Bai advanced on the three interlopers. The crowd parted, forming a path for him.

Chief Bai stopped directly in front of the trio and looked them up and down. Finally, his gaze rested on the one in the middle. "Where have you come from?"

Ordinarily, people shrank under Chief Bai's hawklike gaze. But Luo just smiled politely. "There's a matter I'd like to discuss with you, Chief Bai. But for now, please don't allow me to interrupt the ceremony."

Chief Bai smiled courteously. "Why don't you step to the side so that we can conduct our ceremony? You'll be in our way standing in the middle of the crowd."

Luo, Professor Zhou, and Yue Dongbei said nothing and retreated to the western edge of the clearing.

Chief Bai then turned back to the crowd and loudly asked, "Who here has seen Xue Mingfei?"

"I've seen him," Mr. Wang, who was standing close by, promptly answered. "Last night I came with my offerings, and he was here."

"Ah." Chief Bai lowered his head, contemplating for a moment. Then he lifted his hand dramatically. "We won't wait for him. Let's begin, shall we?"

With those words, Chief Bai marched over to the Temple of the Dragon King, where he donned his costume and led the procession into the temple. Wu Qun and Zhao Liwen followed close behind. Upon reaching the statue of the Rain God, Chief Bai delivered a deeply respectful salute. Wu Qun, Zhao Liwen, and the villagers watching from outside all followed suit. Then, all the residents of Mihong fell to their knees, leaving Luo, Professor Zhou, and Yue Dongbei standing stiffly on the sideline.

Chief Bai knelt on a rush mat before the icon and proclaimed, "Almighty protector of the dharma, most precious patriot and founding father, immortal General Li, the village of Mihong has not seen rain in many months. If it does not rain soon, we will have no harvest! Chief Bai, who rules over 543 households, asks that you shed your godly tears of mercy!"

When he finished speaking, he threw his head with all his strength upon the mat in front of him, and the dull thud could be heard through the square.

The villagers cried out in a sorrowful chorus, "Please shed your godly tears of mercy so that we might eat!" Then they, too, kowtowed in succession.

After this sequence of chanting and kowtowing had been performed three times, the villagers knelt upright, their eyes fixed expectantly on the statue.

Naturally, Luo assumed everyone was waiting for the Rain God to start crying. But the visitors were too far back to see for themselves, which was terribly frustrating.

Suddenly, from inside the temple, Chief Bai could be heard exclaiming, "What?"

Seconds later, there was a commotion in the front row of villagers. As the disturbance spread, the entire crowd stared into the temple, disbelief on their faces.

Someone shouted, "Oh my God! The deity! The deity—is bleeding!"

It was as if a bomb had been dropped. Panic spread through the crowd, people screaming and young children bursting into tears. Mr. Wang, who had a clear view of the temple, was obviously scared out of his mind. His voice wavered as he chanted, "Please have mercy on us! Please have mercy!"

Luo and the others exchanged looks and started running toward the temple. They were about thirty feet away when Chief Bai stepped into the doorway. Wu Qun and Zhao Liwen trailed closely behind him on either side.

"Everyone on their knees!" Chief Bai thundered.

The crowd immediately quieted.

"You three—stay where you are!" Chief Bai pointed a menacing finger at Luo and the others. "This is a matter for our village!"

Luo and the others had no choice. They were guests here, and brazenly violating their host's wishes would have been imprudent in the extreme.

With all eyes on Chief Bai, no one noticed Xue Mingfei emerging from the rainforest to the east. He took a few steps into the square and stumbled into a villager, who spun around and screamed his name. The crowd turned, their eyes following that scream to its source.

Xue Mingfei's bare skin was frighteningly pale—and they could see every inch of it, as he wasn't wearing a shred of clothing. Hunched, he shuffled toward the temple, seeming not to notice the villagers' shocked whispers.

As the man passed, Luo shuddered. He reeked of fear and despair. His lifeless eyes were fixed on the temple, and with every painful step he took, the look of ghastly anticipation on his stiff face grew. It was almost as if he had been to hell, and now the Temple of the Dragon King was his final rescue and redemption.

Chief Bai looked on, astounded, as his assistant trudged slowly toward him, then passed right by, heading into the temple. The chief whirled around. "Xue Mingfei! What's this all about?"

But Xue Mingfei made no reply. A soulless shell, he remained intent on reaching his destination.

"Help him!" Chief Bai ordered.

Wu Qun and Zhao Liwen were terrified, but they couldn't refuse the chief's orders. Flanking Xue Mingfei on either side, they supported his horrifyingly pale body.

Xue Mingfei found himself staring directly at the statue of the Rain God. His body began to shake violently. He lifted a hand and pointed toward the deity, then erupted in a fit of hysterical laughter. "Ha ha ha—ha ha ha—my blood! That's my blood! He—he took my blood! Ha ha ha—"

Then his body convulsed a few times, and Xue Mingfei dropped like a rock.

The screams of the villagers caused the chief to snap out of his shock and grit his teeth. There was a look of fierce determination on his face as he shouted: "There's no need to panic! I'm here!"

The villagers quieted again, but Luo couldn't stand idly by. He sprinted toward the prone man, with Yue Dongbei close behind. The ever-dignified Professor Zhou hesitated a moment, then he rushed over, too.

"What are you doing?" Chief Bai screeched. "Get out of here!"

"I'm a police officer," Luo declared. "I have a duty to protect this man!"

"I don't care who you are—I call the shots here!" Chief Bai barked. "Get them out of here!"

Wu Qun and Zhao Liwen moved to block their path. But Yue Dongbei, never interested in Xue Mingfei's well-being in the first place, was determined to see what was happening to the Rain God. True to form, he had the gall to push Wu Qun aside. "Now, now, out of the way."

Wu Qun's and Zhao Liwen's faces changed, and before anyone knew it, the fierce young men stood before the intruders with knives drawn.

Yue Dongbei's face turned red. "What—what is the meaning of this?"

Luo yanked him backward, saying with earnestness, "We're not here to cause trouble. Right now, there's someone who urgently needs our help."

Professor Zhou took a step forward. "Chief Bai, even though the situation is confusing, you must sort your friends from your enemies. All of us are esteemed in our respective professions. This is Chief Inspector Luo. This is Mr. Yue, a historian. And my name is Zhou. I'm a doctor. Right now, you need our help. Please try to understand."

Professor Zhou stressed the word *doctor*, and Chief Bai seemed to twitch. He glared at Professor Zhou. Not flinching in the least, Professor Zhou returned his look.

Finally, Chief Bai motioned to his men. "Let him look at Xue Mingfei."

Wu Qun and Zhao Liwen put away their knives and retreated behind Chief Bai. Professor Zhou stooped down, taking the man's pulse. Luo squatted nearby with a look of concern.

"His body is very weak," Professor Zhou pronounced grimly. "He could give out at any moment. He's lost too much blood."

"Lost blood?" the chief cried. "How?"

Xue Mingfei lay naked in front of them, not the slightest abrasion on his body. So how could he have lost so much blood?

Suddenly, Xue Mingfei opened his eyes and mumbled: "It's him— he's the one who took my blood . . ."

Chief Bai leaned closer and looked into Xue Mingfei's eerily dilated eyes. "Who did? Who hurt you? Just tell me, and I'll see to it that vengeance is carried out."

The corners of Xue Mingfei's mouth quivered a little. "Vengeance? Yes, he's here for vengeance. He's come back from the dead—using my blood! Demon! He—he won't show us mercy. He's in hell—waiting for us!" Xue Mingfei was already losing consciousness, yet his hand pointed firmly.

Choked with fear, the men turned to look. Xue Mingfei was pointing directly at the statue of General Li!

The previous evening, the candlelight had been too dim for Luo to inspect the statue closely. Now he saw a regal-looking middle-aged man with bushy brows and a thick beard, a prominent nose and intense eyes. He was wearing a gold suit of armor. In his right hand was a longsword, and in his stone eyes, the power of a man not easily overthrown.

Now that power was spilling forth from his eyes in the form of fresh crimson blood!

As the group watched the blood pour down the statue and spatter the temple, Xue Mingfei took his last breath in the mortal world, his death a testament to the demon's bloody reincarnation.

Luo knitted his eyebrows intently. He had imagined the ceremony for a local rain god would be nothing more than a footnote in the greater scheme of his investigation of the illness in Longzhou. But now he wasn't so sure. Could this all stem from the blood vial and the alleged demons?

Professor Zhou, ever the scientist, had no time to entertain such thoughts. He was examining Xue Mingfei's corpse for clues. A curious Yue Dongbei, on the other hand, craned his neck to peer inside the temple. Apparently, neither the guards' knives nor the man's horrific death could deter him.

The square was silent as the grave, the people of Mihong speechless with terror. Their eyes were locked on Chief Bai, who stood in a daze at the entrance of the temple. It was as if time had stopped.

Suddenly, Chief Bai sprang back into motion. He pointed at Xue Mingfei's corpse and asked, "Is he—dead?"

Professor Zhou nodded.

Chief Bai's eyes narrowed, as his face turned resolute. Facing the villagers, he announced, "As you can see, the deity is not crying, but bleeding! I can also tell you that Xue Mingfei has died!"

The crowd erupted, but Chief Bai raised one hand and they fell silent. This chief certainly had control of his people, Luo marveled. Next, Chief Bai turned and strode into the temple, hissing orders to his men: "No one is to enter!"

Brandishing knives and menacing glares, Wu Qun and Zhao Liwen stood in front of the temple.

Inside, Chief Bai knelt in front of the icon. He spoke loudly and clearly, so all could hear. "Our God in the heavens! We in Mihong are loyal and true to you! Today, our God is bleeding. I, Chief Bai, am worried to no end. What have we done to offend our God? Please tell us!"

He lifted his hands in prayer and kowtowed. His head pressed firmly against the rush mat. He remained in that position for a long time.

The villagers prayed along, their sad voices chanting, "Please tell us!"

Luo saw blood still running from the icon's eyes. Was it possible that it might speak? He watched as Chief Bai suddenly sat upright and marched outside, fury in his eyes.

"Who here disobeyed my orders to not come before daybreak and disturb our God?" he barked.

The villagers looked at one another, not daring to say a word.

After a moment, Mr. Wang began kowtowing. His voice was shaking as he spoke. "Me—it was me. I came to bring my offerings, but it was still yesterday—yesterday evening—not actually today—"

Chief Bai's eyes were two daggers. "Was there anyone else?"

"Yes. Yes," Mr. Wang confessed. "Xue Mingfei. Xue Mingfei came after I did."

"That would seem to be the case." Chief Bai heaved a sigh, then looked up at the sky. A sympathetic look crossed his face. Then he hurried back inside the temple and knelt down. "Xue Mingfei has offended our God, and he has paid the price! We beg that our God forgive and show compassion, and bless and protect the people of Mihong by giving us rain and a good harvest for generations to come. Please have mercy on us!"

The assembled villagers kowtowed and chanted along. Chief Bai had convinced them this was the whole story, and their relief was palpable. In unison, they cried, "Please have mercy on us!"

Luo watched Chief Bai and nodded a little. This Chief Bai was the right man for the job, all right!

Chapter 10

A Century of Spiritual Talk

After these hair-raising events, the ceremony was over at last. The crowd dispersed under threatening black clouds, and at midday, it finally started to rain.

The villagers rushed out into the life-saving rain, merrily celebrating the Rain God, some weeping with gratitude. Xue Mingfei's bizarre death was already in the past.

Luo knew that, in isolated places, long-held beliefs could cause people to lose their capacity for independent thought. Here in the village of Mihong, Chief Bai was the highest authority. He had decreed the reason for Xue Mingfei's death, and his people had neither the need nor the courage to question it.

The matter of the Rain God bleeding concerned them even less. In their eyes, the gods were far removed, and communicating with them was something only a wise man like Village Chief Bai could achieve. All they needed was to enjoy stability under the iron fist of their all-knowing leader.

That was why, when Chief Bai hastily had Xue Mingfei's corpse removed and the Temple of the Dragon King sealed off, they didn't ask questions.

But Luo and his companions were more clear-eyed. Back at Mr. Wang's house, they discussed the strange incident.

"Those thugs threatened me with knives! Have they no respect for scholarship?" Fiddling with his digital camera, Yue Dongbei was indignant. "I can't believe they wouldn't let me into the temple. Thank goodness I brought this baby! The telephoto lens is top-notch. Those bumpkins didn't even notice—they've probably never seen one!"

"You got pictures?" Luo hadn't noticed Yue Dongbei's spy work, either.

"But of course. When you're a scholar, you have to be resourceful, and you can only rely on yourself." Yue Dongbei triumphantly pushed the buttons on his camera. "See for yourself! It's bleeding real blood."

Luo took the camera from Yue Dongbei's hands. The image had been zoomed in so that it focused on the red liquid seeping from the Rain God's eyes and coating its cheeks.

As a seasoned police inspector, Luo was no stranger to blood, and based on its color and consistency, the substance in the photographs could be nothing but.

"Professor Zhou, you're a doctor. Tell me what you think."

Luo handed the camera over to Professor Zhou, who studied the images earnestly for a moment, then nodded. "It's highly probable that this is blood."

Luo thought for a minute, then asked, "Does any of it seem dried up?"

Professor Zhou looked closer and spotted three lines of blood underneath the left eye, two of which were long and still dripping. The other was very short, less than an inch long. Yue Dongbei came over and snatched the camera from him, zooming to the highest magnification. The blood in these lines was unquestionably dried and cracking.

"Ha! No doubt whatsoever, it's blood!" Yue Dongbei clapped his hands happily. "How does science explain that?"

Luo, who didn't want a squabble, waved a dismissive hand at them. "Let's not worry about that right now. I want to ask the two of you: What do you think of Chief Bai's conclusion that Xue Mingfei offended the Rain God?"

"Well, it's obviously a cover-up!" Yue Dongbei cackled. "When Xue Mingfei was talking, we all could see the terror in Chief Bai's eyes. But the minute Xue Mingfei was gone, the chief figured out a way to frame him."

"That's an analysis I can actually agree with," Professor Zhou said. "And it was very clever, indeed. If he hadn't handled that situation the way he did, it would've destroyed his reputation for decades to come."

Luo nodded, and as if he were talking to himself, added, "So what was he trying to cover up, exactly?"

"The fact that the demon had reincarnated." Yue Dongbei rolled his eyes. "Didn't you guys hear what Xue Mingfei said?"

"That's not true. And even if it were, there'd be a gaping hole in your theory." Professor Zhou shot a taunting look at Yue Dongbei.

Yue Dongbei didn't seem concerned in the least. "What are you talking about? Tell me, and I'll give you an explanation."

"According to your 'theory,' this 'demonic force' and General Li are one and the same, and were sealed up in the blood vial. So now that the vial has been shattered, the demonic force has come back. But what reason would it have to seek vengeance on Mihong? These villagers are descendants of Li's soldiers, and they worship him as a god."

"Perhaps you've forgotten that they're descendants of the *defeated* soldiers?" Yue Dongbei crowed. "Li had the greatest contempt for those troops who surrendered. His ghost wouldn't pardon them! And then there's the family name Bai . . ."

Luo noticed Yue Dongbei's hesitation. "What about the name Bai?"

"The chief's ancestor, Lieutenant General Bai, was one of Li's top men—" Yue Dongbei began, then paused dramatically. "But the rest is only speculation. As a scholar, I need more facts."

Luo was no history buff, but he'd been paying close attention. "Didn't Mr. Wang tell us that Li left an official behind to make sure the villagers continued to worship his icon? Was that Lieutenant General Bai?"

Yue Dongbei nodded excitedly. "It's very likely. Very likely indeed!"

Luo looked pensive. Then he extended his hand to Professor Zhou. "Let me see the camera."

He examined Yue Dongbei's six photos one by one. Every once in a while, he'd enlarge a portion, inspect it, and think for a few moments. He went through this process repeatedly, very slowly at first, then progressively quicker. Finally, his face lit up.

"Mr. Yue, I don't think what Chief Bai is trying to cover up is a demonic force. Even if what Xue Mingfei said is true and a demonic force really does exist, Chief Bai isn't sure what that force is. When it happened, there was real confusion in his eyes. Not only that, but fear. I'm sorry to disappoint you, but I've solved this particular mystery."

Yue Dongbei scratched his head and looked at Luo earnestly. "I'm very interested in hearing what you have to say, Inspector."

"First of all, my analysis is based on a supposition, which is that the Rain God at the Temple of the Dragon King absolutely does not shed tears on its own. Mr. Yue, though you may believe in Neo-Taoism, we do live in the modern world, and basic common sense is something that we should share."

"Neo-Taoism is a profound system of knowledge," Yue Dongbei replied seriously. "It explores areas that we don't understand, but it does not in any way deny the laws of physics. We saw that icon up close yesterday, and it's nothing but stone. If a piece of stone can shed tears, that wouldn't be Neo-Taoism, that'd be a hoax!"

Luo was surprised by the man's eloquence and resolve.

Professor Zhou was even more astonished. "Oh? So you're not completely unreasonable after all!"

"How many times do I have to say this? I am researching Li Dingguo and his legendary demonic powers. I am a scholar. You, however, have been treating me like a charlatan!"

Luo laughed with relief. "Perfect. So we agree that a stone statue can't cry, but this morning we saw firsthand that there was blood flowing out of its eyes. That can only mean one thing."

Professor Zhou finished the thought for him. "There was someone inside the statue manipulating it."

Luo nodded. "Li must have secretly installed a mechanism inside the statue when it was built, and instructed his official on how to control it. The official only needed a basic grasp of meteorology so he could make the Rain God 'shed tears' when a big storm was coming. This would ensure the people's submission."

"And if the official was Lieutenant General Bai, and Chief Bai is his descendant . . . ," Professor Zhou added.

Yue Dongbei clapped his hands. "It's not certain whether the trusted official was Bai Wenxuan, mind you, but he was the leader of the defeated troops in Mihong."

"Several centuries have passed, and the Bai family's power in Mihong hasn't waned. Clearly, this is no coincidence," Luo said decisively.

"No, this myth has served as the basis of the Bai family's authority for hundreds of years," Professor Zhou sighed. "When things turned bad this morning, Chief Bai was scared that the people would find out the truth, but he thought fast and managed to save the day."

"It makes sense! It makes perfect sense! This analysis corresponds to the facts. It explains everything!" Yue Dongbei gazed at Luo admiringly, then asked, "The interesting question now is why, on this occasion, did blood flow out of the icon? And how do you explain Xue Mingfei's death?"

"Well, first, we need to know what Xue Mingfei was doing at the temple last night." Luo handed back the camera. "Did you two see the broken jar under the altar this morning? Here it is in the photo."

Professor Zhou thought for a moment. "That's right. Xue Mingfei was carrying that jar last night!"

Luo nodded. "At the time, I assumed it was Xue Mingfei's own offering. But why didn't he put it on top of the altar, then? If you zoom in, can you see what's inside?"

Near the mouth of the toppled container were faint traces of water that hadn't yet evaporated. Professor Zhou and Yue Dongbei said at the same time: "Water!"

Luo laughed. "The night before the ceremony, Xue Mingfei brought a jar of water. It obviously wasn't an offering, so what was it for?"

"To fill it up! To fill up the mechanism!" Yue Dongbei blurted out.

Professor Zhou smiled in agreement.

"And where do you think the switch to control the tears is located?" Luo continued.

"I was just thinking about that," Professor Zhou said. "It's probably under the rush mat in front of the statue. When Chief Bai kowtows, he can activate the switch."

"So normally, the mechanism can't have any water inside. Otherwise, villagers going to worship the Rain God would set it off. The water would have to be secretly added the night before the ceremony, by Chief Bai's trusted assistant, and then villagers could not be permitted to enter the temple before the ceremony. His plan was flawless—" Luo paused for a second before continuing. "Except last night, when the unexpected happened."

"What was the unexpected?" Yue Dongbei's eyes widened.

"Most likely, Xue Mingfei encountered an attacker." Luo stroked his chin as he spoke. "The jar was broken, so the attacker hid it underneath the altar. Then the attacker filled the mechanism with blood instead of water, and tested it. That would explain why there was already dried blood under the statue's eye."

Yue Dongbei and Professor Zhou nodded in unison.

"So was it Xue Mingfei's blood?" Yue Dongbei asked.

"That, I have no way of knowing for sure." Luo turned to Professor Zhou. "Professor Zhou, are you certain that Xue Mingfei died from blood loss?"

"That's half the reason, but it isn't the entire reason."

Luo furrowed his brow, puzzled.

"What I mean," Professor Zhou continued, "is that blood loss was a major factor, but there's another cause that can't be overlooked."

"What is that?"

"Shock!" Professor Zhou explained. "When Xue Mingfei arrived this morning, his body was already extremely weak, but he could still stand up on his own—walk, even. But when he saw the Rain God drenched in blood, he collapsed. To put it more precisely, blood loss was the physiological basis for Xue Mingfei's death, whereas shock served as the psychological fuse."

"I see what you're saying." Luo tapped his forehead with his finger. "I have another theory, so tell me if it makes sense to you. Xue Mingfei wasn't aware of his own blood loss, but he received some kind of suggestion that his blood had been stolen by the Rain God. He didn't believe this, so he found the strength to go to the temple. When he discovered that blood really was flowing out of the Rain God statue, it caused such a huge fright that his body gave out."

"That does correspond to what Xue Mingfei said before he died. But how could he lose all that blood without knowing it?" Yue Dongbei looked at Luo expectantly.

Luo turned to Professor Zhou. "You examined the corpse."

Professor Zhou's face had a helpless expression. "I don't know. Normally, with such extreme blood loss, there are severe injuries to the body. But there wasn't the slightest wound to be found."

Luo frowned.

All of the sudden, Yue Dongbei laughed darkly. "You two have finally reached a matter there's no scientific explanation for. You must admit that, in this world, there are still many mysteries. Just because you've never encountered something before doesn't mean that it doesn't exist."

Professor Zhou glared at Yue Dongbei. "Is this another one of your demon theories?"

"Yes. The demon's back! It seeks revenge! Don't you two remember what Xue Mingfei said? A bloody reincarnation! It didn't kill Xue Mingfei outright because it wanted him to deliver the message. It wanted to frighten the people before it exhibited its terrifying powers!" As Yue Dongbei blathered on, excitement spread across his face.

"No . . ." Luo shook his head slowly. "There has to be a clearer motive."

"What kind of motive, then?"

Professor Zhou hadn't finished those words when they heard the sound of rapid footsteps outside. The door was pushed open, and Wu Qun and Zhao Liwen, along with six or seven other tough-looking men, stepped inside.

Chapter 11

Mystery Man

"Chief Bai would like to see you. Please come with us." Wu Qun stepped forward. His tone made it clear this was not a request.

Maintaining his composure, Luo smiled. "That's great, because we have something we'd like to chat with him about, too." Then he stood up.

Professor Zhou, who didn't have any major objections, stood up, too. There was a sour look on Yue Dongbei's face, but he muttered reluctantly, "Fine, let's go. He wants to see us, but he's not coming over himself, huh? They must not be used to receiving guests around here."

Outside, the rain was still coming down. Mr. Wang gave the three of them rush hats to wear, and they followed the chief's men through the village. About fifteen minutes later, several large buildings appeared before them. There, standing at the entrance with his hands clasped behind his back, was Chief Bai.

Then Wu Qun and another man flanked Luo on either side, guiding him toward the guesthouse to the west. The others separated Professor Zhou and Yue Dongbei, escorting them into two other buildings.

"What's the meaning of this?" Yue Dongbei demanded. "What are you doing?"

"Please, if you don't mind," Chief Bai said coolly, "I'd like to ask you each a few questions individually."

Luo understood: Chief Bai harbored a grievance against them, and so he wanted to isolate and interrogate them. Luo reflected on his many years as a police officer and how it was finally his turn to be interrogated. He couldn't help but laugh.

"Do as they say. Don't think too much. Whatever Chief Bai asks you, answer honestly," Luo called to his colleagues.

Yue Dongbei was taken to the guesthouse to the east, while Professor Zhou went straight into the main house, where Chief Bai was standing.

Inside the westernmost building, Luo sat waiting. Wu Qun and the other guard didn't say a word to him, and Luo was relieved to have a little peace and quiet. It was the perfect opportunity to muse on what questions he was about to be asked.

After about twenty minutes, he saw Chief Bai emerge from the center building, then enter the eastern guesthouse, where Yue Dongbei was. Luo noticed that when Chief Bai entered the building, the guards exited. There was no doubt he was hiding secrets from his villagers.

Another twenty minutes passed, and Chief Bai came to see Luo. Without waiting for instructions, Wu Qun and the other man left, shutting the door behind them. Chief Bai sat down across from Luo, his face inscrutable. Luo knew he was feeling things out. Oftentimes, there was more to be learned from appearances than from words. He adopted a gentle and sincere expression as he returned Chief Bai's gaze, showing that he intended no harm.

Finally, Chief Bai spoke. "So you're a police officer?"

Luo nodded. "My name is Luo. I'm from Longzhou."

"The people of this village have been living here for generations. We don't take much of an interest in the outside world. What I want to know right now is, why did you come to Mihong?"

Luo gathered his thoughts, hoping to explain the situation clearly. "I'm investigating a very strange case, and I don't have too many leads.

The key figure in this case passed through Mihong on the way to the Valley of Terror about a year ago, and his trip resulted in a string of incidents that are difficult to explain. This is a picture of him. Perhaps you have seen this person before?"

But Chief Bai did not take the photo Luo extended toward him. He glanced at it, then shook his head, saying, "I don't have much contact with travelers. You should ask Mr. Wang. If he really was in the village, it's likely that he stayed at Mr. Wang's house."

"You're right. Mr. Wang already confirmed it."

Chief Bai looked much more at ease now. "I asked your two friends the same thing, and all of you gave the same answer. There doesn't seem to be any reason for me to distrust you. I've been harsh with you just now and at the temple yesterday morning, and if I've offended you in any way, Chief Inspector Luo, I hope you will forgive me."

Luo thought to himself, *Now's the chance to attack.* And so, with a big smile on his face, he said, "No, I understand. The incident yesterday morning was rather out of the ordinary. As chief, you were naturally suspicious, and we'd just arrived in the village. But we didn't come here to cause trouble, and there's no need to go through this whole business."

Luo's tone was casual, yet there was an incisive glint in his eyes.

Chief Bai's pupils contracted in alarm. "Go through what whole business? I don't understand what you're saying."

"Chief Bai, it's just the two of us—you can speak honestly." Luo suddenly grew serious. "The Rain God statue has its secrets, and that's your business. It doesn't concern me, nor am I here to expose anything. If we share what we know, it will benefit us both."

Chief Bai stared at Luo. After a moment, he chuckled. "Chief Inspector Luo, you're not only a perceptive man, you're a forthright man. Very well, then. You first. What do you know? What do you want to know?"

Luo got straight to the point. "Well, we both know Xue Mingfei's death wasn't the result of offending the Rain God. Someone killed him, and in my view, this person must have a score to settle with you. He not only knows about the mechanism in the statue, but he also plotted this so that you'd be dealt a blow on the day of an important ceremony."

Chief Bai clenched his teeth. The veins in his forehead were visible, and Luo knew he had lingering fears about the incident. If he hadn't thought fast and thrown poor Xue Mingfei under the bus, there was no telling what would have happened. But Chief Bai suppressed his emotions and focused on the man sitting across from him.

The first time he'd seen Luo outside the temple, Chief Bai had sensed something unusual about him. Yet he'd never imagined that this man would possess such keen insight. Within the span of half a day, he'd seen straight through the source of Bai's power. To have such a man as your enemy would be truly dreadful!

But for now, the dangerous inspector could be of use. Bearing this in mind, Chief Bai decided not to waste time with denials. Instead, he asked bluntly, "Who do you think it is?"

"Probably one of the villagers. Think for a moment: If your secret were revealed, who would stand to gain the most?"

"No, it can't be! None of my villagers would dare to challenge my authority. And besides, other than Xue Mingfei, everyone was at the ceremony that morning. And wouldn't Xue Mingfei have identified his attacker on sight?"

"Everyone?" Luo thought for a second. No wonder Chief Bai had been suspicious of the three newcomers. "Is there anyone else around who's not from here?"

"Right now, aside from the three of you, there's one other fellow. But he just arrived this afternoon. The same guide who brought you here swore to it."

Luo forced a smile. "So who else could it be?"

Chief Bai looked even more puzzled. He mumbled, "Unless there really are demonic spirits."

"Demonic spirits? You believe in them, too?"

Chief Bai gave an embarrassed laugh and waved dismissively. "That's how your friend explained it."

Luo shook his head. Yue Dongbei must have given Chief Bai a full rundown of his scholarship. "What do you think of his theories?"

Chief Bai hesitated for a second. "To be honest, this is actually the first time I've ever heard that General Li is the figure the Hamo people call a demonic spirit. For generations, we in Mihong have worshipped him as the Rain God. This is a complete contradiction, of course."

Luo acknowledged this with a grunt. Then, another question occurred to him. "When Xue Mingfei was on his deathbed, he said something like 'The demons have come back!' Don't you find that strange?"

"I would," Chief Bai said thoughtfully, "but in the past year, some of the Hamo people have been fleeing the forest. When they pass through the village, they say that, in the Valley of Terror, 'the demons have come back.' The villagers have started gossiping about it. Even though no one knows the particulars, there's no dispelling these kinds of rumors, which are deliberately cryptic."

Luo was mulling over this analysis when Chief Bai changed the subject: "Very well, Chief Inspector Luo. What's your objective in all this?"

Luo laughed. "I actually don't have one. Perhaps it's just my nature as a police officer! This is a bizarre homicide, and I can't help wanting to get to the bottom of it. Other than that, I just want to have a good relationship with you, Chief Bai. There is something I would like your help with."

"Oh? What is that?"

"We're heading to the Valley of Terror very soon. We're going to need a guide who can speak the Hamo language, and I'd be grateful for your help finding someone. It has to be the most capable candidate, and they can name their price."

"That won't be a problem," Chief Bai answered immediately. Then he swiftly stood up and flung open the door.

"All right, then. See the guests off!" Chief Bai ordered loudly. Wu Qun and the others didn't hesitate in gathering their rain gear and escorting Luo, Professor Zhou, and Yue Dongbei outside.

Chief Bai suddenly lifted his hand. "Hold on a minute."

Everyone turned around, unsure what he was about to do.

"Chief Inspector Luo, you're looking to hire a guide? I know just the man."

Luo smiled. "Is that so? Where is he?"

With a serious face, Chief Bai declared, "Right in front of you. Me, Bai Jiane!"

Luo, his companions, and even the guards exchanged quizzical looks. But Chief Bai didn't appear to be joking.

"In terms of wisdom, in terms of courage, who in Mihong is better qualified? If you want to go to the Valley of Terror, I'm the best guide. And I'll bring two of my assistants, Wu Qun and Zhao Liwen."

Professor Zhou squinted at Chief Bai. "But Chief Bai, we're talking about hiring someone for a job—someone we might have to give orders to."

"Don't worry about that," Chief Bai answered earnestly. "I know how to fulfill my duties as a guide. Give us time to prepare, and we'll set off in three days!"

"Okay! It's settled, then," Professor Zhou agreed somberly, his air scholarly as always.

Chief Bai nodded in silence, then went back inside the building.

"Don't you worry! When our chief promises something will happen, it does," Wu Qun said, guiding them out of the compound.

Luo, Professor Zhou, and Yue Dongbei were already getting to know their way around the village. Declining Wu Qun's offer to escort them, they set out for Mr. Wang's on their own.

"Heh heh, so this Bai fellow must really believe in my theory." They hadn't been on the road long before Yue Dongbei was back at it, triumphantly tooting his own horn. "Think about it: He's the high and mighty chief, so why else would he be so eager to serve as our guide? His real motive is to uncover the secrets of the Valley of Terror, too!"

Professor Zhou shot an annoyed glance at Yue Dongbei before turning to Luo. "Chief Inspector Luo, what do you think?"

"Actually, I agree there's something strange about his offer." Luo paused, then he shook his head. "But for now, it doesn't matter if he has some ulterior motive. Having him accompany us to the Valley of Terror can't hurt, but it can definitely help."

The three of them didn't speak again for quite some time, each absorbed in his own thoughts.

The storm was intensifying. As they followed the path through the village, they could see the people inside their homes, praising the mercy of the Rain God. They seemed lighthearted, genuinely believing that Xue Mingfei's death was a reasonable punishment for having offended the Rain God. None could have imagined any connection between their deity and the demonic spirits in the Hamo village.

A small trickle of a stream had formed in the riverbed, life-giving water quenching the thirst of Mihong's earth. Raindrops pelted the travelers, and in spite of the heat, Luo felt a slight chill as they struck his face. He had the ominous feeling that something was very wrong, but he couldn't say what.

Little did he know that during a summer like this one, more than three hundred years before, a giant rainstorm triggered a series of events that brought about joy and sorrow, tears and bloodshed.

But had that series of events run its course? Or was it destined to follow an endless cycle of death and rebirth in which good and evil were inherently bound together?

Because of the rain, few villagers were out. But when they'd nearly reached Mr. Wang's house, they spotted someone on the path, heading straight toward them.

Head down, the person walked with lightning-quick steps. They could see only his black raincoat, the hood drawn tight as if he was afraid of getting any rainwater on his face. His right hand clutched the hood, pulling it downward, and his eyes were visible only through a slit.

Luo and the others stared, and Luo remembered Chief Bai saying another visitor had arrived this afternoon.

But he was moving so quickly, Luo didn't get a chance to speak. Turning sideways, the man tried to slip between the three of them and bumped right into Yue Dongbei.

"Watch it! You almost knocked me over!"

Slowing down for only a second, he replied in a low voice, "Sorry." Then he rushed off in the opposite direction.

"Who was that? That was kind of bizarre, wasn't it?" Professor Zhou asked. He stared at the man, who was already disappearing into the distance.

"Chief Bai said another visitor arrived this afternoon. Maybe that's him." Luo sounded uncertain. "I wonder if he's staying with Mr. Wang."

"Forget about that jerk. Let's get inside," urged Yue Dongbei.

As soon as they reached their room, Mr. Wang told them, "There's a man looking for you. He just left."

"Looking for us?" Luo asked. "Was he wearing a black raincoat with a hood that covered his face?"

"Yes."

"What did he want?"

Mr. Wang shook his head. "He didn't say."

"Did he wait long?"

"About fifteen minutes."

Luo scanned the room, and his gaze settled on wet footprints. "He came into our room?"

Mr. Wang seemed frightened. "I—I thought it was someone you knew."

"It's fine, it's fine. There's nothing to steal here." Yue Dongbei carelessly plopped down onto the bed and crossed one leg over the other, removing his shoes. "Oh, will you look at this? They're soaked all the way through!"

Mr. Wang picked up Yue Dongbei's shoes. "I'll put all your shoes near the hearth to dry."

Luo smiled and thanked him. As he and Professor Zhou both removed their shoes, he thought to himself, *This Mr. Wang isn't much of a talker, but he sure is diligent and hardworking.*

Mr. Wang took all three pairs of muddy shoes and came back with slippers for them to change into before occupying himself with cooking dinner.

"What do you think that man was really here for? If he was looking for us, why didn't he say anything outside?" Professor Zhou asked, obviously still concerned.

"Didn't Chief Inspector Luo just say? He's a new arrival," Yue Dongbei said, splayed out on the bed. "Maybe he wants to travel with us? Heh heh. He doesn't know we're going to the Valley of Terror."

"I agree with Professor Zhou. It's clear that we're not from around here, so why didn't he at least stop and ask? He was in such a hurry . . ." Luo shook his head. "Tomorrow we'll find out where he's staying and pay him a visit."

Chapter 12

Night Rendezvous

The three travelers were exhausted. They changed out of their soggy clothes and piled onto the kang, the heated brick bed, to relax before dinner. Without meaning to, all of them passed out the moment they lay down.

Luo was the first to wake up, and the sky was already dark. He checked his watch. It was almost eight o'clock, and he was ravenously hungry. Luo walked over to the door and called for Mr. Wang.

"Awake now? Dinner's ready. I saw you were all asleep, so I didn't want to disturb you."

Their dinner was a piping-hot sweet-potato porridge. Mr. Wang had scrambled some eggs and prepared a variety of mountain vegetables. The men devoured the simple meal, unable to contain their praise. Their host, who had already finished eating, watched with a huge smile on his face, happy to see his guests taking such delight in their meal.

Professor Zhou, who had been holding his chopsticks and bowl, suddenly froze. His eyes apprehensively darted around the room.

"What's wrong?" asked Luo, who'd been watching him the entire time.

"I have a feeling like something's not right." Then, in a soft voice, he added, "It's almost like a premonition."

Upon hearing Professor Zhou's remark, both Luo and Yue Dongbei lost interest in their food. They looked around the dim room, which, lit only by flickering candles, was a bit spooky. Out of nowhere, there was a clanking sound at the window, and then it opened by itself. All of them were astounded.

Yue Dongbei called out, "Who's there?"

But outside the window was a world of darkness and nothing but the sound of falling rain.

Mr. Wang walked over to the window and leaned out, looking around. He seemed to be mumbling to himself. "There's nothing, just the wind—" Closing it, he turned to his guests. "Why don't you finish eating? I'll go outside and take a look."

At the door, Mr. Wang hesitated. "Are you sure you want to go to the Valley of Terror?"

Since they'd met, this was the first time Mr. Wang had taken the initiative of asking them a question.

Luo smiled and nodded. "Yes."

Mr. Wang sighed with resignation, then headed outside.

A moment later, his words resonated through the dark, rainy night. "It's really not a peaceful place!"

Luo and the others exchanged looks. They would soon set off on their trek, and no one could predict what awaited them.

The next morning, when Mr. Wang went to fetch his guests' shoes from the stove, he discovered that a hole had been burnt in one pair.

Mr. Wang was racked with guilt. The way that he stood at their door, faltering as he tried to explain, it looked as if he were waiting for a terrible sentence to be handed down.

"They're still wearable. I purposely put charcoal in the stove to keep it lit. I never thought a piece might fall out," moaned Mr. Wang.

The shoes belonged to Professor Zhou, who magnanimously consoled the poor man. "It's not a big deal. I've had these shoes for years, and I was going to throw them out anyway." He dug through his bags. "Look. I brought hiking boots to change into before we got to the forest."

Professor Zhou's response seemed to ease Mr. Wang's conscience. "Thank you for your understanding. I'll have breakfast ready in a second."

After they'd finished breakfast, Luo consulted Professor Zhou and Yue Dongbei. "I was hoping to go find that man from yesterday. Would you be interested in joining me?"

Professor Zhou chuckled. "Don't you think it'd be a little intimidating if all three of us showed up? Anyway, I'm supposed to head over to Chief Bai's place to help him prepare."

Luo nodded. "Fine, so we'll split up. Yue Dongbei, what are your plans?"

"I'm not going, either," Yue Dongbei proclaimed from his spot on the bed. "We're about to go into the forest, to confront obstacles and forces we can scarcely imagine! I'm going to make good use of this time to sleep and conserve my energy."

Luo and Professor Zhou didn't protest, grateful to have some time away.

A short while later, Luo set off. The rain still hadn't stopped, but it wasn't pouring nearly as hard as the day before. Luo asked around and soon learned that the newly arrived guest was staying on the south side of the village, at the home of one Mr. Sun.

Unfortunately, when he arrived, Luo was told the visitor had left about ten minutes prior.

Mr. Sun didn't know where he'd gone or what time he'd be back. Mr. Sun also didn't know where he was from or what he was doing in

Mihong. Luo waited for over an hour, then decided to head back, thinking he'd try another time.

The loneliness of walking in the rain overwhelmed Luo, and he kept hoping to meet a kindred soul. But the path was vast and empty until he reached a fork in the road and saw someone approaching.

Even though both of them wore rush hats and raincoats, Luo could instantly tell that it was Professor Zhou.

"What luck." Luo grinned as they approached each other. "Were you able to meet with Chief Bai?"

"We were just in the middle of full-scale preparations. When you get down to business, the man's actually quite meticulous. He said he'd come get us tomorrow morning. And what about you? Where's that guy from?"

Luo flashed a wry smile. "Ah, he was off somewhere. I waited, but he didn't come back."

"Didn't come back?" Professor Zhou echoed. "Isn't he following you?"

"What?" Luo exclaimed in disbelief.

He turned around. Sure enough, he could make out a figure down the road, straight behind him, standing perfectly still and looking in his direction. The person wore that same black raincoat with the hood that covered his face.

"What's this about? What is he up to?"

"You didn't know he was behind you?" Professor Zhou studied Luo's face, then patted his shoulder firmly. "Come on, let's go find out."

The man saw Luo and Professor Zhou rushing toward him and seemed stunned for a moment. Then he turned and started sprinting in the opposite direction. He slipped into the forest and disappeared without a trace.

"He went that way!" Professor Zhou panted, pointing.

Luo blocked his way. "It's fine. We don't want to risk getting lost. Besides, if he's going to all this trouble to avoid us, it's going to be hard to catch him. Why don't we head back?"

Professor Zhou narrowed his eyes. "This doesn't make any sense. I don't like it one bit."

"Don't worry. He has to have some kind of objective in following me. He hasn't achieved it yet, so he'll be back. All we have to do is wait." Luo chuckled. He turned, and in the most carefree and leisurely manner, started walking back.

Professor Zhou finally laughed, too. He hurried to catch up with Luo. "Very well, then. I will defer to your expert opinion, Chief Inspector Luo."

Luo's assessment turned out to be accurate, as was confirmed that evening.

That afternoon, Mr. Wang had been working in the fields. It was after six o'clock by the time he got home. He didn't so much as wipe his brow before he sought out Luo.

"Chief Inspector Luo, this afternoon I ran into the man who was here yesterday. He asked me to tell you to meet him at nine o'clock tonight at the western end of the village."

Luo shot a look at Professor Zhou that said *I told you so.*

Professor Zhou smiled knowingly. "Ha! Looks like you were right! But—why does he want to meet you alone?"

"What's this guy up to?" Yue Dongbei was likewise suspicious. "Why does he want to meet you at night and in such a remote location?"

Luo had passed through the western end of the village once. It was open farmland, and there were canals everywhere. He could imagine just how desolate the area must be at night.

"Are you sure it's safe? Do you want me to go with you?" Professor Zhou offered.

"Nah, it'll be all right." Luo deliberated for a moment before replying. "He only asked to see me. If two of us go, he might take offense. I'll just be extra careful. In case you've all forgotten, I'm a police officer!"

"Yes, I know, but it's better to make sure you're covered." Professor Zhou lowered his head in contemplation. "How about this? You go there on your own, and I'll find a spot where I can stay hidden and observe from a distance. That way, if anything goes wrong, I can help."

"That's a great idea!" Yue Dongbei added. "We're heading to the Valley of Terror soon. Now's not the time to create complications that could interfere with our plans."

Amused to see his colleagues agreeing for once, Luo gave in.

Later that evening it was pouring harder than ever. The sky had unleashed whipping winds and furious rain. Luo had been hoping that the storm would abate by nine o'clock, but by eight thirty, it appeared that he would have to bite the bullet. He headed out, Professor Zhou trailing at a distance.

Mr. Wang saw the two of them getting their rain gear on. From the other room, he called to them, "Tonight you have to keep your distance from the canals."

But Luo couldn't hear him over the crashing storm. "What? What did you say?"

"It's pouring! Beware the mountain torrents! Stay away from the canals!" Mr. Wang came closer and repeated himself loudly.

The deep concern on Mr. Wang's face reminded Luo of Master Zheng, a guard at the gates of Nanming Mountain who'd fretted over his safety when he ascended the snowy mountain alone. His landlord on Mingze Island, Sun Fachao, had been the same type: salt of the earth. Kindhearted and trustworthy, they'd made his experiences meaningful.

Warmth surged through Luo's heart, and he couldn't find the right words. He gestured to indicate that he understood. Then he plunged into the torrential rain.

Under the pitch-black sky, he had only his flashlight to guide him along the muddy path, and he was extremely cautious. He could hear water gurgling hungrily nearby. With all of the mountain streams converging in the canals, the current would be extremely powerful.

He didn't run into a single person along the way. In this vast, empty world, Luo felt small and insignificant. Every now and then, he'd look back. About two hundred yards behind him was a faint flicker, and Luo knew it was Professor Zhou. The loneliness subsided somewhat.

As he neared the western end of the village, Luo realized why Mr. Wang had been so concerned. The path split in two, with one fork heading toward a mountain pass between two high peaks, practically bordering a section of canal, while the other led uphill and ran alongside an elevated terrace. Having been forewarned by Mr. Wang, Luo opted to go uphill. If he walked farther, he would leave the village. This, then, had to be the designated location. Luo stood to the side and pointed his flashlight back down the road. That way, if the man came from the village, he would be easy to spot.

Some time passed, and then Professor Zhou arrived. He did not signal to Luo, but instead went straight into his hiding place in the fields. He must have been thirty or forty yards away when he found a place to crouch down and turn off his flashlight, disappearing into the night.

Luo looked at his watch. It was nearly nine. The stranger should be arriving at any moment. But as the minutes and seconds passed, there was no sign of anyone on the long, dark path.

Luo frowned, thinking to himself, *What on earth is this guy trying to do? Is he really not going to show up?*

Then a distant, rumbling sound began in the mountain range. Though it wasn't loud, it seemed to signal that something was coming with astonishing momentum—like a colossal army marching over the horizon. Luo was startled. He listened closely for a moment, and it suddenly hit him: the mountain torrents!

In a flash, the sound grew infinitely louder, thundering toward the terrace. Luo lifted his flashlight and shone it toward the upper reaches of the canal. There appeared to be nothing unusual about the rushing rainwater at first. Then, suddenly, there was a burst of white. Out of nowhere, a giant, rumbling wall of floodwater crashed into the canal.

The sound echoed for a long time. Luo still hadn't quite recovered from the shock when someone came up behind him and gently patted him on the shoulder.

"Chief Inspector Luo, are you all right?" It was Professor Zhou.

Luo exhaled deeply. "What a fierce torrent that was!"

Cautiously, he took a few steps closer to the water and lifted his flashlight to get another look. Sure enough, the lower fork of the path was completely submerged. Professor Zhou came up beside him, and the two exchanged a frightened look. If they hadn't heeded Mr. Wang's warning and taken the upper fork, neither of them would still be here.

"Chief Inspector Luo, it's getting late. Are we still going to wait around?"

Luo shook his head. "I don't believe he's going to show up. Let's get out of here before that happens again."

He pointed his flashlight into the darkness, not knowing what to make of it all.

Chapter 13

THE HISTORICAL EVENTS OF MOPAN MOUNTAIN

It was their last day in Mihong. Tomorrow, they would head deep into the forest to find the Valley of Terror.

Early in the morning, the rain subsided. Because Chief Bai had called a meeting, the three travelers were up early.

Luo ate breakfast as quickly as he could. "I have something to take care of—I'll meet you at Chief Bai's right after."

"Trying to find the man who stood you up?" guessed Yue Dongbei.

Luo nodded.

Professor Zhou frowned. "We have a lot to do, and it'd make things easier if you were there."

"Don't worry," Luo replied as he scurried toward the door. "I'll be there before you know it."

He reached Mr. Sun's house just in time to see the master of the house step out the door.

"That guest of yours isn't here, is he?"

"My guest? Oh, he already left."

"Left?" Luo asked incredulously. "Where did he go?"

Mr. Sun shook his head. "How would I know? Probably going to the forest like all the others."

"What time did he leave?"

"Last night," Mr. Sun replied, sounding impatient.

Last night? In that storm?

"Is there anything else? I have a lot of work to do in the fields."

"I won't keep you, then." Frustrated, Luo pursed his lips and headed to Chief Bai's place.

When he arrived, he found Chief Bai, Wu Qun, Zhao Liwen, Professor Zhou, and Yue Dongbei gathered around a square table, some sitting and others standing.

"Come in." Chief Bai waved to Luo. "Now we can get started."

Luo walked to the table. Like the others, he looked to Chief Bai, waiting to see what was next.

Chief Bai fixed his gaze out the window, at the sky. He stared intently for a long time. "Perhaps we need to postpone our departure time."

"Why is that?" Yue Dongbei immediately asked, surprised.

"It's going to rain again, probably for two days straight. There's a chance there will be flooding in Yijian Gorge, which we need to pass through. It would be safer to wait until the rain stops before we leave."

"Since we've already settled on a plan, we should carry it out." Professor Zhou stared coldly at Chief Bai. "Even if there really is flooding, you can find a way around it."

Chief Bai threw up his hands. "This is decided by the heavens. What am I supposed to do?"

"You shouldn't have picked this departure date, then. This is a really annoying way to do things." Professor Zhou grumbled.

Chief Bai didn't say anything for a moment. The mood turned awkward.

Luo broke the silence. "As long as the rain stops, Yijian Gorge won't be blocked off?"

"Based on this level of rainfall, we would have to wait at least a day until the water receded from the gorge."

Luo persisted. "How long will it take for us to reach Yijian Gorge?"

"If we leave first thing tomorrow morning, we'll probably be able to make it there by the afternoon of the following day."

Luo reflected on this. "If the rain doesn't let up by tomorrow morning, then let's postpone. If it stops, let's depart."

Chief Bai nodded. "That's just what I had in mind."

Professor Zhou was still unhappy, but he didn't want to contradict Luo. "Hmph" was all he could manage.

"I've already prepared our food and water supply," Chief Bai continued. "Each person will receive theirs at departure time. It's only appropriate that, as guides, the three of us will carry extra. The Valley of Terror is about thirty miles from here, and there aren't any roads, so the trip will be extremely rough. All of you must be fully prepared for this." Chief Bai glanced over at Yue Dongbei, as if to suggest he didn't expect much from him.

Yue Dongbei stubbornly lifted his chin. "Don't worry, I won't slow you down, even if it kills me."

"How long do you estimate it'll take us to get there?" Luo asked.

"If it were only us, two days would be enough. With you all, I'd say three or four days."

"What should we pack?"

Chief Bai didn't reply. Instead, he asked, "What do you have so far?"

"Well, each of us is bringing a jacket, hiking boots, a backpack, a water bottle, a compass, and some food," Luo enumerated. "The larger items are a tent and three sleeping bags."

"That should do. You can drop those off, and we'll get them packed." Chief Bai waved to Wu Qun. "Bring the map." He faced Luo again. "Though we'll be leading the way, you should familiarize your-selves with the topography. That way, you'll be equipped to handle an emergency."

"Good idea."

Wu Qun returned with a heavy-looking rectangular case about six inches long. It was crafted entirely from silver, with a quaint design featuring horses and soldiers in gold inlay.

"Inside this box is a military topographic map of Yunnan that General Li once used," Chief Bai explained with a smile.

"Oh?" Yue Dongbei snapped to attention. "What an extremely valuable cultural artifact! What are you waiting for? Show us!"

Wu Qun placed the case on the table, then gently lifted the lid. He took out a thick scroll made with animal hide and placed it in Chief Bai's hands.

"That's it—" Yue Dongbei stared. Then it suddenly hit him. "Lambskin! That's right, that's right! Back in those days, they used it for military maps, since it was water-resistant and durable. It was all drawn on lambskin!"

Chief Bai unrolled the scroll, revealing the contents. Indeed, it was made of white lambskin. Because it was so old, the material had started to yellow. However, the brush marks formed a map that was still clearly legible.

Luo and the others closed in around the map. Wu Qun and Zhao Liwen, no doubt already familiar with its contents, didn't move.

"This here is Mihong. And this, here, is our destination: the Valley of Terror." Chief Bai pointed to the respective symbols, clearly marked in red.

"Hmm." Luo studied the directional arrows on the map, conclud-ing, "From the looks of it, the Valley of Terror should be a little over ten degrees southeast of Mihong."

"Eleven point five, to be exact." Chief Bai shot an approving glance at Luo. "This is the route we'll be taking, which will take us past Mopan Mountain, Yijian Gorge, and Qingfeng Pass."

The names of the three locations were clearly written in ceremonial seal script. "Mihong" and "the Valley of Terror" did not appear. But that made sense. The former was based on the legend of General Li, and the latter came from his remaining supporters. These two names wouldn't be found on a map the general himself used for military purposes.

"What does this mean?" Luo pointed to a thick line that went from Mopan Mountain to Yijian Gorge, intersecting with the Valley of Terror along the way, ultimately connecting Qingfeng Pass to the Valley of Terror and continuing eastward.

"Those are the lower reaches of the river in Mihong," Chief Bai explained. "It eventually flows into the Lancang River."

Luo nodded thoughtfully. "So in terms of elevation, the Valley of Terror is lower than Mihong?"

"Right. And actually, the easiest way is to follow the course of the river. But then you'd have to wind around too far, because Mopan Mountain is right smack in the middle. That's why we're going east around Mopan Mountain first, then following the river."

"It looks like Mopan Mountain provides an extended natural barrier for the Valley of Terror." Luo gazed at the map, awestruck.

"Excellent! Excellent!" Yue Dongbei suddenly started clapping. He flashed a thumbs-up at Luo. "There was a time when General Li was at a pass on Mopan Mountain, being pursued by Wu Sangui's troops in what would lead to one huge final confrontation. If some scoundrel hadn't leaked military secrets, Wu Sangui would have been dead and buried on Mopan Mountain."

"Really?" Luo said. "Mr. Yue, please tell us more."

Yue Dongbei wasn't about to pass up an opportunity to show off. He cleared his throat and began narrating in a singsong voice: "It was February of 1659. Li Dingguo's Ming troops fled toward the southwestern border, Wu Sangui hot on their heels. The general was betting that winning had made the Qing troops complacent, and so he decided to lie low in the woods on Mopan Mountain and ambush his enemy. Indeed, the Qing troops were gloating so much that they sauntered right toward the ambush. Just when Li was about to give the order to attack, one of his commanders betrayed his plan to Wu Sangui. Wu Sangui ordered his men to charge the thicket alongside the road, and both sides engaged in a bout of unimaginably fierce fighting. After calling for reinforcements, Li's troops were able to beat back the Qing forces, but it was not the triumph it should have been."

He threw a smug glance at Chief Bai. "Well, Chief Bai? Is anything I said incorrect?"

"It's correct, Mr. Yue. You are a man of true erudition." Chief Bai looked a little surprised.

As he tried to imagine the monstrous clash that must have taken place, Luo couldn't help feeling a shiver of excitement.

"All right already. Let's not go off on a tangent." Professor Zhou, who wasn't terribly interested in the subject, waved at the others. "Let's get back to discussing our departure."

Luo laughed and looked over at Chief Bai.

"Okay. That's our route and the terrain. I think you understand what's involved." Chief Bai turned to Wu Qun. "Put away the map."

Wu Qun stepped forward. Just as he was placing the lambskin scroll back into its case, a piece of paper floated out. It hung gently in the air before landing on the table directly in front of Yue Dongbei, who snatched it up. It was a sheet of ancient rice paper, yellowed with ragged edges. There was writing on one side.

Yue Dongbei stared in wonder, then cried, "My oh my! Chief Bai, I never imagined you would have so many treasures in your possession."

Chief Bai frowned, a confused look in his eyes.

Luo leaned closer. "What is it?"

"If my analysis is correct, this is a note handwritten by Li Dingguo himself! It is invaluable to my research!" Yue Dongbei's eyes shone. "Chief Bai, do you have any more of this sort of thing? Let me have a look—now!"

But Chief Bai simply turned to Wu Qun. "What's this about? Where did this come from?"

There was a bewildered look on Wu Qun's face. "I—I don't know."

"What do you mean?" asked Luo. "This document isn't yours?"

Chief Bai shook his head. "We looked at these maps only yesterday. How did this piece of paper get in the box?"

Zhao Liwen, the assistant who hardly spoke, interjected, "Could it have been there all along without us noticing it?"

Chief Bai was quiet for a moment. He shook his head and asked Yue Dongbei, "What does it say?"

"This note actually appears to be from his journals. We were just talking about the battle at Mopan Mountain, and as luck would have it, this was written on the evening of the battle! I'll read it out loud for you."

> *Battle at Mopan Mountain. My long-awaited plan's end was to be found in bitter struggle. A golden opportunity hath befallen us on this day. The third regiment was in position, entrenched in the valley. If the enemy came, the first was to strike. Then, the earth's eruption, during which the second and third cometh. Assaulted from front and rear, the enemy was to be vanquished! Counter to expectation, secrets hath been disclosed, the plan impeded. All three met in a bloodbath. How it grieves me. My only consolation is that I entered the enemy fray, sliced ten, with seven lashes reaped. The end saw the traitor seized in the field, to go under discipline tomorrow at daybreak. Remove the traitor's tongue, and let him meet his maker.*

Because it was written in Classical Chinese, Luo and the others didn't understand a word. Wu Qun and Zhao Liwen were likewise gaping.

"Now," Chief Bai objected, "Mr. Yue, we're all on the same team. Tell us in plain language what that meant."

There was a smug look on Yue Dongbei's face. "Fine. I'll translate it for you. The first half is General Li's account of the battle at Mopan Mountain, which confirms my research. The second half is quite interesting. It seems that he infiltrated Wu Sangui's ranks, killing ten soldiers and sustaining seven wounds. Eventually, the commander who leaked the ambush plan was captured alive. Li was planning to punish this fellow early the next morning by pulling out his tongue!"

"*'Sliced ten, with seven lashes reaped'*—this Li Dingguo was one fierce fellow." There was admiration in Luo's voice. "I've never heard of pulling out someone's tongue before."

"Heh heh. Classic Li Dingguo! He would take a man and pull out his tongue until it killed him. It was a favorite execution method."

A silence fell over the room, everyone trying to envision the wretched sight of someone undergoing such torture. It was truly bloodcurdling.

With a sigh, Professor Zhou was the first to speak up. "Divulging military secrets is a serious offense, but even so, that kind of punishment is profoundly cruel."

Yue Dongbei was tittering. "Just the beginning of General Li's cruelty, I assure you. If he hadn't been so cruel, why would the Hamo people have considered him a demonic spirit? Even after he died, they put their most vicious curse on him. Heh heh, now that the blood vial has been shattered, they must be trembling in fear at the thought of his reincarnation!"

The others leaned away, disgust on their faces.

Luo was both frank and blunt. "Mr. Yue, it's not appropriate for you to be labeling Li Dingguo a demonic spirit. Even though there was a cruel and barbaric side to his character, his courage and resourcefulness shouldn't be underestimated. He should be considered a hero to the Han people."

But Yue Dongbei wasn't one to back down. He shook his rotund head. "A hero? Chief Inspector Luo, you seem to have forgotten that we're trying to uncover the mystery of the demonic spirits terrorizing Longzhou! I am here helping you! At least you're finally taking an interest in General Li, which will come in handy when we reach the forest."

"Please give me that piece of paper," Chief Bai coldly interrupted. "And don't forget that our people descend from General Li. I think you've spoken enough for today."

Wu Qun and Zhao Liwen were giving Yue Dongbei the evil eye, and he suddenly remembered how the two of them had brandished their knives outside the temple. He shut his mouth and indignantly handed the paper over to Chief Bai.

"Put this away." Chief Bai told Wu Qun. "And go conduct a thorough search to see if there's anything else tucked inside the scroll."

Then he turned and faced Luo and the others. "That's all for today. If the rain stops, we'll meet tomorrow at 8:00 a.m. at the Temple of the Dragon King and depart as scheduled!"

Chapter 14

Deep in the Forest

The next morning, there was no sign of rain, so the travelers prepared to depart. Mr. Wang specially prepared extra eggs to give them a nutrient-rich breakfast. And when it came time to settle the bill, he couldn't help repeatedly warning them to be careful. It was clear that this kindhearted man was deeply worried.

Naturally, Luo and the others were even more uneasy. They were finally heading to the eye of the storm: the Valley of Terror. What awful events had transpired in the past in this forest cut off from the rest of civilization—and what was yet to come?

On the way to the Temple of the Dragon King, the three men were subdued, each lost in his own thoughts.

Luo was frustrated by the mysterious man who had followed him. Who was he, anyway? Where was he from? If he had wanted to make contact, why did he fail to keep the appointment? Was he also going to the Valley of Terror? Could it be possible that he was hurrying to stay ahead of them? And he hadn't hired a guide, so did that mean he already knew his way? There were far too many questions and no easy answers.

Even garrulous Yue Dongbei wasn't himself. The fanatical scholar was finally nearing his goal, and yet he seemed reticent, moody, too distracted to chatter.

And what of Professor Zhou? The renowned professor now found himself on the brink of the wilderness. Luo wondered, not for the first time, why the man had agreed to make this journey. Was he really doing it to track down the cause of the phobia? Or was it just because he wanted to refute Yue Dongbei's theory and defend the principles of scientific knowledge? Could he solve the mystery?

With his two assistants in tow, Chief Bai was already waiting at the Temple of the Dragon King. He stepped forward and greeted them, pointing toward the sky. "It's not going to rain over the next two days. God willing, if this keeps up, this trip of ours will go without a hitch."

Evidently, Chief Bai had put yesterday's disagreement over the departure date behind him.

Professor Zhou smiled lightly, as if to accept this truce, and politely responded, "Luckily for us, Chief Bai knows what he's doing!"

"I'll certainly do my best. Once we set foot in the forest, we're all going to be in this together," Chief Bai said. Then he turned to Wu Qun, who stood beside him. "Parcel out the rations. We need to get going."

"Each package contains enough jerky and crackers to last four days. There should be ample water in the mountains, so we don't need to bring our own. When you've finished what's in your water bottles, I can help you find someplace safe to refill them," Wu Qun explained.

"The rainforest is crawling with mosquitoes, leeches, poisonous ants, and whatnot. So fasten your collars and button your sleeves," Chief Bai advised. He looked at them and saw that the collars of their hiking jackets were secured with elastic loops and their pants were already tucked into their socks and boots. He flashed a smile, then told Zhao Liwen, "Help them put on the garlic juice."

Zhao Liwen took out a small, pungent satchel and began rubbing it against their ankles.

"This way, the insects won't crawl into your boots." Chief Bai took out three pairs of tinted sunglasses. "Here, there's a pair for each of you."

Though they found it a little odd, Luo and the others took them.

Yue Dongbei asked, "What are these for? Is the sun in the forest going to damage our eyes?"

Chief Bai chuckled. "The path is filled with all kinds of brambles. You'll need these to protect your eyes from scratches."

Suddenly, Luo felt a rush of excitement. This trek was going to be educational, indeed! If it weren't for their guide and his wealth of experience, they surely would have encountered countless difficulties.

Under Chief Bai's orders, Wu Qun and Zhao Liwen took the travelers' sleeping bags, which significantly lightened their loads.

They were all set. With his hands clasped behind his back, Chief Bai turned his gaze eastward.

Everyone followed the direction of his gaze and stood a long time in reverent silence. Not far in the distance, a towering mountain peak and a dense forest spread before them.

"Mopan Mountain . . ." Chief Bai pronounced the mountain's name in one long, dramatic breath. Then he stood up straight. "Let's go!"

With that, the chief bounded into the wooded hills behind the Temple of the Dragon King.

Luo and the others trailed closely behind him. Twenty minutes later, they had fully disappeared into the dense mountain undergrowth.

As they approached the mountain, Luo increasingly felt as if he were in another world altogether. The tree canopy overhead almost completely blocked out the sky. Even though it was light outside, the interior of the forest was quite dark. The trees grew in thick copses with hardly a gap in between.

The explorers who'd come before them had left a trail—though to call it that was a stretch, as it was nothing more than faded footprints. Wu Qun hurried to the front of the group, brandishing his machete and continually chopping down the branches and vines that obstructed their path, which also frightened off deadly insects and wild animals hiding in the dark recesses.

Whenever it was unclear which direction the footprints were leading, Chief Bai stepped up and made the decision. The rest of the time, he devoted his energies to looking after Yue Dongbei.

Desperately out of shape, Yue Dongbei looked even clumsier than usual in this setting. They had barely set out, and he was already huffing and puffing, struggling to keep up. But he didn't so much as grumble. He simply buckled down and made a few self-deprecating jokes. The man had formidable grit.

Behind Yue Dongbei came Luo, who was relatively light-footed due to his strenuous police training. He was no stranger to mountaineering—he'd worked on Nanming Mountain before coming to Longzhou—though this was his first time in such a dense rainforest. He occasionally reassured Yue Dongbei and helped pull up Professor Zhou, who walked behind him.

Professor Zhou's pace was not quick, nor were his strides large. However, his steps were strong and steady, and his physical fitness was evident. Whenever strange, new flora appeared along the path, he would stop and collect a few specimens for research.

Zhao Liwen came last. He wasn't big, but his eyes revealed a sharpness. His arms were muscular, the veins bulging as he gripped his machete. Everyone felt safe with him bringing up the rear.

As they ascended, the temperature began to plummet. Because the trek was so physically grueling, everyone worked up a sweat and drank water frequently. Chief Bai watched the three travelers carefully to see how they were holding up. Whenever necessary, he instructed Wu Qun to slow his pace so they could catch their breath. The first time Luo noticed Yue Dongbei struggling, he suggested they stop and take a break.

But Chief Bai refused, telling them, "We should either take a long rest or just keep moving. Taking short breaks will make your body even more tired."

"That's because starting and stopping repeatedly will disrupt the rhythms of your body's metabolism," Professor Zhou added.

Fortunately, though the uphill path was damp and slippery, no one took a spill. With a guide out in front, those behind were able to gauge the steps ahead and minimize the risk of a fall.

This continued straight into the afternoon, when Chief Bai told Wu Qun to stop. Then he turned to the rest of the group. "All right. Let's drink some water and have something to eat."

Yue Dongbei had long been looking forward to those words. Without waiting for Chief Bai to finish, he took out his food rations and plopped down. "Goodness gracious, I am dying. Finally, a break!"

Luo stifled a smile. "We're just getting started. You're going to have to hunker down."

But Yue Dongbei was too busy guzzling the contents of his water bottle to reply.

Luo tore off a piece of the jerky they'd been given, chewing carefully. Made from pickled pork, it was mildly spicy and actually rather palatable. In comparison, the crackers were hard, dry, and bland. They were effective in staving off hunger, and not much else.

Yue Dongbei looked around and scowled. "How are all of you so hungry? I'm too tired to eat."

Professor Zhou laughed. "You drank your water too quickly, so your stomach is full right now. Just wait a while and you'll be fine."

Sure enough, a moment later, Yue Dongbei had recovered. He started wolfing down his food, gobbling up more than anyone else.

"Chief Bai, how far have we traveled?" asked Luo.

"We should be more than halfway up the mountain. If we pick up the pace in the afternoon, we can make it to the eastern slope of Mopan Mountain and find a place to camp for the night."

After lunch, everyone rested for a little while longer, then continued onward.

Yue Dongbei's physical limitations became even more apparent in the afternoon, and the whole group had to travel slower and slower. But they were dead set on not taking any breaks, and so around six o'clock, they finally reached the top of Mopan Mountain.

Luo climbed atop the rocks at the summit and looked down. Before his eyes were hills upon hills covered in lush trees.

Chief Bai joined him. Without waiting for Luo to ask, he pointed to a lowland plain off in the distance, between two mountains. "That's where the Valley of Terror is."

It looked so picturesque, and yet its name was enough to strike fear into anyone's heart. What secrets lay hidden beneath that green veil?

Luo stared for a while before turning and looking back west, in the direction they had come from. The mountains and gullies spread out before him in a panorama. Did General Li stand in this very same place over three hundred years earlier, directing his forces in the tragic battle at Mopan Mountain? Envisioning this tranquil forest as a battlefield, a site where thousands upon thousands of people were killed in a bloody war, Luo couldn't help growing sentimental and pondering how a man's life was but a mere blip in the vast timeline of the universe.

The sky was still clear and bright. For the next half hour, the group made one more big push, heading down the eastern side of the mountain. They passed a clearing with a small cluster of flat rocks.

Chief Bai stopped. "It's getting dark. We'll camp here."

Everyone took off their backpacks. Chief Bai cleared off the area, then Luo, Professor Zhou, and Yue Dongbei pitched the tent. Wu Qun surveyed the surroundings before finding a hole where rainwater had collected. However, it looked muddy and therefore undrinkable. Using his machete, he carved out a reservoir nearby that was about eight inches in diameter and a foot and a half deep. A minute later, the water from the hole had flooded into the reservoir, only now it was visibly cleaner.

Zhao Liwen was searching for fallen branches, splitting them open to find the dry part inside. He then lit a campfire. When the sky turned dark, everyone sat around the fire, finally able to relax.

Everyone's socks and shoes were thoroughly drenched, so the first thing they did was take them off and place them near the fire to dry.

The tranquil moment was interrupted when Yue Dongbei started shrieking hysterically. "Damn it! What the hell is this?!"

Luo ran over to see. Attached to his thick ankles were two giant leeches.

The leeches were about the length of a person's thumb. As they'd been sucking blood for some time, they'd not only grown puffy but were bright red and gleaming. Yue Dongbei clearly had no idea what to do. One of the leeches, now exposed to the open air, plopped off on its own.

Chief Bai chuckled. "Yue Dongbei, your pants weren't sealed tightly enough, so you ended up with a pair of leeches. The more the merrier, might as well drink up!"

"Damn it! How dare they drink the blood of yours truly!" Yue Dongbei cursed. He picked up a twig and flung the leech into the campfire. There was a sizzling sound, followed by the faint scent of blood in the air.

As Yue Dongbei inspected both of his feet, he whispered fearfully, "They're so huge, how could I not have noticed?"

"If you did, then you'd just pull them off, right?" Professor Zhou laughed. "Leeches have an anesthetic on their suckers so you don't feel a thing. And when they're done, they excrete a substance that helps the wound heal. It's a function they developed as a matter of evolution."

"You really can't tell there's a wound," Yue Dongbei marveled after peeling another leech from his ankle. "Well, at least they didn't suck up every last drop. How'd I get so lucky?"

Everyone broke into laughter, marking the end of that minor drama.

The water bottles they had filled before setting off were now empty. Wu Qun filled each bottle from the reservoir he'd made, then added a tablet.

"What is it that you're putting in there?" Luo asked.

"It's a purification tablet," Wu Qun answered calmly. He took a huge gulp from his bottle as if to show it was safe.

Luo took a sip from his own bottle. Sure enough, he could taste bleach.

By the time they finished dinner, night had truly fallen. There wasn't a sliver of light in the entire forest, apart from the campfire. It was as if black ink had washed over their surroundings, blanketing them in darkness. The trilling sound of some unfamiliar insect came from somewhere, lending an atmosphere of loneliness to the scene.

Everyone was quiet for a moment. Then Chief Bai said, "We have a lot of ground to cover tomorrow. We should get to sleep. Why don't all of you squeeze inside your tent, and the three of us will find a place to sleep out here."

Luo knew better than to argue, so he simply replied, "You guys sure are tough."

Chief Bai and his trusted assistants found a flat and comfortable area and laid out the bedding they'd brought. Zhao Liwen took out a bamboo tube and sprinkled some kind of powdered substance around each of their beds.

Luo's nose detected the scent. "Is that—sulfur?"

Chief Bai nodded. "When you sleep out in the open, the campfire keeps the predators away, and sulfur keeps the insects at bay. We're going to put on some mosquito repellent, too, in a second."

Luo smiled faintly. "I hope your efforts aren't in vain. All of us need a good night's rest."

Chief Bai didn't reply. His gaze was fixed on the darkness around them, a solemn expression on his face.

Whether or not he could have predicted it, no one was going to get a good night's rest.

Chapter 15

Skinned, then Stuffed

The tiny tent felt cramped with all three of them packed inside, but there was nothing to be done about it. Exhausted, Yue Dongbei crawled into his sleeping bag and immediately passed out, snoring loudly. Professor Zhou grumbled about the noise, but Yue Dongbei was sound asleep, so what use was there in trying?

Luo scarcely heard it. His weariness overtook him, and he drifted off into slumber.

That slumber didn't last long, though. Out of nowhere, there was a strange noise, as if something had fallen on their tent. Luo, always vigilant, instantly sat up straight.

"What is it?" Professor Zhou asked as they crawled out of their sleeping bags. From the looks of it, he'd hadn't slept a wink.

There was a commotion outside the tent, followed by a beam of light swinging wildly. Chief Bai could be heard hissing, "What's going on here? Each of you take a side and stand guard."

Luo slipped on his shoes and dashed out. Wu Qun and Zhao Liwen were holding knives in their right hands and flashlights in their left. There was a stunned expression on their faces as they peered every which way. Chief Bai stood next to the campfire, his eyes glinting like hooks. He clasped something in his hands.

A chill ran down Luo's spine. The thing Chief Bai held was a two-foot-long live snake. But the snake had been skinned. Only the skin on the tip of its tail remained, hanging limply. Its contorted pink body was engaged in a fierce struggle to live. It was a gruesome sight.

"What happened?" Luo asked, running toward him.

Chief Bai seemed both confused and frightened. After a silence, he looked up at Luo. "This fell onto your tent just now."

Professor Zhou, who had come over, overheard their exchange and saw the live snake. "Is there someone else here?"

Chief Bai didn't say anything, but what he did next seemed to answer the question. With a swing of his arms, he tossed the snake into the campfire. Then he lifted his chin, and like a hawk, scanned his surroundings.

The poor snake writhed wildly in the flames. Soon it stopped moving.

Yue Dongbei emerged from the tent just in time to see the gesture. He was flabbergasted at first, but then let out a sadistic laugh. "Heh heh. Chief Bai, I fed that fire two leeches this evening. That wasn't enough for you, and you had to feed it a snake, too?"

The solemn men paid him no mind, and Yue Dongbei realized that something was wrong. "What—what's going on?"

Suddenly, Wu Qun pointed his flashlight at something. "Chief, come look!"

Everyone followed the light, heading southwest into the woods until they reached an elevated area, where they caught a glimpse of clothing half-hidden in the foliage.

Chief Bai reeled back and reached for his machete, then assumed a defensive posture. He called out, "There's no use in hiding! Come out!"

There was no sign of movement.

"Chief, could it be—could it be—a person?" Both Wu Qun's voice and the beam from his flashlight were quivering.

"What are you so afraid of? It's nothing!" Chief Bai barked. With a flash of his hand, he snatched Wu Qun's flashlight and aimed it once more at the bushes and leaves. "I don't care if you're a ghost. If you don't come out right now, I cannot be responsible for any harm that comes to you!"

No response.

Luo, Professor Zhou, and Yue Dongbei exchanged looks. They hadn't expected something so bizarre to happen their very first night in the woods. It looked as if Chief Bai and his men, despite their wealth of experience, weren't prepared, either.

The standoff continued a while longer. Then Chief Bai swung around and nodded to Zhao Liwen. There was a stern and grave look in his eyes.

Zhao Liwen understood. He took a few steps forward, tensing his right arm. Suddenly, with a flash of silver, he charged into the woods, machete first.

Luo watched him disappear into the darkness. He never would have imagined that this man, who hardly made a peep, would turn so bold and fierce—and much more so than his outspoken counterpart, Wu Qun.

They heard something tumble to the ground, then Zhao Liwen called, "Chief, it's a dummy!"

Everyone ran to catch up. The figure they'd glimpsed now lay atop a pile of leaves. Zhao Liwen stood next to it, inspecting it by the light of his flashlight.

Sure enough, it was a scarecrow stuffed with hay and fully dressed in men's clothing, including a shirt, pants, and shoes. But there was something else about it.

They saw Zhao Liwen stoop over, practically putting his nose against it. "Chief, these clothes have blood all over them!"

Chief Bai stared at the dummy's clothes, and his face muscles began to twitch.

It was then that Wu Qun worked it out, too. "Those clothes—those clothes—they're—"

"That's right," said Luo, ever the detective. "They're the clothes Xue Mingfei was wearing the night before he died!"

Yue Dongbei's eyes widened. He squatted down to take a closer look. "Hmm, the stains really are blood. But are you sure it's Xue Mingfei's?"

No one responded, but everyone was thinking the same thing.

"Who could have done this?" Wu Qun lifted his flashlight, pointing it frantically in all directions, hoping for a signal.

"Stop that!" Chief Bai snapped. "Bring the dummy back to our campsite."

Luo looked at his watch. It was 12:35 a.m. The dummy was carried back to the campfire. Zhao Liwen found some more wood and built up the fire. There was a moment of silent introspection as all of them stared at the blood-soaked dummy.

Professor Zhou broke the silence. His brow was furrowed as he asked Chief Bai, "Could it be that someone's been following us this entire time?"

Chief Bai didn't reply. It was clear that he was distraught. Yue Dongbei stood off to the side, lost in his own musings, cocking his head to one side and mumbling to himself. Luo squatted down and examined the dummy. It had been crudely constructed and just barely resembled a human figure. It appeared to have been made using the grass that grew all over the forest. The giant bloodstains had already dried hard, but the smell was still pungent.

Luo gave the dummy a thorough pat-down, poking through every inch of its clothing. Suddenly, he removed something from its pants pocket and held it up to his eyes. "I think I know how Xue Mingfei died."

"Oh?" Chief Bai got up and walked over to see what Luo was holding. "It's—a leech?"

"That's right." Luo nodded. "It's dried up, but it looks like the same type of leech that got Yue Dongbei."

A light bulb seemed to go off in Professor Zhou's head. "No wonder I couldn't find any wounds to explain his blood loss!"

"But it had to have been a lot of leeches. And then the leeches that sucked his blood must have been chopped into pieces and placed inside the Rain God statue!" Luo held up the leech for Chief Bai to see. "Chief Bai, why don't you see for yourself?"

Chief Bai made a hmph sound. "Yes. I've known for some time."

Luo was stunned at first. Then it hit him. When the ceremony ended, Chief Bai must have inspected the mechanism in the statue and discovered the pulverized leeches.

Chief Bai ground his teeth. "It's not important how Xue Mingfei died. What's important is who killed him and why."

Professor Zhou nodded somberly. "The blood covered icon, the skinned snake, the dummy with blood-soaked clothing. His methods are getting more and more barbaric."

"What?" Yue Dongbei's head swiveled. "What did you say? A skinned snake?"

"Didn't you see?" Professor Zhou glanced over at him. "The snake that Chief Bai threw into the fire had been skinned alive!"

"I get it! I know what he is trying to do!" Yue Dongbei cried out in excitement. "Ha ha ha ha, the past and future collide! I truly am a scholarly genius."

Chief Bai stared at him coldly. "So why don't you tell us, then?"

"It's a symbol, as well as a warning, and it comes from a fearful force that's been sealed away for a long time." Yue Dongbei paused dramatically.

Professor Zhou snorted with impatience. "What kind of symbol? Just spit it out."

Yue Dongbei wore a strange smile as he clearly enunciated each word: "Skinned, then stuffed."

"What does that mean?" Luo prompted.

"It's a punishment invented by the Ming Emperor Zhu Yuanzhang," Yue Dongbei explained, "where the criminal is skinned and then his skin is stuffed with rice straw and propped up on sticks of bamboo for public display."

It dawned on them. The men looked down at the dummy at their feet, stuffed with weeds and twigs, and each one trembled inside.

The skinned snake, the stuffed dummy. Was someone—or something—trying to warn them away from the Valley of Terror?

A silence passed, then Professor Zhou scoffed at Yue Dongbei. "What would Zhu Yuanzhang's punishment have to do with your grand theory about General Li and the demonic spirits?"

"It was invented by Zhu Yuanzhang, but that doesn't mean he was the only one who used it. Among Li's troops, skinning and stuffing was specially reserved for those who surrendered and defected to the enemy side."

Yue Dongbei's tone grew solemn as he stared meaningfully at Chief Bai.

Luo did a quick calculation: Chief Bai's ancestors had been among General Li's troops. When his army was defeated, these ancestors had surrendered. So the punishment—

Chief Bai's eyelids fluttered. He appeared to be suppressing his emotions as he replied menacingly, "Mr. Yue, what makes you think that I suddenly care about your historical theories?"

"It doesn't matter whether you care, Chief Bai, but you had better watch your back."

Chief Bai's face flashed with fury. "What do you mean?"

"General Li was up against all kinds of forces that banded together to annihilate him. Among his troops, the most likely candidate to have been the so-called traitor was none other than his lieutenant general, Bai Wenxuan. And if my hunch is correct, you're a descendant of Lieutenant General Bai."

Chief Bai glared at Yue Dongbei. "That's right. I am. But General Li was dead, and the troops had already surrendered. Calling him a traitor is going too far. It's deeply offensive."

"We both know that's not true." There wasn't a trace of politeness left in Yue Dongbei's tone. "According to historical records, Lieutenant General Bai's 'surrender' took place before his death—and he was immediately rewarded by the emperor! Bai Wenxuan was of extraordinary service to the Qing regime!"

To Luo and Professor Zhou, Yue Dongbei's words came as a bombshell. Could it be that Li Dingguo's most trusted lieutenant general had colluded with the enemy?

It was hard to read the expression on Chief Bai's face, but it appeared as if Yue Dongbei's claims were accurate. After a long silence, Chief Bai asked, "So what you're saying, Mr. Yue, is that this 'demon' is coming after me, personally?"

"First, your trusted aide dies a bizarre death, and at the ceremony, your family's power is nearly destroyed. Now symbols of skinning and stuffing are appearing. Who else do you think this is directed at?" Yue Dongbei was practically bursting with excitement. "There's no doubt about it. From the moment we set out, *he* has been following us to the Valley of Terror. The fearful force has been reemerging at every step. He wants revenge. Even if we can't see him, there is no doubt he is right beside us!"

A gust of wind howled past, underscoring Yue Dongbei's words. The flames of the campfire flickered. Then the wind died down and the forest was tranquil once more, but a cold gloominess had set in.

Suddenly, Chief Bai looked up at the night sky and burst into a fit of wild laughter. It continued for some time, loud at first, then gradually fading until it descended into something resembling the cry of a savage. He clenched his jaw and turned to face the black forest. Then he bellowed, "Come out if you dare! I don't care who or what you are! I, Chief Bai, will be waiting for you!"

The cry seemed to carry to every last dark corner of the wilderness. "I will be waiting for you . . ." The sound lingered for a long time. Was it an echo or a sinister reply from the netherworld?

Chapter 16

PULLING OUT TONGUES

At the campsite, Chief Bai showed no signs of fear.

"Zhao Liwen will be on duty for the next two hours, then Wu Qun can take over. Replenish the campfire and keep your eyes open! If anything happens, holler. Nobody messes with Chief Bai. The rest of you go to sleep."

Chief Bai went back to his bed and closed his eyes. Could he really be so unfazed?

Luo, Professor Zhou, and Yue Dongbei retreated to their tent and crawled back into their sleeping bags, but even though they didn't speak a word, all three knew sleep was an impossibility.

Luo stared into the dark tent, feeling a complicated mix of emotions. He was alert, confused, shocked, and even a bit excited.

There was the scent of something diabolic in the air, and it was growing stronger. Who was their unseen adversary? What was he trying to do?

Luo had no answers. He now felt a tinge of regret. It had been a serious mistake not to have conducted a search of the Temple of the Dragon King when they were in Mihong. There must have been clues left behind. Even if it was only a footprint or a hair, it would have been of immense importance. At the very least, it would have helped to determine what this adversary actually was.

Of course, Chief Bai had forbidden anyone to enter the temple. And all of them had underestimated the importance of the blood on the statue. Prior to this evening, Luo had been partial to the view that the incident at the temple had been a personal attack against Chief Bai's authority, and so he hadn't wanted to enter the fray.

But now the situation had escalated. Could it really be as Yue Dongbei said, that it was all tied to the Valley of Terror's legendary demonic spirits?

If so, had this mysterious adversary actually followed him all the way from Longzhou? That would simply be too terrifying! The implications were enough to make his hair stand on end.

The further he followed that logic, the more bewildered he felt. At the same time, the sheer challenge of it galvanized him. He was a born hunter, and this adversary, so frightening and mysterious, was awakening his most visceral instincts. His prey hadn't left any means of tracking it, but a good hunter had to know when to lay in wait. And Luo had the courage, the intelligence, and the patience to do it.

Adhering to this line of thinking greatly simplified the problem. Luo's next task was to figure out the adversary's next move so that he could be on the lookout and prepare a counterattack.

According to Yue Dongbei's analysis, Chief Bai was almost certainly the next target. But how much credence should Luo give the preposterous man? Furthermore, what if "skinning and stuffing" was just a bluff?

He peeked outside the tent. Zhao Liwen was faintly visible in the firelight, standing up straight and stock-still. Whenever there was even the slightest sound, he would turn on his flashlight and go investigate.

Luo watched and saw how whenever Zhao Liwen reacted to a sound, Chief Bai and Wu Qun would toss and turn in their sleep.

The men of Mihong were on high alert.

Luo, on the other hand, was finally relaxed. For the moment, there was no need for him to keep an eye on things. He decided to rest up for the unknown dangers to come. When he opened his eyes again, it was already the next morning. Beside him, Professor Zhou and Yue Dongbei were still sound asleep.

Luo quietly slipped out of his sleeping bag and stepped outside the tent.

A pure, dewy freshness filled the air. Luo inhaled deeply a few times. It was as if the freshness infiltrated his mind and body, making him feel exceptionally clear-headed.

Chief Bai looked as if he had just woken up, too. He had just rolled up his bedding. Wu Qun held his machete and stood guard. Zhao Liwen was off to the side, extinguishing what little was left of the campfire.

"Chief Inspector Luo, you're up early," Chief Bai said.

"I slept like a rock. All of you must be tired from your hard work," Luo said politely. He crossed to Wu Qun and patted him on the shoulder. "All right, it's daybreak. You can relax now."

Wu Qun looked at Luo nervously out of the corner of his eye, tightening his grip on his machete.

Chief Bai looked over. "What are you doing? Put that knife away. Everyone's water bottles are running low. Why don't you go fill them?"

"Yes, sir!" Wu Qun answered. He placed his machete back in its sheath, then went to collect the water bottles.

With a sheepish laugh, Luo watched him walk away. "I guess Chief Bai is still the boss around here."

Their conversation woke Professor Zhou and Yue Dongbei, who crawled from the tent and, just like Luo, inhaled the fresh air.

"My goodness, I haven't slept outdoors like this in years," Yue Dongbei said as he stretched. "Chief Bai, if I said anything last night that offended you, please forgive me."

"We don't know who the enemy is. There's no time for infighting." There was an impassiveness to Chief Bai's demeanor.

Rubbing his belly, Yue Dongbei strolled around the campsite. He kicked the dummy lightly as he passed. "You rotten thing, you're the reason nobody got a wink of sleep last night!"

"We were lucky to have these two on watch all night." Professor Zhou looked up, searching for a moment. "Where's Wu Qun?"

"He went to refill the water." Luo pointed in the direction of the reservoir. Then he realized Wu Qun had been gone too long. "Hey, shouldn't he be back by now?"

"It's broad daylight. The chances of—" Chief Bai didn't finish what he was saying. The words *something happening* sank to the pit of his stomach.

At that moment, Wu Qun had emerged from the thicket, tripping over his own feet as if he were drunk. He seemed to be out of his senses and in extreme pain. His eyes were practically popping out of their sockets. Even more frightening, his hands were in his mouth, tightly gripping his tongue. The man was yanking out his tongue with all his might!

"What the hell are you doing?" Chief Bai hollered, running toward him. Zhao Liwen was right beside him. The two of them supported Wu Qun as he staggered.

Luo and the others followed close behind.

Wu Qun stared at Chief Bai, shock and distress on his face. It seemed as if he wanted to say something, but he could produce only a whimpering sound. There was a hoarseness to it, such that it didn't seem human.

All the energy in his entire body seemed to be concentrated in his fingers, which had yanked his tongue a full two inches out of his mouth. His fingernails were deeply implanted in his tongue, and blood was oozing out. It was almost as if he believed this wasn't his tongue but a snake that had entered his body.

"Hurry up and stop him! He's going to kill himself!" Professor Zhou cried out in alarm.

Luo stepped forward and tried to pry Wu Qun's fingers free. Chief Bai and Zhao Liwen joined in. But Wu Qun had an iron grip, and it seemed impossible to wrench them loose.

Wu Qun's tongue had virtually been pulled out. His face was completely red, as if he were suffocating, and he was taking unusually rapid breaths.

"Quick, help!" Luo knew it was bad. He shouted out to the others. Professor Zhou and Yue Dongbei became part of the group, and they wrung Wu Qun's stiff fingers, one by one, away from his tongue.

Finally, Wu Qun appeared to have spent all of his energy. His fingers loosened their grip, and the others wrested his tongue free.

However, there was no cause for celebration, for at that very moment, Wu Qun stopped breathing and his eyes froze. His body grew limp. His tongue still hung outside of his mouth. A strange expression spread across his face as death overtook him.

Shocked and angered, Chief Bai watched as another one of his most trusted aides died tragically. He pulled away from the group and removed his machete from his belt, then stormed off in the direction of the water.

The reservoir was only ten yards from the campsite, but the trees hid it from view. When Chief Bai arrived, there was not a single hint of anything out of the ordinary.

Gripping his machete, he scoured his surroundings, eyes flashing with anger. "Damn you! What is it that you want? Show yourself," he growled.

He heard a rustling sound, and indeed, someone appeared. Chief Bai stared intently, ready to attack. Then he saw that it was Luo.

Luo's face was placid, and his eyes were bright and piercing as he carefully surveyed the scene.

Wu Qun had neatly arranged the water bottles along the edge of the pool. One bottle lay at a distance from the others, water spilling out of it. Luo went over and picked it up.

"Is this Wu Qun's?" Luo asked Chief Bai, who nodded in response.

Luo squatted down, but the brush was too thick to check for footprints.

"Let's go back and take a look at the campsite. It doesn't look like there are many clues here," Luo said.

His face ashen, Chief Bai silently followed Luo.

At the campsite, Professor Zhou was examining the corpse while Zhao Liwen stood guard beside him. He seemed to grow more furious every time he looked down and saw his partner's body. Yue Dongbei was off a little way, his hands clasped, looking up at the sky.

"What did you find?" Professor Zhou lifted his head as Luo and Chief Bai neared.

Luo didn't answer right away. Instead, he stooped down to inspect the jacket on the body. One spot was visibly soaked.

With his left hand, Luo picked up Wu Qun's water bottle. With his right, he touched the wet spot. Then he racked his brain, recounting how the events had unfolded, step-by-step: "He filled his own bottle first. Then he immediately started drinking it. It was then that something happened—"

"What happened?" Chief Bai wanted to know.

Luo shook his head, staring at Wu Qun's face. "Why?" he asked himself. "Why was he trying to pull out his tongue?"

He contemplated the question for a while, but there didn't seem to be any leads. "What do you see? Can you pin down the cause of death?" he asked Professor Zhou.

"There aren't any wounds on his body, so no signs that he was attacked. I'm starting to think that pulling out his own tongue caused him to suffocate, which is what killed him, but"—Professor Zhou

140

pointed to Wu Qun's tongue, which was dangling out of his mouth—"there's also something fishy about that."

"What about it?" Luo narrowed his eyes. Chief Bai crouched over and listened closely.

"Look, it's swollen!"

Sure enough, Wu Qun's tongue was much too large, and it looked faintly black.

"What could have caused this? A disease or poison?" Luo asked.

"Right now, it's not clear. This is just an external symptom. But the problem most likely stems from the tongue. In order to find out what happened, we have to conduct special procedures on the corpse." Professor Zhou was looking inquisitively at Chief Bai as he spoke.

Luo understood. If Professor Zhou wanted to do something to the corpse, he needed Chief Bai's permission.

Chief Bai also understood what Professor Zhou was getting at. He resolutely reached into his belt and took out his machete. Then he stepped forward and made an incision in Wu Qun's throat, near the base of his tongue.

Blood poured out.

Luo felt a chill in his heart, and his breath caught in his throat.

Chief Bai gazed at the scene before him, scowling. He clenched his jaw and cut all the way through the skin and muscle in Wu Qun's neck. He then plunged his fingers inside Wu Qun's throat and groped around before pulling the entire tongue out through the opening.

It was a bizarre and frightening sight. The tongue, which had a dark welt on it, was so incredibly swollen that it almost looked like a loaf of bread. To everyone's shock, there was a vividly colored spider right in the middle, pressed against it.

The spider was roughly the size of someone's thumb. On its body was a distinctive hourglass-shaped marking. Though it had been dead for some time, its fangs were securely embedded in Wu Qun's tongue.

Chief Bai's face showed all kinds of different emotions swirling inside of him: shock, helplessness, sorrow. He gingerly removed the spider and laughed darkly. "A black widow."

"Black widow?" Luo couldn't take his eyes off the spider. "That's what it's called?"

Chief Bai nodded. "It's an extremely poisonous species. A bite to the leg, without proper treatment, can kill a person, so you can imagine what happens if it bites a vital area like the tongue."

Luo furrowed his brow. "Does it live in water?"

"No." Chief Bai deliberated for a moment. "Maybe it crawled into the water bottle?"

Luo thought it through. Chief Bai, Wu Qun, and Zhao Liwen had spread sulfur around their beds, but the water bottles had been outside the ring. This dangerous spider had crawled into Wu Qun's water bottle. Wu Qun had filled his own bottle first and swallowed the spider along with the water. Its life in danger, the spider had bitten his tongue, injecting all of its venom. Wu Qun, who was not only in unbearable pain but in shock, instinctively tried to pull out his tongue to get rid of the poison in his throat. But the poison still killed him.

It was all too tragic. Luo shook his head. There was nothing he could say. Professor Zhou and Zhao Liwen were likewise overcome.

"Ha ha. A bit too much of a coincidence, wouldn't you say?" When Yue Dongbei finally opened his mouth, he didn't mince words. "This was portended two days ago."

"Two days ago." Chief Bai gaped at Yue Dongbei. "Two days ago, we were still in Mihong."

Yue Dongbei didn't answer and instead looked up at the sky. Then he sighed dejectedly. "My, I should have known. I was distracted by the whole business of skinning and stuff, but there was an earlier warning that appeared right before our eyes—"

The others exchanged baffled glances.

"Pulling out tongues as a punishment! Have you all forgotten?" Yue Dongbei yelled. "The paper from General Li's journal! He made it perfectly clear that—at dawn on Mopan Mountain—the traitor would be punished by pulling out his tongue!"

Luo quickly went over the events of the past two days in his head. There was one detail he hadn't given much consideration before.

"You said that piece of paper wasn't in the scroll before, right?" His gaze traveled back and forth between Chief Bai and Zhao Liwen.

Zhao Liwen seemed dumbstruck. He simply looked over at Chief Bai.

Chief Bai nodded and said in a low voice, "That's right. I have no idea where it came from."

A hush fell over the group.

"If that paper really was from Li Dingguo's journal, it would be very interesting." Professor Zhou paused. "It's not the sort of thing your average person would have access to."

That was exactly what Luo had been thinking, too. He looked up, signaling for Professor Zhou to continue.

"In fact, I think that only someone who studies history, which is to say, someone who has conducted in-depth research on Li Dingguo, would have this kind of cultural artifact in their possession."

Yue Dongbei was no idiot. His face turned red. "You think it was me?"

"As you've taken such pains to show, you have a wealth of historical information on General Li. Indeed, who has researched him more extensively than you? Now, over the past few days, there's been a series of strange, inexplicable incidents, and isn't that what you've been hoping to see?" Professor Zhou's tone was starting to become aggressive.

"Absurd! How absurd! How could I have planned all of this? You think I arranged for there to be some kind of omen so that I could go and explain it?" Yue Dongbei had gone from embarrassment to anger. "It's true that I want to witness these kinds of things because they build

143

evidence for my theory and enrich my scholarship. But if they were all a show on my part, then what good would it do me? That's not research—that's fraud! You've repeatedly resorted to despicable means to attack me—is this how you scientists treat those whose viewpoints differ from your own?"

Professor Zhou stared icily at the man. He'd been hoping to provoke him into a confession, but he was disappointed. If Yue Dongbei was faking this response, he was a talented actor.

Chief Bai and Luo were also suspicious of Yue Dongbei. Though there was no evidence he'd committed a crime, he'd had an awfully thorough explanation for each of the strange incidents. It was difficult not to speculate that the unseen "mysterious forces" were parts of a plan that Yue Dongbei had guided them toward, step-by-step, and executed.

Yet chatty Yue Dongbei hardly seemed capable of such profound secrets—not to mention double homicide. Luo usually prided himself on being able to accurately assess a person's character. Could he have misjudged this cartoonish man?

Luo was silent for a moment, then he shook his head. There was one problem with suspecting Yue Dongbei. If he had planned and carried out these incidents, then why would he explain their hidden meaning at every juncture? Those explanations had caused everyone to mistrust him, which a criminal mastermind would have had to foresee. It didn't make sense.

Chief Bai broke the deadlock. "Mr. Yue, according to your theories, why would this punishment be inflicted on Wu Qun?"

Though he hesitated, his answer was decisive. "Tongue removal was a punishment that General Li designated for traitors, so I think that Wu Qun must have been linked to some kind of secret being divulged."

"Oh?" Chief Bai's eyes flashed. "What kind of secret?"

Professor Zhou listened with rapt attention.

"That—um." Yue Dongbei scratched his head. He looked slightly embarrassed. "That I can't say, exactly. Perhaps one of Wu Qun's ancestors committed some act of treason against General Li but wasn't punished for it? This is only a guess. I have no historical evidence to support it. I have to think about it more. Let me think about it . . ."

Chief Bai didn't appear to be satisfied with this explanation.

Luo noticed Professor Zhou frowning as well. He considered Yue Dongbei's theories hogwash anyway, so why was he so interested in the answer to this question?

"Right now, there are still a lot of things that are unclear, but let's not point fingers at one another." Luo had been ruminating for some time. "The residents of Mihong are all descendants of General Li's troops, so it wouldn't be surprising if someone had his writings in their possession."

Yue Dongbei nodded, glaring at Professor Zhou out of the corner of his eye. "Chief Inspector Luo may not agree with my views, but he's much more objective than you are. Now there's an actual scholarly approach to investigating the truth!"

Professor Zhou laughed coldly and turned away.

"Fine, then. Let's figure out what we're going to do now." Chief Bai glanced at the spider in his hand, then tossed it aside in disgust.

There was a glint of anger in Zhao Liwen's eyes. His right hand, which gripped his machete, sprang forward. The dead spider, which had just then hit the ground, was sliced to bits.

Chapter 17

An Ominous Catch

The sky was already bright. Everyone sat around the tiny campsite, their expressions solemn. The blood-soaked dummy and Wu Qun's corpse, in all its unsightly horror, lay at their feet.

And their journey to the Valley of Terror had only just begun.

Now they were confronted with a very real question: Should they continue?

Yue Dongbei's stance was the most explicit. "Of course we should. If we've already come this far, are we going to give up halfway? How could you not be interested in the truth behind these mysterious incidents? The answers are in the Valley of Terror, and they're almost within our reach!"

"Here's what I think," began Luo. "We have to go to the Valley of Terror. The more often strange things happen, the more critical it is that we get to the bottom of this mystery. If we turn back now, it may mean that our adversary has achieved his goal. That said—" He paused, then looked at Chief Bai. "Right now, it looks as if there's a serious threat to our safety. All of you can decide whether you wish to stay or go. We've already determined the route. As long as we continue downhill and successfully locate the river, in my own estimation, we'll be able to make it to the Valley of Terror."

"No, no, no. Chief Inspector Luo, there's something you don't understand." Yue Dongbei shook his head frantically. "As things stand now, regardless of whether we go, Chief Bai *has to* go to the Valley of Terror."

The others stared at him, perplexed.

Yue Dongbei looked earnestly at Chief Bai. "It's true that you'll be putting yourself at risk. But running back to Mihong won't solve the problem—Xue Mingfei will still be dead back in Mihong. The demonic forces have returned, and they need to be sealed up all over again. And no one else can do it except the high priest of the Hamo people."

"What you're saying is that we have to find the high priest of the Hamo people and ask for his help?" Chief Bai asked slowly, sounding despondent.

Yue Dongbei shook his head slightly. "It's not that simple. You have to join forces. The Hamo people lost the blood vial, and now all hell has broken loose. The demonic forces aren't going to let them off the hook. But if you can work together, and with my guidance, it's not hopeless. After all, the demonic forces were suppressed by the Hamo people for over three hundred years. It's been done before, so it can be done again."

Chief Bai furrowed his brow.

"I agree. You must not give up," Professor Zhou said. "Since the problem is coming from somewhere in the forest, it should be resolved in the forest. If you run away, the problem is only going to get worse!"

Chief Bai looked up in astonishment, but Professor Zhou's gaze was unwavering.

Chief Bai didn't say anything further. He nodded firmly, then glanced over at Zhao Liwen.

"I will avenge the deaths of Xue Mingfei and Wu Qun!" Though Zhao Liwen's voice wasn't loud, his tone was grim and forbidding.

Chief Bai seemed considerably relieved. Of his few trusted aides, Xue Mingfei was the one he'd been closest to. But in terms of sheer ability, Zhao Liwen was matchless. Though the situation at hand was dire, with a subordinate like him, perhaps there was no need to turn back.

Now that they had reached a consensus, everyone broke down the camp and prepared to continue on their journey. There was no way to bring Wu Qun's corpse, so they worked together to dig a makeshift grave. The residents of Mihong had the highest reverence for nature, and for them, to be buried in the mountains was an enviable sort of homecoming.

Everything was now in order. By the time they got back on the road, it was already almost ten o'clock. Without Wu Qun, Chief Bai himself stepped to the front, and the smaller group moved onward toward the base of the mountain. Morale had declined dramatically since they set out a day earlier. There was little talking, and with the exception of Yue Dongbei, who looked enthusiastic, everyone was in a dark mood.

However, the descent was much easier than their upward climb the day before, and nothing unexpected happened along the way. By around five in the afternoon, they had reached the foot of Mopan Mountain.

"Not too far ahead is Yijian Gorge. If we keep going all the way to the pass, where the gorge meets the valley, that's where we want to be." Chief Bai turned to face the rest of the group.

"Don't worry. I'm in better shape today," Yue Dongbei promptly responded. "I can keep going for another two or three hours."

Chief Bai shook his head. "Once we reach Yijian Gorge, we shouldn't go any farther. It would be extremely dangerous for us to spend the night in the gorge itself in this weather."

As they headed eastward, they could hear the faint sound of running water. Sure enough, just a few minutes later they emerged from the forest, and a panorama unfolded before their eyes.

A river flowed from the southwest, and not far in the distance, it curved eastward. Luo knew that this was the same stream that ran through the village of Mihong. They had traveled east across Mopan Mountain, whereas the river had curved south under the base of the mountain.

This far downstream, the river had grown quite powerful. It was about a hundred feet wide but flowed more gently than it did in Mihong.

The group followed the course of the river as it ran eastward. This phase of their journey was not only leisurely but, because they were near the water, rather pleasant. Though the recent tragedy wasn't forgotten, their spirits were lighter.

After they had walked less than a mile farther, two mountain peaks suddenly emerged. Between them ran a pass that was narrow and winding, such that it was difficult to discern where exactly it ended. The river followed the contour of its twists and turns, and from a distance it looked like a giant snake slithering into a crevice.

Chief Bai stopped and pointed. "Right up ahead of us is Yijian Gorge. We shouldn't go any farther. We should camp here on the floodplains."

Chief Bai didn't need to explain further. Luo took one look at the terrain and understood why they couldn't spend the night in the gorge. It was a narrow crack between the peaks, and it must have been about 150 feet wide. The river occupied more than half the width, and the banks offered a meager amount of space. If they set up camp there and the water level rose during the night, they could easily be engulfed.

"If it hadn't stopped raining yesterday, the river would have overflowed and flooded the gorge, and we would have had nowhere to run." Chief Bai looked at Professor Zhou.

Professor Zhou smiled. "That's how it goes. Man is at the mercy of nature, which decided not to delay our trip."

Everyone busied themselves setting up camp. It was still light out, so there was no rush. Luo, Professor Zhou, and Yue Dongbei put up their tent, while Chief Bai and Zhao Liwen took a walk around the nearby woods and returned with firewood.

Zhao Liwen had also chopped off a two-yard-long stick of bamboo. When everyone started eating dinner, he sat down and started fiddling with the stick, using his machete to carve a hole in it. Then, he produced a gray wire from his bag and inserted it into the hole.

"Hey, why aren't you eating? What are you doing?" Yue Dongbei asked loudly.

But Zhao Liwen's head was down, and he was preoccupied.

It was Chief Bai who explained: "There's something special he wants for dinner."

"Is he going fishing?" Luo guessed.

Sure enough, Zhao Liwen attached a float and speared a piece of cracker on his hook, then went over the river's edge and cast the line.

"Are there a lot of fish in this river?" Professor Zhou asked.

"There are *kanglangyu*."

"What a strange name. Are they unique to this area?" asked Luo.

Chief Bai nodded. "These fish are fierce and strong. They like to travel upstream, which is how they got their name."

"Oh really?" Luo squinted at the water.

The float suddenly jerked, and the line pulled taut. Zhao Liwen snapped to attention. His left hand gripped the bamboo pole while his right removed his machete from his belt.

Luo was stunned. "What, is he going to start a knife fight at the same time?"

"Can you see how tight the line is? If you don't use a special technique, the *kanglangyu* will go wild and tear its jaw trying to break free."

With a flick of the wrist, Zhao Liwen pressed the back of the blade against the line and jerked it back and forth, as if he were playing the violin. This produced a grating noise.

The sound wasn't loud, but it was enough to make Luo bristle. The awful sensation on the hooked fish's mouth was easy enough to imagine. After the blade was jerked four or five more times, the line went completely slack.

Zhao Liwen casually retracted the line and pulled the fish to the surface. The catch was already somewhat limp. It was long, and its head wasn't especially large. Based on its looks, it was hard to imagine that this fish was in fact incredibly strong.

There were quite a few *kanglangyu* in the river. Just a few minutes passed before Zhao Liwen pulled up another. He then laid his rod on the riverbank and brought the catch back to the campsite. He inserted a twig through each fish and roasted them over the fire.

It wasn't long before the mouthwatering aroma wafted through the air. Yue Dongbei had already eaten jerky and crackers, but the scent whetted his appetite once more. Seeing that Zhao Liwen had no plans to share, he let out a tiny laugh. "I want to try some!" He reached out and touched Zhao Liwen's machete, which was lying on the ground.

Instantly, Zhao Liwen's right hand snapped forward and gripped the knife. The blade flashed through the air and pressed against Yue Dongbei's hand.

"What—what are you doing?" Yue Dongbei gasped.

"What's the matter there, buddy? Mr. Yue just wants to borrow your knife for a second." Professor Zhou raised an eyebrow.

But Zhao Liwen just stared at Yue Dongbei with alarm.

"He's really taken to his training. If Mr. Yue wants to go fishing, he can use my knife." Chief Bai tossed his own machete over, shooting a stern look in Zhao Liwen's direction.

Yue Dongbei retreated a few steps and picked up Chief Bai's machete. He grumbled under his breath, then headed toward the river. Luo had remained calm as he observed this strange episode. Zhao Liwen's reaction seemed a bit extreme. Was it possible that he was fierce on the surface but terrified of the "mysterious forces" deep down?

Yue Dongbei walked over to the river's edge and picked up the fishing pole. He affixed a piece of cracker to the hook, then cast the line, just as he'd seen Zhao Liwen do. Watching his awkward movements, Luo laughed and shook his head. It was obvious that Yue Dongbei wasn't very experienced at these sorts of things. After a long while, there was still no fish on the line. Impatient, Yue Dongbei reeled it in. The cracker was still on the hook. Yue Dongbei went a few steps farther down and cast the line once more.

This time, his movements were much more fluid. The hook flew high over the water, and the line formed an arc as the hook splashed down, producing a plopping sound as it pierced the water's surface.

Yue Dongbei eagerly lifted the fishing pole a little. As soon as he did, there was a tugging at his wrists, and the line was pulled taut.

"Heh heh. I caught a fish!" A smile of satisfaction spread across Yue Dongbei's face, and he promptly lifted the knife and began dragging the back of the blade against the line.

"That was fast," Luo whispered, surprised.

Chief Bai and the others likewise stared in disbelief.

But Yue Dongbei was in high spirits. He couldn't wait to pull in the fish. The fishing pole was visibly bending at an angle due to the resistance.

"Hey! Hey! This is a big one!" Yue Dongbei hollered as he turned his head back. "Come help me!"

"The line is taut, and it won't budge. It can't be a fish. My guess is that it's hooked to the weeds at the bottom of the river." There was mockery in his voice as Professor Zhou offered his analysis.

Chief Bai nodded slightly in agreement.

Luo watched Yue Dongbei pull back the fishing rod and yank on the line, frantically struggling. With a smile, he stood up. "I'm going to go help. It's just sad watching him break that fishing pole."

Luo hurried over to Yue Dongbei's side. He gripped the rod with both hands, saying, "Don't yank too hard—easy does it!"

With Luo taking charge, the two of them combined their strength to pull back the fishing rod. They tried again from a few different angles before the line finally quivered, then drifted to the water's surface.

Luo felt the line slacken, but didn't relax his hands. He could feel his heart pounding in his chest. The hook must have snagged something at the bottom of the river.

Luo and Yue Dongbei had only managed to drag the line in two or three yards before they saw something black coming slowly to the surface.

"Hey, that's not a fish. What is it?" Yue Dongbei whispered in astonishment.

Luo's hands kept moving. His unblinking gaze was fixed on the water's surface. As the object came closer, Luo felt a shock of recognition.

Yue Dongbei had come to the same realization. "It's a dead body! What's a dead body doing here?" he shrieked.

When Chief Bai and the others heard those words, they leapt to their feet.

By the time the other men reached the river's edge, Luo and Yue Dongbei had already dragged the body out of the water. The corpse lay facedown on the riverbank. Though thoroughly bloated, it appeared to have been a man.

Chief Bai and Zhao Liwen stood perfectly frozen, stunned looks on their faces. Professor Zhou's mouth hung open in bewilderment. Luo's mind was racing. Then there was Yue Dongbei, who was making a ruckus as usual. "Look at his clothes! It's that man we saw back in Mihong!"

He was right. The corpse wore a black raincoat with a hood. The hood now lay limply to the side, revealing a head of wet, disheveled hair.

"This is the visitor who appeared in Mihong two days ago? How come he died out here?" There was a stupefied look on Chief Bai's face.

Luo was contemplating the same question. But what was more pressing was taking a look at the condition of the corpse.

Luo stepped forward and squatted down next to the body. He gingerly removed the fishing hook that had snagged on the clothing, then flipped over the body.

As it had apparently been underwater for quite some time, the victim's face was pallid and waterlogged. It had begun to decompose. Even so, it was evident that this had been a man in his twenties.

Luo stared at the man's face for an instant. He suddenly gasped. "Professor Zhou, do you know who this is?"

Professor Zhou stroked his chin, deep in thought. "He looks familiar, but I can't recall. I can't place it."

Luo nodded. "It's only natural. After all, you only met him once."

Yue Dongbei scratched his head. "You two know him? Who is it?"

Professor Zhou and the others all looked fixedly at Luo.

"Do you remember the first time I visited your office? I was there that day with Dr. Zhang, but there was also a young man. At the time, I thought he was your student."

"The reporter! It's the reporter for that website!" Professor Zhou erupted. "The one who leaked the incidents to the public!"

"Liu Yun." Luo spoke his name, then filled in the others on the backstory.

"Oh, he's the one who wrote the story I saw online?" Yue Dongbei sighed. "Without him, all of us never would have met!"

"But why did he come all the way out here? And if you know him, why didn't he get in touch with you?" Chief Bai asked.

Luo smiled grimly. "He must have followed us this whole time, looking for some kind of juicy scoop."

"Well, that's dedication." There was a rare look of reverence on Yue Dongbei's face. "If he had that kind of fearlessness and drive as a journalist, then he deserves a lot of respect."

Professor Zhou felt it beneath him to respond, as this was not the time or place for criticism. He frowned. "The question right now is why he died. Could it really be that he climbed Mopan Mountain, then ran into some kind of unexpected trouble? Maybe he was attacked?"

"No!" Luo categorically rejected Professor Zhou's theory. "We just learned firsthand what Mopan Mountain is like. There's no way he could've made it without a guide. Moreover, based on the condition of the corpse, he died at least two days ago."

Professor Zhou studied the body for a moment. "You're right. So maybe he didn't die here, but rather his corpse washed downstream from Mihong."

That made more sense. Yue Dongbei clapped his hands together, adding, "Yes! That's entirely possible. Remember how he asked to meet you that night it was raining? He never showed up. I bet he drowned in the mountain torrents!"

That was what Luo had been thinking, too. But he'd noticed a few things about the corpse. He leaned forward and gave it a closer inspection, then solemnly shook his head. "I'm afraid the cause of death might not be that simple."

"What do you mean?" Professor Zhou sensed that Luo was onto something and leaned in closer.

"Look at this." Luo brushed away the corpse's hair and pointed to the left cheek. "There's a cut right here. He must have been attacked."

The gash ran all the way from his forehead to his earlobe. Even though any traces of blood had been washed away, it was evident that this cut had been made with a sharp tool, and the wound was deep.

Professor Zhou examined the wound, then the nose and mouth, then the eyes. "The cut isn't what killed him. His nose and mouth are full of sediment. He drowned."

"He was attacked? Then he drowned?" Yue Dongbei had assumed his thinking posture once again, looking up at the sky. He was trying to find a link between this man's death and the legend of the demonic spirits. However, this time he seemed unable to come up with anything. After trying in vain for some time, he shook his head.

Squinting, Luo assessed the body with his sharp eyes. Another detail caught his attention.

The outfit looked neat and tidy, except for the left sleeve, which was rolled up. Luo reached out and took hold of the exposed forearm. There were indications of cuts in several places here, too. However, these wounds were much more shallow than the one on his cheek, and the cuts formed the Roman letters *d-a-n.*

The others leaned in with confusion on their faces.

"What's that? Did the attacker leave some kind of mark?" Professor Zhou wondered.

Luo shook his head. "No. He probably didn't stick around and let his attacker carve this mark into him. If he drowned, at least we know he managed to escape the attacker."

"Could he have done it to himself?" asked Professor Zhou, biting his lip in disbelief. "What was he trying to say? Is it information about the attacker? Chief Bai, is there anyone in the village with that name?"

Chief Bai was taken aback. "Someone with the surname Dan?"

"There's no such family name." Luo shook his head firmly so that Chief Bai didn't waste his time thinking any further. "It must be English. Look at the way the letter *d* is closed up with a loop. If it were supposed to be pinyin, it would have been drawn as a straight line."

"English?" Yue Dongbei interjected. "But it wouldn't be a complete word in English."

Luo thought for a moment. He knew the answer, but out of habit, he didn't say it out loud right away.

"It might not be a complete word. If he did it after he was attacked, he probably only got halfway through." Luo led the others through his logic, step-by-step.

"Danger!" Yue Dongbei blurted out. "He was sending a warning!"

"That's right. Here's what I'm thinking—tell me if you think it makes sense." Luo paused to collect his thoughts. "On his way to meet me that night, he was attacked. We can see from the severity of the cut on his face that the attacker was trying to kill him. In the process of flee-ing, he used a small knife that he was carrying or some object he found on the side of the road to write half of a word in English. Not long after, he was swept up in the mountain torrents. Or maybe something else happened. Maybe the attacker pushed him in. He only managed to fin-ish the letters *d-a-n*. Among the words in English that begin with *dan*, one is *dance*, and another is *danger*. Given the circumstances, *danger* is certainly more likely. Of course, he didn't need to tell himself he was in danger. It's a message for whoever found his body. I think that person is me, or should I say, us."

Everyone listened in silence as Luo finished. No one raised any objections.

"So when he made the appointment to meet you, he wanted to warn you that there was danger?" Yue Dongbei took it one step further.

Luo nodded gravely.

Professor Zhou added, "He knew something we didn't, so the attacker wanted to get rid of him."

"He wanted to tell us not to go to the Valley of Terror? Could it be that he knew something terrible would happen along the way?" Yue Dongbei's shoulders were hunched in fear. He glanced over at Chief Bai sympathetically.

"In the end, he managed to send the warning, though it arrived a little too late." Luo looked over at the face of the corpse, which was a sickly white. He spoke softly, with gratitude in his voice.

The young man who constantly pursued secrets had ultimately achieved his goal of uncovering a big one. But he never got the chance to say what it was.

Luckily, Luo had his own way of communicating with the dead. In fact, he had just thought of a question that hadn't yet been raised.

No one noticed that Luo's brow was damp from sweat. Danger was already near.

Chapter 18

THE DEMON TAKES HUMAN FORM

Everyone felt an obligation to bury Liu Yun's body. But there was a difference between Liu Yun and Wu Qun: Since the first makeshift grave was in the mountains, Wu Qun's family would still be able to visit the site. Luo surveyed his surroundings, hoping to find a location that would be easily identifiable.

It didn't take long before he found what he was looking for. Not far from the riverbank, near the edge of the woods, there stood a towering tree. It was well over two hundred feet tall and around six feet in diameter.

Luo realized this tree belonged to a species under protection by federal law, and that it could only be found in the river valleys of Yunnan. Because it stood taller than the surrounding trees, it had earned the lofty-sounding name of *wangtianshu*, or literally, sky-gazing tree. Judging by this one's size and shape, it had to be at least a thousand years old.

A *wangtianshu*! Since this tree had mystical powers to see the farthest reaches of the sky, had it also witnessed the events that had taken place in this forest? If only it could speak. Though it knew all the bitter rivalries and triumphs of the past centuries, the *wangtianshu* kept its secrets.

And so, Liu Yun's body was buried, for the time being, at the base of the tree. The branches and leaves swayed in the mountain breeze, rustling lightly, as if to weep, as if to grieve.

By the time they finished, the sky was completely dark. Everyone sat around the campfire for the second night since leaving the forest. The flickering fire illuminated their grave, anxious faces. Was the fearful "demonic spirit" in some dark corner, secretly watching them? In his eyes, were they weak and helpless as lambs awaiting slaughter?

"It's clear that we're in a dangerous situation." After a long silence, Luo disrupted the oppressive atmosphere. "So it's absolutely vital that we exercise caution tonight."

"You can relax," Chief Bai replied. "The two of us will take turns standing guard the entire night."

"No. We can't have just two people. Everyone needs to help out," Luo responded firmly.

"But aren't two people enough?" Yue Dongbei grimaced.

Luo fixed his gaze on Yue Dongbei. His look was like a dagger.

Yue Dongbei lowered his head. "Fine—whatever you say," he muttered timidly.

"From now on, everyone must do as I say. I'm a police officer, and under extraordinary circumstances like these, I have to take responsibility for the safety of every one of you." Luo's gaze swept over the others, one by one. "Does anyone have anything to say about that?"

No one said a word.

"Okay, then, I'll start by assigning shifts for tonight's watch," Luo continued. "Chief Bai and I will be on duty from 10:00 p.m. to 12:30 a.m. After that, it will be me and Zhao Liwen from 12:30 a.m. to 3:00 a.m. The third shift will be Professor Zhou and Mr. Yue, who will be on duty from 3:00 a.m. to 5:30 a.m. That way, you all have a shift, plus five hours of sleep. I myself will have two shifts, plus two or three hours of sleep. So I'll take a nap before 10:00 p.m., and none of you should be asleep during that time."

Everyone listened to Luo's orders in a daze. Yue Dongbei and Professor Zhou eyed one another, both of them flustered.

Yue Dongbei forced an awkward smile, then turned to Luo. "Chief Inspector Luo, do you think—it would be possible to switch? How about if you and I take the first shift?"

"No, that's not possible. You two need to put aside your differences. This is no time for your silly squabbles."

Luo reached into his holster and took out a black semiautomatic pistol. Though Luo carried it with him at all times, he rarely took it out.

When face-to-face with criminals, intelligence was more important than force. That was the first lesson Luo learned at the police academy. For over a decade, those words had served as his motto. But today, it was time for Luo to take out this familiar and yet strange partner of his.

There was a cold gleam to the gun's barrel. Luo unloaded the clip and removed each of the bullets. He examined them carefully, then reloaded them. Afterward, he spoke solemnly. "Those who are on watch duty must be exceedingly alert. If anything unusual occurs, the first thing you should do is notify the rest of us. If anyone fails to do so, it's hard to say what might happen. Please believe me when I say this."

Everyone sensed the weight of Luo's words, and Yue Dongbei nodded respectfully.

"I've already loaded this gun with bullets. Even as I sleep, I'm going to be holding it," Luo said as he carried the gun back toward the tent. "All right, then. I'm going to rest for a while. Wake me when it's ten."

The sky was growing darker. Chief Bai, Zhao Liwen, Professor Zhou, and Yue Dongbei sat up together until ten. Then Chief Bai and Luo started the first shift.

The night was tranquil, but they knew all kinds of danger lurked in the darkness. At twelve thirty, the second shift began. Then, at three, the third. Everything went according to Luo's plan. When the light of dawn reached their campsite, Luo awoke and exhaled deeply.

Everyone seemed much more relaxed. They broke down the camp and ate a simple breakfast, then started off.

It took the entire morning to cross Yijian Gorge. It was called *yijian*, meaning "a single arrow," because the distance between the two mountain peaks was said to be about the distance of an arrow's flight. The river followed a twisting path through the gorge, which was so narrow that there was no choice but to wade through the water.

However, the scenery in the gorge was riveting. They were surrounded on both sides by verdant hills, and the river gurgled at their side. All along the way, wild creatures descended into the gorge to drink, but upon seeing humans, they retreated to the edge of the woods to watch in alarm.

Around noon, the group finally reached the end of the gorge. Ahead, the terrain turned relatively flat, but it felt as if they were still heading downhill overall.

"This is Qingfeng Pass," Chief Bai announced. "We should take a break for lunch."

"Are we close to our destination?" Luo recalled that Qingfeng Pass had been the last feature listed on the map.

"It'll be another two hours. We're going to follow the river downstream, then turn south and we'll be in the Valley of Terror." Chief Bai stared off into the distance. A moment later, he turned and faced Luo and quietly told him, "If nothing unexpected happens, we'll reach a Hamo village today."

The group found a dry place to rest between the forest and the river, then unpacked and distributed their rations. Everyone's water bottles were almost empty, so Zhao Liwen went to the river, where he carved a tiny reservoir in the ground and filled it with clean water from the river.

Zhao Liwen then went to pick up everyone's water bottles. Just as he was about to leave, Luo suddenly spoke up. "Hold on."

Zhao Liwen stopped in his tracks, confused.

Luo smiled. "Why don't you leave the bottles that belong to the three of us, and we'll fill them ourselves?"

Professor Zhou was clever enough to understand immediately what Luo was getting at. Surprise crossed his face, and he glanced at each of the others.

Zhao Liwen stood frozen, looking to Chief Bai for an answer.

Chief Bai's expression was calm as he spoke. "Chief Inspector Luo, what are you implying?"

Yue Dongbei laughed awkwardly, hoping to help mediate. "We've learned our lesson from what happened to Wu Qun, but still—Chief Inspector Luo, aren't you overreacting a little?"

"Under the circumstances, there's no such thing as overreacting." Professor Zhou, who stood next to Luo, had been mulling it over. "Everyone should follow Chief Inspector Luo's orders."

Chief Bai laughed. "Fine. We'll each take our own bottles."

Zhao Liwen left behind the bottles that belonged to Luo, Professor Zhou, and Yue Dongbei. Though he didn't say a word, it was evident from his demeanor that he was not happy.

Professor Zhou walked over and picked up the water bottles, then handed Luo and Yue Dongbei theirs. "Shall we?"

Luo and Yue Dongbei followed him to the reservoir. They watched Zhao Liwen finish filling up his and Chief Bai's water bottles and then glare at Luo before leaving.

Professor Zhou waited for him to go, then whispered, "Chief Inspector Luo, do you really think they're up to something?"

Luo responded in a low voice, "I don't actually suspect anything. It's just best if we don't leave any room for chance."

Professor Zhou nodded to show that he understood. Then he squatted down and dunked his water bottle.

Yue Dongbei, on the other hand, took issue with the idea. "Why would you suspect those two of being involved in Wu Qun's death? That's nonsense, pure nonsense," he grumbled.

Luo, who didn't want to waste his breath arguing, simply smiled a little. He replenished his own water, then turned and left.

After that, lunch was an awkward affair. Everyone looked down as they ate and drank. No one was in the mood to converse much.

Chief Bai was conflicted. The Valley of Terror was close, and his work as a guide would soon be over. But would the mysterious demonic spirits let him be? He waited until everyone finished their food and drinks, then stood up decisively.

"We've reached the final leg of our journey, and we need to take extra care. Once we reach the Hamo village, we can relax and get some rest."

Luo nodded. They were all getting ready to go when, suddenly, a strange feeling came over him, spreading throughout his body.

It was terror.

Luo looked around in all directions, confused. At that moment, he heard laughter.

It was a dark and sinister laugh. The voice was hoarse and dry, and it pierced his eardrums. The sound seemed to contain a multitude of spine-chilling emotions: sorrow, hatred, despair, fear, cruelty. It was truly terrifying.

All of them were wide-eyed as they looked at the nearby forest, from which the laughter seemed to emanate. Zhao Liwen bit his lip. There was a whoosh of metal as he whipped out his knife and charged the trees.

Chief Bai shouted in a low voice. "Wait, we'll go together!" He took out his own machete and hurried to catch up.

Luo felt his breath quicken. The laughter sounded like a sledgehammer striking over and over again. It was unbearable.

Professor Zhou approached Luo, concerned. "What's the matter, Chief Inspector Luo?"

Luo shook his head painfully, unable to speak. Then he suddenly grabbed Professor Zhou's arm, staring past him.

Professor Zhou swiveled his head abruptly, nearly smacking into Yue Dongbei, whose face was right next to his, twisted in fear. Yue Dongbei's eyes looked blurry and out of focus.

"It's him—he's coming—the demonic spirit," Yue Dongbei stammered, as if forcing the words out from the back of his throat.

Professor Zhou felt a tingling along his scalp. He narrowed his eyes and stared into the dark and eerie forest.

He watched as Zhao Liwen and Chief Bai, wielding their machetes, entered the thicket together.

When the laughter first rang out, Zhao Liwen, too, had been afraid. But then the anger he'd been holding inside overtook him. This was an anger mixed with grief, despair, and pride. Within the short span of the past few days, he had lost two dear colleagues, and he felt a despondence that bordered on madness.

The grotesque ways that Xue Mingfei and Wu Qun had died were now at the forefront of his mind. Was he the next target? He felt like a pig feeding while a contemptuous butcher secretly watched, and it enraged the proud man, making him forget his fear.

I don't care what kind of terrifying powers you have, I'm going to make you run for your life! Zhao Liwen thought as he blindly flung himself toward the laughter.

In comparison, Chief Bai was much calmer but equally resolute. Two of his aides had been killed for reasons that were entirely beyond him, and this adversary's offensive appeared to be directed at him.

Who could it be? How did he know the secrets of the Rain God? What did he want? These questions had to be answered. And now, the chance had finally come. That was why, when Zhao Liwen stormed into the woods, he followed close behind, surveying their surroundings as he ran.

He did not believe this adversary could fend off both of them at the same time. And under such extraordinary circumstances, if he were to lose Zhao Liwen in exchange for a chance to exact vengeance, the sacrifice would be worth it.

And thus, master and servant barreled toward unforeseen danger. Suddenly, the laughter came to a halt, and the woods were peaceful once more. Clutching his machete and looking every which way, Zhao Liwen was like a bloodhound that had lost the trail.

Chief Bai stopped, too, telling him in a low voice, "Stay alert, and be on the lookout."

They were on dangerous terrain. Not only was the brush dense, but the tree canopy blocked the sky. Towering before them was a massive slab of rock twenty-five feet tall. Its surface was quite steep, such that, from the side, it resembled a cliff.

There were several giant trees close to the rock, and they were covered in vines, which had extended onto the rock.

Chief Bai and Zhao Liwen immediately fixed their gazes on the rock. But what captured their interest was not the scenery, but the two columns of text written in giant characters.

Each character was about six inches tall and crimson red. The words were arranged to form two phrases:

One with the demons, joyous and carefree.

May these schemes be hatched, and may you prisoners of terror be!

The handwriting looked somewhat shaky, trailing off near the end of each character, but the words burned like flames in the dark forest.

As descendants of General Li's troops, Chief Bai and Zhao Liwen both knew these nineteen words. Li had used these words to threaten any soldiers who betrayed him. The men stood frozen about six feet away, taking care not to make any conspicuous movements.

Then Zhao Liwen very cautiously approached the underside of the rock and inspected the characters. After his initial shock passed, a look of hatred and disgust crossed his face. He lifted the machete in his hands and lunged toward the words.

Where the blade made contact, the words seemed to shimmer. Chief Bai inched closer and realized the individual strokes of the characters had been composed of red centipedes. The sight of them was sinister and frightening.

Zhao Liwen madly sliced left and right, relentlessly attacking the face of the cliff and butchering some of the centipedes, which fell into the brush. A pungent odor spread through the air.

Chief Bai called out from behind, "That's enough. Stop!"

But Zhao Liwen kept hacking away with all his might, taking out all the emotions that had built up in the past few days—fear, anger, sorrow—on the blameless centipedes.

Nor did the vines escape a cruel end, chopped to bits by Zhao Liwen's blade. From top to bottom, all the vines were sent flying through the air in pieces.

Suddenly, Zhao Liwen felt a tightening around his ankle, as if the vines were reaching up and wrapping themselves around it. He ripped his leg away, freeing his ankle, then sprang into the air and ran toward higher ground, screaming, "Aaaaarggghhh!"

By the time Chief Bai managed to utter, "Watch out!" Zhao Liwen had already disappeared into the swaying trees. Then Zhao Liwen's cries abruptly stopped, and blood started to rain down through the branches and leaves, almost in a gentle shower. Chief Bai looked up as the droplets struck his face. He realized that they were warm, and his own blood ran cold.

Standing near the edge of the forest, Professor Zhou listened anxiously. He'd had a bad feeling about the two men rushing off like that, but he didn't stop them.

Ever since the first night when a skinned snake fell on their tent, Professor Zhou had felt like there was a bomb ticking, that disaster would be upon them at any moment.

Now the time had finally arrived for a face-to-face confrontation.

About two or three minutes later, he heard a frightened whimper, as if in response to a question.

Professor Zhou felt a chill in his heart. He looked at Luo and Yue Dongbei beside him, out of their minds with fear.

Beads of sweat were forming on Professor Zhou's forehead. He had to do something. Yue Dongbei's theories were insane, but there was no denying some kind of mysterious force was at work here. What did *he* want from them? Did Professor Zhou have the courage to confront him?

After some deliberation, Professor Zhou left the floodplain and headed into the forest. He had just set foot in the forest when something struck him on the back of the head, and he tumbled into a pile of leaves.

Luo watched as the professor marched bravely into the woods, but he couldn't move. He felt like a prisoner.

He was surrounded by a thick, dark fog. Everything he had ever feared from the time he was born lurked in the fog, first appearing, then disappearing. They shrieked wildly, flashed sinister smiles, and wept loudly, letting loose all kinds of spine-chilling noises. Every inch of his skin and muscles, every pore on his body was clenched with fear, such that there was no way to run, and nowhere to hide.

An inexpressible, mysterious presence was drifting nearby. It was as if some unimaginable, frightening thing were slowly approaching, coming closer and closer, yet it remained invisible.

The terror in Luo's chest was almost suffocating him. He opened his mouth to scream, but he couldn't hear the sound come out. He summoned his last bit of will to survive, resisting wave upon turbulent wave of fear, but to no avail. Under the unyielding pressure, Luo felt as if his mind had snapped, and at the same time, his heart was violently palpitating, as if it might leap out of his chest altogether. There was no way that he could support his own weight. He was on the brink of collapsing.

That's when the fearful presence revealed itself at last. It was a dark, ghastly shadow. *He* emerged from the fog and slowly approached.

Though he stood right in front of Luo, all Luo could see was a pair of radiant, inhuman eyes shot through with red veins. Those eyes stared at Luo. They conveyed shudder-inducing grief, despair, hatred, and fear.

Then something touched Luo's face, and some sort of liquid started to drip down. Luo could feel it on his lips.

It was sweet and pungent, and slightly warm.

"The demonic spirit! Is this a demonic spirit that's risen from hell?" Luo wanted to shout, but his tongue was stiff.

That was the last thing Luo remembered before he passed out.

Chapter 19

THE HAMO PEOPLE

Luo's head was muddled, and he felt dizzy, as if he'd awakened from a deep sleep. It was as if he were drifting somewhere outside of his body, out of control.

Eventually, he managed to organize his thoughts and regain his senses. Blurry-eyed, Luo looked at the world of light all around him. It felt as though a lifetime had passed.

Where am I? What happened? Luo's mind leapt from one fragment of a memory to the next, trying to piece them together.

They'd set off early in the morning. They'd passed through Yijian Gorge. They'd reached Qingfeng Pass. They'd pitched the tent. They'd taken a break and had a meal. Suddenly, there'd been the sound of laughter. The feeling of fear had spread through him. It'd been like sinking into a dark inferno. His memories stopped there. Then something in him clicked: He had to stay on high alert—whatever it was could still be here! He reached for his holster and pulled out his gun, narrowing his eyes and searching in all directions for his companions.

What he saw before him was even more sobering. He recalled that everyone had been on the floodplain. But now, there was only Yue Dongbei.

Yue Dongbei was not his normal, arrogant self. He sat on the ground staring blankly, his body trembling uncontrollably.

Luo patted him on the shoulder, saying loudly, "Mr. Yue! Mr. Yue!"

Yue Dongbei looked up at Luo. "The demonic spirit, the demonic spirit! It's come back!"

Demonic spirit? Luo furrowed his brow and remembered. The dark shadow emerging from the fog. That pair of bloodred eyes. Had it been a hallucination?

Luo noticed trickles of blood near Yue Dongbei's lips. Yue Dongbei was wiping at them with his thumb.

A dark-red substance was on his own fingertips as well. There was no doubt about it: blood.

Luo had no time to delve deeper into the matter. His most urgent priority was to assess the situation. "Where are the others?" he asked Yue Dongbei.

Yue Dongbei shook his head. "All I know is that laughter came from the forest, and it was like a nightmare. It's all a mess in my head."

So he and Yue Dongbei had experienced the same thing.

Just then, someone emerged from the forest. He clutched the back of his head as he stumbled out groggily.

Luo instantly recognized Professor Zhou, and he rushed over to him.

Professor Zhou stood there with a blank look. His eyes were blurry.

"What happened? Where are Chief Bai and Zhao Liwen?" Luo asked anxiously.

But Professor Zhou didn't answer. He just mumbled, "What about you two? What happened to you?"

Luo waved dismissively. "That's not a question I can answer right now. But tell me, where are Chief Bai and Zhao Liwen?"

Professor Zhou rubbed the back of his head. "I was on my way to find them when something hit me and I passed out. I woke up just now."

Luo examined the back of Professor Zhou's head. A bump had started to form, but there were no other signs of injury. It appeared that he'd been struck with a blunt object.

"Let's go have a look. Together."

Holding his gun, Luo led the three of them into the dark forest. Wordlessly making their way through the dense undergrowth, Luo and the others craned their necks every which way. Luo lifted his left hand, signaling to the others to stop. Then he took a deep breath and shouted, "Chief Bai! Chief Bai!"

His cry frightened some birds, which rustled the leaves and shook the branches overhead as they scattered. An instant later, there was a distant echo, but no reply.

Luo lifted an eyebrow, thinking for a moment. He turned around and asked Professor Zhou, "Where were you attacked? Do you think you can find the spot?"

Professor Zhou nodded, looking around. Then he started walking southeast. Luo and Yue Dongbei trailed him closely. They had walked about thirty feet when Professor Zhou squatted and pointed at a patch of brush covered with footprints. "It was right here."

Luo knelt. Immediately, he found what he'd been looking for: a patch of ground where blood had dripped.

Luo's heart pounded. "Can the two of you help me track the bloodstains?"

Professor Zhou and Yue Dongbei understood right away. They split up and began searching. Just a yard west of the first bloodstain, they found a second.

Continuing in the same direction, they discovered a third. The distance between the bloodstains seemed to be growing shorter. They spanned a total of about fifteen feet and then seemed to disappear.

"I guess there's no use in looking any further." Yue Dongbei sounded slightly impatient. He stood back up. "If we keep going in this direction, we should be on the right track."

Luo shook his head. "No, he didn't come from that direction."

Yue Dongbei curled his lips. "Why do you say that? The bloodstains all lead that way."

"These bloodstains indicate that he stopped here," Luo explained. He looked over at Professor Zhou. "He saw you and stopped, waiting for an opportunity. When your back was turned, he started sneaking up on you. These bloodstains that are closer together show that he moved slowly at first, and when you were within range, he rushed forward and struck you."

Professor Zhou nodded, thinking. "So this trail only reveals the path he took to attack me, not which direction he fled in."

"Right, but figuring that out shouldn't be difficult." Still squatting, Luo took one step south. "Look right here."

Sure enough, a faded bloodstain was directly in front of Luo's foot.

As they extended their search southward, they found that the trail continued for almost another twenty feet. Luo stood there, his gaze firmly fixed on his companions. "Now this seems right. It's this way!"

The trio headed south. The terrain grew increasingly dangerous, and the forest grew denser. A giant rock suddenly appeared, and they stopped, astonishment on their faces.

One with the demons, joyous and carefree.

May these schemes be hatched, and may you prisoners of terror be!

Luo and Professor Zhou turned and looked at Yue Dongbei. They both recalled how, the first time Yue Dongbei had visited Luo's office, he'd shown them a headband worn by one of Li's soldiers that bore the exact same phrase. Yue Dongbei zealously recited the words, walking toward the rock as he did so. He was astounded to see that countless centipedes had clustered together to form the characters. He stared in awe, then reached out his right hand and gently touched one of the characters. A few centipedes crawled onto his fingers. There was warmth and reverence in his voice as he watched them, mumbling, "Did you follow *him* here?"

As if in response, one of the centipedes opened its jaws and bit his finger. Yue Dongbei flinched, crying "Ow!" before pulling back his hand and shaking them off. The one that had bitten Yue Dongbei landed next to Professor Zhou, who stomped on the insect with disgust.

"These are sacred creatures. You shouldn't step on them!" Yue Dongbei, who was sucking his finger, lectured.

"Sacred?" Professor Zhou scoffed. "That's right. That bite is sacred, indeed."

But Yue Dongbei's face was stern as he spoke. "If it's not because of the demonic spirit, then why would these lowly arthropods arrange themselves into an ancient phrase on the face of a rock?"

"Do you really not understand, or are you just playing dumb?" Professor Zhou glared at him. His eyes were piercing. "These little tricks have been around for more than two thousand years."

At first Luo had been amazed, but hearing Professor Zhou's words, he pointed to the rock and asked, "What are you saying, that there's a historical precedent for using these things to form characters?"

"In 202 BC, during the Chu-Han Contention, Liu Bang was in power. His military adviser anticipated that his rival Xiang Yu would flee in the direction of the Wu River, so he sent troops there and used honey to write the words 'Xiang Yu killed himself here' in giant characters. Ants gathered to eat the honey until they formed the characters. Xiang Yu, believing that it was an edict from the heavens, decided to draw his sword and slit his own throat." Professor Zhou turned to Yue Dongbei. "If you call yourself a scholar of history, shouldn't you have heard this before?"

"Ants are ants, though." Yue Dongbei was unconvinced. "You can use honey to attract ants, but what do you use for centipedes?"

"It doesn't matter what you use. It still works the same way." Luo lifted his hand, not wanting Yue Dongbei to get hung up on the point. But deep down, he felt unsure. *What could you use to attract so many centipedes? And who would know such a thing?* Whatever or whoever was behind this mysterious "demonic spirit" knew the forest terrain and wildlife quite well.

"Chief Bai and Zhao Liwen must have been here already." Professor Zhou pointed at the pile of vines on the ground. "Look. These were cut down recently."

Luo nodded in agreement. Then, as he reached out to touch the vines, he felt something fall onto the back of his hand. It was a drop of blood.

Luo looked up in astonishment. Something tiny protruded from the top of the giant rock, almost like an awning. It was also, strikingly, encrusted with crimson blood.

"Up there!" Luo's voice was hushed. With his gun in his hand, he took two steps backward for a wider view. But the top of the rock was hard to make out, as it was covered with lush green foliage.

"Chief Inspector Luo, we can go up this way," said Professor Zhou, gesturing to a slope on the left side of the rock.

"Let's go." Luo immediately took the lead, scrambling up the hill-side. "The two of you stay behind me. Whatever you do, be careful!"

The three of them slowly filed up the steep slope, and two or three minutes later, Luo reached the top.

The area was shaped like a terrace, about thirty feet square. And there were Chief Bai and Zhao Liwen at the far end.

Several tall trees grew next to the terrace. Only their crowns, thick with leaves, were visible. Zhao Liwen's body hung limply from the branches of one.

Chief Bai stood a few steps away, staring. He seemed uninjured, but in a daze.

Professor Zhou and Yue Dongbei stepped onto the terrace. When they saw what had happened, they hung back. There was a long silence, then Luo tried calling, "Chief Bai!"

Chief Bai slowly turned around. He saw the trio and recoiled. Though they had been separated for mere minutes, Chief Bai had transformed into an entirely different person.

When they first met Chief Bai, he had been a shrewd and domineering village chief. When the unexpected had occurred at the temple, he had revealed that he was cunning as well as wise. Even after they entered the forest and encountered danger, he'd shown formidable character. But the person standing before them could be described only one way: defeated.

His face was no longer radiant, and he no longer stood tall. He no longer seemed to be any sort of chief, but rather a poor mountain man, sad and weary from carrying life's burdens.

Luo slowly walked toward the broken man.

Chief Bai's gaze skimmed over Luo for an instant before turning back to the trees. He mumbled, "Zhao Liwen, too . . ."

Indeed, Zhao Liwen was dead, hanging by his right ankle from a vine. The grisly slit along his throat was both wide and deep, exposing his trachea and esophagus.

Because the body had been hung upside down, almost all the blood had drained out. There was a huge pool of blood on the terrace. At the center lay Zhao Liwen's machete.

Without needing Chief Bai to explain, Luo had already worked out how Zhao Liwen had been killed: He'd stepped into a trap below the terrace and been yanked up into the air. The "demonic spirit" had been waiting for him on the terrace. Before his victim could respond, he'd cut Zhao Liwen's throat. When Zhao Liwen's hanging body spun from the vine, blood had poured out, spraying in a giant circle.

Had the blood also soaked the "demonic spirit"? And what had Chief Bai been doing when all of this took place?

"Did you see him?" Luo asked Chief Bai.

Professor Zhou and Yue Dongbei, who had both moved in closer, were now paying rapt attention.

"Him? Yes—the demonic spirit. I saw him." There was a distant look in Chief Bai's eyes, as if his mind were elsewhere.

"Really? You saw him?" Yue Dongbei yelped. Unable to contain himself, he gripped Chief Bai's arms, shaking him as he asked, "What—what did he look like?"

Chief Bai shook his head in dismay. "I couldn't see. He wore a long black coat with a black hat. There was a black cloth over his face. All I could see was his eyes."

"They were bloodred, weren't they? It was him, all right!" Yue Dongbei glanced over at Luo.

But Professor Zhou didn't share Yue Dongbei's excitement. Eyeing Chief Bai, he asked, "If you saw him up close, why did you let him get away?"

Chief Bai tightened his lips as if he were about to laugh. But no sound came out. "He ran. I had no way of holding him back."

"Why not?" Luo wrinkled his eyebrows.

"Three of my men are dead, including Zhao Liwen, the fiercest warrior in Mihong." Chief Bai pointed at the corpse. His voice grew hoarse. "I didn't stand a chance. What did all of you expect me to do? Was I supposed to die in this forest, too? I only agreed to be your guide. I didn't agree to die for you."

"But you did nothing!" Professor Zhou seemed irritated. He lifted the machete that was in his right hand. "This is yours, right? I found it on the hillside! When *he* appeared, you dropped it in fear, didn't you? I never imagined that you were such a coward."

Two nights earlier, when the "demonic spirit" had first threatened them, Chief Bai had wielded that knife proudly and shouted into the forest, laughing. But now, he didn't seem the least bit concerned about Professor Zhou's accusation. There was a strange look in his eyes. "You don't understand. I didn't have the power to resist him."

"Oh, is that right?" Professor Zhou laughed. "If he's so powerful, why did he spare the three of us? What kind of fishy business is this?

Why don't you make him come over, if you can, and offer us up as a sacrifice?"

Professor Zhou hadn't finished what he was saying when, suddenly, they heard footsteps ascending the hillside. Someone was coming.

Luo gripped his gun, and Professor Zhou brandished the machete, both of them inadvertently assuming defensive poses.

A young man leapt up onto the terrace. He was in his early twenties, with a muscular physique and dark skin. When he saw them, he seemed startled. With his right hand, he pulled out a shiny, curved blade, and he addressed them in a strange language, his tone forbidding.

"Hamo!" Chief Bai explained. Then he stepped forward, speaking to the young man as he walked over.

Luo nodded to himself: It sounded like the language he'd heard at the Kunming psychiatric hospital.

The young man listened to Chief Bai's words but kept a watchful eye on Luo and the others. His hostility seemed to have dissipated. Finally, he nodded, returned to the edge of the terrace, and shouted something downhill. Someone answered from below. A few moments later, four more men stepped onto the terrace. Like the first, they were dressed from head to toe in rudimentary clothing made of black hemp. All of them had black cloth headbands tied around their heads, except for the one who stood in front, whose headband and waistband were a striking white. His clothing was an elegant silver.

Chief Bai walked forward with his right arm pressed against his chest. "Lord An Mi!"

There was a look of surprise on the man's face. After returning a formal greeting, he asked, "Village Chief Bai, what are you doing here?" Though he spoke with an accent, his Mandarin Chinese sounded fluent.

Chief Bai gestured toward Luo and the others. "We're here because of the demonic spirit in the Valley of Terror."

The man's expression turned to one of shock. Then he switched to the Hamo language.

Chief Bai replied in Hamo. At first, the two of them seemed to be asking and answering one another's questions. Then, gradually, just Chief Bai was talking. The other clan leader stood by him, listening attentively and occasionally interjecting with a word or two.

Their conversation continued for a long time. Presumably, Chief Bai was telling him in detail about what had happened since they'd set out for the Valley of Terror. The Hamo man furrowed his brow, looking increasingly worried. He occasionally glanced over at Luo and the others, as if he were assessing them.

The other four Hamo men seemed to be his subordinates. They stood in two separate groups and, like Luo and the others, waited patiently.

Finally, the two men finished their conversation, and Chief Bai led the Hamo group over to where Luo and the others stood. As they approached, Chief Bai pointed to the man in silver.

"This is Lord An Mi, the leader of the Hamo people."

Luo had already deduced as much. Greeting him with a polite smile, Luo looked the man up and down.

The Hamo leader was in his thirties. He was slightly taller than Luo. He looked healthy but was by no means brawny. He had a dark complexion, thick brows, and striking eyes. He exuded a natural boldness.

Lord An Mi's mouth twitched a little, as if to convey a general friendliness. However, he did not return Luo's greeting, and instead went over to Zhao Liwen's body, kneeling in front of it, then bowing deeply.

His four attendants did the same. Chief Bai turned to Luo and the others.

"The Hamo people have the highest respect for the dead, especially for those who died courageously in battle."

Luo nodded to show that he understood. Professor Zhou glared icily at Chief Bai, as if to remind him of his earlier display of cowardice.

The Hamo group appeared to be discussing something among themselves. Then, one by one, each of them extended his right index finger, dipped it into the blood, then licked his finger.

"They believe that a person's soul lingers in their blood, and that drinking a warrior's blood will give them strength and courage," Chief Bai explained.

Luo couldn't help thinking of the blood vial. It seemed that the Hamo people had a rather unusual amount of respect for human blood. Having consoled the spirit of the deceased, Lord An Mi stood back up. He looked at Luo, Professor Zhou, and Yue Dongbei successively. Then, in stilted Mandarin, he told them, "The demonic spirit is the enemy of the Hamo people. We are your friends. Now, let us go to the Valley of Terror together."

Chapter 20

The Dinner Banquet

The river ran southeast from Mihong, crossing the border and becoming a tributary of the Lancang River, which flowed into Laos, where it was known as the Mekong River. Throughout this zigzagging journey through ravines and gullies, its waters replenished the riverbanks, sustaining the lives of countless people.

Beyond Qingfeng Pass, the mountains opened into a narrow valley. On the southwestern side was a peaceful pond beside which the Hamo people had lived for generations upon generations.

Compared to the adjacent river basin, however, the pond was a tiny water source. And because there was no access to water in most of the valley's southern region, no one but the Hamo people had lived there for centuries.

The Hamo village curved over a hill next to the pond. From this hill, a depression could be seen in the distance, covered in dense forest. Though it wasn't far away, the Hamo people rarely ventured in that direction.

Three centuries earlier, General Li and his troops had spent three years entrenched in this depression, fighting off the Qing a hundred or more times. Among these endless verdant hills, the generals from both sides were buried.

That part of the mountain basin had thus acquired its name: the Valley of Terror.

By the time Luo and the others arrived at the Hamo village with Lord An Mi, it was nightfall. The sky was clear and bright, and there was a light breeze. The pond's clear water gently shimmered, and log cabins and bamboo pavilions were arrayed along its shore. The scenery was exquisite, and it was as if the Land of Peach Blossoms really did exist.

But Luo still felt uneasy. He looked around suspiciously, fearing something strange hidden within that peaceful village.

The entire journey, Chief Bai had been teaching Luo about the Hamo people. Despite the remoteness of the village, its population had increased over generations, reaching the thousands and far exceeding that of Mihong. The men hunted and fished, and the women farmed and tended livestock. Occasionally, they had limited exchanges with the outside world, and it was in the course of such exchanges that they had become acquainted with the villagers of Mihong. Both sides used the Hamo language to communicate, though some of the Hamo people also spoke Mandarin.

In this traditional village, the priesthood not only oversaw a body of established wisdom and presided over worship activities at festivals and on holidays but also disseminated culture and cured illnesses. The most prestigious and respected among them was the high priest. That title was not hereditary. Rather, a candidate was elected by the other priests, then approved by the village chief.

Priestesses, on the other hand, selected their own successors. Their only responsibility was to protect a sacred resource passed down from generation to generation: blood.

Priestesses never married. When a priestess reached middle age, she chose a wise young girl to serve as her successor. This selection process required mutual agreement, meaning the girl who was selected maintained the right to refuse. Before she made her decision, the priestess stressed to her and her family: If she accepts, she will become responsible for containing the centuries' worth of suffering and hardship endured by our people!

Even so, no one had ever turned down the opportunity. In fact, many Hamo girls saw the title of priestess as the greatest possible honor. Such honor, however, always came at a great cost.

Thinking of the vial of General Li's blood, sealed up by a Hamo priest, Luo had asked Chief Bai to explain what he meant by *great cost*. But Chief Bai had refused to go into detail. Now among the Hamo at last, Luo was eager for the right opportunity to ask the people themselves.

Lord An Mi led Luo and the others straight to his own residence. The entire way there, Hamo clansmen who saw them moved to the side of the road in deference, bowing to their young leader. Lord An Mi gave most of them no more than a passing glance. It was only when he met an elder that he stopped and said a few hurried words.

Though Luo didn't understand the Hamo language, he could tell by the parties' expressions that they were remarking on the unexpected visitors. After brief introductions, the villagers formally greeted them.

After this occurred a few times, Luo whispered to Chief Bai, "What are they saying?"

"Lord An Mi is saying that you are a Han person who possesses extraordinary courage in combating the dark forces." Chief Bai pointed at Professor Zhou and Yue Dongbei. "And those two are Han high priests."

Luo couldn't help laughing out loud. On reflection, he reasoned that warriors and high priests were the closest thing to police officers, scholars, and doctors in the Hamo social structure.

Lord An Mi's residence was located at the center of the village. It consisted of three houses. Even though they were made of adobe, rough wood, and felt, the walls were tall and wide. A courtyard had been fashioned out of adobe. This deep in the mountains, it could easily be considered a luxurious home.

After they entered the courtyard, Lord An Mi did not show everyone to their rooms. Instead, he gave instructions to his four attendants, who immediately began running about busily. They pulled tables and chairs out of the rooms and began setting them up outside. They lit dozens of torches, which they inserted into the ground, filling the entire courtyard with warm, flickering light.

"Our friends from afar, we welcome you to our home. Please have a seat!" Lord An Mi pointed to the table as he spoke. Though his speech was stiff, his expression was sincere.

The Mihong villagers and the Hamo clansmen normally saw one another in the daytime. Three years earlier, when Lord An Mi succeeded the previous clan leader, Chief Bai had personally come to take part in the succession ceremony, which was how the two of them met. Now Chief Bai was the first to step forward and take a seat.

He called out to Luo and the others: "Come. Since Lord An Mi is intent on showing us such tremendous hospitality, we must graciously accept."

Luo flashed a friendly smile at Lord An Mi. He, Professor Zhou, and Yue Dongbei sat down. Then Lord An Mi joined them. There was plenty of room at the table, which was round and about six feet in diameter, and the chairs were comfortably wide.

Luo pointed at the four attendants. "Are they going to sit also?"

Lord An Mi looked at him oddly. "Why would they sit with the guests?" Then he turned and told them something, which they promptly replied to before exiting the courtyard.

Luo shook his head, slightly fazed. He reminded himself that this was a primitive social system, and if the leader didn't strictly enforce the hierarchy, it would be hard to make everyone follow orders.

He looked over at Yue Dongbei, who seemed gleeful, enthralled by the scene. Meanwhile, Professor Zhou kept a straight face. It was unclear what he was thinking.

Chief Bai was the first to speak. "What a coincidence that we ran into you today, Lord An Mi. Were you at Qingfeng Pass as well?"

"You already know that our people have lost an object that is sacred to us." Lord An Mi's face was solemn. "In the past six months, I've gone to the pass many times with my attendants to search for it. Today, we heard cries, so we went to investigate, and we found you."

"You mean the blood vial?" Chief Bai tightened his lips. "I'd heard a rumor that the Hamos had gone to the mountains and lost a sacred object there."

Anger flashed in Lord An Mi's eyes, as if a fire inside of him had just been sparked. He took a deep breath, then spoke through clenched teeth. "The sacred object was stolen by a young Han man. A little over six months ago, someone saw him heading through the forest."

Luo, Professor Zhou, and Yue Dongbei exchanged glances. They were all thinking of the phobia patient at the Kunming psychiatric hospital. Luo took out the photograph of the patient and handed it over to Lord An Mi. "Is this the man?"

The moment Lord An Mi laid eyes on the photo, his expression changed. He slapped it onto the table, then demanded, "Do you know him? Where is he?"

"No, no, we don't know him!" Luo quickly tried to explain. "As a matter of fact, we're here to investigate what he was doing. You might say that he's paid for the theft with his sanity."

"He's crippled by extreme phobia," Professor Zhou solemnly explained.

"Extreme phobia?" Lord An Mi looked conflicted. He picked up the photograph once more and looked at it disgustedly. There was a pause. "Well, it serves him right!"

Yue Dongbei was sweating now, thinking how the young man had set out under his own guidance. Seeing Lord An Mi's fury, he averted his eyes and shifted awkwardly.

"Since you found him, you must know where the object is!" Lord An Mi declared.

"The vial is in Longzhou, but—" Feeling powerless, Luo paused. "It's been shattered."

"What?" Lord An Mi exploded. He sprang to his feet. With a flick of his right hand, he pulled a curved machete seemingly out of thin air and angrily drove its blade straight into the table.

Lord An Mi's attendants stood horrified at the courtyard entrance, afraid to move. Luo and the others were fearfully silent. It was if time had frozen.

Lord An Mi's chest was heaving. Several long minutes passed before he finally sat back down. His eyes were fixed on the machete in the table, and he looked forlorn.

Chief Bai saw the attendants were unsure whether to come closer or leave. He carefully nudged Lord An Mi, who seemed startled, as if he hadn't noticed their presence. Speaking to them in the Hamo language, he waved them over.

Relieved, the attendants crept over to the table, carrying a bottle of liquor, a hot pot, and bowls. As it were, dinner was ready.

The hot pot was filled with a piping-hot stew. A quick glance revealed that the stew contained large chunks of meat, presumably wild game. Someone passed out the bowls and filled them with wine for each guest. The enticing smell of meat and the fragrant aroma of wine flooded the courtyard.

Without waiting for further instructions, the attendants made a rapid exit.

Lord An Mi waited for them to leave, then pointed at the table and snarled, "Did he break it?"

His machete had sliced the photo clean in half. Luo couldn't help shuddering. Suddenly, he felt someone kick his foot. Looking up, he saw Yue Dongbei staring at him bug-eyed, as if he were trying to communicate something.

Luo knew what Yue Dongbei was thinking, but he decided to be honest. "No, it was me who broke the vial."

Lord An Mi let out a sharp cry and his attendants rushed back into the courtyard. They'd been downright obsequious while serving the food, but now they bared their teeth. They were poised to attack, waiting for their leader to say the word.

Lord An Mi grabbed Luo by the collar. "Who are you? What did you do that for?"

Professor Zhou and the others nervously watched Luo, knowing full well how imprudent his confession had been and that it would only cause trouble for them.

Yet Luo remained calm and collected. Without the slightest hint of fear, he looked at Lord An Mi, slowly telling him, "It was a mistake. At the time, I didn't know what the vial was, and I was carrying out my responsibility to prevent a crime."

"Prevent a crime? You released a demon! Do you know what disasters have befallen our clan due to your actions?" Lord An Mi howled.

"I'm deeply sorry," Luo told him sincerely. Then he instantly adopted a more decisive tone. "But the demon has hurt my own people as well, which is why I'm here. It doesn't matter how the problem started. Right now, our common goal is to suppress this demon."

Lord An Mi stared at Luo without saying a word, but his face seemed to relax. Just then, they heard a scratchy voice coming from somewhere nearby.

"If the demon has escaped, it must be the will of the gods. The Hamo warriors fear nothing. Our friends from other clans are here to help us. Lord An Mi must treat them as his own."

Everyone turned their heads to see a wiry old man. It wasn't clear when exactly he'd entered the courtyard. He wore a long black robe with dolman sleeves. There was an air of wisdom and refinement about him.

Lord An Mi let go of Luo.

"Your Holiness, Suo Tulan, please come in." Though Lord An Mi was the clan's leader, he greeted the old man with reverence.

Suo Tulan pointed at the attendants, whose knives were drawn. "Why don't you ask them to leave?"

Lord An Mi lifted his hand, and the attendants put away their machetes before filing out.

Professor Zhou and the others breathed a sigh of relief.

Chief Bai stood up and greeted the old man. "Your Holiness, we're so fortunate that you're here to clear up this misunderstanding."

Suo Tulan bowed in return. "The Hamo people and the people of Mihong have had a profound friendship for centuries. Village Chief Bai, there is no need for such words." His Mandarin was not only flawless but also quite eloquent.

When the attendants had set the table, they'd left an empty seat next to Lord An Mi, presumably for this old man. Suo Tulan sat down, then looked at Luo and the others. "You are friends of Village Chief Bai?"

Chief Bai nodded. "They came here from far away because of the mysterious demon."

Suo Tulan's gaze swept over them until it landed on Luo. "You are an honest and brave man."

"Perhaps, but he made a huge mistake," Lord An Mi sneered. "What's more, a real warrior's weapon is not his head."

Luo simply replied, "A man's power is weakened the moment he draws his weapon."

Lord An Mi frowned, apparently not understanding. At that moment, they heard a loud bang. The machete that Lord An Mi had driven into the table flew five or six feet into the air before clattering to the ground.

With that, Lord An Mi's demeanor changed. He did a double take of the table, which now had a gaping hole in it. The table was still shaking, and the wine in everyone's bowls was sloshing around.

Luo flashed a smile. "That knife really is dangerous. You can't even tell where its blade is."

As it turned out, when all the Hamo men had taken out their machetes, Luo had readied his gun underneath the table. Now that things had simmered down, he could see that the clan leader was impulsive and fickle. If Luo didn't intimidate him somehow, it might be difficult for the two of them to work together. That was why Luo had drawn his gun and shot the machete, sending it flying and showing the young man a thing or two.

Lord An Mi stared at Luo, stunned. When he finally spoke, his tone was respectful. "Very well. It seems you're courageous and clever after all."

"Fine, then. Everyone can lay down their weapons. We have urgent business to attend to." Chief Bai stepped in to mediate.

"Hmph." Lord An Mi nodded, taking advantage of the opportunity to change the subject. "Where did you say Longzhou was? How was the vial broken? Why don't you tell us more?"

Luo explained how he had broken the vial after chasing the relics smuggler, then told them the whole story of the fear epidemic in Longzhou and the young man who went from the forest to the hospital in Kunming.

"So it seems that a Burmese wanted to get his hands on our clan's relic. And when you tried to stop him, you accidentally broke it." Suo Tulan shook his head dejectedly. "If the vial had in fact ended up in Myanmar, the situation wouldn't have been so terrible."

"Why do you say that?" Luo inquired.

"At least the Burmese would have taken care to preserve the vial. They fear the demon even more than we Hamo people. But tell me, how did the Burmese man know that it was in Longzhou?"

"It was the thief who put the Burmese man in touch with the relics dealer, but I don't know exactly how or why. It's a shame we haven't identified the person who brought the vial to Longzhou in the first place. I have another question, though. Why was the Burmese man willing to pay such a high price for this vial? If they're also afraid of the demonic spirit, why not leave it in the safekeeping of the Hamo?"

"The year that we vanquished the demon, the Burmese people near the border helped us. Everyone feared the demon's powers, so when General Li died, we Hamo high priests sealed away the demonic spirit in the vial. The Hamo people took on the responsibility of guarding the demon, which earned us the reverence and respect of the Burmese. Many of the descendants of these Burmese are now involved in a, well, special kind of trade, and they've made a lot of money. But fear of the demon is still passed down from generation to generation."

Though Suo Tulan did not say so explicitly, Luo knew that by "special kind of trade" he was referring to drug trafficking. In light of this, the chain of events made more sense: First, Yue Dongbei's adventurer stole the Hamo's precious relic. Then, a wealthy Burmese drug dealer learned that the vial had gone missing. And, in an extreme act of religious devotion, he had spared no cost in hunting it down. Perhaps he did so to secure peace of mind or to acquire prestige back home.

The vial made its way to Old Hei's source, who seemed to understand full well the extraordinary circumstances surrounding it. This was why he put Old Hei in touch with the Burmese man. But who was this mysterious person behind the scenes?

The others appeared to be contemplating this very question. Lord An Mi pointed to the photo on the table. "So he's the one who stole the vial? But not the one who took it to Longzhou?"

Luo shook his head. He explained that, when the TV crew found him, the man had already lost his ability to function and was almost completely naked. He hadn't taken anything out of the forest with him.

"So what I'm saying," Luo continued, "is that, before this young man was discovered, someone else must have taken the vial from him and then abandoned him in the forest. But who was it? And if the young man had already gone mad with fear, does it have anything to do with this person?"

"At least two things are certain: The mystery person knew the secrets of the vial, and he knew the young man's whereabouts." Professor Zhou, who'd been uncommunicative for a long time, suddenly spoke up.

Luo, who immediately knew what he was insinuating, looked to Yue Dongbei, who was sitting next to him.

Yue Dongbei wriggled nervously in his seat, shooting an annoyed look at Professor Zhou. Because he feared Lord An Mi discovering the connection between him and this young man, he didn't dare to openly refute what Professor Zhou had said. He had no choice but to swallow the accusation and seethe in silence.

Fortunately, Lord An Mi didn't pick up on the subtle exchange. He let out an exasperated sigh. "It doesn't matter who it is. Any blasphemy surrounding this sacred object will only provoke the demon's wrath."

Indeed, Luo thought, *wherever the vial went, terror seemed to follow.* In the string of incidents over the past few days, everyone had distinctly heard the fearsome sound of the demon's footsteps.

"Very well," Suo Tulan pronounced. "We've talked enough about events that have taken place, but they are not the most important thing. Since the demon has already escaped, it is urgent that we look at the situation that now lies before us. Village Chief Bai, I am told that three of your most trusted aides have already been murdered by the demon."

Chief Bai, looking pale and depressed, heaved a deep sigh, then murmured, "Yes, that's right. This demon has been following us the entire way."

"Are you saying that he is near? He suffered a centuries-long curse and was relegated to hell, so it would be difficult for him to come back to life. If he were to choose a target for revenge, we the Hamo people would be at the top of the list." Suo Tulan raised his head and looked up at the night sky.

Though Luo himself didn't believe in such things, he knew Chinese people had long maintained such beliefs regarding the practice of laying the dead to rest. According to these beliefs, this curse was venomous indeed. If it were broken, those responsible had good reason to fear revenge.

Another silence fell over the tiny courtyard. The only sound they could hear was the wail of the northern winds blowing through the mountains. It almost seemed to echo Suo Tulan's words.

The light of fire flickered, unevenly illuminating Lord An Mi's stony face. The look in his eyes was intense yet revealed nothing, as if his mind had drifted off to another place and time.

Luo knew that Lord An Mi was now under enormous pressure. His clan's greatest triumph had been undone, their most guarded relic, stolen, and a demon unleashed to take his revenge. What a catastrophe for this young leader of the Hamo people!

After some time passed, Lord An Mi composed himself and turned his gaze to each of them, one by one. Then he lifted his bowl of wine, threw his head back, and chugged it. Now the bowl was empty, and this warrior's eyes were filled with a lust for battle and an all-encompassing pride.

Under that gaze, Luo felt a stirring within himself, as if a fire deep inside of him were being kindled.

With a flick of his arm, Lord An Mi tossed the bowl onto the ground. It hit the dirt with a clank and smashed into pieces. He raised his face toward the sky and let loose a deranged laugh at the top of his lungs, then began shouting in the Hamo language.

"What is he saying?" Luo asked Chief Bai.

"He's thanking the gods of the Hamo people, thanking them for giving him the important duty of handling this centuries-old curse so that he has the opportunity to become a legendary hero," Chief Bai explained, watching Lord An Mi admiringly.

Those cries seemed to draw upon all of the strength in Lord An Mi's body, and finally, his voice grew hoarse. He looked once more at the others, his heroic spirit now awakened. "Come now! Let us feast on meat and wine! You'll need to bulk up, because the demon's on his way!"

Chapter 21

A Disastrous Curse

Their feast comprised enormous chunks of meat and huge bowls of wine—but there were no utensils. The only solution was to eat with their hands.

There were stewed meats as well as roasted meats. The meat, being fresh from the hunt, was gamey but palatable and novel. The wine, made from local mountain fruit, was incredibly fragrant. All of them indulged in one of humanity's most primitive pleasures and forgot about their worries for the time being. And each individual's drinking habits seemed to reflect his personality as well as his state of mind.

Perhaps it was because he was the oldest that Suo Tulan drank the least. In fact, he didn't take so much as a sip. Instead, he seemed to be simply basking in the convivial atmosphere. When it came time to make a toast, he lifted the bowl to his lips in a purely symbolic gesture, never once tasting the wine.

At the other end of the spectrum, Yue Dongbei took frequent sips. Most of the time, they were small and furtive, and he paid little attention to the others. Whenever someone raised their glass to him, he seemed to shrink back, as if he were uncomfortable and almost wanted to hide.

Professor Zhou did the opposite. He didn't drink much, but when the others wanted to toast, he was most obliging and would empty his bowl.

Chief Bai had a high tolerance for alcohol. He would often raise his bowl in toast, monitoring each of the others closely. It was because of him that Yue Dongbei was forced to chug down two full bowls.

Luo appeared to be going with the flow. When others drank, he drank, too. If they emptied their bowls, he did, too. If they sipped, he sipped. In short, he blended in.

The person who drank the most was their host, Lord An Mi. He emptied bowl after bowl, seeming to drink nonstop. When it came time to toast, he paid no heed whatsoever to how much or how little the other person drank, and simply downed his entire bowl. Yue Dongbei seemed amused by this and raised his bowl to his host several times, and each time, his host complied.

After some time, everyone began to notice the slight chill in the air.

Chief Bai looked up at the sky, then remarked, "It's going to rain."

The others looked up to see a swath of black overhead. An instant later, rain started to pour down from the starless night sky.

Lord An Mi and Suo Tulan exchanged a glance, and their expressions seemed to change at the same time. Lord An Mi set down his half-drunken bowl of wine and rubbed his cheek, letting the icy rainwater soak him.

Considering the weather over the past few days, more rain wasn't surprising. So when Luo noticed the change in the two of them, he suspected something was wrong. Lord An Mi had already stood up. With everyone watching, he took a few steps forward, then picked up the curved machete Luo had sent flying to the ground.

Lord An Mi's eyes were wide as he stared up at the sky. Suddenly, his right arm twitched, and he jabbed his machete straight up into the air.

The powerful strokes of his blade scattered the droplets of rain in a sparkling burst of white. Then he turned and swung in the opposite direction, slicing at an angle, each stroke still pointed skyward.

He took a third slice, then a fourth, continuing to no apparent end. The sight was too much. Though they were not especially quick, the strokes were broad and forceful, and each seemed to take a different trajectory from the previous one. The resulting effect was rather impressive.

"What—what is he trying to do?" Yue Dongbei scratched his head in confusion.

Luo didn't understand, either, so he turned to face Suo Tulan. The high priest's expression was solemn and respectful, and his arms were folded against his chest. His lips moved as if he was reciting something.

Lord An Mi continued swinging his machete, singing a song in the Hamo language all the while. Every so often, as he walked to and fro, he would stumble drunkenly. But he kept taking deep, long breaths, and his voice penetrated the night, traveling into the darkness of the surrounding mountains.

There was a cold breeze, and the rain turned into drizzle. His singing became more desolate, the melody sorrowful. Though Luo did not understand the lyrics, he felt the alcohol he'd drunk coursing through him, and a burning sensation filled his nose. He couldn't resist standing up and clapping along.

Soon after, the song ended, and Lord An Mi put away his machete. With his hands clasped behind his back, he stared off into the distance toward the Valley of Terror. The music lingered, echoing through the mountains and back like the marching sound of a thousand-man army.

Enraptured, Luo asked Suo Tulan, "What kind of song was Lord An Mi singing?"

Suo Tulan's voice was solemn. "It's a Hamo battle hymn. The song is sung by warriors to bid farewell to their families before they set off and to vow to fight to the death."

"It's a wonderful song," Luo said with genuine admiration. "Especially considering the circumstances, Lord An Mi did a great job of raising everyone's spirits."

"It's a song about heroes. It was written by He Layi, the greatest heroine of the Hamo people." Lord An Mi, who had now returned to the table, had overhead their conversation. "The year, when the Hamos sang that song, they won the holy war."

"The holy war?"

"That's right, a holy war!" Lord An Mi puffed up his chest, and the look on his face was one of unassailable pride. He turned to Suo Tulan. "It was the finest hour in our clan's history. Your Holiness, why don't you tell the story to our friends from far away?"

Suo Tulan nodded. There was a distant, profound look in his eyes. In a respectful, pious tone, he began to tell the story. "The holy war took place over three hundred years ago. For the Hamo people, it was a question of life and death, and during a great battle, the warrior A Liya and the heroine He Layi vanquished the horrible demon, rescuing the entire clan."

"Vanquished the demon? Are you talking about killing General Li?" Luo instantly recalled Yue Dongbei's theory.

"That's right." Suo Tulan glanced over at Chief Bai, a mixture of emotions on his face. "Village Chief Bai, the people of Mihong worship the Rain God, but in the eyes of the Hamo people, General Li is the demon who tried to exterminate our entire clan."

The corners of Chief Bai's mouth twitched as if he were about to smile, yet the rest of his face signaled that he was deeply ashamed.

"Exterminate the entire clan?" Yue Dongbei, intrigued by this tidbit that hadn't made it into the history books, hurried over. His face glowed as he asked, "What caused such profound hatred that he would plot to murder you all?"

"It was not because of profound hatred. Before this, the Hamo people were kind to General Li. It was because Li later chose to bite the hand of kindness that things turned so bitter." Lord An Mi clenched his teeth in disgust.

"Kindness?" The more he heard, the more confused Luo felt. "I'm sorry, but I don't know much about history. Would you mind telling me a bit more about what happened between the two sides?"

"Li Dingguo was the Southern Ming general. We, the Hamo people, despite living in a remote region, were governed by the Ming Dynasty," Suo Tulan patiently explained. "Then the Southern Ming forces and the Manchus fought, and a hundred warriors from our clan were enlisted to fight in Li's army during a major battle in the east."

Yue Dongbei laughed darkly. "A hundred? This was the kindness that the Hamo people showed Li Dingguo?"

"You ought not underestimate the power of these hundred warriors." Lord An Mi looked over at Yue Dongbei with pride. "They were few in number, but they formed a cavalry, riding on the backs of divine beasts. On the battlefield, an army of ten thousand was no match for them."

"Divine beasts?" asked Luo Fei. "Do you mean elephants—"

Luo hadn't even finished his question by the time Suo Tulan answered it: "There were many elephants in this forest, and the Hamo warriors tamed the fierce creatures and made them their friends as well as their servants."

"An army of elephants!" Yue Dongbei's eyes flashed with excitement. "So General Li's forces really had an army of elephants?"

"Yes. This elephant army consisted of warriors from our clan. During a major battle in the east, they created a nightmare for the Manchus."

"Ha ha, that's very interesting! Very interesting! So the Manchus came to the southern grasslands. Their most powerful forces were on horseback, but then they met the elephant army, which scared them out of their wits. They couldn't escape. What weapons could they have used?" Yue Dongbei was slapping the table and exhaling loudly. "This is a big discovery. I really have to give you Hamo people credit."

Luo was deep in thought. Suddenly, he clapped and yelled, "I've got it!"

"Got what?" Yue Dongbei asked.

One by one, the others all turned to face Luo.

"The mysterious force is the elephant army!" Luo pointed at Yue Dongbei. "Your thesis mentioned that, according to Manchu folklore, during the battle over a strategic pass in Guangxi, Li's army used a mysterious force to terrorize people, and that this force originated near the Yunnan border. Based on what we know now, this force must be the elephant army of the Hamo people. Think about it: The battle took place during a thunderstorm, so the atmosphere was frightening to begin with. That's when the elephant army suddenly emerged and made their deadly attack. Why wouldn't the Manchu troops be terrified? Lots of people from the north had never even seen an elephant, and as the story was passed on, it naturally got embellished."

"Right, right." Yue Dongbei nodded, a dour expression on his face. "The great battle in the east, the battle over the strategic pass in Guangxi and the elephant army, the terrorizing forces and the Hamo people, the Yunnan border. It really does explain all of these things."

Professor Zhou cackled. "What? Just like that, you're going to abandon your precious demonic spirit?"

Yue Dongbei glared at Professor Zhou. "Who says I'm abandoning my theory? The elephant army only explains the battle over the strategic pass. It doesn't explain how the folklore of the demonic spirit came into being. First of all, why would the Hamo people allow their soldiers to be seen as demons? Furthermore, the elephant army, though fierce, would have moved rather clumsily. In the plains, they could have put forth a strong offensive. But in the mountain forests, they couldn't have been very effective. That means Li's defeated troops were still able to fend for themselves for three years without the aid of the Hamo people or their elephants."

Yue Dongbei's argument made sense. Luo couldn't help but concur.

Suo Tulan frowned at Professor Zhou. "A demon is a demon. How could anyone ever confuse the warriors of our clan with demons?"

"So then what are these demons all of you keep talking about?" Professor Zhou shot back.

"They're wicked and terrifying forces." Suo Tulan's tone had grown somber. "According to the folklore of our clan, they most likely involve poisoning by *gu*."

"Poisoning?" Yue Dongbei cried, his eyes bulging in disbelief.

Professor Zhou wrinkled his brow.

Luo looked puzzled. "What's a *gu*?"

"In physiological terms," Professor Zhou explained, "a *gu* is a kind of insect-derived poison that causes parasites to grow inside the human body, and at the same time, leads to psychosis. According to Chinese folklore, *gu* are parasites that our people cultivated for the purpose of poison, such as for curses in witchcraft and sorcery. It allowed them to physically and mentally control the victim."

Another explanation not dependent on superstition! Luo observed, careful not to let on what he was thinking. He nodded, then asked Suo Tulan, "How does your people's folklore explain these things?"

Yue Dongbei reached out his hand and banged his fist on the table, chiming in as soon as Luo had finished his question. "Yes, tell us in detail. Any conclusion needs to be based on facts. This is very important."

Suo Tulan narrowed his eyes, which made the wrinkles and creases on his face seem deeper. Then he licked his lips and delivered his account. "The year that Li Dingguo's army retreated, there was a battle when they passed Mopan Mountain. Their army had already been reduced to fewer than ten thousand soldiers. Most of the hundred Hamo warriors had been killed. There were only thirteen of them leading the way as Li commanded the troops to the Valley of Terror. As they went through the ravine, the vanguard captured several suspicious-looking men. At first, Li Dingguo presumed they were Manchu spies, and so he tortured and interrogated them. In doing so, he discovered that these men were actually Miao practitioners of *gu*."

Professor Zhou, who had moved in closer to Luo in order to hear, whispered to him, "These *gu* practitioners specialized in poisoning people and causing them to go mad. It was apparently a common means of injuring people among the Miao in Yunnan."

Suo Tulan went on. "It was customary at the time for troops, if they ran into *gu* practitioners or other sorcerers, to kill them in order to prevent bad luck. However, General Li followed no such conventions. He simply cut out the tongues of these *gu* practitioners and conscripted them into his army. Hamo warriors despise these wicked and cunning types, so they chose a representative to approach General Li and ask him to kill the *gu* sorcerers.

"Everyone knew the general's disposition. The more people were around, the more stubbornly he refused to change his mind. So the Hamo representative took advantage of this by approaching his tent late at night, when it was quiet. He went alone so that his chances would be better.

"When the warrior reached his tent, he saw that there was light inside, so he knew General Li was there. Because he didn't want to disturb anyone, he slipped quietly into the tent. What he saw stunned him. The general looked completely disheveled. He was kneeling at an incense table, unable to sit up straight, sobbing. The warrior didn't know whether to stay or go, but then he heard the general call out to him in a despondent voice. What he basically told him was: 'I had no choice under the circumstances but to resort to the demonic powers of *gu* in order to gain strength and the power to terrorize. That's why the army generals and soldiers are all under the control of the demon. What I've done is deeply wrong, and after I die, my soul will be punished beyond all redemption.'"

Suo Tulan paused, as if to give them all some time to process this.

Luo pondered for a minute, then made a conjecture: "So what you're saying is that Li deliberately took these *gu* practitioners into his army and made them use their poisoning techniques in order to acquire mysterious powers?"

Yue Dongbei clapped. "It makes sense! That makes perfect sense!"

Neither Professor Zhou nor Chief Bai replied, but it appeared as though neither of them had any major objections.

Suo Tulan nodded again. "That's how our warrior felt, too. He was shocked and angry, and he stood dumbly at the entrance. When the general finished his weeping, he turned and shouted, 'Who are you?' The warrior fled. He didn't dare to stop until he reached the Hamo campsite.

"Everyone had been waiting for him to come back with good news. When they saw him so disconcerted, they thought it was strange. The warrior couldn't bring himself to explain, so he just told everyone to pack up and leave. By the time the general and his aides had arrived, the Hamos had already entered the forest. Because the terrain was rugged and it was nighttime, the general didn't dare to pursue them. He simply watched the thirteen warriors disappear into the distance and head back to their village. That night was the initial break between our clan and General Li."

"Oh?" Luo had gotten caught up in the story. "So was the battle between you also because of this?"

"You mean the holy war?" Suo Tulan shook his head. "No. When the warriors arrived back in the village, they told the whole story to the chief. Once the chief knew that General Li was using evil powers, he ended their alliance. For the following three years, the general, on many occasions, tried to revive the alliance, but the chief refused. In the war he fought against the Manchus and the Burmese forces, we never took sides. We maintained a neutral stance from beginning to end."

"During the time, there were supposedly hundreds of skirmishes. Is it actually true that General Li never lost?" Luo asked, recalling Yue Dongbei's lectures.

"It may sound like an exaggeration, but it is true," Suo Tulan sighed. "Though the general's soul entered a dark place, he was a mighty warrior. After he obtained those wicked powers, his army was almost unstoppable."

"Wicked powers—" Luo frowned. "I still don't understand. What exactly does that mean?"

"According to what our elders have passed down, the demon possessed the general's troops, giving even rank-and-file soldiers unimaginable strength and courage. On the battlefield, every one of them turned ferocious and displayed astonishing combat abilities. What's more, none of them seemed to fear death. The soldiers who were killed in the battle all died with smiles on their faces."

"One with the demons, joyous and carefree. May these schemes be hatched, and may you prisoners of terror be!" Luo suddenly recalled those words and quietly recited them.

Suo Tulan was beaming. "You know this saying? It was used to describe the troops. They completely submitted to the demon, and in the end, they succumbed to madness. The thirteen Hamo warriors were fortunate to have left when they did. Otherwise, it would have been difficult for them to escape later."

"No!" Lord An Mi interjected. "How would the Hamo warriors ever have submitted to the demonic powers? In the end, General Li died by the blade of our own Hamo warriors, didn't he?"

"You are correct, Chief." Suo Tulan placed his right hand across his chest and bowed respectfully. "It made no difference whether they had demonic powers. When General Li's troops were confronted by the Hamo warriors, it was inevitable that they would be annihilated."

Luo thought for a while. "If you remained neutral, how did the holy war start?"

"That's a long story," Suo Tulan said softly. As they listened to him recount the story, the others felt themselves being carried off to another time and place . . .

Chapter 22

The Plot to Exterminate

The Hamo people have passed this story down for generations. But before we get started, there are a few figures I must introduce.

A Liya was the fiercest Hamo warrior, and he served in General Li's army for many years. He was the one who acted as the representative of the thirteen warriors and witnessed Li's confession.

He Layi was the most beautiful young Hamo woman. She was the daughter of the Hamo chief.

Then there was Bai Wenxuan, Li Dingguo's most trusted lieutenant general. The hundred Hamo warriors had been under his command. During the battle over the strategic pass at Guangxi, A Liya saved his life, so Lieutenant General Bai felt a strong kinship with the Hamo warriors.

In addition to this, you must better understand the Valley of Terror.

Though the Valley of Terror and the Hamo village are in the same mountain basin, there is a stark contrast in the topography of the two areas. The Hamo village is stationed at the lowest point, where the land is flat. It is also close to a water source, which makes it habitable. In contrast, the Valley of Terror is near a hill at an altitude just above sea level. It is covered in dense forest, and its steep terrain is perilous.

The hill between the two areas continues southeast for about a mile before it abruptly ends at a nearly vertical cliff. The face of the cliff is incredibly rough and jagged, and halfway down protrudes a curved ledge that hangs over a lake into which streams run from all directions. In seasons of great rain, the lake overflows, creating a multilayered waterfall that flows to the pond in the Hamo village.

Keeping this landscape in mind, we must go back in time over three hundred years to a Hamo legend that tells what really happened on that summer day.

The war between the armies of Li Dingguo, the Manchus, and the Burmese had gone on for three years. Li had been relying on the dangerous mountain terrain and his mysterious demonic powers to stay undefeated. But the Manchu forces were backed by endless waves of reinforcements stationed outside the Valley of Terror. The two sides were deadlocked, and the Hamo people found themselves at the center of a tug-of-war.

The Hamo people and the Southern Ming troops had been on friendly terms for many years. But ever since Li's army started using wicked sorcery, causing the thirteen warriors to flee, the relationship had been strained. Both Li and the Manchus sent representatives numerous times to lobby for the Hamos' support, but our chief refused to budge. Perhaps this made both sides unhappy, but no one wanted to offend these heroic warriors, who also happened to occupy a geographically advantageous location.

The Hamo leader, who was in his fifties, was honest and wise. Though he did not take part in the war, he paid very close attention to it. Every time there was a skirmish, he would ascend the low hill with two of his aides and monitor the fighting.

During that time, something strange seemed to be happening with Li's army. Their camp kept moving farther northwest. The Hamo chief realized that Li's forces must have been preparing to undertake a larger operation, and each day, he made the trek to the other end of the mountain, setting out early in the morning and returning to the village in the afternoon. But one day, the sky had turned dark and the Hamo chief still hadn't come back.

The clansmen had an ominous feeling. The chief's daughter, He Layi, was so worried that she didn't sleep a wink. The next morning, Li's emissary paid a visit to the village. The emissary was none other than Bai Wenxuan.

A Liya and He Layi met with the high-ranking official. Naturally, A Liya and the lieutenant general were rather moved upon being reunited.

According to Lieutenant General Bai, when the Hamo chief had gone to the other side of the mountain, he'd been spotted by a Manchu reconnaissance soldier. The Manchu soldier called in reinforcements and tried to take the chief prisoner. Outnumbered, the two Hamo aides were killed in battle, and the chief himself was seriously wounded. At this moment of crisis, the general himself rushed to the scene with his own aides, driving away the Manchu troops and rescuing the Hamo chief. After receiving emergency treatment, the Hamo chief's life was no longer in danger, but he was unable to move and needed time to recover. Now Lieutenant General Bai had come with a message from the chief asking He Layi to come to the camp to see him. He had brought the chief's own machete as proof of his words.

Relieved and grateful that her father was safe and sound, He Layi immediately called for a banquet of the highest order in honor of their guest, who had come all the way from the Valley of Terror.

At noon, the hosts and guest were seated, and the three-year freeze in relations now thawed. One by one, the thirteen warriors toasted their former commander, drinking heartily. Lieutenant General Bai, who couldn't say no, was soon feeling rather tipsy.

After numerous rounds of drinks, the other banquet attendees started to disperse, until only He Layi, Lieutenant General Bai, and the thirteen warriors were left. He Layi, whose presence was largely symbolic, had not been drinking and was there only to entertain the guest of honor, whereas Lieutenant General Bai and the others had become increasingly uninhibited as the day went on, growing nostalgic as they shared recollections of their old days on the battlefield. When it came time to tell the story of how A Liya had saved the lieutenant general's life, all of them were moved to tears.

The exchange had left everyone in high spirits. A Liya burst into the battle hymn of those times, and the other warriors joined in. Lieutenant General Bai's mood changed abruptly as he listened. As everyone else sang jauntily, he began to sob unconsolably. The warriors stopped mid song and asked Lieutenant General Bai why he was crying. But the man just kept bawling. A Liya stood up and demanded to know what was troubling their esteemed brother, telling him that there was nothing that the brotherhood would not do for him.

After collecting himself, Lieutenant General Bai fell to his knees before the Hamo clansmen and remained there for some time. The warriors were shocked and promptly kneeled, returning the gesture. Even He Layi had gotten to her feet.

"Lieutenant General Bai, we the Hamo people consider you to be our good friend. If there is something that is troubling you, please don't hesitate to tell us. Our entire clan will do everything we can to help you." Though He Layi had never left the village, she had been painstakingly educated by the high priest, and her Mandarin Chinese was not only mellifluous but fluent. As she spoke, she walked over to Lieutenant General Bai without the slightest affectation and extended her hand to help him to his feet.

Lieutenant General Bai lifted his head and looked at the beautiful Hamo woman who would one day become a legend. With her graceful figure and elegant deportment, along with her white attire, she looked like a celestial goddess.

He Layi's dark and expressive eyes were now fixed on their guest of honor with a pure and otherworldly radiance. Lieutenant General Bai dropped his head again, unable to meet her gaze. His voice was pained.

"All of you have treated me like family, but I owe an apology to the Hamo people. I must apologize to all of my brothers who have gathered here, and to the very lovely Miss He Layi."

He Layi raised an eyebrow, worried. "General Bai, why are you saying all of this?"

"Disaster is imminent for the Hamo people. All of you will soon be drowned!" Finally, Lieutenant General Bai found the courage to speak the truth.

"Drowned?" A Liya stepped in front of Lieutenant General Bai. "What are you saying?"

Having gone this far, Lieutenant General Bai knew there was no point in being evasive. In an act of treachery, he answered bluntly, "Your chief wasn't wounded by a Manchu soldier, but ambushed by two of the general's aides. As we speak, the general is concocting plans to unleash a surprise attack that would obliterate the Hamo people!"

"What?" He Layi took a step back, appalled. "The Hamo people have never wronged General Li, so why—why would he do such a thing?"

"General Li often lashes out at those who betray him." Lieutenant General Bai looked at A Liya and the others. "All of you fled without saying goodbye, and that broke a taboo for him. In the past three years, we've been in a bitter struggle against the Qing and Burmese forces, and the Hamo people have refused to help, which has only made him angrier."

"We fought alongside your troops for years without ever complaining," A Liya angrily retorted. "It's because of the general's own use of sorcery that we left. How can he blame us?"

"No, that can't be the whole reason. General Bai, it's imperative that you tell us everything!" He Layi looked gravely at Lieutenant General Bai.

Lieutenant General Bai sighed. "The lady is not only lovely, but intelligent. You are correct. There is an even more important reason that General Li is doing this."

"What is it?" The warriors waited anxiously to hear what he would say next.

"His troops have exhausted their provisions. In the Valley of Terror, the terrain is rugged and dangerous, and there's no way to replenish much-needed supplies. Your village, on the other hand, is rich with resources . . ." Lieutenant General Bai trailed off.

So General Li had set his sights on this fertile, blessed plot of land. The Hamo felt their hearts sinking. If that was the case, there was no hope of reconciliation or compromise.

There was a silence, and then A Liya declared, "Our people have lived here for generations. If General Li wants to take our land from us, he's going to have to answer to the swords of the Hamo warriors!"

"I know the Hamo warriors are capable of great heroics, but it's no use," Lieutenant General Bai said. "General Li has already rigged the lake along the cliff with gunpowder, to be detonated at his command, so that this village will be flooded!"

There was a visible change in A Liya and the others as they heard this. As all of them had been born and raised there, they knew what havoc the mountain torrents could wreak. If the water collecting in the lake were to come rushing down all at once, it would instantly wipe out their entire village.

A moment later, He Layi recovered from her shock. "What a sinister tactic," she remarked with a sad smile. "But if this is the case, why did he send you here, Lieutenant General Bai?"

"That—" Lieutenant General Bai seemed unwilling to answer the question.

"Lieutenant General Bai, you are a good, kindhearted person." He Layi's dark eyes glimmered. "You must tell us."

Lieutenant General Bai hesitated. His tone was hushed. "Rumors have spread among the troops that the lady, He Layi, is not only the most beautiful among the Hamo people, but anywhere. General Li, being loath to drown her, sent me here to trick her into coming to the Valley of Terror—and leaving her—to the troops."

A Liya was beside himself with rage. He jumped up and drew his sword. "General Li! You shameless devil! I'll show you!"

The other warriors leapt to their feet to follow.

He Layi called out to them, her cry loud and clear: "Stop! You mustn't go!"

All of the warriors stopped in their tracks, and He Layi sighed with relief. "General Li isn't merely vicious, he's a brutal, relentless fighter, and one with an entire army under his command. Do you wish to storm straight to your death?"

"So what should we do, then?" A Liya scowled so fiercely, the veins stood out on his forehead. "Should we just sit here and wait for the floodwaters to drown our entire village?"

He Layi didn't answer. She turned and laid her hands on Lieutenant General Bai's shoulders. There was sincerity in her voice. "Lieutenant General Bai, please stand up."

Lieutenant General Bai stood up dumbly. He Layi led him over to the chair that had been reserved for the guest of honor, then told him, "Please have a seat."

Looking as if he hadn't a clue what was happening, Lieutenant General Bai sat down as he was told.

He Layi took two steps back, then faced him. "Lieutenant General Bai, the lives of the Hamo people, old and young alike, are in your hands. You have a generous heart, and I know that you will help us avert a tragedy."

A Liya was quiet for a second. His heart was pounding. "That's right. No one is closer to the general than Lieutenant General Bai is. If he stands with the Hamo people, it may be possible to reverse the course of those raging floodwaters."

There was an awkward expression on Lieutenant General Bai's face. He remained silent for a long time, then mumbled, "I had a lot to drink, and I leaked a military plan. I'm a traitor to Commander in Chief Li and to the entire Ming Dynasty. If I were to do as the lady asks, I would be committing an act that is beyond all redemption."

"Li Dingguo isn't the commander he once was!" A Liya stepped forward impatiently. "He sold his soul when he exploited the power of *gu*. Now his heart is filled with pure evil, and his troops are under the control of a demonic spirit. Lieutenant General Bai, if you join him in committing genocide, you will truly find yourself beyond all redemption."

Lieutenant General Bai was trembling. There was a crestfallen look on his face, as if he'd just revealed a secret anguish he'd been holding inside.

He Layi seemed similarly despondent. "We the Hamo people live in this mountain village, far removed from the rest of the world. If Li Dingguo wishes to destroy our clan, there is no difference between him and any demonic spirit. He must be punished by the heavens. For his own general to do so would, in the eyes of heaven, only be righting a wrong. So how could it be an act of betrayal? I speak for Hamo people of all generations when I say, Lieutenant General, I beseech you!"

With those words, He Layi got down on her knees and bowed deeply.

A Liya went to He Layi's side and echoed her sentiments: "Lieutenant General, please carry out the will of heaven!"

The other twelve warriors shouted in chorus: "Lieutenant General, please carry out the will of heaven!" There was a clatter as they all tumbled to their knees.

Lieutenant General Bai closed his eyes, turning his face to the sky. Some time passed, then finally, he gave a painful nod. Two teardrops escaped from his eyes, and a messy stream of tears followed.

Soon afterward, He Layi summoned the high priest of the Hamo clan, and they spent the afternoon in discussions. It was nearly nightfall when Lieutenant General Bai left the village and returned to the camp in the Valley of Terror, where he reported that his mission had gone as planned and He Layi would come the following day. Meanwhile, two particularly nimble Hamo warriors had been dispatched as messengers to contact the Qing and Burmese forces.

Chapter 23

The Demon's Death

Early the next morning, He Layi summoned all the young men in the clan and told them about General Li's plot, infusing them with the will to fight to the death.

He Layi and the thirteen warriors set out first. They had prepared four rattan trunks to bring to the Valley of Terror. A Liya and three of the fiercest fighters were to hide inside the trunks, which would be carried by the other nine warriors into Li Dingguo's camp.

Waiting at the camp, Lieutenant General Bai saw the procession approaching. The general's aides had blocked off the entrance to the general's tent and demanded to see what was inside of the trunks.

"The trunks contain a gift for the general from the Hamo people. I've already inspected them." The second Lieutenant General Bai stepped forward, the rank-and-file soldiers cleared the way for their superior and allowed He Layi and the others to enter.

Inside the tent, the general sat at the altar, studying a lambskin map. Two of his bodyguards stood behind him, swords drawn. According to legend, the ruthless, unconquerable demon was clad in armor, and he had a chiseled face and thick brows.

Lieutenant General Bai announced the procession with the utmost graciousness: "Commander in Chief, the lady He Layi of the Hamo people has arrived."

General Li lifted his head. There was sincerity in his eyes as he stood up and looked at He Layi, pressing his right hand against his chest and bowing deeply. "He Layi, I am Li Dingguo, commander of the Southern Ming forces." Behind her, the warriors had set down the rattan trunks, greeting the general with a punctilious bow.

"Commander, it is an honor."

The general peered at He Layi with a satisfied look on his face. "Excellent!" was the only word he uttered. He was tall and well built, and his imposing manner was readily apparent the instant he stood up.

When General Li finished studying He Layi, he turned his gaze to the nine warriors kneeling before him. Boldly, he told them, "All of you departed without saying goodbye. This violates the code of military discipline."

It was as if a current of electricity shot from his eyes. The Hamo warriors had long cast aside their fears of death, but none of them could suppress the ominous feeling that arose from deep within. All of them lowered their heads in fearful silence.

After a brief pause, the general suddenly hollered, "Messenger!"

Instantly, one of his aides appeared inside the tent. "Yes, Commander."

"Bring the lady He Layi to the West Tent and let her see her injured father."

"Yes, sir!" the aide replied. He gestured politely to He Layi. "Please come with me."

He Layi nodded and calmly followed the aide. The warriors all tensed. If, as Lieutenant General Bai had reported, General Li had been plotting to snatch He Layi, they had to act quickly. Their own lives and the lives of everyone in the entire village were at stake. Now was the decisive moment. All of them held their breath, observing the general's every move. There was no room to falter.

Hands clasped behind his back, the general paced to and fro. The air inside the tent was tense. Lieutenant General Bai stood to the side, appearing thoroughly composed, though he was sweating heavily.

Finally, General Li stopped. He pointed at the trunks. "What are those?"

"These are gifts for the commander from the Hamo people," a warrior quickly replied. "They are to repay the commander for saving the village chief's life."

"Hmph." General Li turned and looked at Lieutenant General Bai. "Why don't you open it so I can have a look?"

Lieutenant General Bai removed the lid, then darted out of the way. "Commander, here you are!"

The general glanced over and saw that the trunk was filled with rare medicinal herbs. He nodded. "Fine, then. Put it away."

But Lieutenant General Bai didn't move. "Commander, packed underneath these herbs is what the Hamo people consider their most valuable treasure. It would not be my place, as your humble subordinate, to uncover it. Commander, please come see for yourself!"

"Oh?" General Li stepped forward and leaned over the trunk. He had just reached his right hand inside when he sensed that something was wrong. He furrowed his brow apprehensively. At that very instant, a man burst forth from underneath the herbs. With his left hand, he gripped General Li's right arm. With his right hand, he swung his machete directly at the general's neck. General Li's reflexes were quick, and he dodged. But the blade's trajectory was precise enough to cut into his shoulder. His skin was shredded instantly, and blood spewed everywhere. He howled in pain. With one powerful flick of his right arm, he sent the attacker's blade flying through the air.

The attacker hiding inside the trunk had been none other than A Liya. He saw that the blow he'd landed had not been a fatal one, so he sprang to his feet and charged at General Li with a sword. The two aides inside the tent had already drawn their swords and stepped in front of their commander, shouting, "An assassin!"

As a dozen or so guards stormed into the tent, the other Hamo warriors leapt out of the trunks and raised their weapons. There was chaos as the two sides confronted one another, swarming in a circle.

The general's wound looked rather serious. His armor was already stained with blood. His aides, in an effort to defend him, had surrounded him. He huffed a little, then pulled his sword from his belt and pushed his way out.

One of the Hamo warriors saw what was about to happen and immediately brandished his sword in the general's direction, then charged. He performed a sword dance, luring his opponent toward his blade. Their swords met. The Hamo warrior felt his wrists twisting and his sword swerving out of control. With the quick thrust of a blade, there was a horrific wound near his waist.

General Li had the upper hand, yet he did not follow that blow with another. Instead, he stalked toward Lieutenant General Bai, who stood at the entrance. He retained his composure even as he snarled, "Have you betrayed me?!"

Lieutenant General Bai turned pale. He started backing out of the tent, with General Li closing in.

As they stepped outside, a soldier ran up, then stopped short. "Commander—are you all right?"

Realizing that his own armor was no longer fully intact, the general looked bewildered, then roared, "You leaked my plan!"

The soldier got down on one knee. "Commander, the Manchu forces, the Burmese army, and the Hamo clan have surrounded our camp on three fronts!"

The gravity of the situation now dawned on General Li. He looked up to the sky and let loose a deranged laugh. "Spread the word: My orders are for all units to stay and defend the camp. Anyone who flees answers to my blade."

"Yes, sir!" the soldier responded. But instead of leaving, he stared at General Li and Lieutenant General Bai with a worried and confused look on his face.

"Scram! This matter doesn't concern you!" General Li barked. The soldier bowed deeply, then sprinted to the soldiers' quarters to dispatch orders.

"What is the meaning of this?" The general's eyes bulged as he glared at Lieutenant General Bai.

Now it was Lieutenant General Bai's turn to draw his sword. His emotions were complicated. After a pause, he whispered, "Commander, I'm so sorry."

"Sorry? Fine! Fine, then!" General Li lifted his sword, his eyes flashing with rage.

Back inside the tent, A Liya and the other Hamo warriors fought a grueling battle with the guards. In the end, A Liya was the only man left standing, and he was exhausted and covered in wounds. But there was no time to catch his breath; he gathered the strength to make his way outside the tent to find the wounded but still living General Li.

A battle cry resounded through the Valley of Terror as General Li's troops hurled themselves into battle on all three fronts. In contrast, here at the heart of the camp, there was only silence, even as death filled the air all around.

A trail of bloody footprints began at the tent's entrance and continued thirty paces west. At the end of those footprints stood a towering figure whose face could not be seen, but A Liya knew it was General Li.

Gripping his knife, A Liya tiptoed toward him. But after taking about ten steps, he realized there was someone in front of the general. It was Lieutenant General Bai.

Bloody footprints surrounded the men, testament to a skirmish. Lieutenant General Bai had already lost his longsword, which had been flung far away from him, the blade visibly bent. He was prostrate in front of General Li, with his head pressed against the ground.

General Li held his sword over Lieutenant General Bai's neck, such that he could instantly take the other man's life. But he didn't. Neither of them moved; they were like statues. Blood, which continued to gush from the general's shoulder, dripped onto the grass.

A Liya could hear his own heart pounding. Finally, he crept up on General Li from behind. A Liya held his breath and grasped his sword with both hands. Then he mercilessly drove the blade straight into the other man's torso. There was a faint puffing sound as the blade punctured his flesh, taking the handle along with it.

A Liya's elation soon turned to bewilderment: The blade seemed to have no effect on General Li. It was not until A Liya struggled to pull the sword back out that the general at last toppled over, his eyes turned toward the sky. Blood trickled from his eyes in two streams. As it turned out, he had been dead for some time.

Lieutenant General Bai, still kneeling on the ground, was trembling. Though he hadn't been injured, he was covered in blood.

A Liya ran to his side. "General Bai!"

Lieutenant General Bai lifted his head. His face was completely drained of color. After a long pause, he stammered, "A—A Liya!"

"You can stand up now, General Bai. The demon is dead." A Liya extended a hand to support Lieutenant General Bai, who slowly rose to his feet.

Why had General Li not lowered his sword? Had his strength already been depleted? Or had there been other reasons, unbeknownst to anyone but the two men?

A Liya didn't have time to reflect on these questions, as he saw He Layi running toward him. He hurried to meet her, calling out in the Hamo dialect, "How is the chief?"

He Layi was sobbing. "Father—he was already killed by General Li's forces."

A Liya let loose a cry of pain. He turned and went back over to the general's corpse, then sliced off the head, cursing, "Li Dingguo, you demon! May you burn in hell!"

He Layi, startled by the grisly act, took a step back. "Was it you—who killed him?"

"Yes." The warrior proudly lifted his chin. "My dear and respected He Layi, please stay here. It looks like the safest place for now. I'm going to go end this war." With those words, A Liya raced off toward the front lines.

Though General Li's troops were under attack on three fronts, they had courage and the power to terrify on their side, and they were still making a strong stand when A Liya arrived on the scene. Covered in blood, the Hamo warrior was exhausted and weak, and it seemed as if he might tip over at the touch of a finger. But in his hand was a power-ful weapon.

"Your demon commander is dead!" A Liya shouted with all of the strength in his body. Then he tossed Li Dingguo's head onto the battlefield.

As if a spell had been broken, General Li's troops instantly lost their will to fight. Some of them were killed right then as they stared, stupefied. Others retreated to the forest. Thus concluded the chapter of Chinese history known as the Southern Ming resistance.

The Qing and Burmese forces celebrated their victory. But the Hamo warriors were the happiest of all. They had waged a holy war and won, saving the lives of the entire clan. A Liya was lifted high into the air and became known as the greatest hero in the history of the Hamo people.

However, though he had vanquished Li Dingguo, what remained of the man was still spine-chilling. His eyes, coated in blood, were so full of anger and hatred that no one dared to look into them.

He Layi tried to close his eyes, but they kept reopening. When the head priest saw this, he worriedly told them, "He was filled with grave resentment and died unhappy. Though his body may be dead, the evil of his soul still lingers. I fear that he may come back and wreak havoc."

The Qing troops were unmoved by this, but the Burmese and the Hamo forces, who had been living there for generations, were deeply disturbed. Lieutenant General Bai felt guilty, and there was a look of contrition on his face.

"What should we do, then?" He Layi turned to the high priest.

"In my view, the best solution is to seal away his blood in a vial," the high priest said after a long silence. "Future generations of our clan must be taught to maintain the curse so that his soul forever remains in hell, powerless and unable to harm anyone else."

He Layi shuddered. "The blood vial would be cursed? Would—would that be too vicious of us?"

"A soul so wicked calls for vicious revenge." A Liya was standing beside her. "My dear and respected He Layi, you mustn't worry. What's most important is the protection of our entire clan, and moreover, retribution for the death of our chief."

He Layi was helplessly silent for a long time, and tears welled in her eyes. She did not voice any further objections and thus tacitly gave her consent.

The high priest took General Li's blood and had a vial specially produced for the purpose. The vial, which served as evidence of the Hamo people's tremendous victory over a demon, became the most sacred object of our clan. He Layi should have become the leader of the clan, but she refused. He Layi insisted that A Liya become chief instead, and anointed herself a priestess, keeping watch over the sacred vial.

The day that General Li was killed was declared a religious holiday. Every year on that day, the high priest gathers the entire village, and together we offer sacrifices to the gods and celebrate our victory in the holy war. The most important part of the ceremony is the curse on Li Dingguo's soul. The priestess wears the blood vial on her chest and stands with her back to the rest of the clan, saying, "Your vicious curse be purified as it passes through my body, which is pure, allowing it to stand for justice."

The story of this war and our people's heroism has evolved into the most sacred conviction of the Hamo people, providing us with the moral support to face hardships and hopelessness.

Chapter 24

The Vial Thief

Though the story had ended, everyone sat in contemplation, still caught up in the tale.

After a long silence, Professor Zhou spoke. "Wow, I never imagined that behind this little vial could be such an intense chapter of history." Though he'd scoffed earlier at the mention of demons and curses, he was now genuinely moved.

"So now all of you know how important this sacred object is to our village." Lord An Mi let out a deep breath as he looked at Luo.

Luo knew he was thinking about how the vial had been broken, and in light of what Luo now knew, he felt slightly ashamed. He rubbed his nose for a second, then changed the subject. "Yes, we certainly do— but how could that young man have managed to steal something so important?"

Lord An Mi grew furious once more. "That scoundrel! He took advantage of the Hamo people's hospitality and swindled us!"

"Swindled you?"

"That's right." Suo Tulan, seeing that Lord An Mi was agitated, answered in his place. "He pretended to be a friend to our people."

"What do you mean, he pretended?" Luo inquired.

"A year ago, he appeared in our village. He came alone, and he brought an interesting gift for Lord An Mi. We Hamos always welcome guests from afar. That evening, in this very courtyard, Lord An Mi warmly received him."

"What was he like?" Luo asked, trusting Suo Tulan to be a good judge of character.

Suo Tulan narrowed his eyes, as if he were trying to choose the right words. Then he shook his head gently. "He was a very bad person."

Though his words were simple, their meaning was not. Luo was alarmed; if wise and generous Suo Tulan used the words *very bad*, that meant this was no ordinary person. He glanced at Lord An Mi, whose face was livid as he recalled the man.

Suo Tulan continued, "That night when we were drinking, he seemed forthright and honest. Perhaps it was because of this that we treated him like a close friend."

Luo nodded. "I understand. Did you ask him why he came?"

"Of course I did. And I looked him straight in the eye when I asked. A person can easily lie with his mouth, but with his eyes, it's more difficult. He said that the legend of the holy war and the Valley of Terror had brought him here."

"Did he say who he was or why was he so interested in these subjects?"

"He said he was an explorer, that his life was about uncovering mysteries. As far as his name goes, he said it came before Zhou in *The Hundred Family Names*."

Luo, Professor Zhou, and Yue Dongbei exchanged glances. They had heard these very same words before. It appeared that this was how this young man always introduced himself.

"His name wasn't important," Suo Tulan said. "So we just followed our customs and called him 'Zhou.' Later on, I told him the full story

223

of our holy war, just as I did with you. He stared at me wide-eyed. It was as if he were not only listening but could see it happening."

"See it happening?" Luo repeated, lifting an eyebrow.

"Yes, as if he could see into our souls. That gaze of his was so piercing. If I had hidden something from him or lied to him about anything, he would have known."

"For a guest, though, that seems a little rude. Weren't you upset?"

"No," Suo Tulan answered honestly. "The holy war was the most trying time in our history. I was more than happy to share the story with him, and there was no reason to hold back. The more attentively he listened, the happier I was. Now that I think about it, Zhou seemed to have used this psychological principle to win us over from the start."

Luo shook his head. "Since he traveled such a long way, he must have been truly interested. It's just—did he really want, as he said, to uncover these mysteries?"

"It is obvious that what he wanted was to get his hands on the Hamo people's most sacred object!" Lord An Min shouted. "Why else would he have stuck around so long?"

"Oh? How long was he here?"

"Over three months."

"That really is a long stay." Luo was surprised. "What did he do all that time?"

Suo Tulan replied, "He kept visiting the Valley of Terror. What he was actually doing there day after day, I'm not sure."

"It was all an act. He was buying himself time while he plotted." Lord An Mi's tone was icy. "Eventually, he learned the Hamo language, and he became close friends with Shui Yidie."

"Shui Yidie?" Luo latched on to the new name. "Who's that?"

Lord An Mi didn't answer. It seemed as if he didn't want to talk about it.

Suo Tulan sighed gently and explained, "He's the bodyguard for the priestess. He was supposed to be the most courageous and loyal of all the young men in our tribe. No one ever imagined that he could commit such a horrific crime."

Luo's eyes flashed. "He helped Zhou steal the vial?"

Suo Tulan closed his eyes and nodded, clearly hurt by the betrayal.

"But why did he do it?" Luo blurted out. He could see how Shui Yidie must have had special access to the vial. But what reason could he have had for betraying the entire village and allowing their most sacred object to be sold to a foreign buyer? Was it simply because he and Zhou were friends? That explanation obviously didn't hold water.

Suo Tulan shook his head in dismay. "Even now, we don't fully understand. We've asked Shui Yidie many times, but he won't answer. All he'll say is that it's all his fault and that he'll accept whatever punishment is handed down."

"Where is he now?" Luo detected something suspicious.

"Locked away in the water dungeon."

"I'd like to see him," Luo said flatly. "The sooner, the better."

Suo Tulan didn't respond. He turned and looked at Lord An Mi. Evidently, the decision was not up to him.

After a silence, Lord An Mi finally spoke. "The water dungeon is meant to degrade anyone who holds the title of warrior, regardless of the reason for his having been sent there, because he has degraded the entire Hamo people. This kind of person is unworthy of interacting with others, so he must live forever alone in the dark. But since we're dealing with the reincarnation of a demon, we can go have a look at this person who sold his soul to that demon."

Lord An Mi stood up and led the group through the gates of the courtyard. The chief's attendants lit their torches and formed two lines, leading the way.

The group filed through the rain, heading north. Soon enough, they saw water up ahead: They had arrived at the pond's edge. They traced the shoreline, moving westward. The lights were off in most of the houses in the village, and all was peaceful and still.

As they proceeded, the houses became few and far between. It appeared that they were leaving the village. Luo suddenly spotted the flickering of torches not far off in the distance, illuminating a wide structure.

This structure was made up of seven or eight small rooms, and along the bottom of each were dark wooden beams that suspended it above the pond. A torch was installed on each, and the flames swayed in the wind and rain, lending a spookiness to the atmosphere.

As they approached, a man emerged and greeted Lord An Mi and Suo Tulan. The man, who looked as if he were about thirty years old, was tall and muscular, with a rather menacing face. As he spoke, he looked over Luo and the others. He seemed shocked for an instant, but quickly concealed his emotions.

Lord An Mi spoke with him for a while, as if he was introducing the others. Though his voice was not particularly loud, it carried through the still air, causing some creature in the darkness to suddenly cry out.

That cry pierced the air and instantly brought Luo back to the dark hallway of the hospital in Kunming—it was almost identical to the cry of the young man there. It was filled with the same despair and fright.

This time, though, the sound didn't die down. It echoed and swelled into a chorus of cries. The tranquil pond had dissolved into a scene from a nightmare.

Luo and the others were stunned when Lord An Mi matter-of-factly told them, "Those are people who have succumbed to phobia. They're locked inside these rooms."

Luo and Professor Zhou looked at one another. They both knew: This was the same disease that had struck in Longzhou. According to Lord An Mi, there had been an outbreak among the Hamo villagers as well. So the disease really did originate in the Valley of Terror—they'd been on the right track all along.

"When did these people come down with the disease?" asked Luo.

"It started in the days following the theft of the blood vial. The demonic powers of the valley were reawakened," Lord An Mi answered, a grave expression on his face. "It happened while they were hunting in the valley. The demon stole their souls."

Luo nodded. Then he asked, "It was only right after the blood vial was stolen? No new cases in the six months after that?"

"After that, no one went to the Valley of Terror. And lots of young warriors from our clan, like Di Erjia here, have been guarding the village day and night. The demon doesn't dare come here." As Lord An Mi said those words, his gaze swept over the tall, athletic men standing by, as if to bestow praise on them. One of the men proudly stuck out his chest. Presumably, he was Di Erjia.

Lord An Mi nodded and said something to Di Erjia, who replied, then led all of them toward the row of wooden rooms. After crossing a suspended bridge, they stepped onto a walkway along the front of the rooms.

"These are Hamo water dungeons. In the old days, during the war, they were used to detain captured enemy troops. They were built on water to prevent criminals from escaping. Nowadays, the only people in them are members of our own tribe." Suo Tulan sighed sadly.

The rooms were all connected. There were no windows, but at the front of each were railings so that the unit was not completely sealed off and it was possible for guards to monitor what was going on inside. Luo and the others followed Di Erjia to the far end. They couldn't help looking into the units along the way, but under the flicker of the torches, they saw only contorted faces, accompanied by the relentless sound of bloodcurdling screams.

The last room was set apart from the rest of the structure, and its construction differed from the others. Instead of having four plain walls, the space comprised numerous wooden planks nailed together, even for the ceiling. It would have been more accurate to call it a *cage* than a *room*.

Everyone stopped in their tracks. Yue Dongbei scratched his head and chuckled. "This water dungeon is really something else."

"This one was specially constructed to hold the most dangerous criminals. It's designed to force them to endure the heat of the scorching sun all day long, expose them to wind and rain during storms, and leave them unprotected from mosquitoes and poisonous snakes. Though they are allowed to live, they must suffer a life of pain that is worse than death," Lord An Mi told them trenchantly. His eyes widened, brimming with hatred as he fixed his gaze on the man inside the cage.

Luo and the others followed Lord An Mi's gaze. They saw a man curled up in a corner of the cage, his face pressed against the floor as if he were dead.

Di Erjia shouted a few words. Though he was speaking the Hamo language, Luo could make out something that sounded like "Shui Yidie" in Mandarin, which must have been the man's name. But the man did not respond.

Then Di Erjia sounded like he was cursing. The expression on his face was savage, and his tone was vicious. Suo Tulan shot him a look of rebuke, and Di Erjia promptly stopped, looking embarrassed. Then Suo Tulan looked at Shui Yidie and sighed. In a much gentler tone, he proceeded to speak a string of words in the Hamo language.

This time, Shui Yidie responded. He lifted his head and glanced over. He started to shift around as if he were about to get up, but his movements were slow and strange. After a long struggle, he managed to sit upright and get to his knees. A short while later, his body swayed, as if he were already exerting himself, and finally, he stood up. He tottered toward the group.

Observing this long, drawn-out process, Luo squinted intently, sizing up this bodyguard who'd been assigned to protect the village priestess. He could see only the filthy, tattered rags that covered his body. His facial hair, as well as the hair on his head, had grown long. It was difficult to picture what his face had looked like before or guess how old he was. Since he'd been in this tortured state for so long, his body had grown gaunt, and his cheeks were sunken.

Each step he took was labored. He had almost reached the door, where he was separated from the group by only the wooden fence. His movements were sluggish and awkward, not only because he was frail but, more importantly, because his hands were tightly bound behind his back and his feet were tied with rope, such that he could take only half a step at a time.

Luo couldn't help shaking his head in dismay.

Suo Tulan said quietly, "He's like a tiger. Only the strongest chains will do."

At those words, Shui Yidie slowly lifted his head and looked at them. In the brief instant they made eye contact, Luo understood what Suo Tulan had meant: This was a person who was capable of serious harm.

In spite of having taken a brutal beating, his body being on the verge of collapse, and being tightly tied up, there was still a light in this man's eyes. He knew everyone—his fellow clansmen and Chief Bai—except Luo, Professor Zhou, and Yue Dongbei. He fixed his gaze, which showed guardedness as well as curiosity, on the three of them.

"These three are Han warriors who've come a long distance. They are friends of the Hamo people. The demon has already wreaked havoc on their land. Three of Chief Bai's own aides have been killed by the demon. Do you still feel no remorse for your crime?" Suo Tulan said to Shui Yidie in the Hamo language. His voice was low but not cruel.

Shui Yidie narrowed his eyes. His face held a look of slight surprise as he mumbled, "Demon? There really is a demon?"

Suo Tulan pointed at the guests standing beside him. "Luo and Zhou have come from faraway Longzhou. The sacred object has been broken! Many people there have been harmed like those in our village. The demon has given them a phobia and even frightened some to death! What's more, the demon has been following these men, and it may even appear in the village."

"Zhou?" This name seemed to trigger memories in Shui Yidie. His eyes lit up, and they followed Suo Tulan's gesture toward Professor Zhou. But he quickly shook his head in disappointment upon realizing this was not the man he'd been thinking of. Then he turned to look at Luo, examining his face. This man was likewise unfamiliar to him, but something about him stirred Shui Yidie's soul.

It was hard to describe that something or tell where exactly it came from. It might have been the intelligence in his eyes, his candid smile, or the cool self-confidence in his face. In any case, though this man hadn't said a word, Shui Yidie heard his message: *I've come, I know your secrets, and I'm the only one who can solve your mystery.*

Shui Yidie licked his lips, then asked in a hoarse voice, "Luo, why have you come here?"

Suo Tulan translated.

"Does he understand any Mandarin?" Luo was excited that this man wanted to communicate, and he wanted to speak with him directly.

But Suo Tulan's answer disappointed him. "No, according to the rules that have been handed down for generations, the bodyguard for the priestess is not allowed to learn Mandarin."

Luo pursed his lips, at a loss. It was a strange rule. "Can you help me, then? The man by the name of Zhou, why did he steal the blood vial? And how did he help Zhou?"

Suo Tulan translated, but it was clear he didn't expect much.

Shui Yidie answered almost instantly.

"What did he say?" asked Luo impatiently.

"He admits that he was the one who stole the blood vial and handed it over to the young man. But as far as his reasons, the priestess is the only one he'll tell."

Lord An Mi exploded with rage, shouting in Hamo, "The crime he's committed is no less than unforgivable! If he's not ready to repent, then he ought to suffer the harshest punishment known to this tribe."

Shui Yidie turned and walked up to Lord An Mi. He calmly replied, "Honored and respected Lord An Mi, I'm more than willing to accept any punishment. But according to the rules that were handed down by the heroic A Liya and the magnificent He Layi, the bodyguard must obey the priestess's every command. And only priestesses can carry out the appropriate punishment."

Lord An Mi narrowed his eyes and gritted his teeth. A second later, he smiled darkly. "You've manipulated the rules in order to protect yourself. Fine. Fine. You want to meet with the priestess? Tomorrow I'll grant you your wish. We'll see what she thinks of your betrayal of the entire village."

Shui Yidie lifted his eyebrows, looking pleased. There was surprise in his voice as he retorted loudly: "Has she recovered already?"

Lord An Mi gasped. "Don't you even try. She won't forgive you," he hissed back.

Luo observed their verbal clash from the sideline, with Suo Tulan quietly interpreting. "The priestess hasn't come to see him?"

Suo Tulan looked embarrassed. Before he had a chance to speak, Lord An Mi answered for him: "After the priestess lost the vial, she fell ill. She's been bedridden for the past six months. But in the past two days, she's suddenly been recovering."

"Is that so?" Luo nodded, looking at Shui Yidie in the water dungeon. "There's a few other mysteries that it looks like only the priestess can explain."

"Tomorrow night, the priestess will pay a visit," Lord An Mi conceded. "It's been too long since all of us saw her. When the time comes, we'll bring Shui Yidie out and let the priestess sentence him."

"Wonderful," Luo said with satisfaction. After all, one day wasn't long to wait.

A cold mountain breeze blew through, and the rain grew stronger once again, pattering on the wooden roofs.

Frustrated, Lord An Mi looked up toward the sky. Perhaps he was remembering the giant rainstorm of several centuries past, when the demon had hatched his plot.

Shui Yidie raised his head, too. His eyes were open wide. There was nothing to protect him from the falling rain. Soon he was drenched.

Suo Tulan gently sighed, then told Lord An Mi, "Let us go, Lord An Mi."

Lord An Mi nodded. He looked over at Luo. "We have a place where you can stay. What are your plans?"

Luo promptly seized the opportunity. "We'd like to go to the Valley of Terror and have a look around, if Lord An Mi can help us find a knowledgeable guide."

"Going to the Valley of Terror, eh? Well, there's no one more capable than Di Erjia," Lord An Mi said. "Your Holiness, let's dispatch two more of our warriors to accompany their group. Since the demon is close by, it's best to take extra precautions."

Suo Tulan crossed his arms over his chest. "As you wish, Lord An Mi."

Lord An Mi said nothing more. He led the group back across the wooden bridge. Di Erjia saluted them but did not follow. Forming a line, the group hurried through the rain, leaving the bleak world of the water dungeons behind them.

Suddenly, they heard a hoarse cry coming from the direction of the water dungeons. It sounded like Shui Yidie. Lord An Mi, seemingly alarmed, stopped. He glanced back for an instant before continuing.

"Is that Shui Yidie? What's he saying?" Luo was curious.

Suo Tulan shook his head. Without answering, he followed Lord An Mi.

"He wants Lord An Mi to set him free so that he can protect the priestess and fight the demon." Chief Bai stepped beside Luo. He looked at Lord An Mi and Suo Tulan up ahead. After a pause, he added, "But for now, it's obvious that no one believes him."

Chapter 25

A Trip to the Valley

Lord An Mi put the visitors up in a house next to his own. The house, which had two rooms, normally housed four attendants. Now Luo and the others slept in the inner room, while the attendants slept in the outer one. Though they were packed in rather tightly, it was certainly more comfortable than the two nights they'd spent in the forest.

This arrangement had been at Luo's request. The four attendants between them and the outside world afforded them a sense of protection.

Luo stood at the window for a long time. Occasionally, he could feel droplets of rain, carried by the wind, against his face. The sensation kept his mind alert. Right now, there were so many things that he had to mull over.

After encountering so many setbacks, they had finally arrived in the valley, the origin and center of all the strange incidents. It seemed as if the answer was right in front of him. And yet things had grown only more complicated. Ever since they'd reached Mihong, the demon had made his presence felt. He had killed Zhao Liwen, knocked out Professor Zhou, and scared brave Chief Bai out of his wits. In the forest, he had seemed unconquerable.

Luo himself had felt a fear like nothing he'd experienced before in his life. Even now, as he reflected on it, that fear still lingered. Were these the demonic powers of legends? They had surfaced in General Li's troops several centuries ago, and now they had been resurrected in the Valley of Terror and left a trail of footprints leading all the way to Longzhou. But Luo was still hoping to find a more plausible explanation.

"Professor Zhou, what are your views on sorcery?" Luo asked, turning around.

Professor Zhou had been sitting on one of the beds, staring off in blank consternation. Realizing that Luo was talking to him, he snapped out of his daze and absentmindedly mumbled, "Sorcery?"

"That's right." Luo raised his voice, standing in front of him. "When we were in Longzhou, you gave me a lesson on how fear affects brain chemistry. Today, when Suo Tulan mentioned the general's use of sorcery, the *gu* poisoners he captured, I put the two together. Perhaps it's the key to uncovering the truth behind the incidents in Longzhou at last."

Professor Zhou was silent a moment. "So what you're saying is that the phobia victims are actually victims of sorcery?"

"It's very possible. General Li used sorcery to control the forces under his command. What I want to know now is what this *gu* sorcery really is. How might it be used to control a person's mental state? I'm hoping that you can provide an expert opinion." There was a flicker in Luo's eyes.

"I've never really understood the definition of 'sorcery.'" Professor Zhou bit his lip and leaned back. "The first Chinese character in the word for it contains the radical for *insect*, with the radical for *blood* directly below it. That indicates the presence of a parasite. In the old days, people believed in various myths about the nature of creatures that carry highly toxic venom, as they could bring illness if ingested, which is how that first character came into use. Victims would suffer impaired consciousness or hallucinations. Poisoners often made use of venom from animals such as snakes, scorpions, and lizards, putting it in food to murder or injure their victims."

"So the character for *sorcery* itself connotes poison?" Luo seemed half-lost in thought. "Is it actually possible for poison to cause mental illness like, say, extreme phobia?"

It was then that Yue Dongbei became interested in their conversation. He narrowed his eyes, peering at Professor Zhou. After all, their experience that afternoon had affirmed what he believed with all his heart.

Professor Zhou nodded. "Of course. Poison, from a scientific perspective, is a chemical substance that is unsuitable for the human body. Psychological disorders are basically chemical imbalances in the human body. And there are certainly specific chemicals that can cause phobia as an effect. This is actual science, and it has nothing to do with sorcery, ghosts, or the like."

Yue Dongbei cackled loudly. "There's a criterion in my research, which is a basis in fact. That means not adhering to your own school of thought and clinging to its methodology. In terms of the problem at hand, I'm in agreement with Professor Zhou. However, this does not represent a shift in my scholarly paradigm. My claim that the demon is behind the evil act of poisoning still holds up. However, if the poisoning technique has been out of use for over three hundred years, how do you explain this new phenomenon that has occurred only since the blood vial was broken? And continuing with that logic, how do you explain the mysterious links to General Li in the ominous deaths of Zhao Liwen and the others?"

Luo lowered his head. Indeed, these questions remained unanswered. They had come here to stop the bizarre epidemic of fear in Longzhou. But all their leads had instilled only a greater sense of crisis and uncertainty.

"How did these people ingest poison? It all started in Longzhou . . ." Luo said softly to himself, shaking his head. After another silence, he asked the question that had been at the forefront of his mind: "And who is *he*?"

The others knew Luo was referring to the mysterious apparition that had appeared in the forest. They shivered as they each recalled their own encounters.

"Chief Bai, perhaps you can provide the answer to that question." Suddenly, Professor Zhou spoke up in an icy tone. "Out of everyone, you're the only one who was conscious when he appeared."

Luo also looked suspiciously at Chief Bai. He had wanted to ask the same thing back on the cliff, but then Lord An Mi and the others had arrived, and there hadn't been an opportunity until now.

Chief Bai let out a cynical laugh. "I already told you. I only saw his eyes. I didn't get a look at his face."

"But how did you manage to let him get away?" Professor Zhou pressed him.

"I couldn't stop him. You have no idea how terrifying he was." Chief Bai's voice was trembling. At that moment, there was no semblance of the village chief in him. "His powers, his hatred, all of it was burning in his eyes. No one would ever have dared to challenge him."

"Why didn't he kill you?" Professor Zhou asked. "All of your aides have died, and they've all died in your name!"

At this, Chief Bai was tongue-tied.

Yue Dongbei suddenly chuckled. "Well, isn't this interesting. If you think about it, in Suo Tulan's account of the war, the person General Li most despised was Lieutenant General Bai, wasn't it? General Li was holding his sword over Lieutenant General Bai's neck, but at the last minute, Lieutenant General Bai's life was spared. And likewise, the reincarnated demon hasn't killed Chief Bai!"

Chief Bai looked at Yue Dongbei, nodding slowly, as if in gratitude for the other man's words. He faced Professor Zhou. "The way he carried himself was strange. He drifted in as if he had no physical form and left without leaving footprints. Who knows what he really was?"

"What he was?" Yue Dongbei shook his head. "He's the demon. And I think his motive is rather obvious. It's to seek revenge—on those under his command who betrayed him, on the Hamo people. Otherwise, why else would all your aides have died, while the three of us have emerged safe and sound, without a scratch? He scared us a bit, but he never threatened our lives. It was his way of showing his powers, or perhaps giving us a little warning."

Luo jumped in. "How do you explain the victims in Longzhou, then?"

Yue Dongbei scratched his head, blushing. Embarrassed, he mumbled, "That—that's something I'd have to research further."

"Fine. Why don't we talk about something grounded in reality, then?" Luo waved dismissively, then turned to face Professor Zhou. "If this involved sorcery, then the poison must have been ingested through food, correct?"

"Generally, yes, though not necessarily. It could also have been absorbed through the skin or inhaled, among other means. But it does require physical contact, that's for certain," Professor Zhou replied, erudite as always.

"Hmm," murmured Luo. "So, in your opinion, how were Yue Dongbei and I poisoned this afternoon?"

"You two?" Professor Zhou's face held a look of surprise. "You think someone used sorcery on you this afternoon?"

Luo's expression was grave. "I can't think of any explanation apart from that. At the time, I felt petrified, and I even had hallucinations. Mr. Yue, your experience was similar to mine."

Fear still lingered in Yue Dongbei's voice. "It was terrifying, absolutely terrifying. If it had gone on for even a few minutes longer, I would be in danger of going mad, just like those people in the water dungeon."

"Right. When we were in the forest, you two were indeed acting strange." Professor Zhou tapped his head lightly, trying to remember. "Then I was knocked out. By the time I woke up, the two of you were fine. How did you manage to recover?"

"I wanted to ask you the same question. We did nothing, really. It was like waking up from a bad dream. Based on your expertise, how would you explain that?"

Professor Zhou was silent for a long time. Finally, he shook his head in dismay. "I don't know—could it be that this poisoning method has both long-term and short-term effects? Without knowing what ingredients are used to make that kind of poison, it's difficult to speculate."

Luo nodded sympathetically. "Sure. It really is asking too much without more information. Tomorrow we're going to the Valley of Terror to investigate, and hopefully we'll uncover something."

Yue Dongbei clapped his hands together. "That's right, that's right! According to Hamo legend, most of the ingredients for the poison used in sorcery originate in the valley. Heh, Professor Zhou, if you were able to provide a clear explanation for these mysteries, the ramifications for science would be rather significant."

Professor Zhou snorted. "This is a tropical forest filled with countless peculiar organisms. Finding the right ones will be nearly impossible."

Luo raised an eyebrow, seeing that Professor Zhou was stumped. As he was among those who'd fallen prey to the terrifying force, Luo had no easy explanation for what they'd experienced, either. Then another matter entered his mind.

"Professor Zhou, back in Longzhou, you showed me a substance you'd developed to treat phobia. Did you bring it with you?"

Professor Zhou understood that Luo wanted to use the medication as a protective measure. With a regretful look on his face, he spread his palms. "Like I said, it hasn't undergone clinical trials, so it might not be safe. Anyway, I only made one vial, which I lost—"

"Lost?" Luo echoed. "How could you have lost it?"

Professor Zhou flashed a wry smile. "I don't know, either, but it disappeared in the rush to leave on this trip."

Luo heaved a sigh and shook his head. Trying to hide his disappointment, he looked at the others. "Very well, then. Why don't we all get some rest. We're going to need the energy for tomorrow."

Though all four of them were preoccupied, they hadn't slept much in days, and they drifted off to sleep not long after lying down.

Amazingly, the night passed without incident, though the rainstorm grew stronger. The next morning, breakfast was waiting at their doorstep. Luo thought to himself: *If the Hamo people treat their guests with such hospitality, they must have found the behavior of General Li and this Zhou character rather despicable.*

After breakfast, Suo Tulan and Di Erjia arrived as planned. Two of Lord An Mi's four attendants also prepared to accompany them to the valley. It was still pouring, and the Hamos put on raincoats made out of glossy leaves sewn together to form a comfortable, lightweight layer that was also highly water-repellent.

Di Erjia led the way as they darted into the heavy rain. They quickly traveled through the village and were soon at the pond's edge. But even as Suo Tulan moved with rapid steps, he gazed at the pond's surface, a worried look on his face.

"What is it? What's the matter?" asked Luo. The others stopped and turned to look at them.

"The water is rising," Suo Tulan said softly. "If this keeps up over the next two days, the houses by the shore will be flooded."

Sure enough, the water level of the pond was much higher than it had been yesterday. The most obvious sign could be seen in the trees along the shore, whose roots were now submerged.

All of them stood somberly, watching the pond in the rain. Suddenly, they heard a splash. Something had leaped from a tree branch into the water. Not only had it been tiny and dark, but it had been fast, spraying water everywhere as it dove.

"What was that?" Luo could make out something on the surface of the tree trunks, but it was hard to see anything in the rain except the outline of four or five of them, black and shaped like chili peppers.

Suo Tulan chuckled. "Those are fish."

"Fish?" Luo and the others echoed in astonishment. After all, fish didn't live on trees.

"These fish are native to the Yunnan mountains," Chief Bai explained. "We call them *datouyu*. They normally live in shallow water, and they have suckers on their bodies that allow them to attach to the rocks. Whenever there's a big storm and the water rises to the level of the trees, they climb the tree trunks and attach themselves. When they're frightened, they leap back into the water."

"Fascinating!" Yue Dongbei scurried over. "Oh, this one's climbing up the tree!"

Luo stepped in closer. Indeed, on one of the trees, at about waist height, was a *datouyu*. The fish was about the length of his hand, with a wide black head, yellow body, and narrow tail. A long, broad fin ran down its back. Its thick body seemed capable of powerful movements.

Yue Dongbei slowly extended one hand toward the fish, but the fish sensed his approach. Without warning, it curled its body and flung itself off the tree, grazing Yue Dongbei's hand. The fish disappeared into the water without a trace.

"Almost! Almost got it." Yue Dongbei shook his head in regret. His regret turned to shock as he gasped, "Oh my God, my hand!"

Yue Dongbei's index finger looked as if it had been slashed with a blade, and the wound was beginning to fill with blood. The others gathered around.

Chief Bai chuckled. "These fish have razor-sharp dorsal fins. You have to be careful."

Yue Dongbei glared at him, as the warning had come a little too late.

Fortunately, the cut wasn't deep, and the bleeding subsided. Yue Dongbei grumbled a bit, but seeing that no one took any notice, quickly put the incident behind him.

After they exited the village, the group headed southwest. They hadn't gone very far before the terrain grew steeper and the forest denser. In the distance, Luo saw a low hill and realized that, once they'd crossed it, they would finally reach the legendary Valley of Terror.

Though this section of their journey was challenging due to the rugged terrain, compared to crossing Mopan Mountain, it hardly seemed strenuous at all. There was less of an incline, and there was a clearly demarcated path to follow.

"Do people often travel along this path?" Luo asked.

Among their Hamo companions, only Suo Tulan spoke Mandarin. "Because the valley has abundant natural resources, members of our tribe often go hunting there. After the phobia cases six months ago, however, no one has been hunting there."

"How long did this go on for, in terms of the phobia cases that you saw?"

"Three or four days. Then Lord An Mi made an announcement to the entire village, and almost no one has been over there since."

"Lord An Mi has never gone to investigate?" Based on what Luo had observed, the Hamo people didn't seem much for burying their heads in the sand.

Suo Tulan's reply seemed to confirm his judgment. "Of course he's been there, and more than once. Di Erjia has also gone a few times. But they haven't found any clues. Though Lord An Mi is an extraordinary warrior, there's very little we can do about the situation. Lord An Mi has put Di Erjia in charge of protecting our village. If anyone goes to the valley, he has to accompany them."

Ah, so that's why Di Erjia is leading the group, Luo thought as he studied the man from behind. Indeed, if anything went awry, they'd need someone who was fearless.

Suo Tulan seemed to sense what Luo was thinking. "Di Erjia is a rare breed of Hamo warrior. Early on, he volunteered to take on this particular responsibility. And with him escorting us, you'll see that no one will suffer from phobia afterward. Lord An Mi is grateful for him. He says that the demon himself fears Di Erjia's strength."

The day before, Luo had noticed how much Lord An Mi appreciated Di Erjia. What was strange was Suo Tulan's demeanor. Even as he praised Di Erjia, his glum expression belied his gushing words.

Di Erjia, who appeared to be single-mindedly absorbed in the task of blazing the trail, did not hear the conversation taking place behind him. He seemed not to understand a word of Mandarin.

"Your Holiness, your Mandarin is excellent. Not only is your pronunciation natural, but you choose your words well. I must say, you speak it better than many Han people."

"In order to become a high priest, one must know Mandarin. This is an unwritten rule that has been handed down since the holy war."

"Oh really?" Luo's interest was piqued. "Why is that?"

"Because, according to the codes of our tribe, the priestess must study Mandarin with the high priest. In fact, after the priestess has selected a successor, the very first thing that the successor must do is begin these studies with the high priest. It is only after she has acquired proficiency in reading and writing that the succession ceremony is held."

"The priestess needs to have proficiency in Mandarin?" marveled Luo. "But I remember you saying yesterday that her bodyguard is prohibited from learning it? That seems very strange."

"All of these rules are the work of the founding priestess, He Layi. As she was the chief's daughter, her status was a little higher than that of A Liya. There are many things that we don't understand, but for many generations, no one has ever disobeyed He Layi's rules. That applies to everyone, without exception, even the chief." When he spoke of these two heroes of the holy war, Suo Tulan's expression grew solemn and his tone was reverent.

"Since your Mandarin is fluent, you must communicate regularly with Han people, isn't that right?" Professor Zhou joined their conversation.

But Chief Bai was the one who answered his question. "His Holiness Suo Tulan is a frequent guest in our village. Not long ago, he passed through on his way to the outside."

Suo Tulan nodded. "People from our tribe rarely ever leave. Any contact with the outside world usually involves the priesthood."

Luo asked, "So why did Your Holiness recently travel to the outside?"

Suo Tulan heaved a sigh. "To find the villagers who had fled."

"Oh, right!" Luo recalled how their host in Mihong, Mr. Wang, had mentioned this.

"You know about this?" Suo Tulan looked at Luo quizzically. "When news got out that the sacred object had been lost and that there was a connection to the phobia cases, some members of our tribe fled."

Luo sensed that they were broaching a taboo subject and didn't press him any further. Changing the subject, they proceeded along the road, chattering, until Di Erjia suddenly stopped. Everyone looked up and realized that they had arrived at the top of the low hill.

The Valley of Terror was only a heartbeat away. Perched atop the hill, everyone gazed southwest, where a narrow strip of land contrasted with the surrounding mountains. It almost felt like the countryside.

"This is where General Li's troops were once stationed." Suo Tulan pointed. "Back then, they felled the trees on the slope and turned the entire mountain into a military base. This section of forest has grown back since then."

Indeed, though the forest on the mountainside was dense, few trees were especially tall. Luo surveyed the scenery along the mountainside. Between the two hills demarcating either side of the ravine, there was a narrow pathway that, from a distance, seemed to serve as the perfect entrance.

Luo couldn't help thinking that General Li had been a true master at the art of war. The Hamo village would have been located behind the military base, while there was a natural barrier in front. No wonder the Qing and Burmese forces had been locked in battle with him for three years and only succeeded with the aid of the Hamos, who had helped them encircle the camp.

Suo Tulan turned and pointed southeast. "Look. Atop the cliff is a lake. Whenever there are heavy rains, the lake will rise overnight and overflow in a waterfall."

Luo and the others, who had heard the story of the holy war the night before, already knew that the lake had played a pivotal role in history. They couldn't see the lake itself from where they stood, but they could see water cascading down from the cliff, and it was an awe-inspiring sight.

Below the top of the cliff was another ledge, and so the water cascaded down in two steps, pouring from the lower ledge in an arc that was about a hundred yards long and sprayed onto the northeast area of the hill below before flowing into the pond at the other side of the mountain basin.

After his experience in Mihong, Luo understood the sheer force of such rapids. He could easily imagine how, if the ledge were demolished as General Li had planned, the entire supply of water in the lake would come down in full force, instantly obliterating the Hamo village. He shook his head a little, mumbling to himself, "Flooding the village—what a barbaric idea."

"General Li understood the power of water!" Yue Dongbei took advantage of the opportunity to show off. "In the early years, when General Li was leading the Yunnan army, he started constructing irrigation systems and predicting rainfall. He knew how important water was. Otherwise, the Mihong residents wouldn't still be calling him the Rain God, heh heh."

Luo was startled to realize that the designation had its roots in General Li's very real expertise.

Chief Bai's brow was knitted. He was apparently in no mood to discuss anything related to the Rain God. He changed the subject: "Why don't we descend and have a look at the forest down there?"

Suo Tulan nodded and said something to Di Erjia. Following his instructions, Di Erjia led everyone down to the forest in the valley. The forest here was extremely dense. Leaves spread out overhead like giant umbrellas, forming a protective barrier from rainwater. There was so little sunlight that it almost felt like dusk, and all of them fumbled around for a minute before their eyes adjusted.

In this gloomy atmosphere marking their arrival in the Valley of Terror, where a legendary demon originated, everyone grew tense. Lord An Mi's two attendants carried their machetes on high alert as the group slowly made their way through the dense undergrowth. All of them had just started to relax when Di Erjia stopped abruptly. A split second later, his machete was drawn.

The rest of the group instantly huddled together, each feeling his heart pounding in his chest. All of them followed the direction of Di Erjia's gaze, trying to figure out what was wrong.

Di Erjia kept his left hand behind his back, with his fingers pointed upward. He waved everyone back.

Suo Tulan whispered to Luo, "There's an enemy up ahead."

Luo's right hand was already on his gun. He quickly slid back the trigger lock. Then the two attendants, who had been watching Di Erjia's hand signals, lifted their machetes. Yue Dongbei, Professor Zhou, and Chief Bai all held their breath, anxious and unsure of what was about to unfold.

They could hear the pitter-patter of raindrop on the leaves. Apart from that, there was only silence. It was as if time were standing still.

But that silence did not last long. A second later, there was a rustling sound, followed by a ruckus somewhere in front of them.

Di Erjia calmly pivoted, then charged straight ahead into the grove. Zhao Liwen's tragic death had already taught them a lesson, and Luo wasn't about to hesitate this time around. He pulled out his gun and trailed closely behind Di Erjia. He heard rustling behind him, presumably the others following suit.

They could hear someone running, but the brush was too thick for them to see. No matter how fast they sprinted, the fugitive easily kept a safe distance ahead of them. Yet he did not appear to want to throw them off completely. At times, it was clear that he was slowing down, as if he was waiting for Luo and the rest of the group to catch up.

After noticing this two or three times, Luo grew apprehensive: Something wasn't right. The fugitive was trying to lure them to a certain location. He wanted to tell Di Erjia, but they didn't speak the same language, and the others were too far behind to translate. Finally, Luo stopped in his tracks, watching as Di Erjia continued to claw his way through a thicket. There was a worried look on his face.

This time, their target didn't wait for them. The rustling sound gradually grew fainter. Soon Professor Zhou and Suo Tulan caught up to Luo. By then, the forest had returned to its former stillness.

"What—what happened? That—that—" panted Yue Dongbei.

Understanding what he meant, Luo pointed: "He went that way."

"Why—why didn't—didn't you keep chasing him?" Yue Dongbei was scowling.

Luo lowered his voice and told him firmly: "Our enemy is hidden, while we're out in the open. We shouldn't advance blindly. We have to stick together. Don't wander away from the group."

He had just caught sight of Di Erjia standing a little way ahead and was about to reenter the thicket when Suo Tulan suddenly called out to him: "Luo, hold on a second."

Luo turned and saw the grave expression on his face. "Your Holiness, what is wrong?"

"Don't go any farther." Suo Tulan was squinting. He hesitated, then said slowly and solemnly, "We're approaching the ancient cemetery."

"Ancient cemetery?" No one had mentioned this to him before, but as soon as Luo heard those words, something clicked.

Suo Tulan's explanation confirmed his suspicion. "It's where General Li's troops were buried. Tens of thousands of his followers were laid to rest there. We ought to be careful about treading there."

Though people in the old days customarily returned a body to that person's hometown, General Li had been entrenched in the valley and naturally couldn't leave. It made sense that the site had been transformed into a giant cemetery.

No wonder Di Erjia had stopped and suddenly grown vigilant. Luo recalled how deeply the Hamos respected the dead and hesitated, trying to find the right words. "They're already dead, and there's nothing we can do to change that. We can only be conscious of the crimes that haven't yet taken place. Your Holiness, I came from very far away to put an end to a series of crimes, and the deceased have no reason whatsoever to defend the demon's barbarous actions."

Suo Tulan seemed moved by Luo's words. He nodded vigorously. "Luo, you're right. If the demon really has fled into the cemetery, then we can't turn back now. Let me lead the way."

He stepped out in front. Seeing this, Di Erjia extended his arm and uttered a few worried words in the Hamo language. It was clear that he wanted to stop Suo Tulan from going to the cemetery. Suo Tulan looked back at him, his face emotionless. He seemed calm and self-possessed. Di Erjia angrily dropped his arm and lowered his eyes.

"Please pardon Di Erjia's rudeness and cowardice," the high priest said. "According to Hamo folk songs, this area was once the site of a battle against the demon, and so it is filled with evil demonic powers."

"Oh?" Luo's ears perked up. "What do the folk songs say about it?"

Suo Tulan sang a bit of a song, translating in Mandarin as best he could: *"Here the demon fought, left the place a hellish ruin. See the plume of smoke, marking the fiery demon's river of blood."*

"Interesting. Why don't we go see for ourselves?"

"Follow me." Suo Tulan placed his right arm across his chest and slowly headed toward the cemetery. He gestured ceremoniously after every other step he took, mumbling incantations the entire way to pray for the souls of those who never returned to their homelands.

Chapter 26

GHOST IN THE CEMETERY

With Suo Tulan leading the way, it didn't take long for the group to make their way out of the forest and reach a clearing.

Luo squinted in disbelief. It felt as if he'd entered a strange new world.

There wasn't a single tree in the two-acre clearing. Among the few species of plants, one in particular grew in abundance. No more than three feet tall, it had a straight stalk with only a few stems. At the top of each stem was a flower whose petals were a deep shade of red with black undertones. The plant appeared to be in bloom, and it filled the entire clearing. The raindrops on the petals glistened against the blackish-red background.

Though he didn't know why, Luo suddenly felt uneasy. With a frown, he asked Suo Tulan, "What kind of flowers are these?"

"Blood of ghosts," Suo Tulan quietly replied.

Luo's mouth fell open. "Blood of ghosts?"

"That's right. I believe that's the name in Mandarin." Suo Tulan paused, then added, "This is the only place along this vast mountain range where these flowers grow."

Luo exhaled slowly. The shade of blackish-red really did evoke the image of rotting flesh, or a mix of dirt and blood. The flowers emitted a slightly pungent odor reminiscent of blood, such that it felt as if they were standing in a giant pool of it.

"Blood of ghosts. Fascinating." Yue Dongbei fondled the petals of a flower in front of him. "Flowers growing over dead bodies in an ancient cemetery. I wonder if that's where the terrifying powers come from."

Luo, Professor Zhou, and Chief Bai all froze, recalling their discussion of sorcery and poison from the previous night.

Luo turned to Professor Zhou and cocked an eyebrow.

Professor Zhou shook his head. "I'd have to perform a chemical analysis."

"Hee hee. If that's the case, I'm afraid we'll have to do some deflowering." Yue Dongbei snickered as he tugged at a stem. Despite several tries, the plant did not budge.

"You'd better just cut it," said Professor Zhou.

The Hamo warrior beside him drew his machete and stepped forward, then expertly cut off several stalks.

"Great," said Luo. "I'll take some back to the forensics lab and have them analyzed there, too."

Professor Zhou nodded and gave a handful to Luo and Yue Dongbei. He kept one for himself, which he then examined.

The flower had few petals, but each was broad and thick. When Luo touched one, a liquid flowed out, staining his fingers dark red.

Luo lifted his fingers to his nose. There was a faint floral scent, but it was nothing like the rotting smell that filled the air.

Where could the rotting smell be coming from, then?

Luo leaned over and sniffed like a bloodhound, following the direction of the odor. An instant later, his eyebrows shot up. He moved a few paces to the side, then brushed aside some weeds to reveal something white underneath.

The others gathered around, trying to get a look at what he was holding. It was a bone, and it had come from a fully intact human skeleton.

Luo lifted the bone in the rain, letting the water wash away the dirt that had been covering it. "Human bones. The victim is a man in his thirties. The time of death—at least a century ago."

Straightening his posture, Suo Tulan solemnly looked Luo in the eye. "These weren't here the last time I visited. They must date back to the time of General Li. The deceased would have been laid to rest and their bones buried. They shouldn't have been disturbed." His voice was soothing.

"The deceased," Luo repeated, shaking his head. "They can rest. But we've still got problems to solve. And there are some questions that perhaps only the dead can answer."

Then Luo paused as if he were about to say something else. He handed the bone to Professor Zhou. "Professor Zhou, why don't you have a look?" He tilted his head, thinking.

Professor Zhou turned the bone in his hands a few times, then smiled at Luo. "Chief Inspector Luo, you're no medical expert, but I'd say your assessment is quite accurate."

Luo glanced at Professor Zhou. He seemed slightly disappointed. "This bone is in a rather strange condition, don't you think?"

"Strange condition?" Puzzled, Professor Zhou took another look.

Luo pointed at the bone. "This is a scratch I made with my nail just now."

"Huh?" Professor Zhou examined the scratch. Then suddenly, he exclaimed, "The hardness! That can't be right!"

"Indeed." Luo nodded. "Back when I was in the police academy, we spent a lot of time studying human bones. Every bone has a story, and we learned how to listen."

"How to listen?" Yue Dongbei snickered. "They talk, do they?"

"All you have to do is open your eyes and your mind." Luo looked stonily at Yue Dongbei. "They'll tell you all sorts of things about the deceased, their lives, and even a few things about what's happened since they died. You can't overlook any detail. To a police officer, it can be the key to solving a case."

Yue Dongbei cowered a little, scratching his head before backing down. "Fine, then. What is this bone telling you?"

"It's much softer than it should be, which shows that there's less calcium. At first I thought the deceased must have suffered from rickets or some such disease, but then I ruled out that possibility. First of all, General Li would never have allowed someone with such a disease in his army, since he wouldn't have been much of a combatant. Furthermore, we can see from the skeleton that the deceased had a healthy set of teeth. So I drew a different conclusion, which is that the calcium depletion took place after death."

"After death?" Yue Dongbei seemed confused.

"That's right. It was depleted by the soil." Luo touched the scratch that he'd made, picking up particles of dirt on his fingers and letting the rain wash them away. "That's because the soil in this ecosystem differs from that of the surrounding area. There isn't a single tree growing here. It's a garden of the blood of ghosts."

"Oh!" Yue Dongbei slapped the side of his head. "What you're saying is that the soil here is acidic?"

"That's right." Luo looked at the field of blackish-red flowers. "That means that only acid-resistant organisms can survive on this plot of land."

Professor Zhou squatted down and gathered a handful of dirt. He examined it for a minute. "That's brilliant, Chief Inspector Luo. You figured out the properties of this soil, and you didn't even need a lab."

"And it's all because of this bone and a few inferences about the natural environment. We have to take this a step further and test it. That way, we'll have even more evidence." Luo looked around. "We should be able to find more bones somewhere around here."

"That's not going to be easy," Yue Dongbei muttered as he stepped into the field of flowers and reached under the plants. But soon enough, he made a discovery.

"Look! I found one. It's a thigh bone, isn't it?" Yue Dongbei lifted up a long bone and hooted, "There are a ton of bones here! I guess the general didn't give his soldiers a proper burial after all!"

"Here, let me have a look." Luo took the bone from Yue Dongbei and scratched it, then nodded. "Soft."

"So you're sure it's because of acid in the soil?" Yue Dongbei still seemed skeptical. "Why would just one area on this huge mountain be like this?"

Luo smiled. "You can look to the lyrics of the folk song that His Holiness just sang."

Suo Tulan seemed surprised. "The acid has something to do with the war against the demon?"

Luo shook his head. "It has nothing to do with the demon. Your ancestors witnessed a minor geothermal eruption, and they transformed it into a folk song."

Suo Tulan didn't seem to understand. But Yue Dongbei and Professor Zhou did.

"That's right! The song said there was a plume of smoke and the ground was bloodred. It really does sound like geothermal activity," Professor Zhou said. "It all makes sense."

"The 'fiery demon's river of blood' is a hot spring." Luo took his theory one step further. "Hot springs can be highly acidic, which is why this soil came to be so acidic as well."

"So that's what happened," Yue Dongbei remarked thoughtfully. "There certainly are some important clues to be found in the lyrics of folk songs. You have what it takes to be a great historian. It's a shame that you're a police officer . . ."

Luo ignored Yue Dongbei's words of praise. He was inspecting the thigh bone in his hands. "Professor Yue, didn't you raise some questions earlier?"

"Did I? What did I say?" Confused, Yue Dongbei scratched his head. He seemed fatigued from trying to keep up with Luo.

"These bones aren't on the ground because General Li didn't bury his dead, they're on the ground because someone dug them up."

Chief Bai, who hadn't said a word thus far, interjected, "How can you tell?"

Luo lifted up the bone for everyone to see. "Take a look. There's a scratch right here. It was likely made with a shovel. Of course, during the war, many of the soldiers must have been wounded. But if this injury was sustained while this person was alive, the bone would have been hard, and the injury would have fractured it. But instead, there's a deep scratch carved into the bone. It was most likely made after the bone had softened—due to having absorbed moisture from the eruption of a geyser. Can you smell the rotting odor? The lingering traces of sulfur indicate that these bones were excavated not very long ago."

"That never even occurred to me." Yue Dongbei shook his head. "So you're saying that the bones were dug up recently?"

Luo looked around again. "Not that recently, but maybe last spring, since the blood of ghosts have been in bloom and there aren't any signs of digging."

"So who dug them up? And why?" Yue Dongbei narrowed his eyes at Luo, waiting for him to answer yet another riddle.

But Luo was only human, and after a long period of contemplation, he finally shook his head. "Right now, I have no way of answering that question."

"It doesn't matter who did it. It's disrespectful to the dead and bound to cause trouble," Suo Tulan said soberly. "Luo, the person we're trying to catch isn't here, he's—"

The high priest stopped midsentence and lifted his head, a look of horror on his face. The others all turned and looked into the distance, toward the hilltop.

From there came a mournful wail.

It was a cry of despair and sorrow, of hatred and anguish. In the cold, unrelenting rain, the sound echoed through the valley, lingering for a long time before it finally died away. When they heard it, all of them felt a sharp pain in their stomachs. Di Erjia drew his blade and uttered a few words in disgust.

The muscles in Chief Bai's cheeks were twitching. His voice trembled. "It's him! He's over there!"

Near the top of the hill was a man dressed in black. Was it he who had been wailing?

Luo was stricken with fear as he recalled the stupor and hallucinations he'd felt a few days back. He couldn't make out the other man's features, but he could acutely sense that it was the same mysterious figure who'd brought him into that terrified state.

Yue Dongbei evidently felt the same way. He stood frozen in terror. "It's him. He's watching us. What does he want?" he whispered.

After a silence, Chief Bai broke into nervous laughter. But there was fear and trepidation in his voice. "He's watching his prey! To him we're like sitting ducks, just waiting for him to do as he pleases."

Standing at the hill's crest, the figure in black looked out over the entire valley as if he were at a command post. The group in the cemetery could sense his power.

Luo recovered his senses and pointed toward where the figure stood. "Your Holiness, please show us the way over there!"

Suo Tulan, who seemed to have had the same idea, said something to Di Erjia. Di Erjia gritted his teeth and brandished his machete, then led the group back into the forest.

Because the undergrowth was so dense, it was impossible to see the top of the hill. Everyone kept their eyes on Di Erjia.

It was a short distance to the hilltop, and the incline was not particularly steep, yet it was an exhausting ascent through the woods. It took them about ten minutes to reach their destination.

By then, there was nothing there to see. The figure in black had disappeared. Di Erjia refused to give up. He stormed to the edge.

Suo Tulan stepped forward, following him. "There's a cave here. Let's go have a look," he told the others.

Sure enough, about a dozen paces away they could see a ten-foot opening. The cave entrance was partially hidden behind trees and barely detectable from a distance.

"During the battle against the Qing forces, the general had this cave dug as his command center," Suo Tulan explained.

But Luo's mind was elsewhere. He grabbed Di Erjia, who was eager to head into the cave, and pointed at the vines near the entrance. The vines were tangled and appeared to have been stepped on. It was clear that someone had just gone inside.

Di Erjia cautiously slowed his pace. Luo trailed closely behind him, and the two of them adopted a defensive formation. The two Hamo warriors were about to enter the cave with the rest of the group, but Suo Tulan instructed them otherwise: "The two of you stand guard at the entrance. Don't come in."

They acknowledged his orders, then unsheathed their knives and assumed posts on either side of the entrance.

Since the cave was man-made rather than natural, the floor was level, and they could sense moisture in the soil underfoot. There was no light inside, so Luo and the others pulled out their flashlights and pointed them at the cave walls. The cave was not particularly large, and the ceiling was a little over fifteen feet high. A quick glance revealed that no one was inside.

Luo suddenly thought of something and called out to the others, "No one move!" He lowered the beam of his flashlight, pointing it at the ground in front of him. There were visible footprints.

Though the footprints were indistinct, it was clear that they belonged to a human being. Luo squatted and assessed their size. "This is a big fellow, at least six feet tall."

The cave appeared empty, so Professor Zhou and Yue Dongbei pointed their flashlights at the floor. About six feet away from them on the cave floor was a giant hole. Piles of dirt surrounded the hole, and the footsteps seemed to lead right to it. It was clear that the hole had just been dug.

Di Erjia hollered in alarm.

"What's the matter?" asked Luo, turning to Suo Tulan.

Suo Tulan was deathly pale.

"Your Holiness, please tell us, what is it?" Luo persisted.

After what felt like an eternity, Suo Tulan weakly answered, "This hole is a tomb."

The others were stricken with fear as they took a closer look at the hole. Indeed, it was clearly constructed to fit a human body.

"A tomb? Whose tomb is it?" Luo asked.

Suo Tulan smiled wryly. "All the Hamo people know that this cave contains the tomb of the demon himself, Li Dingguo."

"Li Dingguo!" Luo and the others cried out in unison.

Suo Tulan nodded. "After the high priest drew blood from Li Dingguo's body, a simple tomb for the body was built inside this cave in accordance with the curse."

"Why, there are no historical records of Li Dingguo's final resting place. I'd never imagined I'd make such an important discovery!" Yue Dongbei rubbed his hands together excitedly. A moment later, however, he looked disappointed. "So why isn't his corpse inside?"

Indeed, the hole was empty.

"Could it be that the man we saw ran off with the corpse? What could he have been thinking?" Luo asked himself, frowning.

Suo Tulan sighed deeply, then turned and headed for the exit. Di Erjia immediately followed him. Professor Zhou and Yue Dongbei, who had grown tired of the cave's dank atmosphere, exited soon after. Only Luo was left. He inspected the inside of the cave, hoping to uncover some valuable clues.

He even rummaged through the pile of excavated dirt beside the tomb. But apart from the footprints, there was nothing to be found.

When Luo emerged, his clothes covered in dirt, Suo Tulan was sitting cross-legged under a giant tree. His eyes were fixed on some point in front of him. He appeared to be meditating.

Luo approached him, then traced Suo Tulan's line of sight to a withered tree decaying amid the weeds.

"Your Holiness, what you are thinking about?" Luo cautiously whispered.

There was a sudden glint in Suo Tulan's eyes, as if he'd snapped out of his meditative state. He stood up and went over to the withered tree, from which he picked a mushroom. He handed it to Luo.

"Luo, death does not necessarily mean the end. To the contrary, it can be a fresh beginning."

Chapter 27

BETWEEN GOOD AND EVIL

"Maybe the tomb wasn't excavated!" Yue Dongbei couldn't contain his excitement. The second he had a thought, he shared it.

The group had returned to the Hamo village that afternoon. After having something to eat with Suo Tulan and the other tribesmen, Luo and the others went back to their room to get some rest.

But none of them were able to shake off that morning's events. They were all subdued until Yue Dongbei broke the silence.

"You probably think that this figure in black dug up the tomb and ran off with General Li's remains. But I have an outrageous theory, which—heh heh—I'm sure none of you will believe."

Professor Zhou glanced at him. "Go ahead. Don't keep us in suspense. You've got so many outrageous theories, what's one more? Tell us."

Yue Dongbei lowered his voice, as if to heighten the intrigue. "The disappearance of that mysterious figure in black and of General Li's remains are one and the same."

Luo knew instantly where this was heading, but he didn't let on.

Yue Dongbei bit his lip. "This might sound strange, perhaps stranger than any theories you've ever heard before—but it has a basis. See, this figure in black appeared in the last few days, and General Li's remains disappeared only recently. What's more, I can't think of anyone, apart from General Li himself, who would know the secrets behind so many mysteries—from the Rain God mechanism, the strange appearance of General Li's note, the skinning and stuffing, the pulling out of tongues, the centipedes on the rock. Then he himself appeared outside the cave. Don't you think it's strange that he seems to have been with us every step of the way? Everything that has happened since the cursed blood vial was shattered—and I say this as a scholar of metaphysics—makes it impossible for me to deny the connections. This figure in black is the reincarnation of the demon who has been burning with vengeance: Li Dingguo!"

Professor Zhou didn't give Yue Dongbei the pleasure of a strong reaction. He merely smiled. "So you're saying that General Li dug himself out of his own grave?"

Yue Dongbei responded to this mockery with a cold glare. "I'm not joking. History books from all over the world contain legends of reincarnation. Do you suppose that all these legends are pure hogwash? At the very least, I've conducted more research than you have in this field."

"That's enough," Luo said. "Did you see the footprints?"

"Footprints?" Yue Dongbei squinted. "You mean the footprints inside the cave?"

"They were footprints made with a size nine hiking boot. The lines along the sole left clear prints in the dirt. So clear, in fact, that you can see the Nike logo in the middle. Do you suppose those were the shoes General Li was wearing?" Luo smiled. "Sometimes it's better to investigate closely than to have a fertile imagination."

"Nikes? Really?" Embarrassed, Yue Dongbei rubbed his nose. "Then who was that person? He couldn't have come out of nowhere. And why did he make off with General Li's remains?"

Luo was silent. He'd thought long and hard about the question but didn't have an answer.

Then Professor Zhou spoke up. "This person's identity may be a mystery, but he's appeared before us, and he's left footprints. It's a shame he managed to escape today. I wonder where he's hiding."

Chief Bai let out a deep breath. "Let's not worry about that. Since we can't find him, he's going to find us again."

Just then, a cold draft entered their room. Luo stood up and walked over to the window. He stared off into the distance. Under the wind and pouring rain, the mountain range was covered in lush vegetation, where all kinds of plants and animals thrived in tranquility. Meanwhile, they found themselves trapped indoors, where an oppressive mood had overtaken them all.

Looking at the top of the hill, Luo thought about how all of them had seen the figure in black from the cemetery. He had been perched atop the hill looking down at them. Though he had been far away, he'd still managed to strike fear in all of them through the sheer hatred and fury in his gaze, which had rendered each and every one of them help-less and defenseless as a newborn.

Luo was acutely aware that a crisis was brewing. But how could he respond when he still didn't know who their adversary was or what he wanted?

By nightfall, the rain had eased. Luo wanted to take a walk around the village, but he realized there'd be a language barrier. He asked Chief Bai to accompany him to help translate.

The two of them left the house and strolled through the village. Many of the villagers were busily going about their daily routines, but they all seemed to recognize Chief Bai and offered polite greetings.

"Chief Bai, it appears as though you're a man of great status in the Hamo village," Luo told him.

Chief Bai laughed. "Our villages have had good relations for gen-erations. The Hamo people know that my family descended from Lieutenant General Bai."

"Right. The Hamo people must be incredibly grateful to all the Bais." Luo nodded. Then he had a sudden recollection. "Chief Bai, since you're a descendant of Lieutenant General Bai, there's a question that you might be able to answer for me."

"What is it?" Chief Bai stopped and looked at Luo.

Luo didn't mince words. "Why didn't General Li kill Lieutenant General Bai?"

Chief Bai appeared to be looking at the mountains in the distance. After a long silence, he replied, his voice trembling with emotion. "To the Hamo people, General Li is undoubtedly a demon. But in the village of Mihong, he has been a hero, even a god, for generations. Alas, what we call good and evil, success and failure, is never black and white. In fact, they are inseparable in human nature."

And, with a sad sigh, he told Luo the story of the final moments between General Li and Bai Wenxuan, the lieutenant general who had betrayed him.

The roar of battle filled the Valley of Terror as the Qing, Burmese, and Hamo fighters joined forces against their common enemy.

With all of General Li's troops defending the base, the center of camp was deserted. Only two people could be seen: Li and Lieutenant General Bai.

Gripping his longsword, the general made his way toward Lieutenant General Bai step-by-step. His armor was already soaked in blood. His eyes brimmed with rage. Though he had suffered a serious wound, he still emanated enough ferocity to make anyone cower in fear. Lieutenant General Bai's face was pale as he backed away.

"Lieutenant General Bai!" General Li bellowed. "You've betrayed me. Why not come forward to duel me?"

Lieutenant General Bai stared at the trail of blood on the ground. Gritting his teeth, he drew his sword.

General Li growled. With an astonishing force, he swung straight at Lieutenant General Bai, and there was a clank as their swords met. Lieutenant General Bai was overwhelmed by his opponent's sheer strength, which broke his grip. His fingers loosened, and the sword flew away from him, a warped piece of metal.

He suddenly found himself with General Li's cold blade at his throat. Lieutenant General Bai closed his eyes in despair, waiting for death. But the blade didn't move. Then he heard the general's hoarse voice saying, "So—why?"

Lieutenant General Bai grew weak, and he fell to his knees, wailing, "Commander!"

"Why did you do it?" General Li barked, his eyes practically bursting out of their sockets.

"Commander—" Lieutenant General Bai was bent over at his commander's feet. "My troops have been trapped in the forest for so long with no hope of ever winning. And I couldn't bear to watch the kindhearted Hamo people be wiped out in a senseless war."

General Li's sword was still pressed against Lieutenant General Bai's throat. He could have taken the other man's life in a split second. His rage was apparent in his voice. "Today is the day that we will set off the explosion by the lake. If things go as planned, this could be a turning point. I never imagined that you—that you would be the one to thwart me!"

Lieutenant General Bai lifted his head to look at the general and bravely told him, "If things go as planned, how would it help? We're less than ten thousand strong, and the Yongli Emperor has been assassinated by Wu Sangui. Commander, we don't stand a chance. Only you have the power to decide our fate."

These words seemed to touch a sore spot in General Li, who quivered. His eyes flared, and out of the corners trickled a mix of blood and tears. After a long silence, he said coldly, "I've spent my entire life soaked in blood. I've fought for the people, and I've fought alone, with no one to help me. Now, even you, Lieutenant General Bai, have turned your back on me."

Lieutenant General Bai didn't know how to answer. He only smiled sadly. "Commander, why don't you kill me?"

"Kill you?" General Li sighed deeply. "Everyone for generations to come will think of me as a murderous tyrant. But given the present circumstances, what good would it do for me to kill you? No. Go find your troops and surrender to the Qing forces."

"What?" Lieutenant General Bai's jaw dropped in disbelief.

General Li lowered his voice. "Surrender to the Qing forces and give the troops a rest. The mechanism is hidden in the village of Mihong. You can recuperate there until you see another opportunity to defend our land."

Lieutenant General Bai understood what the general was getting at. "Commander—"

General Li laughed coldly. "Would you want to become one of the most reviled figures in the Ming Dynasty?"

"If that's the case, I'd like to ask the Commander a favor."

"What is that?"

"Give me your demonic powers. It would be of great help."

General Li shook his head. "They're only geysers—natural hot springs. I have no choice but to use such nonsense to control the rank-and-file soldiers. It's not a type of power that can be shared. I've assigned soldiers to guard the Miao *gu* sorcerers. If we lose, they'll be killed. And that's a secret that should remain buried for eternity in hell."

"What?" Lieutenant General Bai was stunned.

"Lieutenant General Bai!" General Li exploded. "You've committed a grave crime! Do you know why I haven't killed you?"

Lieutenant General Bai bowed his head. "Yes, sir."

"Very well. The Rain God mechanism will be maintained by the Bai family forever, and the people will hold out against the Manchus in their hearts. You must not forget who conferred this authority upon you. If you are ever disloyal again, I will take away the basis for your authority."

"Yes, sir. That will never happen."

"Good, good." There was sadness in General Li's hoarse laughter. It stopped abruptly, and there was only silence as tears of blood ran down his cheeks.

"So General Li spared your ancestor to preserve the last vestiges of the Southern Ming in the hopes that the dynasty would one day return to power?" After hearing Chief Bai's account, Luo was filled with a new admiration. "It makes no difference if he's a hero or a demon—on his deathbed, he showed tremendous courage, and based on that, General Li was truly extraordinary."

"Hero? Demon?" repeated Chief Bai. After a silence, he laughed quietly. "Perhaps those words have never referred to two separate aspects of a person's character. All matters regarding human beings and their actions are subject to debate. Three centuries ago, if the general had prevailed, the land of the Han people would have been revitalized, and he would have been revered as a great hero by subsequent generations. It's a shame that, in the end, he had to die in the forest, and that the victors of war painted him as a demon in their history books."

"He fought for the people. It's admirable." With those words, Luo looked up at the beautiful, tranquil scenery of the village and shook his head. "But there's no doubt that flooding the Hamo village was a ruthless plan. You can't blame the Hamo people for killing what they considered a demon and cursing him for eternity."

Chief Bai sighed. "Everyone has their reasons. When you learn to see it from their perspective, lots of things start to make more sense."

Luo nodded in agreement. But something else was troubling him. "The figure in black killed your aides, but he hasn't come after you. Is that related to your ancestry? It must have made someone unhappy that General Li put your family in charge of Mihong."

Chief Bai seemed caught off guard. He looked embarrassed. "To sustain an isolated village is easier said than done. The Bai family had to refuse the support of the Qing government and be willing to lie low in Mihong for centuries. And you're right, Chief Inspector Luo; not everyone has been pleased. Have you noticed that today the village is bustling compared to yesterday?"

Chief Bai obviously wanted to change the subject, but he spoke the truth. It was dusk, but the path was crowded with people hurrying by. It was evident from the villagers' faces that they were looking forward to some kind of event.

"They're probably on their way to see the priestess," Luo guessed.

"The priestess?"

"Don't you remember what Lord An Mi said yesterday? The people haven't see their priestess in a long time, and she's making her first appearance tonight." Luo smiled. "This could be a good opportunity for us. I have some questions that I'd like to ask her."

Chief Bai was silent. He frowned and shook his head. Just then, several Hamo people passed, and Chief Bai approached them and asked in the Hamo language, "Are you going to see the priestess?"

"Yes, we are," a middle-aged woman replied respectfully. "The priestess has been ill for so long, and the village hasn't held a single ceremony. Now she's finally recovered, so tonight the entire tribe will go pay a visit. Please don't believe the awful rumors."

Luo, who had joined them, listened as Chief Bai translated for him. "What awful rumors?"

"That the priestess was murdered by the reincarnated demon," Chief Bai answered Luo's question. "There have been many Hamo people who heard the rumor and fled, passing through Mihong on their way."

"It's utter nonsense!" a Hamo man standing beside them suddenly piped up. "The demon may have reincarnated, but the priestess wasn't by any means killed."

The man, who was in his forties, looked honest and forthright.

Luo looked at him in astonishment. "You speak Mandarin?"

The man introduced himself: "My name is Meng Sha. I spent the past few months in Mengla, and I just returned to the village."

"Oh." Luo nodded. "You're one of the people who fled."

A look of shame crossed Meng Sha's face. "The gods will punish cowards like myself. I've been fortunate. The priestess rescued me."

Luo and Chief Bai exchanged a glance, unsure what he meant by "punishment" or "rescue."

But Meng Sha explained. "Those of us who fled have had trouble adjusting to life outside. The Han people living in the county seat look down on us. They don't believe in our gods, and they've never even heard of the Hamo people's holy war. Every day there was a struggle, and I couldn't earn a living. I couldn't afford a place to live, so I slept under a bridge. In the end, I fell ill. I lay on the freezing-cold riverbed with no one to help me for three days. I nearly died."

As he spoke of his hardships, Meng Sha's eyes grew red. Luo had to stifle his own emotions. He simply couldn't imagine how difficult it must have been for this tribal villager to make his way in modern society, given the stark differences in language, belief, and culture.

"What happened after that?" Chief Bai asked gently.

"The high priest found me. He cured my illness and brought me back to the village," Meng Sha answered. "But by that time I was utterly filled with despair. The demon had reincarnated, and my village was facing catastrophe. I lost the courage to go on. In fact, if the priestess hadn't appeared, I'd surely be dead right now."

"The priestess? Did she go to Mihong with Suo Tulan?" Luo was surprised. "But I thought she'd been ill for the past six months?"

Chief Bai raised an eyebrow. "Suo Tulan stayed with me in Mihong, but I didn't see the priestess."

"The priestess wasn't well enough to leave the village, but her soul came to rescue me." There was piousness in Meng Sha's voice. "When I was on the brink of death, I could detect her presence. She was stunning in her white robes and with her benevolent powers. My eyes opened wide, and I saw her walking toward me. She placed her hand on my forehead and said: 'Come with me. We'll go back to the village. Everything will be fine. The demon was defeated by the mighty A Liya and He Layi, and the spirits of the warriors will always protect the Hamo people.'"

The other Hamo people who had been standing and listening had placed their arms across their chests and were now saluting to the sky. "The spirits of the warriors will always protect the Hamo people."

"It was the priestess who saved me. After I recovered, I returned to the village. I won't leave until the demon has been defeated!" Meng Sha's eyes welled with tears as he spoke.

The priestess? Could he have been hallucinating? Luo had his own hypothesis. "When did the priestess appear? After you woke up, did you see her?"

"No." Meng Sha shook his head, smiling. "But tonight I'll see her."

"Can we all go together?" Luo asked sincerely. "I would very much like to meet your priestess."

"Of course. Our benevolent priestess helps anyone who is suffering and in need," Meng Sha replied, beaming.

"Thank you." Luo smiled and turned toward Chief Bai. "Let's go."

"You go ahead. I'll join you later," Chief Bai said quietly. "I have an old friend in the village, and I'd like to pay him a visit."

Luo nodded. Together with Meng Sha and the others, he went to the sacred grounds on the south side of the village. Chief Bai waited for them to turn the corner before he left.

Chapter 28

THE PRIESTESS REEMERGES

Soon Chief Bai had left the village and entered the forest, heading back down the path to the valley they'd taken that morning. It was dusk, and the forest was especially dark. Chief Bai stopped in front of a tree. One thick branch had blade marks on it. Chief Bai didn't go any farther. Feeling uneasy, he turned and headed back a little way. He seemed to be waiting for something, and at the same time, he seemed afraid. The forest was growing darker and quieter.

Suddenly, Chief Bai recoiled. His eyes opened wide, and he froze. A rustling came from somewhere deep in the forest.

"He's coming," Chief Bai whispered.

His eyes were fixed in the direction of the rustling. It was *him*. Emerging from the dark forest, the ghost walked toward Chief Bai, his intense hatred filling the air. The forest was dead silent, with no signs of life.

Chief Bai felt a tremendous pressure bearing down on him. Barely able to breathe, he broke into a cold sweat. He knew that his adversary was filled with a rage that compelled him to rip his victims to pieces. Chief Bai's machete was on his belt. He felt a growing feverishness.

Perhaps this was an opportunity, as his adversary would likely be caught off guard.

With that idea in mind and beads of sweat forming on his forehead, Chief Bai's right hand twitched.

"Don't try to fight me. You know very well my powers. You know even better what it would mean if you lost." The hoarse, sinister words seemed to resound from the depths of hell.

Chief Bai's heart froze. The courage he'd managed to summon waned.

He collapsed, falling to his knees on a mass of rotting leaves. His lineage had conferred the authority to rule the village of Mihong since birth. He was unaccustomed to bowing down to others. But in the cool breeze on the hills, he experienced for the first time the awareness of a higher authority, and he threw himself to the ground. And when he did so a second time, it was much easier than the first.

The figure in black slowly approached, then stopped and stood in front of Chief Bai. "The Bai family once made a vow. Do you remember?"

"Yes, I remember. I am your loyal servant. I will do anything you say, and I will make up for any wrongs I have committed in the past. I seek your forgiveness." Chief Bai pressed his head against the ground. Three centuries earlier, Lieutenant General Bai had been in this exact same position, kowtowing at General Li's feet.

"Very well. You will do as I say, and it will allay my anger." The figure in black placed his hand on Chief Bai's shoulder.

Honored by this gesture, Chief Bai sat up and lifted his head. He looked into eyes the color of blood.

"Even so, my fury is enough to swallow you in its flames," said the hoarse voice. "You cannot imagine the pain and torment of being banished to hell. Nor do you even understand the grave wrongdoings that the Bai family committed during the holy war!"

Chief Bai looked slightly puzzled, as if he didn't understand those last words.

The figure in black leaned over and whispered in Chief Bai's ear.

Chief Bai trembled as he tried to defend himself. "No, it can't be."

"I have evidence to show you," the figure in black said coldly. "But first, there are a few matters that I'd like you to take care of, and I hope you don't disappoint me."

Chief Bai nodded silently. He knew that he had no choice.

The Hamo people's sacred grounds were located on the edge of the village. The grounds were slightly larger than those of the Temple of the Dragon King in Mihong. On the east side were two square altars. They were designed so that worshippers would face the light of dawn during early morning festivities. The south side bordered the forest, and there was a hill to the southwest that stood between the village and the Valley of Terror.

By the time Luo and Meng Sha arrived, the grounds were already packed. The crowd stood in two orderly groups, with the men in front and the women in back. Meng Sha and the others promptly led Luo into the crowd of Hamo worshippers. Luo walked around slowly, surveying his surroundings and taking mental notes. Suddenly, he heard someone calling his name.

"Chief Inspector Luo, over here! Over here!"

Luo spotted Yue Dongbei standing on the west side of the grounds, waving. Four chairs were arranged in a row, and he and Professor Zhou sat next to one another.

When Luo came over, Yue Dongbei proudly told him, "Have a seat. The Hamos reserved these seats for us."

Luo nodded and took a seat next to Professor Zhou, who asked, "Where did Chief Bai go?"

"He's dropping by a friend's house. He should be here shortly."

Professor Zhou lifted an eyebrow, as if he didn't quite believe it.

Around the altar and throughout the grounds, torches were mounted on top of wood posts. As the sky darkened, two men entered the grounds from either side of the south end and lit the torches. Within an instant, the area was brightly lit.

Luo recognized the men—they were the two attendants Lord An Mi had sent to accompany them to the valley. The two other attendants were nowhere to be seen.

The attendants returned to the south end, standing guard on either side. Then Lord An Mi and Suo Tulan entered the grounds from the west end, walking toward the altar. The crowd parted to let them through.

When he reached the altar, Suo Tulan stopped and stood before the crowd. A line of men stood behind him, and they appeared to be the other Hamo priests. Lord An Mi ascended the steps to the altar. When he was halfway up the steps, he looked over at Luo and the others and saluted them. The three of them stood up and returned the greeting.

"Where is Village Chief Bai?" Lord An Mi suddenly asked, looking slightly upset.

Luo was about to answer when Chief Bai called out, "Pardon my lateness, Lord An Mi."

This ally of the Hamo people was standing next to the chairs. He was sweating profusely, as if he'd hurried over.

Lord An Mi smiled and nodded, then said nothing more. He finished climbing to the altar platform, where he faced the tribe. There was a stateliness about Lord An Mi as he stood under the glow of the torches, his head held high and his face solemn.

The tribespeople waited in the night. With all of them assembled, silence filled the air. Under Suo Tulan's lead, the priests bowed and addressed their leader in the Hamo language: "Honorable and courageous Lord An Mi."

The entire crowd followed suit: "Honorable and courageous Lord An Mi." Their voices rang out clearly and in unison, resounding in the quietude of the surrounding mountains.

When the echo had died away, Lord An Mi addressed the assembly: "A wretched thief has stolen the blood vial, and the demon has reincarnated in the valley. The Hamo people's great holy war has resumed, and we have no choice but to prevail!"

With those words, Lord An Mi drew his sword and lifted it above his head, sounding out a battle cry at the top of his lungs. Each of the men standing on the platform drew his own sword and did the same. As the thousands of people in the crowd joined in, their cry grew into a thundering roar. Luo and the others felt themselves getting swept up in the excitement.

"We are not alone," Lord An Mi thundered. "We must rebuild the alliance of the holy war three centuries past. Our allies are Chief Bai of Mihong, the Han warriors, and the priesthood!" Lord An Mi gestured toward them, and the crowd turned, erupting in cheers.

Lord An Mi signaled for them to quiet down, then looked to the back of the crowd. His expression grew sober and respectful. Everyone turned their heads, full of anticipation.

"The priestess is with us." Lord An Mi pressed his right arm against his chest, then turned to the west and bowed. From that direction, a woman in flowing white robes emerged. Amid the surrounding darkness, it was an extraordinary sight. The Hamo people immediately parted, forming a path to let her through and crying out her name: "Ya Kuma!"

Ya Kuma? Luo instantly recalled where he'd heard this name before and glanced at Professor Zhou, who had turned to him at the same time. Though they didn't exchange a word, the two of them knew what the other was thinking. Their suspicions had been right.

Sure enough, Ya Kuma was the name that the man in the Kunming hospital had been crying out. His voice had been filled with such fear, pain, despair, and anger that it was impossible to forget.

The answer was near at hand. Perhaps Ya Kuma herself knew the answer.

Ya Kuma made her way down the path that the crowd had created. Her movements were graceful and befitting a lofty figure. Her white robes flowed around her, giving her a noble and elegant air. No one in the crowd could resist staring, but her face was covered by a veil of the same white fabric that revealed only her forehead and bright eyes and contrasted with her long jet-black hair. Her onlookers were left with the sense of having entered a dreamlike dimension.

Ya Kuma was closely followed by a man wielding a machete. The man was tall and he moved assertively, his face beaming with pride. It was none other than Di Erjia, who had accompanied their group to the valley that morning.

A moment later, the two of them were on the altar platform. Ya Kuma stood next to Lord An Mi, while Di Erjia remained no more than a few steps behind her.

Ya Kuma gazed at her fellow tribespeople, then spoke. "For the past six months, I've been very ill. But in my heart I've been thinking of all of you at every moment. The blood vial has been stolen, and the demon has come back to life. But our Hamo warriors will not allow the demon to hurt me or anyone else in this tribe."

For the Hamo people, this gentle voice was familiar and soothing. They burst into celebratory cheers.

"For the past six months, Di Erjia has taken on the enormous responsibility of guarding our village against the demon." Ya Kuma gestured to the warrior behind her. "Starting today, I would like to make him the new bodyguard of the priestess. He will accompany me wherever I go."

Di Erjia stuck out his chest, tremendous pride written all over his face. He'd obtained the highest honor among Hamo warriors, such that even Lord An Mi and the high priest Suo Tulan had no authority over his actions, for he obeyed only the priestess herself. During the ceremony, only he was permitted to accompany her as she ascended the altar platform. Today, he had achieved every Hamo man's dream.

But the Hamo people did not necessarily approve of this sudden decision by the priestess. There was tittering from below, then one of the priests bowed and said, "Honored and respected priestess, Your Holiness Ya Kuma, in accordance with the traditional code of our tribe, the appointment of the bodyguard is a decision that must be made with care, as it calls for fighting skills as well as wisdom, courage, and loyalty. The appointment of Di Erjia is a rather hasty move. Though Shui Yidie has committed a grave crime, the priestess has not tried him for it. Strictly speaking, he has not yet been stripped of his title."

Before Ya Kuma had the chance to reply, Lord An Mi interjected. "Right now we are experiencing an emergency. There are matters that need to be handled immediately. Ever since Di Erjia started patrolling the valley, our tribe hasn't been harmed by the demon. I believe he is well suited to serve as the bodyguard for the priestess. As for Shui Yidie, Ya Kuma will try him for his crimes today."

After he spoke, Lord An Mi clapped twice, and from a corner along the western end, near the pond, came a line of three men.

The man in front hobbled along, dressed in rags. It was none other than Shui Yidie. His hands were tied behind his back, and shackles were on his ankles. Lord An Mi's two other attendants followed him, brandishing machetes.

The three men made their way through the crowd and headed toward the platform. When Shui Yidie passed by, his fellow tribespeople shrank away from him. It was apparent from their faces that they regarded him as a traitor whom they reviled as well as feared.

Shui Yidie struggled to keep moving. He squinted at Ya Kuma the entire time. Finally, he stopped in front of the high priest and lifted his head. His voice trembled. "Ya Kuma, are you really all right?"

"Yes." Ya Kuma's tone was impassive. "Because the gods protect me, it's not possible for evil spirits to harm me."

"But why are you wearing a veil?" Shui Yidie asked.

"The priestess has just recovered and must beware of the cold," Lord An Mi snapped. "If the Hamo people are concerned, then perhaps the priestess can remove her veil for a second."

Ya Kuma nodded. Then, with one hand, she removed the right side of her veil, revealing her beautiful face.

Shui Yidie dropped to his knees, choking back sobs. "Your Holiness! Ya Kuma—Ya Kuma!" Though tears streamed down his face, it was clear that he was crying out of happiness.

The sound of relieved sobs spread through the crowd.

But the person most affected was Luo. He leapt to his feet. "Xu Xiaowen!"

Everyone turned and stared at Luo. The priestess turned as well, and she looked at Luo with her dark eyes, surprised. Now Luo was able to see her features clearly. He was certain this was the young woman he'd met at the hospital in Kunming.

Suo Tulan stepped forward. His voice was disapproving. "Luo, this is a very important occasion for the Hamo people. Please do not interrupt the ceremony."

The priestess looked Luo up and down with no indication that she recognized him, then turned away, pulling the veil back over her face.

Luo's mind was reeling. He stood there, flabbergasted. Embarrassed, he felt someone tugging on his jacket. He looked down to see Professor Zhou staring at him, then sat back down. "Professor Zhou, did you see that?"

Professor Zhou shook his head in disbelief, then added in a low voice, "It doesn't make sense. I guess we'll see what happens."

Luo, who had regained his composure, agreed. They couldn't derail the ceremony.

Chief Bai, who was sitting next to Luo and translating for him, told him in a grave tone, "Chief Inspector Luo, the priestess is the most respected figure among the Hamo people. You must take care not to cause offense."

And Yue Dongbei, who wasn't aware of the backstory, teased Luo: "What happened, Chief Inspector Luo? Did you just lose your cool because of a woman?"

Though he felt guilty, Luo had no time for jokes. *Ah, Luo,* he told himself, *what's the matter with you today? Where's your head?*

Seeing that Luo had taken his seat again, the Hamo people asked no further questions—perhaps they didn't recognize "Xu Xiaowen" as a name and they assumed that he'd cried out at the sight of the priestess's lovely face.

A cool breeze blew as the audience turned their attention back to Shui Yidie, and they heard Ya Kuma coldly tell him: "Shui Yidie, you've committed a crime. What do you have to say for yourself?"

Shui Yidie stopped crying. He looked up at Ya Kuma. "I only wish the priestess good health. I take full responsibility for the crime I've committed."

"Very good. What you've done is evil, but you're as courageous as you've always been." Ya Kuma nodded. "Because of this, Di Erjia will carry out your punishment."

Shui Yidie was stunned. "Di Erjia?"

"That's right. He's taken your place as the bodyguard of the priestess." Lord An Mi turned, revealing Di Erjia, who stared straight at Shui Yidie.

Di Erjia took his cue. He stepped down from the platform and walked toward Shui Yidie, his eyes glittering. A sadistic smile was on his face.

There was grief in Shui Yidie's eyes. "Your Holiness, you haven't forsaken me, have you? To me, that would be a fate worse than death."

But Di Erjia had already reached Shui Yidie's side. Shui Yidie looked up at his successor. The piousness and sorrow that had been on his face a second earlier were now gone, replaced by hatred and disgust.

Di Erjia was evidently upset at this response. He leaned over and snarled, "You don't scare me. Do you still think you're the priestess's favorite? You're not. Your glory days are far behind you. Didn't you say something about death? Well, it just so happens that we're looking forward to yours."

Di Erjia reached into his belt and turned to the audience. "Shui Yidie was the priestess's bodyguard, but he helped the enemy steal the tribe's sacred object. His crime is unforgivable. According to our tribe's code, he must die. The priestess has taken mercy on him and given him the opportunity to commit suicide in order to cleanse himself of his wrongdoings."

The Hamo people began whispering among themselves, and a buzz spread through the crowd. But no one objected. Chief Bai translated for Luo, who stared back at him. "They're going to take this man's life, just like that?"

Chief Bai waved dismissively. "In these remote mountain villages, tribal rules are much more powerful than the law. Chief Inspector Luo, please don't interfere."

Luo let out a deep breath. He felt uneasy, but there was nothing he could do.

Di Erjia removed from his belt several round berries and held them out. "Shui Yidie, why don't you do as you're told and eat these?"

"What are those?" Luo asked.

"They're poisonous berries," Chief Bai explained. "The Hamos used to use them to sedate wild elephants."

"Since he has to kill himself, why not give him a sword so he can make it quick? Why does it have to be so complicated?" laughed Yue Dongbei.

"Shui Yidie is said to be the most fearsome bodyguard in three centuries. Giving Shui Yidie a sword is like giving a tiger fangs." Chief Bai seemed awestruck.

Yue Dongbei snickered, unimpressed. "Why? What would happen?"

When Shui Yidie saw what was in Di Erjia's hand, he was shocked. He looked up at Ya Kuma on the platform. "Your Holiness, can this be your true intention? You wish for your loyal Shui Yidie to die?"

Ya Kuma was silent. Then she nodded. "Yes. That is my intention."

Lord An Mi hissed at Shui Yidie. "What's the matter, are you afraid to die?"

Shui Yidie smiled. "I will forever be the most loyal servant that the priestess has ever known. If it is the priestess's wish that I die, then it would be the greatest honor for me."

The priestess seemed moved by his response. There was hesitation in her eyes. She turned and looked at Lord An Mi, who said to her, "Your Holiness, please consider what is best for the tribe."

Ya Kuma nodded, then looked back at Shui Yidie kneeling below. "Eat the berries. Cleanse your soul of your wrongdoings!"

A strange look crossed Shui Yidie's face. "Now?"

"Yes, now!"

"Your Holiness, you can take everything, including my life. But—" Shui Yidie hesitated. "Aren't you forgetting something?"

"What?" Ya Kuma was surprised. "You can leave knowing that Lord An Mi and I will look after your family."

"No! No!" Shui Yidie cried out. Still on his knees, he edged forward, staring at Ya Kuma in horror. "Your Holiness, what is the meaning of this?" he asked anxiously. "Have you forgotten that you've been entrusted with the burden of tradition?"

"Burden of tradition?" Ya Kuma seemed puzzled. She looked at Lord An Mi helplessly.

"That's enough!" snapped Lord An Mi. "There'll be no more of this nonsense from you. Are you going to eat them, or are we going to force-feed you?"

Shui Yidie looked up at Ya Kuma. The expression on his face gradually changed, and finally, he appeared resolved. He nodded slowly. "Fine. I'll eat them." His voice was emotionless.

Gloating, Di Erjia extended his hand toward Shui Yidie's mouth. The bright-red berries had an ominous glow under the light of the torches.

Shui Yidie chewed slowly. Soon after, his face twitched, and he began to writhe in pain. After twisting from side to side for a spell, he fell to the ground with a thud and didn't move. A red fluid ran out of his mouth. It was unclear whether it was blood or juice from the berries.

Di Erjia, who seemed relieved, let out a deep breath. He leaned over to make sure that Shui Yidie was no longer breathing.

At that very moment, Shui Yidie lunged at him. He had somehow managed to free his hands and, within a split second, he had taken hold of Di Erjia's sword.

Lord An Mi's reflexes were quick, and he barked, "Kill him!"

The two attendants drew their swords and attacked Shui Yidie, who rolled away from the gleaming metal. With a flash of the sword, he sliced the shackles from his ankles.

Shui Yidie spat out the berries and turned around, sword drawn, eyes sparkling. The convict who had accepted his execution just seconds earlier was now a formidable opponent.

The Hamo people surrounding him were frightened.

Lord An Mi gritted his teeth and shouted angrily, "Don't panic! Surround him!"

Under the instructions of High Priest Suo Tulan, men stepped forward from the crowd and formed a circle around Shui Yidie. As they had come to see the priestess, none of them had brought their swords. Shui Yidie was renowned for his fighting prowess, and no one dared to attack him.

Lord An Mi called his attendants, and the four of them bore down on Shui Yidie from all four directions. Being the chief's personal attendants, they, too, were quick-footed as well as skilled at sword fighting. Yet they proved no match for their opponent.

The attendant to the south charged first. He suffered a wound to the leg, and blood began to flow. He gasped in pain and tumbled back into the crowd.

Di Erjia stepped forward and took the fallen attendant's sword, then entered the circle. Shui Yidie stared him down, his eyes burning with rage. With the flick of his hand, Shui Yidie gestured for the remaining attendants to stand back. Then, brandishing his weapon, he unleashed his attack on Di Erjia.

Di Erjia was unable to dodge and only just managed to block the charge with his own sword. But his opponent overpowered him, and he felt his hand shaking as the sword slipped out of his grip and flew through the air toward Lord An Mi.

"Lord An Mi, look out!" someone screamed.

The Hamo leader was unflustered. As the sword sailed toward him, he reached into his belt and drew his own blade, deflecting the thrown sword and sending it back toward Shui Yidie, who was forced to jump back, distracting him from Di Erjia.

Di Erjia, in a panicked attempt to retreat, took a step back and stumbled on the fallen attendant, tumbling to the ground in a pitiful heap. A look of deep humiliation crossed his face. "Lord An Mi, thank you for saving my life."

The top clansman grunted in acknowledgment and stepped down from the platform. He looked at the other attendants. "Step back." The attendants bowed, then retreated. Only Lord An Mi and Shui Yidie remained in the circle.

Shui Yidie beckoned him with a wave of the hand. "Honored and respected Lord An Mi."

Lord An Mi glared at him. "If you still consider me to be the leader of this tribe, then put down your sword!"

Shui Yidie gnashed his teeth. "Please forgive me. I cannot obey your wishes."

Lord An Mi cackled. "Very well, very well."

The crowd dispersed as the swords clashed and the two fiercest Hamo warriors battled one another.

But this was no fair fight. Shui Yidie seemed to be impaired by deference to his superior and remained on the defensive, while Lord An Mi grew more fearless with every blow he delivered. Soon overwhelmed, Shui Yidie was weakening.

Watching the battle from a close distance, Luo silently shook his head. At this rate, Shui Yidie was going to meet a bloody end.

Shui Yidie had the same realization. There was a flash in his eyes, and at the precise second when Lord An Mi's defenses were down, he suddenly launched a vicious strike. Lord An Mi, who'd been caught off guard, immediately stepped back. He was shaken.

But Shui Yidie did not go for the kill. Instead, he leapt onto the altar platform, where the only person remaining was Ya Kuma. Shui Yidie walked directly up to her and lifted his sword to her throat.

Moments before, this same man had been weeping and expressing his willingness to die for the priestess. Now, contrary to all expectations, Shui Yidie had turned that gesture of respect on its head. Everyone was in utter shock.

Alarmed, Luo unconsciously reached for his gun.

Chief Bai quickly placed his hand on Luo's wrist. "Careful! You mustn't risk harming the priestess!"

Luo tightly gripped his gun and watched anxiously.

After a silence, they heard Suo Tulan's hoarse voice. "Shui Yidie, what is the meaning of this? Have you gone mad?"

"I have no intention of harming the priestess. I simply wanted to escort her as she left the premises," Shui Yidie replied, pushing the priestess toward the altar.

Ya Kuma's face was pale. She'd gone from being the object of worship to a frightened, helpless captive.

Lord An Mi gripped his sword. His eyes burned with rage. But there was little he could do besides watch the two of them head toward the crowd gathered at the south end.

"Excuse us." Shui Yidie spoke quietly, but the people fled as if it were a threat.

Ya Kuma, who had collected herself, looked him in the eye. "Shui Yidie, what you have done today is an act of betrayal to the entire tribe. You will never be forgiven."

Shui Yidie laughed darkly. Then, with the flick of his blade, he cut off his left index finger. Blood flowed everywhere.

Ya Kuma was stunned. "What—what are you doing?"

Shui Yidie, who withstood the tremendous pain, looked out at his fellow tribespeople and shouted, "I, Shui Yidie, have defied my superiors, a crime for which I must die a thousand deaths. But today is not the day. When my duty is complete, only then will I return and receive my punishment. Until then, I will leave this finger as a token of my vow. Let the high priest put my blood in a vial and place a curse on me!"

With those words, he charged toward the hills to the south. An instant later, he had disappeared into the dark forest.

Chapter 29

A Familiar Face

The priestess's first appearance since her illness had been expected to be a joyous occasion, but the scene at the sacred grounds had unfolded quite differently. The fiercest and most loyal warrior in the tribe had confronted Lord An Mi and Ya Kuma with sword in hand, then successfully escaped into the forest. This not only dealt a serious blow to the dignity of the chief and the priestess, but also filled every single member of the tribe with terror.

It was unclear whether the rising wind had dimmed the torches or if they had simply run out of fuel. The flames flickered for a while before they disappeared into the darkness.

"Lord An Mi, should we follow him?" The attendants stared in the direction that Shui Yidie had gone.

Lord An Mi was livid. "There's no chance of catching up to him. And given what just happened, why should I expect anything from you?"

The attendants hung their heads in shame.

Then Ya Kuma returned to the altar with Di Erjia, who was supporting her as she walked.

Lord An Mi came forward to greet her. "Your Holiness, aren't hurt, are you?"

Ya Kuma shook her head. "I'm fine."

Though she tried to pretend as if nothing had happened, Luo could tell that she was still shaken.

Lord An Mi seemed relieved. He turned to Di Erjia. "See to it that the priestess gets home safely."

Di Erjia acknowledged the chief's orders. Then he heard Luo calling out to them.

"Please wait!"

Ya Kuma stopped and turned to Luo, gazing at him impassively.

Lord An Mi raised an eyebrow. "Luo, what can we do for you?"

"I just want to have a few words with the priestess. Perhaps ask a few questions." Luo approached them. His eyes were fixed on Ya Kuma.

"I'm sorry. I'm very tired. I must go," Ya Kuma replied in fluent Mandarin, returning Luo's gaze.

"Luo, your behavior this evening was highly inappropriate." Lord An Mi blocked Luo's path. His voice was forbidding. "It's time for you to leave!"

With an apologetic look on his face, Luo watched as Ya Kuma headed back to the village. Then he had an idea.

"It's been a long day. Why doesn't everyone go home? All of us will be with the priestess in spirit, and the gods will be with us in spirit," Lord An Mi told the tribe. Then he looked at Suo Tulan. "Your Holiness, we have some matters to discuss."

Suo Tulan bowed, then left with Lord An Mi and his attendants. The other tribespeople waited until their chief was far in the distance before they left, talking among themselves in tight bunches.

"Professor Zhou, do you remember Xu Xiaowen?" Luo asked Professor Zhou.

"Vaguely." Professor Zhou paused. "There is something deeply puzzling about this situation."

"Xu Xiaowen? What are you talking about?" asked Yue Dongbei, turning his head. "Tell me what's going on. Tell me everything. There are no secrets between us!"

Luo signaled to Professor Zhou. "Why don't you explain to him?" Then he darted into the crowd of Hamo villagers, hurrying to catch up to the middle-aged man he'd spoken to earlier.

Meng Sha saw Luo coming toward him and stopped. "Luo, how are you?"

Luo didn't have time for niceties and promptly asked the question on his mind: "Did you get a good look at the priestess's face just now, when she lifted her veil?"

"Yes, I did! Her Holiness was the one who saved me when I was on my deathbed!"

"Are you sure she was the priestess? Are you sure she's the same priestess you saw before?"

"Of course!" Meng Sha replied instantly. "Everyone in our tribe has known her since the day that she became the priestess. We all remember Her Holiness's face."

"She hasn't ever left the village, has she?" Luo continued. "She never left for a long time?"

"How would that be possible?" Meng Sha stared at Luo as if he didn't understand. "The priestess always stays with the tribe. When she wasn't ill, we always saw her in the village, sharing in our joys and sorrows."

"Is that so? All right—all right." Luo fell silent. Then something else occurred to him. "There's a cave near the Valley of Terror that's home to General Li's tomb. Do most people know about that?"

"Everyone knows," Meng Sha answered. There was suddenly a strange look on his face. He pulled Luo closer and in a low voice told him: "But about six months ago, the tomb was discovered to be empty."

"Six months ago?" Luo looked at him, astonished. That morning, it had been clear that the tomb had been excavated recently, not six months earlier.

Seeing that Luo was speechless, Meng Sha added earnestly, "Some people hunt in the valley and take shelter in the cave when it rains. Something strange happened: When the tomb was dug up, there were no remains inside. When Lord An Mi learned of this, he prohibited members of the tribe from entering the cave. A few days later, when the demon caused the priestess and some of our tribespeople to fall ill, word went around that the sacred object was missing. It was because of this that I and others fled the village."

Luo lifted his eyebrows in wonder. Could it be that the tomb was excavated more than once? But if so, why?

"I'd like to pay a visit to the priestess, but I don't know where she is." He looked at Meng Sha.

Meng Sha smiled. "Come with me. I'll take you to where she lives."

Luo followed Meng Sha through the village until they reached the pond. Where the village backed up into a steep mountain slope was a path leading to a small wooden house. The lights were still on inside.

"Since it's late, I'm not sure if the priestess will see you." Meng Sha pointed at the house.

"What a great location—all this peace and quiet to yourself," Luo sighed.

"With mountains on one side, water on the other, and a bodyguard in the front room, this is the safest location in the entire village," Meng Sha told him proudly.

Another question sprang into Luo's mind. "During the six months that the priestess was ill, did anyone come to see her?"

Meng Sha shook his head. "Ordinary tribespeople weren't allowed to. Only Lord An Mi and His Holiness Suo Tulan were allowed here to take care of her."

"Oh, I see." Luo didn't say anything more. He and Meng Sha parted ways, and Luo proceeded alone to the small house.

Di Erjia stood at the front door holding a torch. It was his first day in the role of the priestess's bodyguard. He'd been waiting for this day a long time, and now he'd finally realized his dream.

But it hadn't gone smoothly. A prisoner whose hands and feet were bound had managed to take his sword, wound one of the attendants, and hold the sword to the priestess's throat. This was a source of great shame for the priestess's bodyguard.

Di Erjia silently cursed Shui Yidie. He'd pay for these deeds someday.

There was no denying that Shui Yidie was a fearsome opponent. A year earlier, when all the warriors had been vying for the role of bodyguard, Di Erjia had learned firsthand just how ferocious Shui Yidie was. The trials had left Di Erjia disheartened, and he had nearly abandoned all hopes of ever achieving his dream.

In fact, he'd packed his bags and traveled to Mihong, ashamed to face his village after losing to Shui Yidie. But then something happened that changed his destiny.

"Di Erjia, you're a warrior, and warriors always keep their chins up!" Those words had come from the village chief of Mihong, Chief Bai.

Di Erjia remembered how dejected he'd been, saying, "No, I don't think there's any hope for me. Shui Yidie is the fiercest warrior my people have seen in a century. I can't best him. Plus, the priestess likes him."

"Must you defeat him by sheer strength alone? We need a plan, and that will take time. The heavens look fondly on those who persevere and can bestow great fortune beyond your wildest imagination." There was a sinister flicker in Chief Bai's eyes. "Right now, your good luck has just begun. We are your friends, and we support you."

Standing behind Chief Bai were his fierce attendants: Xue Mingfei, Wu Qun, and Zhao Liwen.

That day, Di Erjia had decided to continue down the path to his dream.

The sound of light footsteps interrupted Di Erjia's recollections. His eyes widened in alarm as he saw Luo walking toward him. Who was this person, anyway? His gaze was penetrating, almost as if he could read minds. Was he an enemy? Hadn't he come with Chief Bai? Could it be that something had happened?

As Di Erjia's imagination ran wild, Luo came up to him. Though he wasn't eager to speak to this man face-to-face, Di Erjia collected himself and stuck out his chest. "Halt. What is your business here?"

Luo frowned, recalling that the priestess's bodyguard didn't speak Mandarin. As he floundered, the door of the wooden house creaked open. Ya Kuma slowly made her way outside and spoke to Di Erjia, who immediately retreated.

"Chief Inspector Luo, please come inside so we can speak." Ya Kuma looked at Luo, her eyes glimmering. In flawless Mandarin, she told him, "I knew you were coming. I've been waiting for you."

Luo felt a surge of relief but didn't let it show. He followed Ya Kuma into the house.

The small house had few furnishings aside from a wooden table, chairs, and a cupboard. The window facing the pond was open, and on the windowsill was a pot of white flowers. Luo couldn't recall the name of the flowers, but their breathtaking scent was carried into the room by the breeze, and it made the desolate mountainside seem more hospitable.

An oil lamp burned on the table. The priestess adjusted it so that it was bright, then gestured toward a chair. "Chief Inspector Luo, please have a seat."

Luo surveyed his surroundings. He noticed that there was a bed close by, and that some sort of powder had been sprinkled around it.

"It doesn't look like you've moved in yet," he remarked.

"Oh?" The priestess raised an eyebrow, then sat down across from Luo.

Luo pointed at the powder. "Is that sulfur? I thought mountain people like the Hamos don't use such things, since the insects that crawl into bed aren't usually harmful."

"You're right, but it puts my mind at ease. It's not terribly pleasant to have insects crawling across my face when I sleep."

Luo turned his gaze to the woman sitting before him. After a brief silence, he asked, "What should I call you? Xu Xiaowen? Ya Kuma? Your Holiness?"

"I'm Xu Xiaowen," the priestess replied. "We met in Kunming. Ya Kuma is my twin sister."

"Your sister?" Luo lowered his head, trying to understand. "So you're posing as her? Where is she?"

There was grief in Xu Xiaowen's eyes. "She died six months ago."

That had been precisely Luo's guess. "How did she die?"

"I don't know the particulars." Xu Xiaowen smiled sadly. "You probably think I know all kinds of secrets, but in reality, I know about as much as you do. My guess is that you came here hoping that I could provide the answers to some mysteries. I didn't expect you to come all the way to the mountainside. Thank God someone is here to help me."

Luo was perplexed by Xu Xiaowen's words. He stared into her eyes. "I need you to tell me everything you know. Can you do that?"

"At the ceremony just now, I pretended I didn't recognize you so that the tribespeople wouldn't realize who I am. I'm not hiding anything from you." Now speaking frankly, Xu Xiaowen looked at Luo. "But that's really all I can tell you. I've been here for less than a week, and before that, I spent more than ten years living outside of this village."

"What?" If she'd been away for more than ten years, she was practically an outsider. Luo hadn't expected this. "During the time that you were away, did you keep in touch with the tribe?"

"His Holiness Suo Tulan checked in on me every few years. You might say that I'm an unlucky child. My mother died giving birth to us. When I was three, my father became sick and died, leaving me and my sister orphans."

Luo didn't say anything, but the look in his eyes conveyed sympathy and concern.

Xu Xiaowen smiled gratefully before continuing with her story. "The previous priestess took us in. She was a kind and loving woman, and she raised us as if we were her own children. When we were six, she decided that she would choose one of us as her successor."

"Do you regret that it wasn't you?" Luo spread his hands.

"Regret it? No, that's not the case at all. You don't understand—" Xu Xiaowen's expression was grave. "My sister suffered enormous hardships."

"Hardships?" Luo didn't understand. After all, the priestess was worshipped by the entire tribe.

"That's right." Xu Xiaowen gazed out the window, her mind seeming to drift. "Even to this day, I still remember how things were. One night, in this house, the priestess called us to her side."

Luo listened intently as she reminisced. The tranquility around them made it easy to imagine the events that had taken place ten years earlier.

The priestess had already grown old, and the hair at her temples was white. Standing before her were two innocent and adorable six-year-old girls, their eyes twinkling. It was obvious that they didn't know the fate ahead of them.

"Girls, now is the time for you to make a choice." The priestess's eyes conveyed both warmth and helplessness. "I want to raise one of you to become the next priestess. Who will it be?"

Neither answered. They both stared at her, wide-eyed.

The priestess sighed. "You must think deeply about this. The one who is chosen will experience great hardships for the rest of her life, but it's up to her to carry on tradition."

The girls didn't understand this, either, but the sober look on the priestess's face made it clear that being chosen was not a good thing.

"I'll do it. I'm older," Ya Kuma earnestly said. Though she was born only a few minutes before her sister, she knew that older siblings had to take care of younger ones.

The priestess smiled gratefully. She stroked Ya Kuma's hair. "Good girl." Then she looked over at the younger sister. "I'll do everything to give you the best life I can, to make up for your sister sacrificing herself for the sake of the tribe. You won't be able to come back to this village, but I hope that you'll never forget your sister."

Little Xu Xiaowen gazed at the priestess, then at Ya Kuma. Though she didn't understand, she nodded.

"So that's when you left the village?" Luo guessed.

"That's right. His Holiness took me to Kunming." Xu Xiaowen finally looked away from the window. "There was a scholar who specialized in the tribal languages of Yunnan, and he was a friend of the Hamo people. The high priest entrusted me to this scholar, and I was raised by his family. My adoptive parents were kind to me. I received a good education and went to college. I had a good life. As I grew older, I started to understand that my sister had suffered in my stead. I thought about the village all the time, and I missed the priestess and my sister. But whenever the high priest came to see me, he always had a message from the priestess: Don't come back. It was clear that her life was hard. That was until two weeks ago, when everything changed."

"Two weeks ago? After we came to Kunming?"

Xu Xiaowen nodded. "That's right. Three days after you left, the high priest came to see me. He seemed very sad, and he told me something had happened and that I had to come immediately."

"Did he give you any details?"

"He said that the sacred object had been stolen, that the demon had broken free and was wreaking havoc in the village, and that Ya Kuma had been killed." Xu Xiaowen paused. "But that's not even the worst part. The foundations of their society have been shaken, and the villagers are so afraid that they're fleeing."

Luo sighed. "So Suo Tulan said you had to return and take your sister's place so that the people would have the courage to fight the demon?"

Xu Xiaowen was quiet. "Does any of this make sense to you? I'm an educated person. How am I supposed to believe that this is the work of a demon?"

Luo didn't know how to answer. He looked at her curiously as she continued.

"Of course I don't believe it. But I came back because the tribe needed me. I've already lost my sister. Why else am I helping the tribe? Though I don't know what the demon really is, I know that the Hamo warriors are brave and their spirits won't be broken, and that they'll triumph over the enemy."

Xu Xiaowen was filled with conviction as she spoke, and there was admiration in her eyes. At first Luo was moved, but then he thought of a question: "You were very young when you left the village. What do you know about the demon?"

"Before this, almost nothing. When I was a child, the priestess never told us about the holy war or the demon. I only know about these things now because the high priest told me!"

It was just as Luo had expected.

She continued, "In fact, when the mental patient in Kunming started talking about the Valley of Terror and the demon, I had no idea what he was talking about."

"But he cried out Ya Kuma's name," Luo said. "Didn't you think that was strange?"

Xu Xiaowen shook her head. "I only knew my sister's nickname. We were so young when we were separated that we never even heard each other's full name!"

"And how long have you been back in the village?"

Xu Xiaowen reflected for a second, then replied, "I think today is the eighth day. These past few days, the high priest has been teaching me the rites that the priestess conducts so that when I meet with the tribespeople in the evening, they don't realize I'm not her."

"You really don't seem like the same person as the student I met in Kunming," Luo told her, smiling. "Wait, did you put on the veil because you weren't confident you could pull it off?"

Xu Xiaowen laughed. Luo had guessed right.

But the light mood didn't last long, as Luo asked a question that disrupted it: "Why did you want to kill Shui Yidie?"

Xu Xiaowen smiled. "That wasn't my decision to make. I'd never even seen this person before in my life. Lord An Mi and His Holiness Suo Tulan told me what to do. They said that Shui Yidie and a man from the Han tribe conspired to steal the sacred object, which allowed the demon to reincarnate. My sister went to the Valley of Terror to recover the sacred object, and that's when the demon killed her."

"The Han man who stole the vial was that same patient in Kunming," Luo explained.

"Really?" Xu Xiaowen's eyes widened. "No wonder he kept saying things about the demon. What was he trying to do?"

"That's the biggest question we have right now." Luo tapped lightly on the table, then said quietly, "That man has succumbed to the disease, and Ya Kuma is dead, which means that the only person who can explain what happened is Shui Yidie. It's a good thing you didn't kill him."

Xu Xiaowen looked ashamed. "I know. It was a rash decision. I blamed him for my sister's death, so I wanted revenge. But now I feel differently."

"Why is that?" Luo's gaze softened.

"When I was on the altar platform looking at him, I couldn't get past the look in his eyes. He seemed so concerned and so loyal. I'm positive that it wasn't an act."

"But then he lifted his sword to your throat."

Xu Xiaowen's answer was unwavering. "That's because he knew that I wasn't really Ya Kuma."

Luo thought about it for a second, then nodded. "Right. When he said that you were entrusted with the burden of tradition, your response was all wrong. I'd be willing to bet that you're right, and if that's the case, it's unlikely that Shui Yidie is guilty of betraying Ya Kuma and causing her death."

Xu Xiaowen looked expectantly at Luo. "Please help us get to the bottom of this mystery. I know you can do it. I know I can count on you."

Luo was startled and moved by the look in her eyes. Though this was only the second time that they had met, she seemed to understand him.

"Why?" Luo couldn't help asking. "To your tribe, I'm an outsider. We've barely spoken. Why would you trust me?"

There was a smug expression on Xu Xiaowen's face. For a brief instant, she seemed like a young university student again. "Growing up with the priestess and then as an outsider in Kunming, I learned a lot about reading people. From the moment I met you, I could tell that, though you're reserved, you're a good person inside, and you're skilled at helping people uncover the secrets behind long-hidden mysteries."

Luo blushed, then changed the subject. "The key now is to find Shui Yidie."

"We'll need the help of Lord An Mi in order to track him down." Xu Xiaowen's face was now solemn. "Are you aware that the chief and the others are intent on putting Shui Yidie to death? They're convinced that he betrayed the tribe, and if he is allowed to live, my identity will be exposed."

Luo stroked his chin. He pondered for a minute. When he finally lifted his head, there was a calm confidence in his eyes. "It might not be that difficult to find him, but"—Luo looked at Xu Xiaowen—"can you write in the Hamo language?"

"Yes."

"Great!" Luo clapped. "I need you to write a note pardoning Shui Yidie."

"A note pardoning Shui Yidie." Xu Xiaowen sounded hesitant. "Do I have the authority to do that?"

"Of course you do!" Luo was brimming with confidence. "Don't forget: You're not Xu Xiaowen, you're the honored and respected priestess, Ya Kuma."

Chapter 30

ENTERING PRISON

It was already late, and the forest was pitch black. The far-off howls of night creatures made the atmosphere sinister.

Luo walked alone down the winding path through the valley. He'd brought a flashlight, but the unfamiliar, dense forest made for a difficult journey. Luo remained on high alert, knowing that the deadly figure in black could be anywhere. Though he felt cold, perspiration was beginning to seep through his jacket.

The goal of his journey was to find the man who'd fled, Shui Yidie. Given that this man was a fugitive, Luo tried to move as stealthily as possible, not wanting to frighten him off.

After making his way over a particularly treacherous pass, Luo finally arrived at his destination: General Li's tomb. He paused at the entrance to catch his breath, then cautiously entered the cave.

Inside, it was dark and silent. The air was filled with the aura of death. More than three hundred years earlier, Li Dingguo, the man whom the Hamo people called a demon, had been buried here. But a curse had apparently left his soul unable to rest.

Luo pointed his flashlight at the ground and found a new set of footprints in the dirt near the grave. These footprints were slightly smaller than those made by the Nikes. The pattern along the soles was visible, and it matched the shoes typically worn by Hamo warriors.

Luo felt a stab of hope: Shui Yidie must have been here. His guess had been correct.

But he was still befuddled about the cave itself. Why did the pile of dirt appear to have been freshly dug? The first time he'd come out to the Valley of Terror, there hadn't been a moment when the group had separated except when they entered the cave and Suo Tulan told the chief's attendants to wait outside. Could it be that there were secrets regarding the cave itself? Suo Tulan and Di Erjia had entered. But perhaps the secrets had been concealed from Lord An Mi's attendants.

What were they?

For one, there was the secret of Xu Xiaowen pretending to be Ya Kuma. What did it mean, then, that Di Erjia had suddenly been chosen as her new bodyguard?

Standing there in the dank cave, Luo reviewed what he knew: Six months earlier, the blood vial was stolen and General Li's tomb was dug up. Ya Kuma went to the valley to find the blood vial, but she met a tragic fate at the hands of the reincarnated demon. Lord An Mi and Suo Tulan covered up her death, so her corpse hadn't been returned to the village and laid to rest. In all likelihood, it had been buried in a safe place where no one would discover it and realize what had happened.

So there was one probable conclusion: Six months earlier, the corpse buried inside the cave wasn't General Li, but Ya Kuma. This secret was known only by Lord An Mi, Suo Tulan, and Di Erjia. That was why Suo Tulan and Di Erjia had been so alarmed when they discovered that the tomb was empty.

Furthermore, Luo had to consider the possibility that, if Ya Kuma had been buried in the cave, she may have died there as well. If that was so, something highly out of the ordinary had happened.

Next, Luo considered Shui Yidie's perspective. After discovering that the priestess was an impostor, his first instinct must have been to search for the real Ya Kuma. And these new footprints served as evidence that Shui Yidie had indeed come here. Luo knelt down and touched the dirt forming one footprint with his finger. It was cool and moist, suggesting that whoever entered the cave had left wet footprints not long before.

Luo felt his heart pounding: That meant he couldn't be far off. He was hiding in the wilderness, somewhere in the dark night, and it would be impossible to find him. There was only one solution: to make Shui Yidie come to the cave.

Luo stood up and walked outside, where a ledge protruded from the cliff. Centuries ago, General Li had stood in this same spot and commanded his troops in countless battles. No one would have imagined that, hundreds of years later, it would serve as the scene of yet another tragedy.

Facing the vast mountain range, Luo took a deep breath, then shouted at the top of his lungs: "Ya Kuma!"

The cry shattered the silence, echoing through the valley for a long time. If anyone was hiding nearby, the sound surely would reach them. Luo took a few steps forward to the very edge and turned on his flashlight, setting it on the ground pointing up to illuminate himself. In that world of darkness, it was the most effective way to attract attention.

Luo spread his arms wide. He wanted the entire valley to look up at him, this lone human being standing defenseless on the cliff's edge. He wanted anyone who came forward to know that he wasn't going to hurt them.

Then he heard the sound of light footsteps. Luo kicked the flashlight so it pointed in that direction, and the beam revealed none other than Shui Yidie, who gripped his machete in a defensive posture as he walked toward Luo. There was a look of surprise and confusion on his face.

He walked closer and closer to Luo, until finally, the two men could see each other's faces. "Luo." Shui Yidie sounded stunned.

Luo smiled and nodded. He placed his hands on his head to show that he had no intention of harm.

Shui Yidie stopped about three paces away. He held the machete in front of his chest. "What are you doing here?"

Luo didn't understand the Hamo language, but he could guess what the other man was saying. He repeated the priestess's name gently: "Ya Kuma."

Shui Yidie stared at Luo. His eyes were full of curiosity.

Luo slowly lifted his hand. In it was the pardon note that Xu Xiaowen had written in the Hamo language back at the wooden house.

Shui Yidie took the letter in his hands. He noticed Luo moving and, in a split second, the machete was at Luo's throat. Luo pointed at the flashlight and waited for the other man's suspicion to ease, then leaned over and picked up the flashlight, which he aimed at the note.

Shui Yidie held the letter with his left hand and the machete with his right, keeping it near Luo's neck. Using the light that Luo had offered, he began reading the letter.

"Shui Yidie: The priestess Ya Kuma has died. I am her twin sister, the new priestess. There are many things I want to ask you about the truth behind Ya Kuma's death and the demon's rampage. Earlier, I harbored suspicions toward you, but after tonight's ceremony, I see that you are loyal and courageous. I want to ask you to return and help me and to resume your rightful position as the priestess's bodyguard. I promise that you will be safe. Luo is my friend. He will bring you to me."

Shui Yidie began to tremble. Tears streamed from his eyes. "Her Holiness—Ya Kuma—she's really dead?"

Luo extended a hand and rested it on Shui Yidie's shoulder. Shui Yidie lifted his chin and looked at Luo. Though Luo did not speak, the look in his eyes expressed several complex emotions: condolences, trust, and a courage that hinted at a common enemy.

This man was strange, thought Shui Yidie. His eyes had a mysterious quality, as if he could communicate with the hearts and souls of others. Shui Yidie slowly lowered his machete.

The two men stared at one another. Then, Luo spoke in the Hamo language: "We need your help."

Luo had just learned this phrase from Xu Xiaowen. He said it slowly, and his pronunciation wasn't accurate, but his voice conveyed a disarming sincerity. Shui Yidie was moved by the gesture. He nodded at Luo.

Returning the greeting, Luo nodded back at him. Then he began walking north, back toward the village. Shui Yidie followed closely behind him. The Hamo warrior who had just escaped death had put his life in the hands of an outsider whom he hardly knew. This decision would play a key role in the reversal of fortune that had just been set in motion.

By the time the two men descended the mountain and returned to the village, it was the middle of the night. They did not anticipate the scene that awaited them at the village entrance.

Dozens of torches burned. Lord An Mi, Suo Tulan, Professor Zhou, Yue Dongbei, Chief Bai, and Xu Xiaowen all stood along the path to the village as if waiting for something. Behind them was a large group of Hamo warriors.

Seeing this from a distance, Shui Yidie began to have misgivings. He slowed his pace and grabbed Luo.

Luo was likewise confused. Xu Xiaowen had agreed not to tell anyone that he had gone to find Shui Yidie. So what was this all about?

After thinking for a minute, Luo signaled for Shui Yidie to wait. Then he walked alone toward the village entrance.

With the eyes of the entire crowd upon him, Luo emerged from the forest. Lord An Mi's expression changed, and he lifted his hand. The Hamo warriors charged forward, encircling Luo.

Luo remained perfectly composed as Lord An Mi and the others surrounded him. His tone was dour as he told them, "The priestess has already pardoned Shui Yidie. You have no right to harm him."

"Shui Yidie?" Lord An Mi raised his eyebrows. "Did you find him?"

Luo turned and pointed toward the dark forest. "He's watching us. But I don't think there's any way that you'll capture him."

Lord An Mi immediately turned toward the forest and shouted, "Shui Yidie, the priestess has pardoned you. Your role as the priestess's bodyguard has been restored. We have no control over you. Come out from the forest. There's no need to hide!"

When Shui Yidie heard those words, his heart pounded with joy. He knew that Lord An Mi harbored many incorrect notions about him, but the young chief was an honest man, and he would not go back on his word. Without further hesitation, Shui Yidie returned his machete to his belt, straightened his jacket, and strode out of the forest. The group of warriors, who were wielding their machetes, didn't move an inch.

Shui Yidie greeted Lord An Mi, saying, "Lord An Mi, there are no enemies here. Please ask them to put their swords down."

Lord An Mi stared coldly at Shui Yidie. "That's not a matter for you to worry about. Why don't you take care of your own business as the priestess's bodyguard?"

Shui Yidie stepped back and bowed. Then he went over to Xu Xiaowen's side and knelt on the ground.

Xu Xiaowen immediately helped him back up. "Please. It's not necessary." Then she clutched Shui Yidie's left hand and covered his cut-off finger with a mud-like paste. The wound had not yet healed, and blood still flowed from it.

Xu Xiaowen wiped the wound clean using her own white robes, then tore off a strip and tied it around his finger as a bandage, telling him, "This will do for now. When we return home, we'll apply ointment to it and it will heal. We all trust that you are loyal and will never do such a thing again."

Shui Yidie was overcome with emotion. He choked back sobs. "Your Holiness—I have always been your loyal servant."

Xu Xiaowen smiled faintly but said nothing more. She turned and gazed over at Luo. There was a look of worry on her face.

It was then that Luo knew for sure something was wrong. He surveyed the others. Not only Xu Xiaowen but Suo Tulan, Professor Zhou, Yue Dongbei, and Chief Bai were all staring at him. Their expressions differed; each looked alarmed, astonished, or skeptical.

Luo's heart froze with fear. He understood: These Hamo warriors had come for him.

Lord An Mi stepped in front of Luo. His countenance was grim. He held up something to Luo. "Luo, can you tell me what this is?"

Luo squinted. It was a faded white scroll, just like the one that they had seen in Mihong. "A lambskin map?"

"To be exact, it's a lambskin map of the Valley of Terror." Lord An Mi unrolled it so that Luo could have a closer look. The map showed the topography of the mountain range in the Valley of Terror, with major features marked. Where there was blank space on the map, there were densely packed lines of letters and symbols whose meaning Luo was unable to discern even after studying them for some time.

"What do these things mean?" Luo couldn't help asking.

"You don't know?" Lord An Mi looked Luo in the eye. "Didn't you bring this map?"

"Me?" Though Luo was intelligent, he was still confused.

Lord An Mi was silent. Then he took out another object and handed it to Luo. "Do you recognize this?" It was an eight-inch pen-knife. Luo did recognize this object, as he had bought it before departing Longzhou.

"That's my camping knife," Luo said softly. Then his jaw dropped. The knife was covered with blood that was not yet dry. The torches flickered, casting a somber glow around them.

"Di Erjia is dead." There was anger in Lord An Mi's eyes. "Stabbed in the neck with this knife."

"You think that I killed him?" Luo gasped. "But you can see that I was just in the Valley of Terror."

"When you met with the priestess, Di Erjia came and reported it to me. I had him follow you out of the village, but he never came back. I sent two of my attendants to search for him an hour ago. They found his body on the mountain trail not far from here. The killer left this map with his body." Lord An Mi stared at Luo and said coldly, "Since the beginning, I've told you that there are matters you shouldn't involve yourself in. Now it seems that the situation has worsened well beyond your imagination."

Luo grasped the seriousness of the situation, and his mind spun. How had this happened? Since they'd arrived in the Hamo village, that knife had been stored in his backpack, so how could Di Erjia have been stabbed with it? Luo had been framed. Protesting too much would only further raise suspicions.

Luo returned Lord An Mi's gaze and told him frankly, "I only have two things to say: I didn't kill Di Erjia, and I need to know what you are planning to do."

The fact that Luo was unfazed did seem to lessen Lord An Mi's suspicion somewhat. He replied, "I'm going put you in the water dungeon until I find Di Erjia's killer. Perhaps it was you, and perhaps it wasn't. Until we know for sure, you won't be harmed, but you can no longer be allowed to move freely."

Luo nodded. He knew that there was no negotiating with Lord An Mi.

"No, Lord An Mi. You can't do that," Xu Xiaowen pleaded. "Trust me. He's a friend of the Hamo people."

"Your Holiness," Lord An Mi replied without a trace of emotion, "you may determine whether Shui Yidie lives or dies, but you have no authority to stop me from detaining this man. I am the leader of the Hamo people, and I must look out for the safety of the entire tribe."

Xu Xiaowen bit her lip. She seemed to want to say something more, but Luo's stare stopped her.

Luo turned his gaze to Lord An Mi and smiled politely. "Lord An Mi, though I know that I am innocent, I am not angered by your decision. In fact, if I were in your place, I would do the same thing. Before you take me to the water dungeon, I would like to have a few words with my friends. Would that be all right with you?"

Lord An Mi nodded. But he added, "You may not leave the circle."

Luo slowly walked over to where Professor Zhou, Yue Dongbei, and Chief Bai stood. The three of them were Han people who had come to the Hamo village together. The expressions on their faces showed their unease.

Yue Dongbei's face was twitching. He managed an embarrassed smile. "Chief Inspector Luo, what happened? How did this happen?"

Chief Bai sighed. "I believe you when you say you didn't kill him."

Professor Zhou didn't say a word. He simply looked at Luo and waited for him to speak.

Luo scanned their faces. Then he said, slowly and clearly, "One of you has framed me."

Yue Dongbei waved dismissively. "No, I'd never do such a thing."

"What I'd like to know is if any of you went out on your own after the ceremony."

"I went to see some friends," Chief Bai said casually, "but I didn't leave the village. My friends will attest to that."

"That doesn't mean that you were with your friends the entire time," Yue Dongbei said to Chief Bai, then turned to Professor Zhou. "You left the house. What were you doing?"

"I went for a stroll." Professor Zhou let out an exasperated sigh. "To be honest, I just didn't want to be in the same room as you. I didn't go far. I went, and when I came back, you weren't there."

"I just went to the bathroom. Apart from that, I didn't go anywhere!" Yue Dongbei seemed embarrassed as he defended himself.

"So you three weren't together?" Luo raised an eyebrow. He hadn't expected the situation to be this complicated. He lowered his head, thinking. "From now on, the three of you should split up."

"What?" Professor Zhou and the others looked at each other in confusion.

"I'm talking about when you go to sleep at night," Luo explained. "Otherwise, there's a chance that one of you will harm the others."

Professor Zhou stared at him in alarm. "You're saying that whoever framed you is conspiring against the rest of us?"

Luo nodded. "In fact, when I discovered the body of that journalist who followed us, Liu Yun, I was already sure that the danger was lurking near. Liu Yun had wanted to tell me something, which is why he wanted to meet me alone and why he tried to carve that word on his arm. Since then, I've been on high alert, but now I have to go to the water dungeon, and perhaps that is what someone was hoping would happen."

Professor Zhou and the others were silent. They anxiously looked one another up and down.

"But shouldn't we stick together?" Yue Dongbei asked. "If there's two of us, it'll be easier to handle the third."

Luo shook his head. "No, it's better to split up. Everyone has to watch out for themselves."

"Why?" Professor Zhou didn't seem to understand, either.

"With things as they are, I can't keep my concerns to myself anymore." Luo's eyes shone as he turned his gaze to Chief Bai. "Chief Bai, if you have anything to get off your chest, now's the time."

Chief Bai slowly raised his eyebrows. "Chief Inspector Luo, what exactly are you saying?"

"Let's take a look at the issue of Liu Yun, shall we? Why was he so cautious in Mihong?" Luo's gaze swept over Professor Zhou's and Yue Dongbei's faces. "Why did he have to meet with me alone? I've been racking my brains, and there's only one explanation: He discovered a secret that would have a much bigger impact on the situation. That was the case in Mihong, at least."

At first, Chief Bai was startled. Then he let out a dark cackle. "Chief Inspector Luo, are you accusing me of killing that journalist?"

"It was just a suspicion, so I never came out and said it. But it would be wrong if I didn't say anything at this point. If you have nothing to do with this incident, then I sincerely apologize. But"—Luo gave them all a severe look—"if my guess is correct, then the three of you shouldn't stick together."

He'd made himself clear. If anything happened to Professor Zhou or Yue Dongbei, the killer's identity would be revealed.

With those words, he turned. "Lord An Mi, why don't you hand-cuff me? I won't resist."

Lord An Mi lifted a hand, and his four attendants tied up Luo and led him away.

Luo couldn't resist a cynical laugh. He'd never imagined that, after more than a decade of being a police officer, he would finally experience what it was like to be in jail.

Chapter 31

CLUES EMERGE

When the first glimmer of dawn appeared that morning, most of the villagers were fast asleep, but one person quietly left the village. The tall, lanky man with thick brows was none other than Mihong's village chief and Lieutenant General Bai's descendant. Taking long strides, Chief Bai hurried back toward the place he'd been the day before and where he had agreed to meet the figure in black.

Chief Bai placed two giant clay vessels on the ground, then silently waited. Before long, the figure in black appeared before him.

"Did you bring what I asked for?" The figure in black looked at the vessels, his tone forbidding.

Deferentially, Chief Bai moved aside. "Yes."

The figure in black opened one of the vessels and examined its contents, then nodded, satisfied. "Very good. I will consider pardoning the Bai family for its crimes."

Chief Bai threw himself on his knees, bowing fervently. Then, after some time, he lifted his head. The figure in black was already gone.

If this cursed business had been resolved earlier, I wouldn't have to do this. I'd be living like an ordinary villager, he thought as he descended the hill on his way back.

After three centuries of peace, the events of the past had come back to haunt the Bai family, and the consequences were tragic. According to the instructions handed down by his ancestors, subsequent generations of the Bai family were to reside deep in the mountains, where they alone would hold the secrets of the demonic powers that could manipulate minds and reinforce authority and wealth. Now the secret behind those powers was being uncovered, and the status held for dozens of past generations was being questioned. Someone had appeared out of nowhere with a plot to render it completely meaningless.

Chief Bai was unable to accept the recent string of deaths as mere coincidence. He could even accept the fact that it had been karma. When his forefather Lieutenant General Bai began the first chapter in a series of karmic exchanges over three hundred years ago, it had been decided early on that the secret of their legacy would someday be buried once and for all.

And now it had. It did not matter what this certain someone wanted as long as it finally came to an end.

It was pitiful indeed, never knowing where one's fate was headed next. As for Chief Bai, he hadn't expected to run into Professor Zhou on the road.

Professor Zhou was standing with his hands behind his back. His expression was flinty. "What were you doing in the mountains so early?"

There was a pause. "I went to see *him*," Chief Bai replied matter-of-factly. "I have to do whatever he says."

"You have to do everything *he* says?" Professor Zhou didn't hide the fact that he was annoyed. "Are you an idiot? You're going to be the death of us all. You need to get back over here and help figure out a way to get rid of him."

"Get rid of him?" Chief Bai cackled. "The forest is his empire. What can the two of us possibly do? He was confined to the depths of hell, and he managed to find a way to reincarnate. It's the will of the heavens. They've allowed him to take revenge. The legacy of the past three hundred years is about to come to an end. Listen to me—the most sensible thing for you to do is to step aside. This is outside your area of expertise."

"'Outside my expertise?' How can that be?" Professor Zhou exhaled loudly. "Luo is incredibly perceptive and insightful. He's managed to find evidence that *he* left behind and uncover all kinds of secrets. Does he seem to think that this is outside of my expertise?"

"He's locked away in the water dungeon! What can he do?" Chief Bai glared at Professor Zhou. "Do you think that getting rid of *him* will keep all these secrets hidden? The situation is quite to the contrary."

Professor Zhou narrowed his eyes. "What are you saying?"

"He's already drawn up the documents. If things don't go according to plan, he'll make the documents public," Chief Bai said gravely. "That's why our only recourse is to help him realize his wishes and pray that he shows us mercy."

"Is that so?" Professor Zhou's face was deathly pale. "Does he know all of our connections?"

"It's not that serious." When Chief Bai saw the look of despair on Professor Zhou's face, he almost wanted to laugh. He patted Professor Zhou's shoulder, then consoled him. "Just think about it. If he already knew, would he have let you go at Qingfeng Pass?"

"Fine." Professor Zhou was somewhat relieved. Then he noticed a faint smile on Chief Bai's face.

A few hours later, Luo was waking up inside the water dungeon that had previously held Shui Yidie. The ceiling and all four sides were lined with wooden slabs that provided no shelter from the wind or rain. With his hands tied, Luo lay on the cold, wet floor. When he opened his eyes, he saw a giant tree on the shore. One of its branches, which extended over the water dungeon, was swaying.

Having struggled to fall asleep in such conditions, Luo could scarcely imagine how Shui Yidie managed to survive six months of detainment. It was both physically and mentally grueling. But Shui Yidie had persevered, and his ability to seize an opportunity to escape demonstrated a courage and will that was truly admirable.

The one thing that consoled Luo was the fact that, despite his immobility and physical discomfort, his mind was still sharp. He had just awakened and felt somewhat rested.

In his mind, he laid out all the clues and leads that had emerged since his trip to the Valley of Terror—from the past, from the present, in history, in folklore, in reality. Whatever connections he'd made so far had proved useless. If he looked at the big picture, there was no unifying explanation.

There were also logical links that were missing. The various clues formed an intricate web tied together by preposterous myths, revealing only a glimpse of the truth.

Luo already knew where the links ought to fit, but those were the areas shrouded in mystery. Over and over again, he closed his eyes and went over the events at Qingfeng Pass in his mind. He envisioned the dark fog, the bloodshot eyes that had stared at him, trying to get a clear picture.

Who was *he*? What was he trying to do? That question was at the center of the entire mystery. Luo sensed that a major incident had occurred. And just when he was about to uncover the solution, he'd been framed. It was humiliating, and he hadn't seen it coming. His adversary had been close and had concealed himself well. Figuring out the adversary's identity was just a matter of time, so Luo had let his guard down, hoping his adversary would do the same and slip up. But Luo hadn't expected him to launch a preemptive attack.

Before being locked in the water dungeon, Luo had received permission from Lord An Mi to inspect Di Erjia's body. Di Erjia's head was turned to the left. He had apparently died from a wound to the nape of his neck on the right side.

It was possible that, as Di Erjia walked by himself toward the forest, the attacker had snuck up behind him and put him in a headlock with his left arm, covering his mouth, then used a blade in his right hand to stab him—all in one swift motion.

But Di Erjia was a formidable warrior, and executing such a maneuver would have been no easy feat. Among the three of them, only Chief Bai would have been capable of it.

Indeed, in explaining his whereabouts the night before, Chief Bai had also been the least convincing. Before and after the ceremony for the priestess, he had claimed to have been visiting a few friends. What had he really been doing?

Luo pondered these questions until noon, when Xu Xiaowen and Shui Yidie arrived, interrupting his thoughts.

Two of Lord An Mi's attendants were responsible for guarding the water dungeon, and one of them, who wore colorful robes, saw Shui Yidie. Both guards were slightly aloof and embarrassed, but upon seeing that the priestess was at his side, they remained on their best behavior. Shui Yidie, for his own part, was magnanimous.

In a friendly tone, he told them, "My fellow Hamo warriors, I am grateful for all you have done to ensure the safety of our tribe, and on behalf of the priestess, I thank you." His words were sincere, as if he'd already forgotten that, the night before, they'd been planning to take his life. This gesture put his counterparts at ease, and the two of them returned the greeting before politely informing Xu Xiaowen, "Your Holiness, we've been instructed by Lord An Mi to watch the prisoner and ensure that nothing unexpected happens."

"Luo is our friend. He is innocent. Lord An Mi will release him soon." Xu Xiaowen stared at them, then added lightly, "But I won't be troubling you. I'm only here to give him some food."

The two attendants stepped aside, but their eyes remained fixed on the basket in Shui Yidie's hands.

Luo scrambled to his feet and went over to the wooden bars. "It's you." He sounded relieved.

"I brought you something to eat." Xu Xiaowen switched to Mandarin, and her voice sounded warmer. "I tried to come sooner, but this morning something happened—one of your friends was killed."

"Who?" Luo was stunned.

"Chief Bai."

Luo froze for a second, trying to work it out. Chief Bai's secret— the Rain God statue—had been exposed, so perhaps he'd had his aides killed to make sure they wouldn't talk. As it was impossible to defend himself now that suspicions had been raised within their own group, he had apparently decided that there was only one way to assert his innocence.

Luo shook his head helplessly. "Where did it happen? How?"

Xu Xiaowen gestured for him to wait, then glanced at her bodyguard. Shui Yidie presented a clay bowl filled with a meat dish that was still steaming hot. The aroma drifted through the air. Luo hadn't eaten since the night before, and his stomach immediately began to rumble.

Xu Xiaowen took the bowl from him, then looked at Luo wide-eyed. "Pardon me, Chief Inspector Luo, but there's no way that I can untie your hands. Is it okay if I feed you?"

Blushing, Luo looked down. But given the circumstances, there was no choice. He nodded.

Xu Xiaowen flashed a smile and lifted a piece of meat through the fence, saying, "I'll tell you everything I know about the situation. You don't need to say anything. Just listen. Right now your job is to put some food in your stomach. After that, you'll feel better, and you can help us capture this criminal."

Her concern and trust moved Luo. He felt warm waves of courage rising and spreading through him.

Luo opened his mouth and accepted the bite of meat, brushing against her smooth, delicate hand. Xu Xiaowen blushed and pulled back her hand, then continued.

"About Chief Bai—his body was discovered on a mountain trail not far from the village. He was stabbed once in the chest, but he didn't die immediately. He kept going deeper into the forest for a few dozen yards. There was a trail of blood."

Xu Xiaowen's words had deliberately shifted the focus away from who was to blame, but Luo's mind was already at work.

"Also, lots of people have been saying that, last night after the ceremony, Chief Bai went to their houses to ask for kerosene."

"Kerosene?" Luo cried through an unchewed mouthful of food.

"That's right. It would have amounted to a lot of kerosene." Xu Xiaowen tilted her head. "I wonder what he was planning to do with it."

Luo hurriedly swallowed his food. "Did you go back to the house and search for clues there?"

Xu Xiaowen took a teacup from Shui Yidie's hands and lifted it into the water dungeon so that Luo could drink. "Lord An Mi and the others searched it, but they didn't find the kerosene. Early this morning, some of the tribespeople saw Chief Bai carrying two clay vessels as he left the village. Then later he was found dead on the path. Could it be that the kerosene was in those vessels?"

"Did they find the vessels in the forest?"

"No. They weren't anywhere near his body, at least. Lord An Mi sent more people to search, but I don't know if they found anything." Xu Xiaowen offered Luo more tea and food, waiting on him attentively.

"Could it be that *he* took them?" Luo mumbled to himself after a silence.

Xu Xiaowen had no idea whom Luo was referring to. She squinted at him, then suggested her own theory: "Perhaps whoever took the kerosene and whoever killed Chief Bai are the same person?"

"If the only wound was in his chest, his guard was down, so the attacker must have been someone he knew. And the wound didn't immediately kill him, so the attacker's maneuver wasn't well rehearsed. Chief Bai, while he was critically injured, headed farther into the forest. That means the attacker must have gone toward the village." Luo sorted out the facts one by one. "In light of what we know, it must have been that man, who was actually—"

"Who?"

Luo shook his head, reluctant to state his conclusions so hastily.

Seeing his reluctance, Xu Xiaowen didn't ask any more questions. Instead, she waited for Luo to finish eating, then wiped her hands and removed a slip of paper from her robes, handing it through the fence to Luo and telling him: "When I was cleaning my room on the first day that I arrived in the village, I found this in a drawer. At first I didn't think anything of it, but this morning Shui Yidie told me the story behind this piece of paper, which I thought was strange."

Luo scanned the paper, an eyebrow lifted in suspicion. It was old and faded, and there was a message written on it in clear letters: "It comes before Zhou in *The Hundred Family Names*."

Those were the exact words the young man at the Kunming hospital had used to introduce himself.

"Tell me what's so strange about the story behind this." Luo was impatient.

"According to Shui Yidie, the man who stole the blood vial spent almost six months in the village. He had gotten to know quite a few people, but he hadn't met Ya Kuma. That was because my sister lived in seclusion, and most villagers didn't see her often, much less some man from a different tribe. Six months ago, this man suddenly asked to see the priestess, but my sister declined. So then he wrote the message on this slip of paper and had Shui Yidie relay it. The funny thing is that, after my sister saw this slip of paper, she changed her mind and immediately told Shui Yidie to let him into the house. It was because of this that everything went wrong."

Luo felt his heart pounding. He had never stopped wondering about the words of the man in Kunming, but he had never found another clue that might explain it. Apparently, there was a hidden meaning in the words that had gotten through to Ya Kuma.

Luo stared at the slip of paper for a long time, reading the words to himself over and over. His mind was racing. Suddenly, it was as if a ray of sunlight pierced through the fog.

He could hardly refrain from yelling in excitement.

This was the link. He had finally uncovered a real, concrete link.

Xu Xiaowen watched Luo's expression change, her eyes widening. "What is it? What did you figure out?"

"It was him. It was him, after all." Luo tested his theory against all the existing evidence. He nodded firmly. "Yes, it has to be him."

"Who are you talking about?" Xu Xiaowen pleaded.

"Who would be so interested in General Li's legend that he took a long journey deep into the forest? Who would resort to any means not only to steal the blood vial, but the general's remains? Who would know the secret of the Rain God statue and use it to control Chief Bai? Who would maintain General Li's relics, including his personal journal? Who would be inextricably entangled in this business, such that he became a scourge to both Mihong and the Hamo people?" Luo pursed his lips. "The answer is on this slip of paper."

"You mean it was that young man?" Xu Xiaowen examined the slip of paper again. "Is his family name Zhou? Wait—is he related to Professor Zhou?"

"No." Luo shook his head. "His last name isn't Zhou. This fellow is clever. It's a little puzzle that he used to hide his identity, and at the same time, communicate it to your sister."

"'It comes before Zhou in *The Hundred Family Names*.'" Xu Xiaowen mulled it over, mumbling to herself. She looked up at Luo expectantly.

"If his family name were Zhou, why would he have said it comes before Zhou? That's the key: 'comes before.' Just think of what name comes right before Zhou."

"In *The Hundred Family Names*?" Xu Xiaowen frowned a little, then recited the names: "Zhao, Qian, Sun, Li, Zhou, Wu, Zheng, Wang. Zhou comes after Li. It's the fifth name."

Luo's eyes flashed.

Xu Xiaowen stopped. "Oh my God. He's a descendant of Li Dingguo?"

Shui Yidie and the two attendants looked over, concerned. Xu Xiaowen quickly composed herself. Fortunately, none of them understood Mandarin.

"That's right." Luo nodded.

"Could he be the one behind it all? Was he avenging his ancestors? And if so, why was he the first to contract the illness? After he fell ill, he was brought to the Kunming hospital, so how could he have been responsible for everything that's happened since?"

These were questions that Luo did not yet have the answers to. He hesitated before speaking. "The motives behind what happened afterward are likely known to him alone. When we saw him in Kunming, he was ill and he was locked up, but he may not be either of those things anymore. And we do know that this illness isn't incurable."

"That's right. Professor Zhou has a drug for fear," Xu Xiaowen said, recalling the conversation at the Kunming hospital. "But at the hospital, he was against using it because it was untested and wouldn't be ethical."

It was precisely because of this that Luo had suggested trying to get consent from the patient's family. He had never imagined the search for them would bring Yue Dongbei to him and take Luo on a journey to the far edge of Yunnan.

"Professor Zhou may not have been willing to test it on that patient then, but he and I have always been on good terms—anyway, he lost the medicine. I wonder if he lost it in Kunming." Luo contemplated this for a second. "Okay, let's not worry about that right now. Can you tell me what happened after this descendant of Li Dingguo's and Ya Kuma met?"

"Again, I only heard about it from Shui Yidie, but I trust that he's telling the truth." Xu Xiaowen glanced over her shoulder at her bodyguard. Though he wasn't especially tall, he had a commanding presence and an air of faithfulness.

Luo likewise looked at Shui Yidie before nodding in agreement with Xu Xiaowen's assessment.

"After the young man went inside the priestess's house, Ya Kuma came out and asked Shui Yidie to stand guard outside. She and this man spoke for a long time. He was there from the evening until the sun came up. Shui Yidie didn't know what they talked about, but judging by some minor details, it didn't seem to be an ordinary meeting."

"Tell me about those details." As far as Luo was concerned, details were the thing that never failed to reveal the essence of a matter.

"When the young man finally emerged, his expression was grave. He seemed to be deep in thought. Before he left, he bowed deeply toward the house. There was a look of respect and gratitude on his face, and even tears in the corners of his eyes. Shui Yidie said that he and this man were friendly, and he'd never seen anything like it before."

"Hmm." Luo was quiet. "And then what?"

"After the young man left, Ya Kuma called Shui Yidie inside the house and asked him to make preparations for a trip to the Valley of Terror the next day."

"Did they go to General Li's cave?" Luo asked, narrowing his eyes.

"That's exactly what they did." Xu Xiaowen looked at Luo with admiration. "As you probably guessed, the young man was with them. They went late at night, as if they didn't want anyone to know. When they arrived, Ya Kuma told Shui Yidie to wait outside. He waited all night. It was nearly dawn when Ya Kuma came out. The young man stayed inside the cave. Then Ya Kuma and Shui Yidie returned to the village just as everyone else was waking up. That entire day, Ya Kuma was uneasy. She kept looking out the window as if she were waiting for something."

"She was waiting for that man?" Luo guessed.

"That's what Shui Yidie and I both think," Xu Xiaowen replied with a nod. "But he never showed up. Then in the afternoon, some of the tribespeople went hunting in the valley, and they returned with bad news. They said that General Li's tomb had been dug up and that the remains were missing."

"It was raining that day, right?"

"Huh? How do you know?" Xu Xiaowen looked at him with concern. "Shui Yidie didn't say anything about that."

Luo chuckled. "It's not because I was the one who dug up the tomb, don't worry. I just heard that hunters take shelter in the cave when it rains, which is how it was discovered that the tomb was excavated. But please go on."

There was a look of relief on Xu Xiaowen's face. "When she heard the news, Ya Kuma became anxious and didn't know what to do. After a while, she said to Shui Yidie, 'I heard that you were friendly with that young man. What were your impressions of him?' Shui Yidie replied, 'He seems like an honest and courageous member of the Han tribe. If he made a promise, he would keep it.'"

"That's quite a high appraisal." Luo glanced at Shui Yidie suspiciously.

Xu Xiaowen lowered her voice. "But it's also possible that he misjudged this man—because he never showed up. That evening, Lord An Mi and Di Erjia came to the priestess's house and asked where the sacred object was."

"Who is Di Erjia, anyway? It seems like Lord An Mi holds him in high regard."

"He competed against Shui Yidie for the role of bodyguard but lost. He's been unhappy about it since. Shui Yidie thinks that he betrayed Ya Kuma to gain the trust of Lord An Mi."

"What do you mean, he betrayed her?"

"Think about it. Ya Kuma met with this young man and secretly went to the valley with him. A problem was discovered with General Li's tomb, but it didn't make sense to suspect the priestess. But Lord An Mi came in and demanded to see the sacred object, so someone had to have informed him. Shui Yidie thinks it was Di Erjia."

Luo nodded in silence. No wonder Shui Yidie's eyes had been brimming with rage the night before when he'd fought with Di Erjia. "Did Ya Kuma give the sacred object to the man?"

"Most likely." There was sorrow on Xu Xiaowen's face. "My sister couldn't produce the sacred object. She had no choice but to bring Lord An Mi and Di Erjia to the cave. But this time, she had Shui Yidie stay in the village, and she left something in his care."

"What was it?"

"The priestess's so-called burden of tradition."

"Burden of tradition?" Luo had heard Shui Yidie use this term at the ceremony. He raised an eyebrow. "What is that, actually?"

Xu Xiaowen shook her head. "I don't know. Even Shui Yidie doesn't know. Ya Kuma was able to avoid Lord An Mi and Di Erjia for a short time, and that's when she handed Shui Yidie an ancient letter. Ya Kuma told him that he had to guard this letter until she returned safely, but if she did not return, he was to give it to the next priestess. Not even the village chief and the high priest know the contents of the letter. It concerns the fate of the entire village."

"It's that serious?"

"Yes, it's extremely serious." Xu Xiaowen smiled sadly and looked over at Shui Yidie. "Now you know why he could tell yesterday that I was only pretending to be Ya Kuma."

"Do you have the letter now?" Luo asked.

She nodded. "Shui Yidie gave it to me this morning."

"Have you read it?"

"Not yet." Xu Xiaowen was silent a moment, then added in a low voice, "My sister's last words to Shui Yidie were: 'Once a priestess reads the letter, she carries the burden of the entire tribe on her shoulders.' I don't know if I can take on that responsibility."

Luo's heart pounded. Until very recently, Xu Xiaowen had been a college student living in modern society, enjoying life and looking forward to a bright future. It would take a great deal of strength for her to take on this mysterious, terrible burden.

Luo changed the subject. "After Ya Kuma went with them to the valley, what happened?"

"After they left, Shui Yidie found a hiding place for the letter, then he anxiously waited for the priestess to come back. In the morning, Lord An Mi, Suo Tulan, and Di Erjia came. Lord An Mi's face was filled with grief. Without any explanation whatsoever, he had his attendants tie up Shui Yidie and lock him in the water dungeon. You know the rest of the story. A mysterious phantom appeared in the valley. Lots of tribespeople were affected by the fear illness, and others fled. But the people didn't know about any of this. They were simply told that the priestess was very ill. Only Lord An Mi and Suo Tulan can explain why my sister died."

"Do you suspect them?" Luo asked.

Xu Xiaowen looked intently into his eyes. "What do you think?"

After a brief silence, Luo spoke again. "In any case, you shouldn't do anything rash. The situation is far more complicated than I had imagined. Though you have Shui Yidie to protect you . . ."

His words trailed off, but the look in his eyes, which were filled with tenderness and concern, said it all.

Xu Xiaowen bit her lip. "I understand. I'll wait for you to get out of here. I need your help." With those words, her eyes glimmered and her tone grew mysterious. "I know you'll get out. Shui Yidie wanted me to tell you that the fish on the trees here are delicious."

"Fish?" Luo was confused. He lifted his head and looked all around, then laughed. "Oh right, fish. I heard."

Xu Xiaowen nodded and said nothing more before leaving with Shui Yidie.

The two attendants had been watching Xu Xiaowen's every move, though they seemed less tense than before. As far as they knew, the priestess had delivered food, and that was that.

Chapter 32

JAILBREAK

Late in the afternoon, one of the attendants guarding the water dungeon went to the village to pick up food, leaving the only other—whose leg had been injured in the sword fight—to watch Luo. Over the course of the day, apart from the visit by the priestess and Shui Yidie, nothing had happened, and the attendant was fairly relaxed.

Luo stood up and trudged over to the door. He peered out at the guard, his lips twitching as if he wanted to say something. The other man immediately noticed and scowled, then walked over and stared at him through the fence suspiciously.

Luo stared back intently, as if he urgently needed something. But his voice was soft and barely audible, producing only a faint whisper. "Ya Kuma—Ya Kuma—"

Alarmed, the attendant leaned forward and put his ear next to the fence so that he could hear better.

After all, what could the prisoner do with his hands tied behind his back?

Then, Luo's right fist suddenly shot through a crack in the fence and slammed into the other man's temple. He didn't so much as utter a sound before collapsing to the ground.

Back in his police-academy days, Luo had undergone special combat training. He knew that this blow would knock out the other man for at least ten minutes. He quickly patted down the attendant and found the key, then unlocked the door. He dragged the attendant into the water dungeon, then exchanged jackets with him. He tied up the other man's hands and feet with rope and stuffed a cloth into his mouth, then rolled him over so that he lay facedown. When Luo was finished, he took the attendant's machete and left, locking the door on his way out.

Ever since being thrown in the water dungeon, Luo had been wondering how Shui Yidie, whose hands were tied, had managed to suddenly break free at the ceremony.

Then, thanks to Xu Xiaowen's subtle hint, Luo figured out the answer: The fish known as *datouyu.*

It had been raining hard for days on end, causing the pond's water level to rise. And, as he'd learned, these strange fish used the suckers on their bodies to crawl up trees and hang from the branches.

Several long branches extended over the water dungeon. Luo had lain on the floor motionless, quietly waiting for several hours for a fish to appear on a branch overhead.

These fish were timid and easily frightened. All Luo had to do was cough loudly a few times, and a scared fish had flung itself off the branch. Though it had been aiming for the water, it had fallen short, and it landed on the floor of his cage.

Luo had pinned down the wriggling fish, then picked it up in his hands. As Yue Dongbei had demonstrated, the fish had a long, sharp fin that ran down its back, which Luo then used to cut through the rope tied around his wrists. After that, he'd just waited for an opportunity to escape.

Since he was now dressed like one of the locals, Luo was able to move through the village quickly, his head lowered and hood up to avoid detection. Even as he hurried along, he never stopped thinking for a moment.

The identity of the young man, which had been an enormous mystery, had been uncovered at last: He was General Li's descendant. Like his forefather three centuries earlier, this young man was intelligent and capable. But it also seemed that he was similar to General Li in other ways: He was brutal, dangerous, and mysterious.

Luo wasn't sure what had happened to this man in the past six months, how he had returned to the valley and carried out the string of terrifying attacks. Regardless, he had to be stopped, and the bloodshed had to come to an end.

What Luo particularly wanted to know was what this man planned to do next. To know that, Luo had to figure out his motives. People always had a reason for doing something. Luo wasn't ready to dismiss these recent events as simply the product of a centuries-old grudge.

What had this young man and Ya Kuma talked about six months before?

Why had the young man become the first victim of the demonic powers? How was this linked to the blood vial's transport to Longzhou and the terrible outbreak there? What were the circumstances surrounding the death of the priestess Ya Kuma?

Luo was determined to find the answers to these questions. He arrived at Suo Tulan's house. The high priest was a pensive, wise man, and so his house was located in a quiet, secluded area of the village. This was convenient for Luo.

The front door was unlocked. Luo stormed inside, immediately shutting the door behind him. Suo Tulan stood at the window, lost in meditation. He turned around in surprise. He was a highly respected figure, and not even the village chief or the priestess would barge in on him like this.

Luo walked toward Suo Tulan and, with a flick of the wrist, removed the hood he'd been wearing and reached into his belt for his machete.

Suo Tulan, realizing that it was Luo, calmed down after a second. His mouth twitched as if he were about to smile.

"Luo, why don't you put your sword down? I trust that you won't use such a thing on an old man."

Suo Tulan's reply caused Luo to lower his guard a little, and he did put away the sword, bowing apologetically. "Pardon my manners, Your Holiness. I want to make it clear that I am not here as your enemy. But you must know that I've just escaped from the water dungeon, and it's only a matter of time before the tribe's warriors find and capture me."

Suo Tulan's eyes flashed. "Did the priestess or Shui Yidie help you escape?"

Luo wasn't about to reveal the fact that he'd spoken to Xu Xiaowen. He shook his head. "No, no one helped me. I used the fin of the *datouyu* to cut the rope around my wrists, then I took advantage of a slipup on the part of the guard."

Suo Tulan pondered for a while, then sighed deeply. "So it seems that the water dungeon does little to restrain beasts after all. But Luo, you should not have escaped, even though I know you weren't the one who killed Di Erjia."

"Oh?" Luo raised his eyebrows. "You believe that I'm innocent?"

"You're no fool. You wouldn't kill a man and leave your own knife in the victim's body. Besides, Di Erjia knew these mountains far better than you. He followed you the entire time. How could you have stabbed him in the throat from behind?" Suo Tulan spoke in a leisurely tone.

"That makes sense." Luo nodded. "Why didn't you speak up when Lord An Mi sent me to the water dungeon?"

"Because I don't want you in my village," Suo Tulan said frankly. "Luo, you're too curious for your own good. There are some matters that are none of your business."

"Are you referring to my bringing Shui Yidie back to the village?"

"Shui Yidie is a loyal and courageous man. Lord An Mi wanted to put him to death. I did not fully agree. His escape into the forest was really the best outcome, but you found him and brought him back to the priestess." Suo Tulan shook his head in exasperation. "You must already know that the current priestess is not Ya Kuma. After we came under threat, Lord An Mi and I put a great deal of thought into the question of how to maintain unity within the tribe, and Shui Yidie's return jeopardizes that unity. You must know that, when he and the priestess protect one another, the tribe has no authority to control them. If certain information is disclosed, there will be grave consequences that you simply cannot imagine."

"Certain information?" Luo narrowed his eyes. "Like the truth about Ya Kuma's death?"

Suo Tulan wrinkled his brow, alarmed. "What are you saying?"

"Ya Kuma entered the cave with Lord An Mi and Di Erjia, but she never came out. Her remains were buried in the cave. Perhaps the circumstances surrounding her death were not as simple as the explanation you gave to the new priestess."

Suo Tulan looked astonished. "Do you suspect that Lord An Mi killed Ya Kuma?"

Luo said nothing.

"That's an outrageous accusation!" Suo Tulan cried out. "Is this what the priestess and Shui Yidie also believe?"

"I can't say that they don't."

Luo's words had triggered a cataclysmic reaction in Suo Tulan, who was wide-eyed and shaking his head in disbelief. "These kinds of suspicions could tear apart the entire village!"

"So why don't you tell me what really happened when Ya Kuma went to the valley with them?" Luo's eyes were intensely bright, urging on the other man. "Oftentimes, hiding the truth brings about the opposite of the intended effect."

"No, I can't tell you that." Suo Tulan seemed to be struggling to contain his emotions. His face had turned pale. "If this secret were to get out, the entire village—their convictions, their will to fight—would crumble in an instant."

Luo could see that the only way to get this critical information would be for each side to have absolute trust in the other. After a minute of thought, Luo changed his tack, asking, "Do you know the real identity of that young man who stole the blood vial, the one you call Zhou?"

Suo Tulan shook his head, puzzled.

"He's a descendant of General Li."

"What?" Suo Tulan seemed to be reeling. "It's him—it really is him!"

"And he's back!" Luo stared at Suo Tulan. His voice was low. "He's hiding in some dark corner of the forest, watching our every move. Do you remember what happened when we were at the tomb? He was wailing, and then he stared down on us with hatred in his eyes. I had the distinct feeling that he was plotting something, that something terrible was about to take place."

"Right." Recalling that episode, Suo Tulan felt his stomach churning. "He was full of hatred. He wanted revenge—"

"Trust me. I'm your friend." Luo told him sincerely. "I'm not here to harm anyone in your village. I just want to stop him, which is why I need you to tell me what happened. I want to help you."

Suo Tulan was silent for a long while. It was clear that he was deeply conflicted. Luo waited patiently, communicating only with his eyes, until his hypnotic gaze finally managed to break through the other man's defenses.

The high priest sighed deeply. He hesitated, then as if he was forcing out the words, told Luo, "Ya Kuma betrayed the mission of the priestess. She betrayed our entire village."

There were tears in the corners of the old man's eyes. He closed them in pain.

"Betrayed?" Luo's suspicion had been correct. "So the sacred object wasn't stolen, it was given to General Li's descendant by Ya Kuma?"

"Not only that, but she brought this cursed scoundrel to the tomb and let him excavate the general's remains. Over the past few centuries, there has never been a priestess who would actually hand over the sacred object, which contains an evil spirit, to a descendant of the enemy. The honor and achievements of the priestess during General Li's time were obliterated in a single instant." Suo Tulan's expression revealed bitter resentment and deep confusion. "Through the ages, the role of priestess has been the most prestigious status that any woman can hold. I simply don't understand how she could do such a thing. Did the welfare and safety of the entire village mean that little to her?"

"So why did she actually do it?"

"No one really knows." Suo Tulan shook his head. He paused. "Lord An Mi's theory is that Ya Kuma and this young man were having an affair."

"An affair?" This possibility had occurred to Luo earlier, but it seemed far-fetched.

"This young man by the name of Li is evil, but during his time in the Hamo village, he acted very proper, brave, and wise. As I've said before, many tribespeople befriended him. It's possible that Ya Kuma, who was a young woman with no experience of men, was tricked by him. According to Di Erjia's reports, Ya Kuma and this young man were alone together in the priestess's house all night and then went to General Li's tomb the next day. If this is indeed the case, it is the biggest scandal the tribe has seen in hundreds of years."

Luo was dismayed. None of the clues had pointed in this direction. The priestess had colluded with the enemy. If this information were to spread among the tribespeople, their pride in their ancient culture would undoubtedly be shattered. No wonder Lord An Mi and Suo Tulan had come up with this scheme, falsifying appearances and fabricating lies.

Even so, Luo persisted in asking questions. "What did Ya Kuma herself have to say about why she did it?"

Suo Tulan smiled sadly. "She was given an opportunity to explain. After she and Lord An Mi went to the cave, she stood at the entrance without saying a word. No matter how the chief interrogated her, she wouldn't answer. She seemed to be waiting for that young man all night, but he never showed. When it was morning and the sun rose, she finally gave up and spoke. Those words were her last."

"What did she say?"

"She said, 'All of this is my fault. Shui Yidie had nothing to do with it. I regret what I've done to the tribe. I must pay for it with my life.' Then she grabbed Lord An Mi's machete and slashed her own throat with it," Suo Tulan said with dismay.

"That's how the chief says she died?" Luo's eyes narrowed. "She killed herself?"

"That's right." As if he were trying to avoid further pain, Suo Tulan looked out the window to some distant place, then said in a low voice, "I watched Ya Kuma grow up. I taught her Mandarin, along with all kinds of other knowledge. I told her the history of the holy war and its glories. She was a bright child. After she became the priestess, she earned the love and respect of the Hamo people through her conduct. If the evidence weren't irrefutable, I'd never believe that she would commit such a grave crime against the village. She had to have been tricked. After the descendant of that demon achieved his aim, he shamelessly left. I can only imagine the hurt and despair our poor priestess felt on her deathbed."

Thinking of everyone's love for this graceful priestess, Luo couldn't help sharing in Suo Tulan's sorrow.

After a brief silence, Suo Tulan turned and looked at Luo. "The person who is angriest of all about this is Lord An Mi. Though he doesn't know about this young man being a descendant of General Li, he does believe that Ya Kuma began a personal relationship with him, which was a betrayal of the entire tribe. For Lord An Mi, this was already a tremendous disgrace. Your meeting with the priestess last night also broke a rule set by the village chief. And even if you had nothing to do with Di Erjia's death, you didn't stay in your cell!"

Luo was startled. There was a pained, embarrassed smile on his face. He was about to explain when suddenly they heard the sound of an explosion in the distance. Though it wasn't loud, the sound was distinct and striking. Surely everyone in the village had heard it. Luo darted over to the window, leaning out in the direction the sound had come from.

"It's coming from the valley. Is it guns?" Suo Tulan asked worriedly.

Luo shook his head. The sound was muffled, different from that of a gun being fired. What could it be, then?

"It's him. He's here." Luo turned and looked at Suo Tulan. "There's no time to waste. I have to go out there and find him."

"It will be dark soon," Suo Tulan counseled. "You don't know the terrain well. Now is a dangerous time to go out."

But Luo had already made up his mind. "No, I have to go. We can't wait around like sitting ducks. I need your help. I need you to help me leave the village without being captured."

As the high priest of the tribe, Suo Tulan did not wish to defy the chief's orders. But right now, there was a formidable enemy in their midst, and the safety of the entire village was at stake. After a silence, he finally nodded. "Fine. I'll show you to the mountain trail."

Chapter 33

EXPLOSION AT THE LAKE

A few minutes later, two men wearing the robes of Hamo priests emerged from the house, heading southwest. Everyone they passed made way for the high priest, Suo Tulan, and behind him, a man who seemed unaccustomed to the mountain breeze, for his black hood was pulled down over his face. Only a pair of dark eyes were visible in the dusk light.

It was dinnertime, when most tribespeople were at home, but young and middle-aged men could be seen rushing about the village. From their conversations, it could be gleaned that the prisoner had escaped and that there had been some sort of commotion in the valley. Lord An Mi had already given orders that all Hamo warriors were to report to the sacred grounds for further instructions.

When Suo Tulan and Luo arrived at the mountain trail just outside the village, they parted ways, with Luo setting off to the Valley of Terror and Suo Tulan heading to the sacred grounds to join Lord An Mi and the ranks of tribesmen he was assembling.

By the time Luo entered the forest, the sky was already dark, and it may as well have been night. When Luo had been imprisoned, Lord An Mi had stripped him of his belongings, including his gun. Now he was equipped only with the torch that Suo Tulan had lent him, and he groped his way along the trail using its warm glow. Fortunately, this section of the trail was not particularly tortuous or rough, and Luo had already taken it twice before. It felt as if he had hardly taken a breath before he arrived at his destination: General Li's cave.

The rumbling noise they had heard earlier seemed to have emanated from that small space. No matter how Luo approached the question, the cave was the first thing that sprang to his mind. When he arrived, he immediately knew he'd been right.

The interior was dark, but there was one area from which gunpowder smoke was steadily streaming. Luo switched his torch to his left hand and held his machete in his right as he cautiously ventured deeper inside.

There was no ventilation in the cave, and the smoke was thick. Luo quickly scanned his surroundings, but no one was there. Luo put his machete back in his belt, then squatted down to look for any new footprints.

The pile of dirt was still there, and it didn't look like it had changed since the day before. About three feet to the left of it was something unusual.

It was a slip of paper tucked underneath a stone. In the dim cave, the bright-white paper would have easily attracted anyone's attention. Luo promptly walked over and picked it up. But he couldn't read the characters.

That's right, Luo thought. The Hamo language. The culprit had wanted to draw a member of the Hamo tribe here, which was why he'd used their language. But what did he want to say, and to whom?

Luo put the slip of paper in his pocket. He'd have to wait until he returned to the village to find Suo Tulan or Xu Xiaowen to help read it.

Luo lowered the torch and held it near his right hand, noticing black stains on his fingers and the back of his hand. He rubbed his fingertips together. It was dirt from the cave floor, but it had been scorched.

A realization came to him. He looked at the ground where the slip of paper had been. Not only was there a black patch of dirt, but there was also a hole that had been created through some force.

Like an explosion. Luo was almost certain of it, as that would also explain the sound he'd just heard. Taking another look, he saw a fine black line that extended from the hole all the way outside the cave. Luo touched the substance that formed the black line. Though scorched, it was still somewhat hard. When he brought the torch closer, he could make out charred fibers that appeared to have been twisted together. The strings appeared to have been woven from bark.

Bark wasn't a highly flammable material. Luo recalled the kerosene that Chief Bai had collected from the villagers. The culprit must have soaked the bark in kerosene to create a fuse, which he used to set off explosives. What did he want to blow up? There was no obvious target inside the cave, and the explosion that had just taken place was relatively small, with very little impact. So it had likely been a test—a successful one. What, then, was he planning to blow up next? As Luo pondered that question, beads of sweat began to trickle down from his scalp.

When the guard who'd gone out for dinner came back to the water dungeon, he didn't see his partner. He searched everywhere, calling out his name, but there was no response. The prisoner inside the furthest water dungeon had dragged himself to the side of the cell, where he hurled himself against the wall, producing a racket that attracted the guard's attention. He edged closer and saw that the prisoner's hands and feet were tied and that his mouth was stuffed with a rag—and that the prisoner was none other than his own partner.

When he learned that Luo had escaped, Lord An Mi immediately gathered a team to conduct a search. He had underscored the possibility of the priestess's house as a potential hiding place, but it never occurred to him that Luo had fled to the high priest instead. But before long, there was the strange and sudden sound of an explosion from the valley. These two successive incidents struck Lord An Mi as extremely ominous. He ordered the whole village to promptly gather at the sacred grounds.

Shui Yidie had returned, Di Erjia had been murdered, Chief Bai had been murdered, Luo had broken free, and there was a mysterious explosion in the valley. A confrontation with the demonic spirit would put the lives of all of the villagers at stake. The young chief's already enormous burden was only growing. But who else could accept such a responsibility?

Lord An Mi didn't have an ounce of hesitation or fear. He was the tribal chief and a descendant of the great warrior A Liya. Heroism was in his blood, and that knowledge gave him unshakable confidence. He believed that he could defeat any opponent.

The difference between this and the holy war was that, this time, the demonic spirit was in hiding, and he didn't leave so much as a trace. This required Lord An Mi to summon all his courage. This battle would be decided not only by courage but by wisdom.

Some matters among the tribespeople worried him. The first involved Shui Yidie, whose boundless loyalty to the priestess created an unspoken and embarrassing opposition to his chief. Shui Yidie clearly knew that Ya Kuma had died, so what could he be thinking? More importantly, would his thinking influence Xu Xiaowen?

Reflecting on these questions, Lord An Mi couldn't help but direct his anger at Luo. This troublesome member of the Han tribe had bested him on several occasions. Where was he now? All Lord An Mi could do was hope that Suo Tulan's assessment had been correct: that Luo was indeed their friend and not their enemy.

But the other two members of the Han tribe gave him no reason to relax, either. Their exchange in the minutes before Luo had been taken to the water dungeon had alarmed Lord An Mi. Fortunately, these two seemed easier to handle. Lord An Mi had already sent someone to bring them to the sacred grounds in the name of protecting them—though, in reality, it was to monitor them. In a crisis like this, any internal discord or disturbance could be life-threatening. Lord An Mi was sure of this.

Suo Tulan was the last to appear at the sacred grounds. When he arrived, Lord An Mi felt slightly more at ease. This wise old man had always been of the most critical assistance to him. In the wake of Ya Kuma's betrayal and suicide, which could have brought upheaval to the entire village, Suo Tulan had managed to find Xu Xiaowen, a feat that saved the tribe from ruin. Lord An Mi hoped that he would be able to count on Suo Tulan's help again now.

Suo Tulan saw the expectant look in Lord An Mi's eyes and stepped forward, bowing. "Lord An Mi, what are your plans?"

"We need to launch an attack." Lord An Mi's tone suggested that he was seeking the other man's counsel. "Not immediately. I hope that we can set out first thing in the morning."

"You are wise to wait." Suo Tulan nodded in agreement. "The darkness provides the enemy with an advantage. If we attack at night, it would only benefit him."

"Since Your Holiness agrees, I'll make arrangements accordingly." Lord An Mi waved, and his four attendants hurried over. "The four of you are to organize the warriors into two groups. The first group will go rest for now and accompany me to the valley in the morning. The second group will be in charge of reconnaissance and safety. Its members will be posted at checkpoints along every road. You must also assign two additional guards to accompany the priestess. One will look out for her safety, and the other will ensure that she has no further contact with Luo." He looked at Suo Tulan. "Your Holiness, what are your thoughts?"

But Suo Tulan was squinting in astonishment toward the southern edge of the forest. "Is that—Luo? Is he coming back?"

Lord An Mi spun around and followed Suo Tulan's line of sight. Sure enough, there was someone on the trail heading toward them. The light of the torch revealed his face: Indeed, it was Luo.

Xu Xiaowen had also been observing the situation, and she cried out, "Chief Inspector Luo!"

Nearby, Professor Zhou and Yue Dongbei were gaping in confusion and worry.

Luo's pace quickened, and with all eyes on him, he hurried through the crowd. He was visibly sweating, and his clothing was torn and covered in dirt.

Professor Zhou and Yue Dongbei raised their eyebrows and exchanged a look. They hadn't seen Luo this frazzled since the incident at Qingfeng Pass.

Puzzled, Lord An Mi shook his head. He quietly instructed his attendants, "Grab him."

The attendants obeyed, but by then, there was no need. Luo tossed aside his torch and collapsed on the ground in exhaustion. He was panting and struggled to speak.

"Hurry—hurry." Suo Tulan waved to the attendants. "Bring him over here."

The attendants carried Luo over to them. Xu Xiaowen and the others gathered around. Xu Xiaowen's heart was filled with deep worry, but while serving in the role of the priestess, there was no way she could express it. She gazed at him, her eyes brimming with concern.

"Hurry!" wheezed Luo. "We have to evacuate the village and go uphill! Everyone!"

Lord An Mi's mien was imposing. "And why is that?"

"He's planning to blow up the lake and flood the village!" Because he was weak, Luo spoke softly. But his words sent shock waves through everyone around him.

After remaining frozen for a moment, Suo Tulan looked at Lord An Mi with urgency. "Chief?"

Lord An Mi's eyes darted back and forth. Though he was filled with rage, he was the tribal leader, and especially at this time of crisis, he wanted to keep calm. "How can I be sure that I can trust you?" He stared at Luo.

"The map—the map," Luo struggled to reply. "The map that was on Di Erjia's body!"

Lord An Mi took the map out of his pocket.

"Look. Right here."

Seeing the mark Luo pointed to, Lord An Mi studied the map for a minute. "That's right. That's the lake. But what does this prove?"

"That mark symbolizes fire. It means that there's an explosion planned—the one that General Li was plotting!" Luo gulped for air. "He found explosives and conducted a test. All that kerosene was for the explosives. He's already gone!"

Hearing those words, Lord An Mi could no longer stand by idly. He straightened his posture while the others looked on with horror on their faces.

"We have to get out of here before it's too late!" Luo cried with all the strength remaining in his body.

But it was already too late. He hadn't finished speaking when there was a ground-shaking explosion from the direction of the lake. Following the sound of the explosion, the ledge along the precipice crumbled into pieces, setting loose all the water in the lake, which crashed down in a flash of white rapids in the dark night.

For an instant, no one moved. They all stared at the wall of water, a deathly pallor on their faces.

Chapter 34

THE DECISIVE BATTLE

The explosion at the lake had unleashed a terrifying flood. The lake, which had been filled with water from the massive rains, pummeled down the cliff with the unrelenting fury of a powerful army. The flood was impossible to defend against. Once the raging water hit the roads, the village would be engulfed in an instant and disappear without a trace.

Following the crash of water came a loud noise from the valley that resounded for a long time.

Luo and the others stood in horror, gazing into the distance at the face of the cliff and the flooded ravine below, transfixed, as if this were somehow a dream.

Indeed, they had all experienced a dream—a nightmare in which death awaited them.

But death seemed to be playing a joke on them. Just as quickly as the threat appeared, it disappeared over the horizon.

The water from the lake didn't obliterate the Hamo people. Instead, most of it was diverted toward the hill in the Valley of Terror, and it flowed southwest toward the ravine. Having narrowly escaped death, everyone around Lord An Mi and Luo looked stunned. Even more surprised were the people in the crowd, who hadn't been informed what was happening. For as long as anyone could remember, the water atop the precipice had always flowed to the village pond, so why had the floodwaters rushed toward the valley instead?

Luo had a flash of insight: It was a matter of potential energy. The potential energy stored in the lake was what had allowed the Hamo village to avoid disaster.

When the ledge was blown up, the river current had been unleashed, and in the process of falling, the water had gained velocity. When it crashed into the smooth, curved rock mass directly below, the water sprayed off the rocks, traveling a long distance before striking the hill in the valley and draining into the ravine.

The principle behind this was similar to that of a faucet. If the handle were turned only slightly, the water pressure would be weak, and the curve of the spout would further reduce the water's velocity to a trickle that would fall straight down. On the other hand, if the handle were turned all the way, the water pressure would be strong, and the curve of the spout would be capable of directing the water forward in a long, solid stream.

Though Lord An Mi could not explain these principles of physics, he similarly understood what was happening. After recovering from his initial shock, he was filled with gratitude and relief, and he couldn't help crying out, "The mountain torrents have been sent to the valley! The demon attempted to destroy our village, but the gods have protected the Hamo people! The demon's plan has been foiled!"

As if awakening from a dream, the crowd joined the chief and exploded into a chorus of cheers.

Yue Dongbei wiped the sweat from his bald scalp and whispered, "How frightening! How frightening, indeed! I could've died!"

Xu Xiaowen was slowly regaining her composure. It was then that she realized she'd unwittingly placed her hand on top of Luo's. Her face turned red. Fortunately, everyone was too distracted to notice. She pulled her hand away, stealing a quick glance at Luo.

But Luo's attention was focused elsewhere. His brow was furrowed in contemplation. Then something occurred to him, and he reached into his pocket and took out the slip of paper he'd found inside the cave.

Luo turned to Suo Tulan. "Your Holiness, would you mind telling me what this says?"

Suo Tulan took the slip of paper and scanned it, then handed it over to Lord An Mi. "Lord An Mi, this is for you."

As Lord An Mi quickly skimmed the note, something seemed to take him over. He stared icily at Luo. "Who gave this to you?"

"No one gave it to me," Luo replied truthfully. "I found it in the cave."

Lord An Mi did not reply and simply stared at Luo, his eyes filled with deep distrust.

"Lord An Mi, we must trust our friend who has come from afar," Xu Xiaowen couldn't help interjecting. "If he weren't here to help us, why would he have risked life and limb to warn us of the explosion at the lake?"

Lord An Mi knew there was sense to what Xu Xiaowen was saying, but the situation surrounding Ya Kuma had created all kinds of problems for him. He grunted as if he were unimpressed, then returned his gaze to the slip of paper.

This time he studied it closely, a look of concentration on his face. Then he looked up at Suo Tulan. "Your Holiness, what do you advise?"

Suo Tulan was silent for a long time. Then he shook his head slowly. "It must be a trap. You'd better not go."

Lord An Mi smiled for a second, then suddenly turned around, lifting the paper high in the air and shouting to his fellow tribespeople, "Do you remember the young man who stole the sacred object six months ago? Well, he's a descendant of the demon himself, General Li! Now he's returned, and he's challenged me to a duel!"

A buzz spread among the tribespeople as everyone turned to their neighbors and began discussing the shocking news.

Lord An Mi held the slip of paper in front of him and began reading its contents out loud: "Hamo Lord An Mi, I am Li Yanhui, a descendant of the great hero General Li. We have a three-hundred-year-old score to settle, and we must bring it to a conclusion once and for all. After tonight's catastrophe, I will be waiting for you in the valley. You must come alone. We will duel in the cave, and I will show you what it means to be defeated."

The sound of cursing emanated from the crowd. Then someone shouted, "'Hero' is an honor that only we the Hamo people can give! How dare this spineless demon call himself a hero!"

Lord An Mi lifted his hand and signaled for the crowd to calm down, then spoke again. "The enemy has summoned me to a duel in the valley. His Holiness Suo Tulan advises me not to go. But I am a descendant of A Liya, so how could I possibly fear the powers of the demon? I will show him who the real hero is!"

The rhetorical force of the clan leader's words ignited the crowd. All four attendants raised their machetes into the air, chanting, "Lord An Mi, we will join you!"

But Lord An Mi waved them back. "No! I alone will go. The enemy will be alone, and if we win by outnumbering him, it will make a mockery of our tribe." He snorted. "And if he were intimidated by the sight of our Hamo warriors, he might continue to hide in the forest, causing us further troubles."

The rest of the tribespeople joined him in laughter. In their eyes, the chief was the mightiest Hamo warrior, and no opponent could appear before him without meeting an ugly end.

Xu Xiaowen and Suo Tulan were both frowning in dismay, worried about the Hamo chief's extreme confidence.

Lord An Mi noticed and turned to Suo Tulan. "Your Holiness, there is no need for you to worry. What you must do now is preside over my send-off with a proper cup of wine. Then you will wait for me to return with good news."

The wine was brought in no time. Suo Tulan filled a cup to the brim for Lord An Mi, who downed it in one gulp, his cheeks glowing. Then he tossed the cup to the ground, shattering it. "My fellow Hamo warriors, as soon as I leave, the protection of the village is in your hands. You must do all that is in your power to prevent our cunning enemy from infiltrating."

Hearing the others echo his command, Lord An Mi nodded in satisfaction, then called for his four attendants, with whom he consulted privately. Then he looked at Luo. "Luo, I'm afraid that I'm going to have to trouble you until this matter is fully resolved."

Luo, who knew what he was getting at, could only smile wryly and shake his head. The four attendants came over and tied his hands and feet.

Then Lord An Mi felt at ease once more. He took a torch, and as the rest of the tribe looked on with respect and anticipation, set off on his journey to the Valley of Terror.

During the holy war more than three hundred years earlier, A Liya had launched a surprise attack on General Li and personally cut off his head. In the present, by a stroke of fate, their descendants were matched in a duel to the death.

But in the decisive battle this time, who would clinch victory? Lord An Mi was full of pride, a torch in his left hand and his machete tightly gripped in his right. His footsteps were quiet, his gaze fixed. There was an imposing air about him that made it clear that nothing could stand in his way.

Ferociousness, wisdom, and anger, coupled with a sense of justice, honor, and duty—Lord An Mi possessed all the traits a hero needed in order to emerge from a duel victorious.

Who would have ever imagined that the leading role in the battle would be played by the young man who'd been in the Kunming hospital, a man who was the descendant of General Li? What kind of state was this Li Yanhui in, physically and mentally? And what did he mean by summoning the chief after the explosion? Wasn't the flood meant to carry him off?

Apart from the warriors who had been assigned to patrol the village, almost all of the tribespeople remained at the sacred grounds, waiting for their leader to return. The priestess had recuperated, the demon was about to be defeated, and six months of protracted terror and unrest would cease after this night.

They needed to win. Those who had grown up hearing stories of the holy war—the heroic epic of the village—had built their lives on this glory, and it had served as a spiritual pillar for them. If that pillar were to collapse, what would it mean for these people who had carved out an existence for themselves deep in the forest?

Meng Sha was in the crowd, and his life experience had been quite different from the others'. That was why he stared fixedly at the path leading to the village entrance, his expression ever pious but his gaze anxious.

Luo felt the same way as he waited. In trying to find the cause of the illness in Longzhou, he'd gotten entangled in a confusing tribal conflict that dated back centuries. He felt as if he were at the eye of a storm, watching it wreak havoc all around him.

It was a feeling that Luo had never experienced before, and he felt a trace of helpless sadness. The only thing he could do now was try to protect those who were innocent from being swallowed by the storm.

Ya Kuma, Chief Bai, Di Erjia, Xue Mingfei, Wu Qun, Zhao Liwen, Yu Ziqiang, Chen Bin, Liu Yun, and all the others. The storm had already claimed many victims. What did it have in store for those who were still alive?

Luo's gaze swept over the crowd of Hamo villagers until it finally stopped on Xu Xiaowen. Their eyes locked. There was comfort and trust in her smile. That smile made Luo's heart ache, for he had a bad premonition, a feeling that the situation was out of his control.

Luo's mood had undergone a peculiar change. For the first time, his innate curiosity had been suppressed by his emotions. He suddenly found himself hoping that Lord An Mi would resolve the problem once and for all, even if it meant that all of these mysteries would be buried forever.

For hours, the crowd waited faithfully. Then Lord An Mi finally returned.

It was late at night, without a star in the sky, and the mountain breeze was cool. Lord An Mi's torch could be seen in the darkness, heading toward the crowd one step at a time. His footsteps were slow, as if he were exhausted, but everything else about the way he carried himself seemed normal, and he did not appear to be injured.

"Lord An Mi has returned!" The anxious tribespeople erupted in cheers, sure their valiant leader had defeated the demon.

But Lord An Mi seemed not to hear his people's cries. He simply continued slowly, his head lowered, staring at the ground in front of him. Apart from placing one foot before the other, he hardly moved a muscle and almost seemed wooden. When he finally arrived, the smiles disappeared. Everyone could tell that something was wrong.

Lord An Mi had returned, but only physically. It was as if his soul weren't there: His pride, confidence, courage, and even his dignity had completely vanished. His back was hunched as if he were a petty criminal in chains. He had left the village a hero, but he'd come back a shell.

"Lord An Mi!" Suo Tulan stepped forward and greeted him. He sounded uneasy.

Lord An Mi stopped and lifted his head. Then he turned and gazed at his fellow tribespeople, who stood all around him. There was a vacant look in his eyes, which no longer had the same light in them. The people who adored him had become strangers.

"Lord An Mi, what's the matter? Did you see him?" Luo called out loudly.

The question seemed to awaken Lord An Mi somewhat. He turned to face the attendants who were guarding Luo. "Let him go. Di Erjia's death has nothing to do with him. He was always doomed."

The attendants promptly untied Luo, who rubbed his sore wrists as he stared suspiciously at the transformed leader.

Everyone was confused, but few dared speak. Suo Tulan seemed to ruminate for a moment before he came a step closer and asked the question that was on everyone's mind: "Lord An Mi, did you defeat the demon?"

The tribal leader's body trembled as if something had struck and injured him deep inside. He mumbled to himself, "Did I defeat the demon?"

Suddenly, he began cackling uncontrollably. It was not a joyous laughter but one filled with sorrow and derision. The way he stared at Suo Tulan conveyed utter despair.

"Lord An Mi, why are you laughing?" Suo Tulan sounded almost panicked.

The Hamo leader did not speak. The sound of his laughter grew louder and sadder until it was a howl of pain. Everyone around him had been holding their breath, and now they started to whisper. The villagers looked frightened and alarmed.

Shui Yidie furrowed his brow. He stepped forward and shouted above the crowd's buzz, "Lord An Mi!"

Lord An Mi's laughter abruptly came to a halt. His expression was blank as he looked vacantly at Shui Yidie.

Shui Yidie did not abandon his manners. He bowed. "Lord An Mi, what has happened to you? Even if you lost, the Hamo warriors have survived for centuries, and the spirit of the holy war that has been handed down for generations has also survived. The almighty A Liya and He Layi still bless and protect us, and in the end, victory belongs to us. The demon will go the way of his forefather, in that he, too, will be punished for his crimes."

Shui Yidie's words were persuasive, and they offered the tribespeople solace. They all looked at Lord An Mi, waiting for their leader to reply.

But still Lord An Mi stood there blankly.

"Lord An Mi, please tell us what to do!" Shui Yidie tried once more. "Just say the word, and I will be the first to storm the Valley of Terror, even if it means risking life and limb to ensure that the demon is finished!"

The clanging of metal could be heard all across the sacred grounds as machetes were drawn in answer to Shui Yidie's statement.

Lord An Mi had an answer of his own as well. He tossed aside his torch and pulled out his own machete. It was the same sword that had been handed down for generations and had once been used by A Liya to decapitate General Li. Lord An Mi caressed the blade for a long time before letting out a cry of pain. Then he suddenly turned the sword toward himself and drove the blade straight into his own chest with all his might. The scene erupted into chaos as cries of shock and grief filled the air.

Suo Tulan crumpled to the ground.

Shui Yidie fell to his knees. "Lord An Mi!"

Luo was horrified. Because he was nearby and had quick reflexes, he raced forward and caught Lord An Mi before he toppled over. The four attendants were close behind him. Unsure of what to do, they fell into a line at their leader's knees.

Xu Xiaowen arrived swiftly as well. She was choked up as she wailed, "Lord An Mi, why? Why did you have to do this?"

Lord An Mi's eyes suddenly sprang to life, and he struggled to push Luo away and throw himself before Xu Xiaowen.

Without a second thought, Xu Xiaowen squatted down and placed her hands on his shoulders. "Lord An Mi—"

Lord An Mi stared intently at her. "Your Holiness—you must promise me."

"Promise what?"

"To save"—Lord An Mi turned toward the panic-stricken crowd—"to save our people."

There was no time for Xu Xiaowen to think, and she promptly replied, "I promise you, I'll do it. Only I can."

"Only you can. Only you can do it." A look of relief crossed Lord An Mi's face, and he fell limply into her arms.

Blood flowed from the wound in Lord An Mi's chest onto Xu Xiaowen's white robes. She cried his name as she looked over at Luo.

"Professor Zhou!" Luo helped Xu Xiaowen lift up Lord An Mi, yelling, "Emergency! We need help!"

Professor Zhou and Yue Dongbei rushed over. Professor Zhou inspected Lord An Mi's injury, then shook his head helplessly.

"No, don't save me." Lord An Mi pushed Professor Zhou's hands away. He gazed piously at Xu Xiaowen. "Your Holiness, please forgive me. I am weak—I lack the courage to bear—"

His voice was fading.

"To bear what?" Luo instantly asked.

"Hardships and suffering—" Lord An Mi suddenly gripped Xu Xiaowen's hand, exerting all the strength in him as he spoke. "Please—you must bear, Your Holiness, the burden of tradition." With those words, Lord An Mi inhaled, continuing to stare fixedly at Xu Xiaowen, his eyes open wide. It was not until she nodded vigorously that he exhaled his last breath and slowly closed his eyes.

"Lord An Mi!" Suo Tulan's face crumpled, and he began to weep, tumbling to the ground again. Shui Yidie quickly helped him to his feet. Mournful cries spread through the crowd. The bravest Hamo warrior, the beloved leader of the tribe, had died, and the enemy still loomed. A sense of hopelessness enveloped each and every member of the crowd.

Luo tried to reconstruct what had happened. In the three or four hours that Lord An Mi had been gone, he had evidently received a deadly psychological blow. That blow had caused arrogant, fierce Lord An Mi to take his own life.

What could have happened to rob him of his honor and dignity?

Luo considered this question as he examined Lord An Mi's lifeless body. Apart from the machete wound, there wasn't a trace of another injury, nor even any indication of a struggle.

So what had taken place at the duel?

Then Luo noticed that Lord An Mi was clutching something in his right hand. Luo gently pried away his fingers and removed it from his grip.

It was a yellowing leather scroll—the same lambskin map that had been found on Di Erjia's body.

Had this map been left by Li Yanhui? What was he trying to say? Though Luo had seen it twice before, much had changed since then. He unrolled it and took another look.

The map illustrated the terrain of the Valley of Terror, with marks in red ink along certain areas. In the southern region, there was a red symbol next to the pond, which undoubtedly represented the Hamo village, and a red symbol along the southern slope of the central hill where the valley was located, roughly where Li's army had been stationed. Further south, beyond the valley, was a mountain pass between two hills. Since the terrain there was dangerous, the pass served as a gateway to the valley from the south.

The mountain pass had also been marked in red, as it was where the Qing forces had set up their base. Wu Sangui had seized that gateway, trapping General Li's troops in the valley.

Another red symbol marked the location of the lake above the cliff. But this one was different from the others. The symbol was a red flame, and among its possible meanings, one stood out to Luo: It was where the general had been plotting to detonate explosives.

A line ran north from the lake along the cliff. This line, which was drawn in black ink, ran from the hill through the valley and ended at the Qing base at the mountain pass. After the explosion that had occurred earlier, this was the precise course the water had taken.

The white areas of the map were filled with strange scribbling that included words and numbers, along with dense paragraphs comprising numerous symbols crammed together. Luo didn't recognize these symbols, but he could make out sketches among them, like two lines joined by a rounded arc, which represented the part of the cliff that met the ledge. Everything snapped into focus, and Luo couldn't help letting out a gasp. This map revealed an ancient plot. The water released by the explosion would flow toward the mountain pass to the south. That meant it hadn't been a matter of good fortune for the Hamo people, but rather part of the original plan.

General Li had placed explosives at the lake not to destroy the Hamo village, but to destroy the Qing base at the southern mountain pass!

Before Li Yanhui had placed explosives at the lake, he had planted the map in the village. Could he have been presenting it as evidence of General Li's intent?

Indeed, this interpretation made sense. It was convincing because the map had appeared before the explosion itself, and Li Yanhui had known that the water would never reach the Hamo village. It also made sense that the duel request had been sent before the explosion had taken place—Li Yanhui knew Lord An Mi wouldn't be killed in the flood.

Luo looked up in astonishment. This enormous secret had been preserved for centuries, and even now it was still being safely withheld from all the people around him.

A Liya had wrongly killed General Li. If this was true, then the legend of the Hamo people's great holy war had no significance at all. In fact, the entire village would be disgraced.

Luo's mind spun. He knew that he should not be the one to disclose the secret. To him, it was simply an error of history, but to the Hamo people, it affected the convictions and spiritual beliefs they had held for centuries. They, like Lord An Mi, would lose their sense of honor and their courage to fight.

Luo's gaze swept over the Hamo tribespeople around him, the moral dilemma shining in his eyes. He stared at Meng Sha, Lord An Mi's attendants, Suo Tulan, and Shui Yidie before he finally turned his gaze to Xu Xiaowen.

Xu Xiaowen had already set down Lord An Mi's body and was now sitting on the ground. She took a letter out of a lambskin pouch that Shui Yidie was holding.

Judging by its appearance, it was clearly an old letter. Luo knew instantly: This was the so-called burden of tradition. And he was pretty sure he knew its contents.

At Suo Tulan's request, all of the tribespeople respectfully took a step back. Only Shui Yidie remained on guard at Xu Xiaowen's side. Xu Xiaowen opened the letter and lifted it in front of her.

"No, don't read it," Luo called hoarsely, taking a step toward her.

Xu Xiaowen turned her head toward Luo, her eyes wide. She thought of something that Ya Kuma had told Shui Yidie: "The priestess must be completely mentally prepared. Once she chooses to open the letter, she carries the burden of the entire tribe on her shoulders. There is no turning back."

Shui Yidie drew his machete and held it in front of Luo. It was clear he was not to be disobeyed.

"Luo, please step back," Suo Tulan reprimanded him. "According to the code of our tribe, when the priestess reads about the burden, only her bodyguard can stand guard at her side. All others must keep their distance."

Luo smiled wryly and shook his head. Of course, the burden was written in Mandarin. The priestess could understand it, but since her bodyguard was not permitted to study the language, the contents of the letter would be known to the priestess only. That was why the secret had never been leaked throughout the centuries.

Xu Xiaowen looked at Luo. For an instant, hesitation swept over her. But then she saw her tribespeople. Their faces were full of fear, their peace of mind shattered. Now everyone was watching her, full of anticipation. She was their last hope.

Finally, she gathered her resolve, smiled apologetically at Luo, and began reading the fateful letter in front of her.

She read in silence, the beautifully penned characters taking her back in time to the events of three centuries past. She found herself in the midst of long-standing grudges and enduring bonds, of virtue and depravity, and waves of shock rippled through her mind as she took it all in. Two glistening tears formed at the corners of her eyes and rolled down her cheeks.

Once she had read the entire contents of the letter, Xu Xiaowen stood up. The breeze gently lifted her long locks into the air. After her tears had dried, she stood tall, a look of resolve on her face.

Luo was astounded. She had completed her transformation from an earnest, callow student to a powerful leader capable of bearing the burden of the entire village—as heroic as any priestess of legend.

Chapter 35

HISTORICAL TRUTHS

After weeks of rain, the weather finally changed. Rays of early morning sun penetrated the clouds, sending light all across the mountain range and valley. Raindrops lingered on the foliage, shimmering as the trees and their branches swayed in the wind. The natural world had been reinvigorated.

The Hamo people were in an analogous state of mind. The unease and fear of the past six months had dissipated. The morning after Lord An Mi's death, all of the tribespeople gathered again on the sacred grounds, their eyes fixed on the two people at the altar.

On the left was the gaunt old man who served as their high priest, Suo Tulan. His right hand was across his chest, and he looked toward the blue sky as he spoke: "The gods have blessed the Hamo people with courage. It is on this piece of land that we live our lives, working hard and living peacefully, far from worldly strife, and we do not fear any evil. The glory of the holy war that we have inherited and the heroism of the almighty A Liya and He Layi are still with us today. The spirit of the Hamo people has not faded away."

The Hamo tribespeople raised their heads high, beaming with dignity and self-confidence. Some of the men pressed their arms across their chest, and the crowd erupted into cheers.

Suo Tulan spread his arms and pressed his palms downward, gesturing for quiet. His expression was solemn, and his next words contained no small amount of sadness: "The demon has killed our most courageous warrior, our mighty Lord An Mi, who was a descendant of A Liya. He died for our village, and he will forever be a hero to this tribe."

Di Erjia had likewise died, but Suo Tulan did not mention his name. It had been Di Erjia's tattling that had led to Ya Kuma's death and allowed him to curry favor with Lord An Mi, and thus Suo Tulan regarded him with indifference. Of course, as far as Di Erjia went, there many matters Suo Tulan knew nothing about.

Lord An Mi's death was undoubtedly the biggest blow the tribe had been dealt. Though their chief's strange behavior and his suicide had left them confounded, his years of strong, fair leadership had earned him their boundless affection. Not only that, but people had for centuries conferred a special prestige to the descendants of A Liya. Now that Lord An Mi was gone, A Liya's bloodline had come to an end. Who would the tribe turn to now?

As the tribespeople reflected on this question, their faces revealed a tremendous uncertainty and helplessness that cast a dark cloud over their earlier joy. Many of the women wept quietly.

Suo Tulan clasped his hands together and bowed in a gesture of respect to the dead. Then, after he stood straight once more, his expression changed from one of sorrow to one of indignation.

"The demon must be punished for his crimes. His wicked soul must undergo the most vicious curse so that he can only wander the furthest reaches of hell for eternity, unable to rest in peace." As he spoke, Suo Tulan reached into his robes and pulled out an object, which he held high in the air. "The sacred object has been resealed! This contains the demon blood of Li Dingguo's descendant, the villain who menaced our people and killed our chief!"

The object was sleek, black, and spiked. It was identical to the vial that Luo had confiscated six months earlier. This new blood vial, which had been based on occult arts handed down over generations of high priests, had taken Suo Tulan a full day and night to produce.

But as far as the people knew, the sacred object had simply reappeared—an enormous triumph. They nodded, their faces somber.

"My fellow Hamo people, there is no need to hold back your anger and hatred—you are free to curse this wretched demon as brutally as you like. Light and dark are irreconcilable forces, and all of you hold within yourselves the weight of justice. It is because of a just victory that we are gathered on this special occasion. We must carry out this punishment under the eyes of the gods!" With those words, Suo Tulan soberly turned and looked at Xu Xiaowen, who stood on his right.

Xu Xiaowen's white robes fluttered in the wind, and the sun illuminated her face, giving her an air of purity and holiness. She took the sacred object from Suo Tulan's hand and pressed the tiny vial firmly against her chest.

"The boundless purity of Her Holiness, Ya Kuma, will serve as attestation to our justice. Gods, you have witnessed everything that has happened. I ask you to render your verdict! The Hamo people have vested their powers in the bosom of the priestess so that we may attack the forces of darkness and ensure that they never again see the light of day!"

As Suo Tulan continued his homily, Xu Xiaowen slowly turned her back to the crowd. She recalled the words she'd finally read the night before, the words He Layi had left behind in her letter detailing the burden of tradition the priestess must bear.

The sky is already dark, and everyone in our tribe is fast asleep. In the past few days, we have been gathered on the sacred grounds with our torches, celebrating our great victory. A Liya and I have become heroes in the eyes of our people. A Liya was raised high by his fellow warriors, and the highest honor was conferred upon him. Amid these festivities, no one noticed that I quietly left. Everyone believes that we killed a brutal demon and saved the village from disaster, but I know that the reality is otherwise. There is no way for me to inform anyone of this situation, not even the courageous and loyal A Liya or His Holiness. Right now, only the deceased soul of my father can understand my pain. I cannot deny that, with the aid of Lieutenant General Bai, we successfully executed our plan. But the terrible thing is, this victory marks the beginning of a tragedy. If only we'd known that General Li never had any intention of harming us. He sent an attendant to take me to my father, which according to Lieutenant General Bai, was a lie and sign that he was about to strike. So A Liya and the other warriors hid inside our baskets, waiting for an opportunity to launch a deadly attack.

When the attendant brought me to the west end of the camp, he told me that my father was there. I took advantage of the moment when he was bowing to me to draw the dagger I'd been carrying and drive it straight into his heart. He was caught completely off guard. He slumped and fell to the ground without a sound.

I didn't have time to deal with his dead body. I rushed into the tent and found he hadn't been lying to me: My father lay in a bed in the corner. His chest was wrapped in thick bandages. It was clear that he'd been seriously injured.

Seeing me enter, my father was surprised and delighted. "My dearest daughter, you've finally come."

I flung myself down at my father's side. "Father, what happened? Are you seriously hurt?"

"It's nothing." My father, who was in high spirits, waved dismissively. "When I was younger, I was the toughest warrior in the whole tribe."

"Let's get out of here, then," I urged him. "A Liya has already launched his attack!"

My father looked stunned. "What attack?"

"The reason General Li has been holding you hostage is so that he can capture me. He's planning an explosion at the lake that would flood our village. A Liya and the others have infiltrated the general's tent. We've joined forces with the Burmese and the Qing to overthrow the demon!"

"What?" Hearing these words, my father seemed to forget entirely about his injuries, and he sat up in bed. "Who told you this?"

"Lieutenant General Bai. He leaked General Li's evil plot."

My father slammed his fist onto the side of the bed. "Nonsense! Commander Li has plans to flood the Qing base. I sent for you so that we could discuss how to cooperate with him in fighting off the Qing forces."

"Fighting off the Qing forces?" I was stunned. "You weren't captured by General Li?"

"Foolish girl." There was anger as well as sadness in my father's eyes as he looked at me. "It was Commander Li who saved my life! Yesterday I was ambushed by Qing

soldiers. I didn't stand a chance. Fortunately, Commander Li was patrolling the area and single-handedly took on all eight Qing fighters and rescued me. Afterward, we agreed on a plan to flood the Qing base. How could you have believed the lies of this lowly creature? This is bound to end in disaster."

I gaped at him, unable to believe my ears.

"Hurry and stop A Liya!" my father snapped at me. But because of his condition, he began coughing violently.

I felt as if I had awakened from a dream. By the time I stepped outside the tent, the camp had devolved into chaos. I knew that the Qing troops and our Hamo warriors had already launched their offensive in the valley, and my heart sank.

One of General Li's subordinates stood there seething, his eyes red and a sword in his hands. Perhaps he had witnessed the bloody confrontation between A Liya and General Li. Visibly injured, he slowly hobbled toward me.

"Why, you ungrateful Hamo people!" Cursing through his teeth, he lunged at me with his sword. The burning rage in his eyes prompted me to stand up to him with courage, and I stood unflinching as the blade came near.

Just then my father, who had dragged himself out of bed, pushed me out of the way and fell to the ground. The soldier turned his sword and plunged it straight into my father's chest.

In a second, my world had been completely turned upside down. "Father!" I cried, tears welling in my eyes.

The soldier pulled the blood-covered sword out of my father's body. My father, on the brink of death, used all the strength left in him to grab the man's leg.

"Don't worry about me." My father's voice was hoarse. *"Hurry! Go! You must stop the battle—"*

My heart was shattered by regret and sorrow. I knew that the damage had already been done, and it was all because I had believed Lieutenant General Bai's lies. All that remained was the chance of stopping A Liya from killing General Li. But what about my father? How could I leave him?

My father shouted angrily, *"Don't just stand there! I'm telling you to leave! Are you deaf?"*

The soldier was unable to wrest free from my father's grip, and so he stabbed my father again. I felt as if my own body had been stabbed, as there was suddenly a sharp pain in my heart. My father could no longer speak. He simply stared at me, frozen.

I understood, and carrying the weight of anguish, I turned and bolted wildly toward General Li's tent.

But it was too late. By the time I got there, the general was already dead. His eyes were open wide, as if he were staring angrily at the sky, asking why he had been the victim of such injustice.

I stood there, dejected. My mind went blank. I saw A Liya behead General Li and go to the battlefield.

The camp was eerily silent. Only Lieutenant General Bai and I remained with the general's dead body. Lieutenant General Bai's face was pale, as if he'd witnessed something truly horrifying.

This man was the mastermind behind the bloodbath. I stormed toward him, incensed. *"You despicable liar! Why did you do this?"*

"How did you find out?" Lieutenant General Bai turned and looked at me. *"It's true. I tricked you. I've*

been planning to surrender to the Qing forces for some time."

"You are the true demon," I snarled through gritted teeth, gripping my dagger and running toward him.

Lieutenant General Bai dodged, then grabbed my wrist and snatched the dagger away from me. I tried to throw him off, but to no avail. He looked at me as if frustrated, and muttered, "I'm a demon? So I betrayed the great Ming Dynasty, fine. But what sense was there in continuing this war? Even if we managed to defeat the Qing troops stationed at the mountain pass, what good would that do? The outcome has been decided. Resisting at all costs will change nothing. I've told the general countless times. His answer was: 'Die honorably in the wilderness. There is no surrender.' But I refuse to die in the wilderness, and when all is said and done, Lieutenant General Bai will be a name in the history books."

His excitement grew with every word. His eyes glazed over maniacally. Unable to reason with him, I shook my head, knowing the fear must be visible on my face.

"Are you hurt?" Lieutenant General Bai suddenly let go of my wrist. "I'm not going to kill you. There's no point. My mission has been accomplished. You could tell your tribespeople the truth, but that would bring disaster, wouldn't it?"

Those last words cut straight through me. Indeed, the general had already died at A Liya's hands, and the Qing forces would soon claim victory. The truth could bring my tribespeople only humiliation, anger, and regret. What's more, they would have done anything to avenge my father's death and punish Lieutenant General Bai's deceit, and as his soldiers would now be allying themselves *with the mighty Qing forces, this would have amounted to suicide.*

"I'm leaving this place, finally. What I've accomplished is no less than earth-shattering. The only thing is—I have yet to possess demonic powers." Lieutenant General Bai looked at me as if he were trying to make me understand, but all he received in return was my hateful glare.

And then he left. He knelt down on the ground and bowed three times to General Li's corpse before he turned and headed off toward the foot of the mountain. Though his plot had succeeded, he walked away a very lonely man. I prayed that he would never acquire those demonic powers, that they would vanish forever.

As Lieutenant General Bai had predicted, the war came to an end that day. The tragedy, however, did not.

General Li did not die peacefully. His eyes were open wide and filled with a rage that never dissipated. This caused a panic within the tribe. Everyone believed that General Li killed my father. Their tremendous fear was compounded by their belief in the vicious and evil plot to flood the village. After a consultation with the high priest, it was decided that General Li's blood would be sealed away in a vial and his soul would be savagely cursed.

I am the only one who knows that this decision is extremely cruel and unfair to General Li. But there is no way that I can say so. My tribespeople fought a fierce battle and emerged victorious. They saved the village. If I were to tell them that not only was their victory of no importance, but that there was blood on their hands, what would happen? The Hamo warriors believe in honor and justice above all else. The truth would upend those beliefs, just as Lieutenant General Bai said, and the resulting chaos would send the entire village to its destruction.

What should I do, then? I have no other choice but to stay strong and bear this burden alone. I hope that the gods and my father in heaven will give me their understanding and forgive me for my mistake.

I am clearly not worthy of serving in my father's footsteps as tribal chief. So A Liya will take on this responsibility. He is courageous and a true warrior, and he represents the brilliance of the Hamo people.

As for myself, I will protect the vial and General Li's blood. Its vicious curse and I will keep one another company for life.

Chapter 36

GENERAL LI'S DESCENDANTS

So ended He Layi's letter, and thus General Li's curse and the glorious legend of the holy war were inextricably bound in the Hamo folklore handed down for three centuries. Though the blood vial had been shattered, a new sacred object that would store the blood of General Li's descendant had been made, and on this early morning, it was in Xu Xiaowen's hands.

Her thoughts returning to the ceremony, Xu Xiaowen seemed to feel the spirit of He Layi and all the other priestesses who had come before her and each taken her turn standing on the altar with the vial pressed against her chest. Afterward, each would turn her back to the crowd, cradling the vial in a secret, symbolic gesture that meant no curse, however vicious, should harm the misunderstood soul contained inside.

Under the guidance of Suo Tulan, the tribespeople all lowered their heads and closed their eyes. The annual ceremony had begun, and their anger, contempt, and overwhelming desire for justice all culminated in this curse.

Xu Xiaowen, too, closed her eyes, feeling the cool vial pressed against her chest. Like every other priestess before her, she whispered with utter devotion in her voice: "Dearest gods, you have always blessed us and protected the brave and honest Hamo people. Please let me use my purity to carry out their curse so that this heroic soul does not undergo any further harm. Please do not punish those tribespeople who are ignorant of the truth and who have been deceived by me, for all suffering must pass through me, a burden that I, Xu Xiaowen, willingly undertake as the priestess."

When this portion of the ceremony concluded, her expression changed and her manner grew somber. She appeared to have attained a state of impenetrability, a quality that gave her an awe-inspiring physical presence. This portion of the ceremony was a test in which she would withstand three centuries' worth of trials and tribulations.

Xu Xiaowen gazed down at her fellow tribespeople. She saw Luo standing in the southeastern corner of the grounds.

When Luo looked at Xu Xiaowen, he noticed that she was staring straight at him, but only for a split second.

It was beyond all doubt that Xu Xiaowen was no longer the bubbly college student she'd been not long before. She had accepted the burden of the Hamo priestess.

Luo lifted his hand as if he wanted to reach out, though there was nothing there.

After scanning the entire crowd, the priestess began to speak to them. "Lord An Mi is no longer with us. The village needs a successor. Shui Yidie is a loyal and courageous warrior. As you all have heard, yesterday he personally killed the demon. Only he is qualified to become our new chief!"

These words were precisely what everyone secretly wanted to hear. The tribespeople erupted in cheers. Shui Yidie stood below the altar, waiting to make his entrance. A group of men hoisted him up and threw him high into the air in a celebratory toss reserved for only a true hero.

"Honored and respected Chief Shui Yidie." At Suo Tulan's command, every member of the tribe conferred the highest title to this young man who had just days earlier been locked away in the water dungeon.

There was a hint of a sardonic smile on Luo's face as he recollected the events of the previous night.

After Lord An Mi's horrific death and after reading the letter detailing the burden, Xu Xiaowen had immediately taken Shui Yidie to the Valley of Terror. Once Luo had decoded the secret contained in the map, the truth behind many mysteries had been revealed, but there were other matters that required additional explanation and evidence. Since he was now a free man and could travel as he pleased, Luo wanted to accompany them to find Li Yanhui.

Xu Xiaowen had objected, and he understood her misgivings. He told her quietly, "You don't need to hide anything from me. I already know the secrets about General Li's death."

"Do you?" Xu Xiaowen trembled. It was the first time Luo had seen her look so dismayed. "There's nothing I can hide from you, is there?"

"You have to trust me. I can keep a secret. Not only that, but you need my help right now." The look in Luo's eyes was sincere.

After considering it for a minute, Xu Xiaowen nodded. "Okay, let's go."

On their way to the valley, Xu Xiaowen gave Luo a detailed account of the contents of the letter, confirming several of his guesses. For Luo, some of the details sparked new ideas, and he wrinkled his brow, turning them over in his mind and slowly trying to form a complete picture from the many pieces.

"So what's your plan?" Luo asked Xu Xiaowen.

"I only have a request for him, which is to stop dwelling on the events of the past and to leave our tribe alone. I'm willing to accept whatever punishment he sees fit on behalf of the whole village."

Luo shook his head. "He doesn't want to harm you or your tribe any further."

Xu Xiaowen seemed taken aback. "So what does he want?"

"That's a whole different story." Luo paused. "I have a few ideas, but since we're going to see him soon enough, it might be best if he answers that question himself."

Xu Xiaowen nodded. "It doesn't matter why he did it. When it comes down to it, he murdered a lot of people. Plus, he used his demonic powers to harm my tribe. There were also all those victims in Longzhou. That's why my conclusion is that he still harbors ill will toward our tribe."

"You're wrong," Luo corrected her. "The demonic powers have nothing to do with him. In fact, he was one of their victims. On his deathbed, the general expressed regret over using those powers, and he even killed all those *gu* sorcerers he'd conscripted, who were their originators. But He Layi's letter mentions a certain someone who still maintained a strong interest in preserving those powers."

"You mean—Lieutenant General Bai?" Once prompted by Luo, Xu Xiaowen seemed to understand.

Luo nodded. "Precisely! After Lieutenant General Bai surrendered to the Qing forces, he spent the rest of his life searching for those powers in the valley. Though he failed, his ambitions were handed down generation after generation."

"So Chief Bai finally found the secret to those powers and used them to harm people?"

"At the very least, he played a leading role." Luo spoke with tremendous certainty. "Of course, there were a few people who helped him."

"Who else?"

Luo's eyes glimmered, but he did not answer. They'd reached the top of the low hill and were already nearing the cave. They now had a broader view of the landscape.

There was a faint flicker of light near the cave entrance. Luo breathed a sigh of relief: He was inside. Xu Xiaowen and Shui Yidie clearly sensed it as well, and the three of them quickened their pace. Before long, they were at the entrance. Xu Xiaowen stopped and looked at Luo inquisitively, as if unsure whether to proceed.

Just then, they heard a voice coming from inside: "Please come in. I'm not going to hurt you. I've been waiting for you for a long time."

Luo stepped in front of Xu Xiaowen, whispering, "Follow me."

Xu Xiaowen contemplated for a second, then turned to Shui Yidie beside her, telling him in the Hamo language, "You stand guard here. Remember, no one is to overhear our conversation."

Obeying her orders, Shui Yidie wielded his sword and stood outside the cave. Then Luo, followed closely by Xu Xiaowen, ventured deep into the cave. The tomb was in the same excavated state, but next to it was a raging bonfire. Behind the bonfire sat a man wearing a black mountaineering outfit and a hood that covered his face. Luo tensed. A memory drifted into his mind of the moment when they had reached Qingfeng Pass. Sure enough, this figure in black had appeared in his hallucinations. Luo would never forget those red eyes. As the two of them approached, the man lifted his head and said in a raspy voice, "Have a seat. The ground is damp, but the fire should make things more comfortable."

Xu Xiaowen and Luo exchanged a glance, then sat down in front of the man.

The man seemed to be looking at Xu Xiaowen. Because his hood was pulled down, the light from the bonfire illuminated only the bottom half of his face. Then there was the slightest trace of a dark smile on his face. "You must be Ya Kuma's sister. You two—you look very similar."

"You know who I am?"

"Your sister told me about you," he replied casually. His thoughts seemed to drift for a moment. "She had me go to Kunming to see you—heh. But there was a change of plans. Who would have guessed?"

At the mention of her sister, Xu Xiaowen couldn't help getting a little choked up, and her eyes reddened.

The man turned to Luo. "You're here, too? Chief Inspector Luo, right?" He paused. "Very good. There was something that I wanted to give her to give you, but this makes things easier."

Luo's eyes shone. "Something to give me?"

"Indeed, I have something that you want." He handed Luo an envelope. "I know that there has been an outbreak of illness in Longzhou. I've obtained some information about it over the past six months, and it's written inside. I think it should help you crack the case."

Luo took the envelope from him and said sincerely, "Thank you."

Xu Xiaowen had been sitting there, looking him up and down the entire time. Finally, she couldn't help asking, "Are you Li Yanhui? Why don't you take off your hood?"

The man nodded. "Yes. My name comes before Zhou in *The Hundred Family Names*. I'm a descendant of Li Dingguo. As far as this hood is concerned, I don't mind taking it off. But I want you both to be prepared. My appearance may disturb you."

Li Yanhui removed his hood, revealing what might be considered a rather handsome face. He looked just shy of thirty. He no longer seemed afflicted with despair and fear as he had been at the Kunming hospital.

But what drew their attention were his eyes. They were completely red, all the veins visible, as if he were some sort of wild beast. This was evidently the main reason why he'd been so frightening.

Recalling what had taken place earlier in the valley, Luo found himself unable to look away from those eyes.

Xu Xiaowen asked in astonishment, "What happened to your eyes?"

"In my attempt to rid myself of the phobia, I took too much medicine, and this was a side effect." Li Yanhui laughed bitterly, then looked over at Luo. "Chief Inspector Luo, at first I was worried that you would end up like me. But it appears that very little medicine is required to cure the illness. It didn't seem to have much of an effect on you."

Li Yanhui took out a tiny vial. Luo instantly recognized it as the same one Professor Zhou had shown him at the forensic center. At the same time, Li Yanhui's words reminded Luo of his hallucinations at Qingfeng Pass, when he had felt a hand on his face and a sweet, pungent liquid on his lips.

"So it was the medicine that saved us." Luo's eyes conveyed gratitude.

"Yes. I saw what was happening to you and your chubby friend in the forest, and I had a hunch that it was Chief Bai's doing. After killing Zhao Liwen, I saw Chief Bai in the forest from behind and knocked him out. Then I immediately treated you two. The medicine is quite effective."

Luo let out a deep breath. Back at Qingfeng Pass, he had been on the lookout for tampering with their food and drink, but he hadn't anticipated this. How did this man manage to pull it off?

"I actually saved the three of you before Qingfeng Pass, but that incident didn't seem to register with you."

Li Yanhui's words sent Luo's mind spinning. Dumbfounded for an instant, he retraced his memories before it finally dawned on him.

"That first night on the mountain! You dropped a skinned snake onto our tent, and we all ran out, terrified. Chief Bai and his men were already dressed and brandishing their machetes. At the time, I was impressed that they responded so quickly, but now that I think about it, they must have been planning to attack us before you stopped them." Luo's heart pounded. "Where did you get the medicine from?"

Li Yanhui's answer was vague. "I—I'm not sure. All I know is that the hospital used it to cure me. When I asked for details, they were evasive. They were anxious to discharge me, but they let me take the rest of the medicine when I left."

"Is that the vial Professor Zhou lost?" Xu Xiaowen's eyes widened. "Could it be that the hospital stole it?"

Luo lowered his head but didn't reply. Indeed, there was something fishy about this.

Li Yanhui waved the detail away and looked at Xu Xiaowen. "There's a very important issue between us that needs to be settled."

Xu Xiaowen fidgeted uncomfortably, but she did not look away from him.

"Since you've come here, that means you already know the priestess's burden, correct?"

Xu Xiaowen nodded solemnly.

Li Yanhui turned to Luo. He looked surprised and inquisitive at the same time.

Xu Xiaowen knew what he was thinking and explained, "No, I didn't tell him. He figured out the truth on his own. He knew who you were before you even revealed your identity to Lord An Mi."

"Oh?" Li Yanhui stared at Luo in astonishment. "Chief Inspector Luo, you really are extraordinarily perceptive. It's a good thing that you came here today, and I hope that you can correct the history books and restore my heroic forefather's good name, and at the same time, bear witness to the resumption of the friendship between the Li family and the priestess."

Luo nodded vigorously. "I'll do my best. But as far as the events of the past six months are concerned, there are still many details I don't grasp. For instance, why did you clash with Chief Bai and the others, and what exactly are the demonic powers?"

"And how did my sister really die?" added Xu Xiaowen, voicing the question that had been foremost on her mind.

"I'll tell you both. I've already done everything I'd like to, of course, but the story doesn't end there." Li Yanhui's tone was pensive, and he looked Xu Xiaowen in the eye. Then, lowering his voice, he began to recount the strange events that had led him to this point.

Until a year ago, Li Yanhui had not been aware of the implications of his ancestry. He was an avid and accomplished outdoorsman, and he became well known in explorer circles. He was physically fit and intelligent, and he had undergone specialized training in combat and survival tactics. He loved the rugged outdoors and the forest, and whenever he was in such an environment, he felt carefree and on top of the world. Little did he know, his talents reflected a natural calling.

He had been planning to venture deep into the forest at the Yunnan border. When he went online to gather information, he discovered Yue Dongbei's research on the Valley of Terror, and he developed a serious interest in the subject, as the central figure of the research was none other than his own ancestor, Li Dingguo. Li Yanhui possessed some relics that had once belonged to his forefather, and when he was a child, his family had told stories mentioning their connection to the village of Mihong. He could not believe that his forefather was the savage demon described in Yue Dongbei's theories. Therefore, he treated this trip as an opportunity to uncover the truth behind Li Dingguo's death.

Li Yanhui then paid a visit to Yue Dongbei, from whom he managed to obtain no small amount of information. Soon afterward, he set off on his journey. In order to conceal his identity, whenever anyone asked for his name, he began to offer a stock response: "My name comes before Zhou in *The Hundred Family Names.*"

Li Yanhui retraced his forefather's footsteps all the way to the Hamo village, where he learned that the priestess had been entrusted with the role of preserving the sacred vial that contained General Li's blood, and that the legends of the holy war were a living, breathing part of the culture.

But Li Yanhui was suspicious about these legends. During the several months he spent in the village, he studied the local language and went to the valley and the lake to search for clues.

Deciphering the marks left on General Li's military map, Li Yanhui finally uncovered the most well-kept secret in this chapter of history. That day, he asked to see the Hamo priestess, Ya Kuma, in order to explain this matter and ask her to break the curse on his ancestor's blood vial.

What surprised him was that the priestess actually understood the situation far better than he did, and that generation after generation of priestesses had been anticipating the arrival of someone like him.

Li Yanhui and Ya Kuma's conversation lasted all night. The historical truths revealed were heartbreaking: In order to maintain the dignity of the Hamo people and to preserve the soul of a hero who had been wrongly persecuted, three centuries of priestesses had each, alone, borne the burden of the secret. This deeply moved Li Yanhui.

But there had to be a way out. According to folklore, if General Li's remains were moved outside the cave and the blood of his descendant was sprinkled on them, the curse on the blood vial would be lifted without causing any damage to the Hamos' sacred object.

The evening after their conversation, Ya Kuma quietly brought Li Yanhui to the tomb. Together, they excavated the commander's remains, and another long discussion ensued. They were the only two people in the entire world who knew the truth behind this chapter of history, and they poured their hearts out to one another. Though this was only their second meeting, each felt as if they had known the other in a past life. Soon it was dawn, and Ya Kuma had to get back to the village before her absence was noticed. According to their agreement, after Li Yanhui had broken the curse, he would bury the remains once more, then return the blood vial to Ya Kuma.

But this was not to be. Li Yanhui carried General Li's remains down to the ancient cemetery full of red flowers at the bottom of the hill, where his forefather would be laid to rest once and for all. Once the process was complete and the curse was broken, Li Yanhui suddenly discovered that he had company—several other people had snuck into the cemetery.

Li Yanhui hid in the dark, watching them. It was Chief Bai and his three aides: Xue Mingfei, Wu Qun, and Zhao Liwen. Their conversation stunned Li Yanhui.

They had come in pursuit of the demonic powers, and they seemed to have grasped the source: poison. They wanted to use the poison to formulate a new type of recreational drug. Unfortunately, in addition to causing hallucinations and a kind of high, the drug triggered the sensation of fear. But they had faith that an outside expert could resolve that issue before the drug reached the market. They planned to first circulate the drug within the Hamo tribe, which would serve as a small-scale test group. Then the outside expert could analyze a sample and try to eliminate its panic-inducing side effects. According to their plans, within six months, a prototype of the drug could be covertly distributed in Longzhou, where a large-scale experiment would take place. The expert would conduct a more detailed analysis of a small number of affected people before developing what would ultimately become a fairly safe—and extremely lucrative—product.

Upon hearing their wicked plans, Li Yanhui was incensed. But in his haste, he hadn't been careful to cover his footprints, which led Chief Bai and the others to discover and surround him. Outnumbered, he was taken prisoner. They interrogated him, trying to uncover his identity, but Li Yanhui refused to say a word. Because he was carrying information about the Rain God's secrets, Chief Bai knew that he was a descendant of Li Dingguo and decided that he had to be killed to avoid further trouble.

When they discovered that he was carrying the sacred blood vial, Chief Bai immediately sent Wu Qun to relay this information to the Hamo tribesman Di Erjia. After Di Erjia had lost the competition to become the priestess's bodyguard, Chief Bai had been able to buy his allegiance and effectively use him as a pawn. Di Erjia was extremely pleased when he received this information from Wu Qun: Now it was his turn to triumph.

Di Erjia paid a visit to Lord An Mi and told him that he had seen Ya Kuma give the sacred object to this young man from another tribe. Lord An Mi was skeptical, but then a hunter from the tribe came with the news that Li Dingguo's tomb had been excavated. Lord An Mi was forced to act. He brought Di Erjia to the priestess's house to ask what had happened.

When Ya Kuma was unable to produce the blood vial, Lord An Mi's alarm transformed into anger. Ya Kuma accompanied Lord An Mi to the cave, nourishing one last thread of hope that Li Yanhui would return.

But Li Yanhui was down in the ancient cemetery, bound and gagged. Because the cave entrance was near the edge of the cliff, Li Yanhui could see Ya Kuma standing outside, waiting in misery. He felt as if a knife had been plunged and twisted in his heart. He was worried about her, but his desperate cries were nothing more than a muffled whimper.

Ya Kuma did not know why Li Yanhui had gone missing, and on that cold, dark night, her heart gradually gave up all hope. Lord An Mi stood before her, angrily demanding answers that she had no way of providing. In the end, just before the break of dawn, she turned to suicide as a means of escaping a world that had never given her much joy to begin with.

Shui Yidie was imprisoned in the water dungeon as a result. Di Erjia took over his post in the tribe and became Lord An Mi's trusted aide. The news quickly reached Wu Qun, who passed it on to Chief Bai, who was extremely pleased with this outcome. In fact, when they carried out their plans to test the drug on the Hamo people, Di Erjia served in a critical role, both covering for them and collaborating with them.

Chief Bai and his henchmen brazenly discussed their plans back at their camp in the cemetery, laughing about how much money they stood to make. When they spoke of how Ya Kuma had died only days earlier, Li Yanhui's heart filled with despair and burning rage. Even after he slipped deep into a state of terror, that fire was never extinguished.

Chief Bai decided to make Li Yanhui their first test subject, forcing him to ingest an extract of the fear-inducing substance. Then they waited for the expert to arrive and take a blood sample for analysis.

Thus, Li Yanhui became the first victim of madness. After his unraveling, Chief Bai no longer guarded him as closely. But it was then that Li Yanhui, who was trained in long-term survival tactics, exploded, breaking free of his bindings and escaping into the deep forest. About two weeks later, he was at Qingfeng Pass when a television crew from Kunming discovered him, took him back to the city, and then sent him to the mental institution.

For the next six months, Li Yanhui was locked inside a room at the hospital. Tormented day and night by fear, he lost his ability to think. Only two thoughts remained lodged deep inside his mind:

"A demon from the Valley of Terror will descend on Longzhou!"

"Ya Kuma!"

Six months later, under circumstances never made clear to Li Yanhui, the Kunming hospital used the drug that Professor Zhou had developed on him, ending the terrible episode at last. Throughout his gradual process of recovery, his thoughts returned to Ya Kuma, and his desire for revenge became his strongest impetus, sustaining his will to survive.

Li Yanhui recognized the incidents in Longzhou as related to his plight, so he followed Luo and the others to Mihong. At the Temple of the Dragon King, Xue Mingfei became the first victim on his path to revenge. The notion of a bloody reincarnation was exactly how Li Yanhui wished his enemies to view his return.

Then, during their journey to the valley, Li Yanhui employed the punishment known as "pulling out tongues" on Di Erjia's informant, Wu Qun. In the process, he left hints of General Li's presence, intending to point Luo and the others toward a heroic view of his forefather, knowing Yue Dongbei would be thrilled to provide historical context.

After killing Zhao Liwen, Li Yanhui caught Chief Bai alone. Once the chief realized who it was and how savagely he'd murdered his men, Chief Bai fell apart, convinced Li Yanhui really must be the reincarnation of the general, back to punish the descendant of traitorous Lieutenant General Bai. He threw himself at Li Yanhui's feet, promising loyalty and begging for forgiveness.

The group was about to enter the Hamo village, and Li Yanhui needed help in order to execute the next stage of his plan, so he temporarily pardoned Chief Bai on the condition that he obey orders. Chief Bai didn't dare defy him. His only hope was that Li Yanhui's plan would proceed without a hitch so that he would be content and show mercy.

When Luo and the others went to the valley with Di Erjia, Li Yanhui lured them to the ancient cemetery in the hopes that they would discover clues that revealed the crimes of Chief Bai and his aides. Then he went to the cave and excavated Ya Kuma's remains. Overwhelmed with grief, he'd stood on the ledge of the cliff and let out a mournful wail.

There were still two names left on his list of targets: Di Erjia and Lord An Mi.

Di Erjia's wrongdoings had been less severe than the others' and all under the orders of Chief Bai, so Li Yanhui prescribed a straightforward punishment for him: He slit his throat with a knife. At the same time, he left the map detailing the explosion at the lake on Di Erjia's corpse. This was part of his plan to punish Lord An Mi. As far as Li Yanhui was concerned, Lord An Mi's obstinacy had pushed Ya Kuma to her death. The Hamo chief had inherited a false sense of glory, and in order to sustain that false glory and preserve the beliefs of the tribe, Ya Kuma had killed herself without ever revealing the historical truth. But as a victim of history, she was left with not a shred of honor or pity, her remains buried in the cursed cave. This was a situation that Li Yanhui could not condone. He resolved to strip Lord An Mi of his glory and his dignity, forcing him to confront Ya Kuma's death in a twisted act of warfare.

And Li Yanhui had succeeded. Faced with this cold, hard reality, Lord An Mi saw his pride and his beliefs collapse in a single instant. The illustrious aura that had surrounded his tribe for centuries had been dealt a deadly blow. By the time the Hamo chief returned to the sacred grounds, he was consumed by despair, disgrace, and guilt. The exact pain that Ya Kuma had so long felt was now foisted upon him, but unlike the wise priestess, the arrogant young leader could not bear it even for an hour.

Listening to Li Yanhui's account, Luo was able to clear up numerous mysteries that had eluded him. His only regrets were that Li Yanhui had never seen the outside expert and he did not know the exact source of the demonic powers, though they clearly originated from the plot of land on which the ancient cemetery had been built.

"Can you forgive my people?" Xu Xiaowen's eyes were wide as she looked at Li Yanhui. "You wanted revenge, and you got it. What I want to ask you is to help me keep this a secret from the tribe."

"Keep this a secret?" Li Yanhui suddenly cackled. "But what good would that do at this point? For the Hamo people, the sacred object has already been lost, and the leader is dead. The glory of the holy war has been marred. If my guess is correct, your people are grieving, and they're terrified. How can they regain their pride and dignity? How can they rebuild their beliefs anew?"

Xu Xiaowen froze. There was confusion in her eyes. It was true: Even if Li Yanhui were to keep his mouth shut, she would still need to confront the problems created by everything that had already happened.

Li Yanhui removed a letter from his bag and handed it to Xu Xiaowen. "Take this, but don't read it just yet." He turned to Luo. "Chief Inspector Luo, what are your thoughts?"

"About what?"

"I've killed a lot of people. And you're a policeman." Li Yanhui paused. "How do you plan to deal with me?"

"There may have been cause to kill those people," Luo said, "but you're not the law, and you didn't have the authority to take their lives."

"So you're going to arrest me and have the law decide?"

Luo didn't answer. It was evident that his response was affirmative.

Li Yanhui suddenly burst into a strange fit of laughter. "I have a better idea."

"What's that?"

As soon as Luo spoke those words, Li Yanhui sprang toward Luo, and his right arm swung forward. The sword in his hand made contact with Luo's head. Not having anticipated such a turn of events, Luo was defenseless. He tumbled to the cold, damp floor of the cave. Xu Xiaowen shrieked and threw herself on top of Luo, putting herself between the two men.

"What are you doing?" she asked.

At the priestess's cry, Shui Yidie abandoned his post and stormed inside the cave.

Li Yanhui laughed again, then lunged straight at Shui Yidie, who greeted him with his own blade. Li Yanhui's chest was left wide open and unprotected, and with only a single pass, Shui Yidie stabbed him in the heart. Li Yanhui stumbled, then fell limply to the ground. Luo touched his throbbing head and checked to see if he was bleeding. He wasn't. Only the dull edge of the blade had struck his head. Luo was dumbfounded—as was Shui Yidie. Back when he and Li Yanhui were on good terms, they had held a few friendly sword fights and found themselves evenly matched. How was it that this time his opponent had lost so quickly?

The answer was in the letter that Li Yanhui had given to Xu Xiaowen. It was brief but clear.

> *After I die, seal away my blood in the vial. Whoever kills me should become the new tribal chief and new hero. I told Ya Kuma, "I will bring the blood vial back. The burden endured by the priestesses of past centuries will not have been in vain. These falsehoods have been perpetuated out of benevolence, and they must be continued." I have not broken my word to your esteemed sister. In the end, I have kept my promise.*

Shui Yidie was never made aware of this, of course. Even when the tribe was celebrating and raising him up high, there was still a confused look on his face. But that confusion faded quickly when the title of tribal chief was conferred on him, and a sense of honor and pride swept over him.

During that joyful ceremony at the sacred grounds, Luo stood on the sideline, watching. He shook his head.

Ya Kuma dead, Lord An Mi dead, Chief Bai dead, and now Li Yanhui dead. Almost everyone involved in this drama had died, and the story hadn't even reached its ending.

Then and there, Luo couldn't help recalling the words that His Holiness Suo Tulan had once spoken to him outside the cave: "Luo, death does not necessarily mean the end. To the contrary, it can be a fresh beginning."

Chapter 37

Case Closed

The Hamo people's lively celebration lasted several days. They rejoiced in the demon's death, the resealing of the blood vial, and the birth of the new hero. They celebrated a great victory in a new holy war.

There was no way that Luo could enjoy the festivities. Deep down, he was filled with sorrow.

Yue Dongbei, on the other hand, was thrilled. The events of the past days had provided him with loads of material for his research, and he had recorded every last detail, along with his own theories and analyses.

Professor Zhou was already packing his bags.

"Time to leave," he told his two travel companions. "The events taking place now have nothing to do with us. The murderer has been killed, so we don't need to worry about that problem anymore. Right now, I have get back to Longzhou as soon as possible and get back to work. I want to take these plant samples and have them analyzed by the lab."

Professor Zhou was talking about the blood of ghosts that they'd collected from the ancient cemetery. Though the flower had been soaking in water for the past few days, the dark-red petals still retained their mysterious splendor, which showed no signs of waning.

Luo looked at Professor Zhou, then at the flowers. He was silent and seemed to be thinking.

Yue Dongbei chuckled. "Chief Inspector Luo, are you reluctant to leave?"

Luo turned. "What do you mean?"

"That woman, Xu Xiaowen," Yue Dongbei giggled, as boorish as ever. "Ever since she first appeared, you've been different."

"It's true," Professor Zhou added with a smile. "That day at the ceremony on the sacred ground, you completely forgot yourself. You were always so cool and collected up until that point, but you never quite recovered after that."

Luo was embarrassed. He had no idea how to respond.

"Heh heh heh." Yue Dongbei snickered. "Chief Inspector Luo, I never imagined that you'd be stumped by our questions. Of course, this kind of situation is quite normal! The blossoming of a relationship is a beautiful thing. You can rely on your logical mind as much as you like, but you'll never be able to understand."

"Xu Xiaowen—" Professor Zhou smiled, recalling their meeting just three weeks earlier at the Kunming hospital, then shook his head and sighed. "She's the Hamo priestess now. Life is full of changes that you can't predict."

Luo felt a tiny stab of pain in his heart. The moment Xu Xiaowen opened the letter describing the burden, her destiny was forever changed.

"Life is full of changes, eh?" Yue Dongbei smirked. "I say take destiny into your own hands! Chief Inspector Luo, if you like this woman, then you should take her with you. What is this tribal code, this priestess business? Once you leave this tiny village, it's a bunch of baloney! Xu Xiaowen is Xu Xiaowen. Heh heh. Maybe my book can have a drawn-out romantic subplot!"

But Luo had a sour look on his face. "All right, that's enough. You two start getting ready. We'll leave tomorrow."

With those words, he turned and headed for the door.

Yue Dongbei swallowed indignantly. "Wait—where are you going?"

"I have some business to take care of." Luo had recovered his cool and collected demeanor. "You two don't need to come."

After he stepped out of the house, Luo left the village and took an out-of-the-way trail toward the valley. But this time, his destination wasn't the cave; it was the ancient cemetery on the hillside.

The blood of ghosts flowers that had been in full bloom on his last visit hadn't fared well in the flood, and most of them had withered.

What was the source of the mysterious powers?

Luo paced around the ancient gravesite for a while, then headed to its perimeter, where an evergreen shrub grew. Its branches were thick and densely covered in lush leaves, which even the harsh mountain torrents hadn't managed to rip away.

Under the shrub were two nondescript dirt mounds. Luo stopped in front of them in a moment of respect and solemnity. According to Li Yanhui, these were the final graves of General Li and Ya Kuma.

The cemetery had been located near a command post. That way, General Li could rest and see below him the thousands of soldiers whose souls would forever keep him company.

"Die honorably in the wilderness," the great general had said. "There is no surrender." But in the end, he did not die honorably; instead, he left a lifelong ambition to preserve the Ming Dynasty sadly unfulfilled.

"I've fought for the people, and I've fought alone, with no one to help me." Though more than three hundred years had passed, this hero's lament on his deathbed still seemed to echo through the valley.

Even though he was but one man, General Li had possessed the courage of a thousand soldiers. But his plans were ill-fated, his allies were useless, and in the end, his own most trusted confidant had betrayed him. How could one man be expected to triumph over such circumstances?

The story of Ya Kuma was another tragedy. While she'd had to uphold a lie, speaking the truth required even more courage and came at a greater cost. Lord An Mi had suspected Ya Kuma and Li Yanhui of an affair. However, the relationship was not between her and him, but rather between her tribe and his family. It was a relationship that transcended the river of time as well as the chasm of death.

Luo spent a long time at the cemetery, thinking fondly of the two people buried under the shrub.

By the time he returned to the village, it was dusk. The tribespeople had gradually left the celebration and returned home for dinner. The smoke from their kitchen chimneys filled the air.

Luo did not return to the house where he was staying but instead headed toward the priestess's house. Before he left, he had to see Xu Xiaowen alone, as they still had matters to discuss. Luo had a strange feeling that he'd only rarely experienced. He didn't know what to do or what the outcome of this visit would be.

A week later he, Professor Zhou, and Yue Dongbei finally made it back to Kunming.

With the frightening history of the forest behind them, the bustling city seemed almost surreal.

The three of them promptly found a hotel and booked their flight back to Longzhou for the very next day. The long and arduous trek back through the mountains had left them all exhausted. After a hot shower, Professor Zhou and Yue Dongbei retired to their rooms and fell asleep. But Luo had no time for such luxuries. He rushed to the

Kunming hospital to see if Dr. Liu could answer his final, urgent questions.

As they discussed Li Yanhui's treatment, there was an embarrassed look on the doctor's face.

"Technically speaking, this is a medical accident. The patient recovered, but not because of our treatment."

There was one particular point Luo was focused on: "Where did the medicine come from?"

"I don't know." Dr. Liu shook his head. "The patients in this hospital undergo monitoring and treatment on a daily basis. The treatment is generally medication based on a doctor's prescription, and the nurses are responsible for administering it. In this case, medication had only been administered for two or three days when the nurse reported that the patient had made a dramatic recovery. I was astonished, and so I went to see for myself. That was when I discovered the patient had been administered a substance from a vial that was not my prescription, and furthermore, not labeled. It could not have come from our institution."

"So could it have been the nurse?"

Dr. Liu shrugged helplessly. "Who knows? The young man's situation was complicated. Every day, we had to dispatch three nurses: two strong, athletic male nurses who could restrain him and a female nurse who administered the medication. If anyone was responsible for misconduct, it would likely be one of those three, but we have no system for conducting a probe to find out. Fortunately, the effects of the drug were more positive than negative, but there were side effects, so we told the patient that whether he continues to take the drug is up to him."

"Oh." Luo thought this over. "I'd like to see the female nurse."

The young nurse was named Zhao Ying, and she apparently had a lot to get off her chest. "I'd just started this job. It was the first time I ever administered medication to a patient. I didn't think I'd become the scapegoat so soon. Me commit misconduct? Seriously? If I went around tampering with medication, would I still be working here?"

Luo chuckled. "I know the medication wasn't yours. But didn't you find it strange that the drug container wasn't labeled? Shouldn't the dosage be written down somewhere?"

"I thought I'd lost the sheet of paper." Aware that Luo was a policeman, Zhao Ying answered honestly. "And I was scared of being yelled at, so I didn't ask the doctor. When I gave the medication to the patient, I used only a little. That patient hadn't gotten any better at all in six months, so I didn't think it would be a problem if I only gave him a little."

Dr. Liu stood by, listening and shaking his head in dismay.

Luo didn't ease up. "The sheet containing the doctor's orders was lost? It never occurred to you to verify the type of medication you were administering?"

"The sheet was missing, and the vial didn't have a label." Zhao Ying lowered her head. Her voice was small. "Like I said, it was my first time ever giving medication to a patient. The instant they opened the door, the patient started screaming at the top of his lungs. My hands were shaking, and so was the entire tray I was carrying. The paper and some of the medicine fell on the floor. I managed to find the vial, but sometimes the patients grab the paper and rip it up—"

Indeed! Luo's heart was pounding. "What was the date?"

"My first day here"—Zhao Ying appeared to be thinking—"was August 15th."

"That was the day that you visited," Dr. Liu observed.

"Right! That's right! So that's what happened." Luo clapped his hands. There was a look of realization on his face.

Dr. Liu was perplexed. "What do you mean? What happened?"

"That vial belonged to Professor Zhou."

"Professor Zhou?" Dr. Liu asked. "Yes. He said he had developed a new type of treatment. Could he have left it here? He wouldn't do that. He's a professional."

"He would never do so intentionally. But he had it in his pocket." Luo patted his chest pocket. "Do you remember when the patient grabbed him? It took two people to pull him off."

"Ah!" Dr. Liu recalled the episode and understood. "The medication fell out and rolled onto the floor!"

Luo nodded. "Most likely. And afterward, when Ms. Zhao gathered the medication on the floor, she picked it up. As a result, the patient was cured."

Knowing that the hospital had not been at fault, Dr. Liu was in a better mood, and he smiled. "Ha. If that's the case, then this has been a stroke of good luck."

Good luck? Luo inwardly breathed a sigh of relief. Indeed, given everything he knew now, only a stroke of extraordinary fortune could explain how things had turned out.

On the plane back to Longzhou, Luo told Professor Zhou about how the drug container had fallen from his pocket in Kunming. Professor Zhou seemed stunned. Finally, he laughed out loud and shook his head. "How could this have happened? Don't you think it's quite a coincidence?"

"Indeed," Luo told him as he took out the container and set it in front of him. "Professor Zhou, you're a brilliant man. But luck played a trick on you. You went through all that trouble of making elaborate plans and following them scrupulously, so who would have imagined that this little container would ruin everything?"

"Plans?" Professor Zhou froze. "What plans are you talking about?"

"Without this container, Li Yanhui would still be in the Kunming hospital. Without it, Yue Dongbei and I would have become victims of the illness. Without it, your plans would have gone without a hitch. But you lost it. There's an old proverb that goes: 'Careful how you use your shield; it may be used as a weapon against you.' It mystifies some people to this very day."

Yue Dongbei had been listening to their conversation. Eyes wide, he stared at the container. "Chief Inspector Luo, are you saying that when we experienced those terrifying hallucinations at Qingfeng Pass, it was drug induced?"

Luo nodded.

Yue Dongbei turned to Professor Zhou. "So what role have you been playing in all of this?"

"You should ask Chief Inspector Luo." Professor Zhou artfully dodged the question. "I'd like to hear about it myself."

Luo put away the container, as it would eventually be used as evidence in court. Then he stroked his chin. "After the journalist Liu Yun's body surfaced, I sensed that Chief Bai might be the culprit. I also found one of you suspicious. So I was extra cautious with all of the arrangements I made throughout the day, even keeping a close eye on food and drink. Even so, we were poisoned at Qingfeng Pass. By you, Professor Zhou."

Professor Zhou shook his head in disbelief. "You were carrying the food, and everyone was carrying their own water. How could I have done it?"

"It would have made no sense to put it in solid food. It needed to be in the drinking water. Everyone filled their water bottles from the reservoir, but only Yue Dongbei and I were poisoned. And we were also the last two people to fill our water bottles. Therefore, the person who filled his bottle before us is a suspect."

"Right, right, right!" Yue Dongbei pointed at Professor Zhou angrily. "You hid the drugs in your own bottle, then you put them in the water when it was your turn!"

Professor Zhou snapped, "Mr. Yue, is this conjecture another hypothesis based on your so-called scholarly methods?"

"Conjecture?" Luo interjected, smiling at Professor Zhou. "Yes, and I have more conjectures. Take Di Erjia's death, for example. My conjecture is that you were the one who framed me."

Suddenly, Professor Zhou smiled back at Luo. "I'd really love to hear how you came to that conclusion. It should be a rather interesting intellectual exercise."

"I originally thought that one of you killed Di Erjia with the intention of framing me. But then there was evidence suggesting that it was, in fact, Li Yanhui. Still, my camping knife was found on the body, and there's no way that Li Yanhui could have put it there. That means one of you followed me and happened to see Di Erjia's murder, at which time you came up with a plot to frame me and returned to get the knife. Professor Zhou, you said yourself that after the three of us split up, you went back to the house."

"Oh, all right. That makes sense." Professor Zhou nodded. There was a glint in his eyes. "But is that all?"

"Shoes," Luo said. "Your shoes."

Professor Zhou frowned and looked at his feet. He was wearing hiking boots. Though they had been through water and across rough terrain over the past few days, there was nothing unusual about them.

Yue Dongbei scratched his head in confusion. "What about his shoes?"

"Not this pair. The old pair," Luo prompted him. "Among the three of us, only you brought an extra pair of shoes. Then a hole got burned in them."

Professor Zhou laughed. "But what does that prove? I burned the hole myself? So that I could wear my new boots?"

"Let's back up and take a look at the sequence of events in Mihong. Liu Yun arrived on the day of the Rain God ceremony. That afternoon, when we were 'invited' to see Chief Bai, Liu Yun went into our room.

That evening, your old shoes got burned. The next morning, I went looking for Liu Yun, and you headed to Chief Bai's place, supposedly 'to help him prepare.' Liu Yun was following me on the road, but then I ran into you, Professor Zhou. Liu Yun saw you and fled, then tried to make arrangements to meet me alone. I've realized now that it's because you and Chief Bai divulged some secrets during your meeting that morning—perhaps your plans for Yue Dongbei and me?—that Liu Yun wanted to warn me about. But how did Liu Yun know what you two talked about? That question had me stumped for a long time. It wasn't until we got back to Kunming last night that I suddenly remembered your shoes. I found something in the tongue of the left one."

Luo extended his right hand. In his palm was a tiny disc like a watch battery. "Liu Yun planted this bug in your new shoes, then made sure your old ones were ruined. He originally wanted to eavesdrop on our conversations so he could publish more salacious stories. He never expected to uncover secrets that would endanger even himself. When Liu Yun arranged to meet me alone, you immediately sensed that something was wrong and insisted on coming along to 'protect' me. Then, when Chief Bai delayed the start of the trip, you were strangely rude to him. You didn't know it at the time, but the delay was because, at the time of our appointment, Chief Bai was hunting down Liu Yun."

"Interesting. Interesting." Professor Zhou eyed the device. "But these bugs don't record. They only transmit sound, isn't that right?"

Luo nodded. "That's right."

"Then there's no real evidence for anything you're saying," Professor Zhou sneered. "I'm disgusted by your allegations!"

Yue Dongbei gazed expectantly at Luo, desperately hoping that he was about to drop an even bigger bomb. "But why would Professor Zhou do all that? What was his motive?"

"Right. Motive." Luo cleared his throat. "I struggled with that myself until I finally had the opportunity to talk with Li Yanhui. Having learned about your plans from Chief Bai and his aides when they captured him, he helped me connect all the pieces. Mr. Yue, you must be puzzled right now, but let me explain it all to you from the beginning.

"A year or so ago, a celebrated psychiatry professor came across your fascinating historical work. But what interested him were not the mysteries of General Li's life and death, but the man's so-called demonic powers. He deduced that these powers were the product of some hallucinatory substance. To learn more, he traveled to the Yunnan border, where he met a man whose family had been trying to obtain those powers for generations: Chief Bai. Chief Bai brought him to the Valley of Terror, and the two of them eventually found a substance that could induce certain sensations that were both stimulating and pleasant. The professor then had the idea of producing a new drug that, with the aid of Chief Bai, would be put on the black market in Yunnan, with the two parties sharing the profits.

"But there was one problem. The drug's side effect was extreme phobia, which meant additional research and development was required. The professor gathered samples and returned to Longzhou. He then went back to the valley in February to test the drug on the Hamo tribe. In August, the professor used a more developed version of the drug to conduct a larger-scale test in Longzhou. He distributed the drug at schools, hotels, and other places where all kinds of people gather, allowing it to be tested on a wider demographic. Most people experienced its intended effects as a recreational stimulant, while a small number—and all of those who received a large dose, as we did—succumbed to extreme phobia. These people, of course, became the professor's patients as well as his research subjects—except for those unlucky few who died and brought the whole mess to my attention.

"Oh, and I forgot about the Hamos' sacred blood vial. Li Yanhui had gotten it from Ya Kuma, so it fell into the hands of Chief Bai and his men when they captured him. Most likely, this same professor brought the vial to Longzhou and arranged for it to be sold on the black market, hoping for a little extra money even before the drug was in full-scale production. What terrible luck for him that I accidentally shot it—a million dollars lost and a meddling detective and historian in his way! You see, when we traced the origins of the blood vial to the Valley of Terror, the professor was with us the entire way, for his objective was to conceal the truth. In the process, he was willing to resort to any means necessary, including killing his own ally, Chief Bai."

After he finished speaking, Luo turned to Yue Dongbei, whose eyes were wide and whose mouth was gaping. He stared at Professor Zhou with genuine terror in his eyes.

Professor Zhou glared at Luo. "A fascinating theory. But you still haven't produced a shred of hard evidence!"

"Yesterday, I called the bureau and had them search your lab. They found some suspicious substances, which they then tested. The substances produce both stimulant and phobia-like effects."

"Ah." With a bitter laugh, Professor Zhou shook his head. "It's normal to have these kinds of substances in my lab. There's no way you can prove that those are linked to the powers from the Valley of Terror. Chief Inspector Luo, your evidence is missing a crucial link."

"This link?" Luo reached into his backpack and pulled out a dark, round object covered in mud.

All the blood drained from Professor Zhou's face.

"Professor, if the substances in your lab contain the same components that are in this, I'm sure the judge can draw his own conclusions." Though his tone was nonchalant, Luo knew he'd dealt Professor Zhou a fatal blow.

"What—what is that?" Yue Dongbei reached out and touched the object.

"It's the fruit produced by the blood of ghosts. But it grows on the roots. According to Li Yanhui, the demonic powers originated in the ancient cemetery. But Professor Zhou here only cut off the stalks for us to bring back for testing, when a scientist would surely know to take the whole plant. Plus, there were the human bones we found—someone had been digging. So, before we left, I went back and found these."

Luo stopped. He turned his head and looked out the window. The plane had begun its descent.

"Professor Zhou, I hope you have everything you need. Someone is waiting for you," Luo said, pointing toward the tarmac.

Standing in the sun, Luo's team waited in their police uniforms, a swath of darkness that was, in fact, full of light.

Epilogue

Yue Dongbei sat across from Luo in his office at the police station with a stunned look on his face, having just heard all the rest of the story about Lieutenant General Bai's deceit and the Hamo people's tragic mistake.

By now, Luo was well acquainted with Yue Dongbei's melodramatic ways. He quietly waited for a gleeful, smug expression to appear before the man launched into his usual blustering.

But this time, something completely unexpected came out. "Why didn't you take her with you?" Yue Dongbei blurted out.

There was a silence before Luo responded. "What?"

"That woman, Xu Xiaowen. Why didn't you take her with you? You already know the holy war business is a sham. Why didn't you expose it? How can you stand to let a lovely young woman endure such suffering? And what about General Li and Li Yanhui, whose reputations have been slandered?"

"I've told you everything, and you now can rewrite the history of General Li so that everyone recognizes his rightful place as a hero—which was Li Yanhui's wish. But you must promise that no one, including you, will ever let this book fall into the hands of the Hamo tribe, for it will overturn their way of life." Luo paused. "As far as Xu Xiaowen is concerned, it's her choice to stay in the village and guard the secret. She would never abandon her people amid such tragedy—"

"She can't do it, but you can!" Yue Dongbei interrupted him, his face flushed. "All you need to do is reveal the truth and everything will come to an end, and no innocent, well-meaning person will have to be enslaved by this huge secret. You have to help her! I really can't believe you actually left her there on her own!"

Yue Dongbei's words touched a sore spot in Luo's heart. After a long silence, he smiled bitterly. "I know what you're saying, but—I can't do it. Trust me, if she'd given even the slightest hint that it was what she wanted, I would have taken her away in a second. But her mind was made up. What right do I have to impose my own selfish desires on someone else?"

"You're going to regret it." For the first time, it was Yue Dongbei's turn to scold Luo. "When you're my age, which will be sooner than you think, you'll regret it. A nice girl came into your life, and you had a chance with her, but you made the wrong decision. Someday you'll find yourself drunk and muttering to yourself, wondering what could have been if you hadn't been such a lowly coward. It doesn't matter what you go on to achieve in life—it'll happen all the same."

A lowly coward? This was the first time that Luo had ever heard himself described that way. His mind was spinning.

"All right. I'm going to rewrite General Li's biography, and I will keep my word. But Chief Inspector Luo, my opinion of you has changed today. You've disappointed me." Yue Dongbei huffed before getting up and leaving.

Luo was astounded. He stood up and walked over to the window, where he felt a gentle breeze on his face. Before leaving the Hamo village, he had paid one last visit to Xu Xiaowen, and their conversation was burned into his mind.

"Is it worth it to you, to keep living this lie?"

"If it were only about me, of course not. But when I think of my sister, or of Li Yanhui, or of the tribespeople, what am I supposed to do? You may think of it as living a lie or even a hideous fraud, but that's because you don't understand our village. You met Meng Sha, who tried living in the city, didn't you? Have you seen how people like him, whose beliefs were so shaken they left the village, have fared? My people are not like your people. In the outside world, there are plenty of people who have no beliefs whatsoever, and all of you can live that way. But the Hamo people have nothing other than their beliefs. Even if those beliefs are false, the tribespeople still need them. If those pillars were to crumble, I simply can't imagine how harsh and cruel the world would be for us."

With those words, "my people" and "your people," she had made it clear: They stood on opposite sides of a chasm. No matter how much time passed, whenever Luo recalled that conversation, his heart still ached.

Exhaling slowly, he gazed at the horizon in the far distance. On this clear, beautiful day, how many others out there were living a lie?

AFTERWORD

First manuscript completed on October 27, 2006, in Yanjiao, Hebei Province

Over six months, from April to October, I completed *Valley of Terror*, my longest work to date.

I started out trying to write an ordinary novel, with no intention of ever making it this long or making use of this much historical information.

Then something happened at the end of May.

I was writing chapter 7, and I needed to know the legend surrounding the demonic powers, as well as the history of the Southern Ming's resistance against the Qing forces. When I searched online, I became intrigued by Li Dingguo.

> *The aloof orphan turned a loyal, steadfast man / Reaching for the sky, he single-handedly took it in his grasp / Making his name in the Battle of Mopan / A light concealed among shadows, his true brilliance is matched only by the sun.*

—An ode to General Li written by a late–Ming Dynasty literati scholar

He is no less than a tragic personage. If you browse through the historical information on him, you'll find that he possesses all the qualities of a hero: fierceness, resourcefulness, ambition, righteousness. And yet he seemed to have been born in the wrong place and at the wrong time. Li Dingguo was born into the peasant army that staged a rebellion during the late Ming Dynasty, and after the Qing government came into power, he demonstrated astute judgment in taking the big picture into account, forming an alliance with the remaining Southern Ming troops to build a resistance. It resulted in major victories in Guangxi and Hengzhou that left two famed princes dead and devastated an army comprising tens of thousands. For the Ming forces, those victories marked an unprecedented triumph over the Qing army.

Sun Kewang, the Southern Ming warlord, held sway at the time, but he felt threatened by Li Dingguo's military might. He wrote a letter inviting the general to Yuanzhou to discuss war strategies, but it was a ploy. General Li realized this, and in order to avoid internal conflict, he withdrew his troops from Hunan and headed to Liangguang. Sun Kewang sent his forces to Hunan, where the Qing army annihilated them.

Li was a brilliant strategist. Having a breadth of firsthand experience, he launched an offensive from Guangdong, then reached out to Zheng Chenggong, who had been occupying Taiwan. During a bloody siege that hardly lasted six months, the surrounded Qing army was all but decimated. But Zheng Chenggong, out of sheer self-interest, had been slow to dispatch his own troops, and before they arrived, the Qing reinforcements were already there. Li's troops struggled against them, losing their entire front line, though they managed to recapture Guangdong. Adhering to their plans and forging ahead to Jiangnan, the troops were dealt a massive defeat. The Southern Ming's hopes of restoring its power had once again been thwarted.

Sun Kewang accelerated his efforts at capturing the throne. Two years later, he assembled an army of more than 140,000 to put down General Li, who found himself isolated by this move until his lieutenant general, Bai Wenxuan, joined him. In the end, Sun Kewang and twenty-some other officials fled to Changsha and surrendered to the Qing.

The Southern Ming's enormous power had been greatly diminished by internecine strife. The Qing army made Duo Ni its commander, while Wu Sangui, Zhuo Butai, and Hong Chengchou carried out a three-front assault. Sun Kewang's remaining troops seized the occasion to revive internal rivalries. Beset with difficulties inside its ranks as well as across enemy lines, the Southern Ming troops experienced an upheaval from which they were never able to recover.

Amid such dire circumstances, General Li managed to rebuild his ailing army. He selected six thousand soldiers to stage an ambush at Mopan Mountain[1], to the west of the Salween River, on all three attacking fronts. Wu Sangui's troops entered the scene with no knowledge of what was to come. It was at this decisive moment that the Southern Ming official Lu Guisheng committed an act of betrayal and informed Wu Sangui of the impending surprise attack, transforming what would have been an ambush into a bloody battle. Two-thirds of Li's soldiers were killed, and the battle took a similar toll on the Qing forces. At least ten of the military generals at the provincial level were killed along with thousands of their soldiers, and Wu Sangui ended his pursuit for the time being.

The Yongli Emperor, devoid of courage, fled across the border to Burma with his aides. Li refused to cross into Burma and gathered his remaining troops on the western border of Yunnan in preparation for

---

1   Note: The actual location of Mopan Mountain is not in Mengla, but in Tengchong, Yunnan.

one last stand against the Qing. The Burmese forces, believing that the Southern Ming had already been defeated, tried to take advantage of the situation to plunder the remaining troops. Lieutenant General Bai was enraged. He congregated the soldiers and unleashed a counterattack. The main Burmese army (which, according to historical data, comprised tens of thousands of soldiers, though the figures could be inflated) faced their opponents on the other bank of the river, prepared for a head-on clash. The Ming troops crossed the river and routed the Burmese forces with only several hundred fighters on horseback. Their surprise attack was said to have claimed the lives of at least ten thousand Burmese soldiers. The Burmese officials had no choice but to bring out the Yongli Emperor and make him order Lieutenant General Bai's troops to retreat.

Given such circumstances, many of the Ming generals and other officials were despondent, and one by one, they surrendered to the Qing. Lieutenant General Bai was the last to surrender. Only General Li never wavered.

When the Yongli Emperor was killed by Wu Sangui, General Li was deeply saddened. In the end, he fell ill on his forty-first birthday. More than ten days later, the general gathered his family and remaining soldiers, telling them: "Die peacefully in the wilderness. There is no surrender." With those words, he drew his last breath and died.

Li Dingguo led a tragic life, and even after his death, his circumstances remained tragic.

Having been born into an army of peasants, he was not eligible for enfeoffment, and having ended his life in defeat, he was not given due respect in the history books.

Yet some people see Li Dingguo as the greatest commander of the Ming and Qing Dynasties and argue that his character and abilities surpassed those of his contemporaries, such as Li Zicheng and Zheng Chenggong. But even so, there are more who have never heard his name.

After reading through all of this information, I formulated a different approach to writing *Valley of Terror*. I took a hiatus for more than a month (naturally, this was because of the World Cup), and instead of writing about the General Li that everyone knows, I decided to write about a tragic hero born in the wrong place at the wrong time.

ABOUT THE AUTHOR

A leading contemporary master of suspense in China, Zhou Haohui is the author of more than ten novels exploring the intersection of human nature, criminal motive, and the art of detective work. His books include *Killing Notice*, *The Evil Hypnotist*, *The Horrific Picture*, and *The Ghost Mountain*. His works have been translated into French, English, Korean, and Japanese, and many have been adapted for film and television. Born in Yangzhou City, Jiangsu Province, Zhou received his master's degree in engineering from Tsinghua University.

ABOUT THE TRANSLATOR

Bonnie Huie has translated several novels from Chinese, including titles by bestselling Hong Kong author Amy Cheung and Taiwanese counter-cultural icon Qiu Miaojin. She also translated the work of Okinawan political novelist Tatsuhiro Ōshiro. She is a recipient of a PEN/Heim Translation Fund Grant and was nominated for a Pushcart Prize for her rendition of the short story "Under the Cherry Blossoms" by Japanese modernist Motojirō Kajii.

Made in the USA
Monee, IL
30 January 2024

52099925R00239